MASTER OF PLEASURE

Godric placed his hands on the tree behind her, enclosing her in a prison of muscle. His body enveloped hers, and his comforting campfirelike scent surrounded her. He leaned forward until his chest grazed hers.

White-hot sensation skittered down her spine.

"It would not be like that at all," he whispered, brushing her forehead with his lips. "I feel how your skin responds to my touch. I feel your heartbeat."

"That is anger and fear."

His hands traced a slow trail down her shoulder. Leaning away, he allowed enough room between their bodies to rake his fingernail softly across her nipple. Sensation arced from her breast to her woman's core.

"This, my lady, is neither anger nor fear," he murmured.

Although the dress and shift were between them, she felt naked. She gasped and pushed him back, not wanting to experience the desire curling in her stomach.

He took a tendril of her hair and twirled it between his fingers. The strand glistened red-gold in the sunlight. "Your passion matches your hair."

She shook her head. "Everyone knows red hair is unlucky."

"Men make their own luck by following their passion. And yours awakens each time I touch you . . ."

MASTER OF PLEASURE

JESSICA TRAPP

ZEBRA BOOKS
Kensington Publishing Corp.
www.kensingtonbooks.com

ZEBRA BOOKS are published by

Kensington Publishing Corp.
850 Third Avenue
New York, NY 10022

All Kensington titles, imprints, and distributed lines are available at special quantity discounts for bulk purchases for sales promotion, premiums, fund-raising, educational, or institutional use.

Special book excerpts or customized printings can also be created to fit specific needs. For details, write or phone the office of the Kensington Special Sales Manager: Special Sales Department. Kensington Publishing Corp., 850 Third Avenue, New York, NY 10022. Attn. Phone: 1-800-221-2647.

ISBN 0-8217-7861-7

First Printing: June 2005
10 9 8 7 6 5 4 3 2 1

Printed in the United States of America

To Joe Trapp:
I am yours and you are mine.
You are ever and always my hero.

Acknowledgments

I could write an entire book filled with people I am grateful for. This list barely grazes the surface.

Thank you, Joe, for your unconditional love, for believing in me, and for a million other things.

Thank you, James, for being the best kid on the face of the earth.

Thank you, Mom, for holding my hand and never wavering in your support. Thank you, Dad, for your help.

Thank you, Babette de Jongh, Betty Pichardo, and Paulette Heidbreder, for your support, friendship, and the darn tough critique. My life is infinitely changed for the better because of you. Thank you, Kay Austin, for your editorial advice and your friendship. Thank you, Lori Mathias, for your help through the years. Thank you Debbie Scheel, Deanne Gatewood, and Dawn Temple—for being you.

Thank you to every contest judge and person who ever offered me advice on writing. I appreciate the time and effort you spent helping me.

Thank you, Rita Gallagher, for making such a difference.

Thank you, Sha-Shana Crichton and John Scognamiglio, for taking on a new author.

CHAPTER 1

Whitestone Castle, November 1470

Lady Meiriona watched a tiny, black spider spin silky strands in the door frame as she waited to betray her bridegroom.

Her slippered foot tapped impatiently against the chapel's red and black tiled floor. If only she could make her father understand the betrothal should be broken by diplomacy instead of force.

From her seat on the front bench, she glanced from her father's hiding place at the front of the church to the chapel's open door and back again. Why did men not understand that violence only begets more violence?

"Promise me you won't kill him, Father. Force him to sign the papers and be done with it."

"I will do what I think is best," her father's voice boomed from behind a wooden screen painted with biblical lore. Bright colors splashed across the partition depicting the image of a woman nailing a man's head to the ground.

The church's incense-tinged air burned Meiriona's nostrils and dread churned in her stomach. Mayhap she was the woman in the painting and the man her bridegroom. She folded her hands together, covering their trembling in the green velvet of her kirtle.

"I hate being bait, Father. Surely the contract can be broken another way."

"There is no other way." Her father's angry voice resounded through the dark, empty sanctuary. Although he hid in shadows, she felt his agitation. "Edward forced the betrothal on us, and by force we will break it. You will sit there until this is over."

Meiriona stiffened; the metal of her girdle scraped against the pew, biting into her flesh. "I am no longer a child, Father." Her voice sounded defiant, even to her own ears. She despised being a pawn.

"You are barely fifteen."

"Old enough to be married," she countered.

Her father's tall, gaunt figure emerged from behind the painted screen, hands balled into fists. Chain mail clinked, and his crimson surcoat billowed as he stalked toward her, his bristly gray beard quivering with rage. Gray strands hung in front of his thin face, as though he had jammed on his helmet without bothering to first sweep his hair aside.

"Defy me and I will kill the bastard for certes!" He slammed his armored fist against the white cloth atop the thick wooden altar. A candle stand crashed to the tiles, sending unlit tapers skittering across the floor.

Meiriona patted her crisp wimple in a telltale gesture of nervousness but met his gaze without flinching. Why did men prefer war when diplomacy could accomplish the same goal? Already the graveyards overflowed with casualties from this conflict between the house of Lancaster and the house of York.

Her father stormed across the bloodred carpet that ran down the aisle of the cold chapel. He stopped directly before her. "Lo, daughter, are you a Lancaster or a Yorkist?"

"Father, please. You *know* my loyalty is true." She stared at him, her fingers running along the edge of the oak bench. "But Henry has regained the throne. Mayhap we can break the betrothal contract *legally.*"

"Legally! Bah!" He shook his gauntlet-clad fist at the air, fighting monstrous unseen demons. "Was your mother raped *legally*?"

Meiriona cringed and set her jaw to dam the tears she never allowed to fall. "I cleaned the blood off Mother's thighs myself after that Yorkist dog took her. Do *not* doubt my sincerity."

Her father leaned forward suddenly to kiss her forehead, an expression of fierce love glowing in his eyes. "You are so much like your mother. When I married my Catrin she was fire and flash. Red hair and green eyes. I will not betray her memory by allowing you to marry a Yorkist."

She tugged at his faded red surcoat, straightening it for him as she often did. "Mayhap King Henry would agree with us that this marriage should not take place, but do not usurp his authority by slaying this man."

Her father shook his head. The metal of his helmet gleamed and bounced colored lights around the elaborate chapel as morning light shone in through ornate stained-glass windows.

"I am too soft with you," he grumbled.

"You have never been soft," she assured him. "But Godric of Montgomery is innocent."

"Ha!" Her father's shoulders straightened with new life. His eyes bulged like an enraged bull's. "No Yorkist is innocent. They are murderers and traitors from birth. May they all burn eternally for their betrayal of our pious King Henry and what they did to my Catrin!"

"Father! Please!" She shivered, wishing he would turn back into the laughing, compassionate papa he had been before her mother's rape and subsequent death in childbirth. Since that time, his tempers were all too recurrent.

A trumpet sounded and her father quieted. "The Yorkist bastard will be here in a moment, and all will be over."

Tearing her gaze from her father's, she peered through the open doorway. A tall figure, walking with the arrogant swagger of a man newly knighted, strode toward the chapel.

"Lo, daughter, he comes!"

Blood drained from her face as she looked upon her betrothed for the first time. With a surge of guilt, her heart went out to the man walking alone across the trampled grass. He was a bastard, a man with no family. Her father had summoned him to come posthaste, under the pretense that the wedding must take place immediately. Perhaps her bridegroom had no one to accompany him on short notice, even to his own wedding.

She clutched the sleeve of her father's surcoat. "Promise me you will not kill him, or I will warn him."

Her father glared at her. "Fine." He righted the candle stand and kicked the fallen tapers beneath the hem of the altar skirt. A cruel smile crossed his raw-boned features. Like a suffocating mantle, a feeling of impending dread fell over her.

"Do not forget your duty, daughter." He hurried to his hiding place behind the screen, mail jangling as he went.

She perched on the front bench, her raw nerves stretched tight as she composed her face into a mask of blandness. She felt like a quivering rabbit, ensnared for bait while the hunters awaited a hungry predator to approach.

Her betrothed reached the doorway in long measured strides. The spider scampered to avoid him as he ducked beneath the low arched door frame.

Meiriona gasped, her whole body aware of the crackling shift his presence made in the air. Backlit with the halo of sunshine, he was an archangel: beautiful, masculine, powerful, dangerous.

He stepped into the sanctuary and her mouth went dry.

Dressed in wedding finery, silver knight-spurs gleaming, he was the most striking man she had ever seen. A blue surcoat with yellow embroidery emphasized broad shoulders. His hose and high boots revealed long, muscular legs. Near a lean waist, his large, callused hands stroked doeskin riding gloves. Guilt pulled at her conscience when she realized he wore no sword.

Blunt-cut, shoulder-length, black hair framed angular features. An aristocratic nose and dark eyebrows gave him a daunting presence, but his eyes danced with intelligence and deep sensuality. Generous full lips softened his features.

What would it be like to be kissed by those lips? She swallowed; her heart pounded and she wished she could stop looking at him.

He stared back at her expectantly. "Lady Meiriona?"

Her heart leapt into her throat at the deep husky timbre of his voice. "Aye."

He bowed. "Godric of Montgomery." He indicated the ornately painted chapel with the sweep of one muscled arm. "Why are you alone here in the dark? We are to be married."

Her hands trembled within the folds of her skirt. "I cannot marry a Yorkist," she whispered.

"What was that?" He stepped closer, masculine arrogance dominating the space between them. "I did not hear you."

She cleared her throat, suppressing the urge to jump and run. Even without a sword, he seemed frightfully capable of ripping one's heart out.

"My apologies, sir. I am disquieted at being a bride." She swept her eyes sideways to hide the lie.

When she did, her gaze rested on a large painted statue of Jesus nestled among the shadows. His unblinking stare condemned her, and she sucked in her breath. Did God really need the huge sum her father had bribed the priest with to annul the betrothal?

"Where is the wedding party?" Godric's deep voice ripped through her thoughts.

Her gaze snapped back to his. Midnight blue eyes fringed with pirate black lashes pierced her.

Heart pounding, she spared a glance at the screen hiding her father. "They will be here shortly."

The knight nodded, as if satisfied with her simplistic answer. "I had not expected the heiress of Whitestone to be so beautiful."

Her stomach flipped at the compliment. Surely only the devil himself would be so beguiling. "Sir, I beg you, do not say such things."

"But it is true." He extended his hand, the muscles of his sword arm dancing as he reached for her.

She licked her dry lips, fascinated with the size of his muscled limb. It was large, tanned, and seductively powerful.

He took her hand and chuckled softly. "You like what you see?" The husky tone of his voice was filled with overconfidence.

"I do not," she lied, feeling her cheeks on fire. She knew not even the whisper of lead powder could hide her blush. She clamped her lips closed in irritation. She was no overheated milksop who blushed and stammered when a man paid her a compliment. She wanted to snatch her hand back but she dared not—he might become suspicious.

He winked at her, gave her a roguish grin, and ignored her lie. It was as if they shared some keen secret. He looked as though he could read her inner desires, see right through her modest green gown *and* the yellow shift beneath it.

"My lady," he murmured, leaning close. "You need not fear the private desires between a man and a woman."

She shivered. He smelled like fresh rain, wild wind, and the comforting smoke of a campfire. She felt a fervid longing for the impossible.

"This is not right between us," she whispered more to herself than to him.

Godric stroked her fingertips with his callused hand, and her body tingled with traitorous desire. "Nothing could be more right between husband and wife."

She turned her face away, heart racing as her private emotions warred with logic and loyalty.

"All will be well between us, my lady." He lifted her hand, and his lips, soft as spring heather, kissed her palm.

She jerked back as if burned, but he held her hand tight.

The faint, metallic scrape of her father's sword leaving its scabbard echoed through the quiet sanctuary.

Godric glanced over his shoulder.

Shrieking a war cry, her father leapt from his hiding place, sword extended. An instant later, armored soldiers crashed into the church, surrounding them.

She sprang forward as her father lunged at her bridegroom.

Godric pushed her behind his own body, shielding her from harm. He drew a short dagger from his boot and held it ready. Her father advanced, the point of his sword aimed straight at Godric's heart. Men crowded into the chapel, swords drawn. The scent of leather and sweat overwhelmed the scent of incense.

Sweet Mary! What had she done?

Meiriona slipped between Godric and her father. "Nay, Father! We can accomplish this another way!"

Godric's gaze pinned her. "Accomplish what?"

She glanced from him to her father and back again. "I cannot marry you." Her hand touched Godric's forearm, a silent plea that he would understand.

"My daughter will never marry a bastard!"

Godric's expression turned from confusion to disbelief. "What?"

She shivered under his gaze and turned to her father. "This is not—"

"Silence, daughter!"

Sunlight gleamed off the men's upraised swords, causing a rainbow of dancing lights to flicker across the altar.

Godric's gaze turned on her, icy as the tip of Snowdonia. Anger and tension hunched his shoulders.

"You mean you were here in the dark as *bait*?" The grip on her hand tightened. The civility disappeared from his midnight blue eyes, replaced by the wariness of a cornered wolf.

"I had no choice."

"No choice?" he roared.

She cringed; his blood would be on her hands if he chose to fight. One man did not stand a chance against so many armed knights.

"Please! Just sign the papers!"

"What papers?"

"To break the betrothal. My father has them drawn already."

The force of the hatred in his eyes nearly knocked her to the pew.

"You are mine," he stated, so quietly it was as though he were shouting. Moving with the lightning reflexes of a warrior, he snagged her waist, yanking her close.

She landed fully against his body, her head not even reaching the top of his broad shoulders.

Her father roared and lunged forward.

The flat of her bridegroom's dagger, cold and inflexible, dug into her back and held her father at bay. Pressed against Godric's body, she felt his wrath as their heartbeats thumped against each other. With a defiant glare at her father, he dragged the wimple from her head and kissed her boldly. Her heavy auburn hair spilled around her, over her shoulders and down her back. Logic demanded she resist, but his mouth laid claim on hers, searing her with its touch.

His lips were not soft as they had been on her palm, but challenging and severe. Yet his breath tasted sweet as honeyed mead.

An uncomfortable heat radiated through her limbs when his tongue flicked across her lips, demanding entrance.

Vaguely, she heard her father bellow in the background. Godric's arm tightened, his knife hard against her back. Then time pitched into a dizzy flurry and she lost awareness of everything but his mouth and the impractical desire it demanded from her soul.

Abruptly he pushed her away.

Breathless, she tried to compose her thoughts, but they seemed as tangled as her hair. Her father's gaze bore into her, condemning her. Shame burned her cheeks. She had not even struggled to get away from the kiss.

Godric assessed her as though he had just staked claim.

She stretched her fingers to wipe the ferocity from his face. Fury radiated from him, and her nerve evaporated. Her hand fell lifelessly to her side.

"Get him out of here," she breathed, wrenching

free from his hold. She scurried from the chapel like a coward, brushing the spider in the process. Long strands of web clung to her hair as she ran toward her chamber.

"I will come for you. You are mine!" His voice rang through the courtyard after her. "You will pay for this."

Five years later. Turkish prison.

Pain pulled Godric Montgomery slowly back to consciousness. Throbbing temples and a sharp ringing in his ears proved he yet lived. He cursed the thought. Better to face the devil in hell than the life of slavery he now had.

"Get up, you oaf." A woman's disembodied voice spoke from the darkness. Meiriona?

Images drifted through his mind: the chapel, his betrothed, her father, the betrayal, then a ship and the slave block. But the thoughts were as impossible to catch as mist. He tried opening his eyes, but one was swollen shut and the other let in only a thin ray of the dim torchlight.

"Awaken, dog." A foot nudged his rib cage and pain shot through his chest.

Turning his head to the side, he tasted filth from the prison's floor on his lips. He spat to remove the mingled tastes of grime and blood and struggled to speak.

"Meiriona?" he rasped, his words feeling like gravel in his throat.

Reality flooded back to him. Nay, the woman's voice could not belong to the conniving little bitch who had sold him to this life of slavery. His betrothed, curse her dark soul, was an ocean away—likely tucked into a warm feather bed while he rotted on the frigid, unrelenting floor of a Turkish prison.

"Your lady cannot help you."

Meiriona? *His* lady? Aye, it was true, but not in the way this woman supposed. He would repay Meiriona for the last five years he had suffered. The desire for revenge burned stronger than the agony of his body.

He pushed himself to his knees and found he was naked. His back stung, every movement afire with pain.

How many lashes had the slave master given him this time? Forty? Fifty? After thirty he had lost count and lost consciousness under the uncompromising whip.

"Hurry. The guards will return soon."

He shook his head to clear the cobwebs, wincing at the sting the movement caused. Peering through one eye, he stared at the woman. She was of medium height. A dark veil concealed her hair and obscured her face. A long black garment covered everything but her hands. She hovered above him, a black demon with a lone candle lighting the way to hell.

"Who are you?"

"My name is not your concern. I have been sent by Princess Nadira."

"Nadira?" A prickle of unease raised the hair on his nape. His affair with Nadira was the cause of these past four months of torture in this underground hellhole.

Before that, he had merely been a slave in the sultan's palace, a position he abhorred. The princess and her maidens had found him to be a novelty—a distraction from the boredom of too much wealth and leisure. He had been brought to them by stealth in the dead of night. They'd toyed with him until he felt more studhorse than man.

A curse on treacherous women. He had given them pleasure, and they sent him to the rack in payment.

Godric rubbed a hand across his aching chest. The hair had grown back over the past months. Before that time, the women had applied a mixture of sugar and beeswax to rip the hair out by the roots before oiling him. It was not much consolation, but at least he was becoming a man again.

"Princess Nadira bids you well."

He gave a short, bitter laugh. "Does she? Did she bid me well when she accused me of rape and turned me over to those curs for a lashing?"

The woman tsked. "Nadira is a princess. And you"—she pushed aside her veil and spat on the ground—"you are a dog. You had no right to take her like one of your English whores."

He rose suddenly, his fist closing around her slender wrist. "Watch your tongue ere I rip it out. I have nothing to lose."

She shuddered and pulled her veil to further conceal her features. "The princess sent me to free you." She hurled the words at him like a curse. "Harm me and you will die here with your own excrement as your only companion."

Godric lessened his hold on her wrist. "Nadira sent you to *free* me?"

She nodded as if the very thought was ugsome. "I would that your body rot here, but the princess bids otherwise."

"Where is your princess now?"

"Asleep in her bed. Are you so prideful to think she would come for you herself? You are nothing to her."

Godric did not doubt the truth of the statement. He had only been a toy for the princess, one easily thrown away when it became inconvenient.

"Why is she freeing me?"

"You are to be executed on the morrow." Wrenching her hand from Godric's grasp, she turned abruptly on her heels. "Follow me or die. It matters naught to me."

She pushed the iron bars of the prison's door.

Unlocked.

Mayhap the woman spoke the truth. Or mayhap it was a trap. She held the door open, beckoning him to follow, but he eyed her warily. Only a fool trusted women. And he was a fool no longer.

Was some greater hell awaiting him if he followed? He planted his feet on the uneven floor, heedless of his nakedness.

"If Nadira cares naught, why am I being freed?"

"A slave may not question his mistress's decisions. It will come clear soon enough."

Clapping a hand onto her slender shoulders, he said, "Betray me, and I will kill you before they capture me."

"Kill me, and you will never see your cursed England again. Release me, dog. I brought you clothing."

He had no choice. He would die for certes should he stay here, forgotten in a filthy cell below the sultan's palace. The devil take him if he was a fool for trusting a woman once again.

He followed her into the musty-smelling hallway beyond the iron bars of the cell. Every movement pained him. She stooped to fetch a bundle that was pushed against the rough stone walls and thrust it at him. "Put these on."

He swiftly complied. The breeches reached only midcalf on his long limbs, and the shirt fit too snug across his shoulders. The linen stuck to the clotted blood on his back, but he voiced no complaint.

She nodded approval when he was dressed. Darkness closed around them as they made their way silently along the dank underground corridor. Colorless roaches scampered away as Godric and the woman turned corners. Water dripped from the ceiling, its echo unnaturally loud. The air smelled ancient and fetid.

Scattered along the hallway at intervals, other cells were carved out of stone and barred with iron. Skeletons lay in several of these. Rats nibbled on what flesh remained on the bones.

At last Godric and his silent guide entered a section of hallway where the uneven floor stones sloped upward and the air smelled fresher. The last bit they crawled on hands and knees but finally worked their way free of the catacombs and into the welcoming moonlit night.

Godric breathed in the night air. Fresh jasmine scented the breeze.

Freedom.

Five years since he last tasted freedom. He wanted to relish it like a starved man would a feast.

A lone man on horseback awaited them. He held the reins in one hand and a wad of rags with the other.

The woman snatched a water bladder from the horse's saddle and hurled it at Godric. "Cleanse your hands, filthy swine."

Godric narrowed his eyes but complied.

She spoke rapidly to the rider in Arabic. He swung down from the steed and handed her the bundle. She thrust it at Godric. "Here is the reason for your freedom."

Godric took it, the package feeling small and warm in his hand. "What is it?"

The top rag slid to one side and a wrinkly, red infant stared up at him. "By God's holy rood." He almost dropped the child in his surprise. "You are giving me a baby?"

"Your daughter," the woman accused.

"My"—he frowned and kept a tight hold on the baby, fearing it might break—"daughter?"

"Are you an imbecile? Did you not know how the sultan discovered your affair with the princess?"

Godric could not tear his gaze from the infant. It weighed almost nothing. "I have been locked in the catacombs. I was told of Nadira's accusations, not of pregnancy."

"You cannot blame the princess for imprisoning you. She only did what she must."

The bundle squirmed and the infant wrinkled her nose. Her tiny body fit in the palm of his hand. Saints! What if he dropped her?

He clutched her to his chest. But what if he was holding her too roughly? Sweet Mother of God, he had never held a baby before. How was one supposed to do it?

The baby's eyes dropped closed as a deep sleep came over her—peaceful, trusting. Had he sworn earlier all females were conniving and treacherous? He had been wrong. This one was guileless. Precious. He felt . . . awed, humbled. The baby was a piece of heaven in the midst of hell.

His gaze snapped back to the woman. "What does this mean?"

"Go back to your cursed England. Take your bastard child."

Bastard? How many times had he heard himself called by that name? He ached inside, feeling his failure. He had promised ne'er to sire a child out of wedlock for that very reason. And here, cradled in his arms, was the proof of his selfish pleasure.

A wave of possession and protection rippled through him. This was his child.

His child.

He must take her to England, secure her a place in the world. His chest ached where his heart would have been if he still had one. But his heart had been ripped away long ago.

Nay, he could not take his daughter. He had failed her already with his selfish rutting; he would not fail her again.

"A child belongs with its mother." He knew he should push the infant into the woman's hands.

But he did not. Instead, he brought the baby to his face and inhaled her sweet little-girl scent.

The woman shrugged. "Take the brat or leave her here on the ground for the wolves to eat. I care not. A bastard cannot be raised in the palace." She turned to the man who had been riding the horse. "Come, we have done our duty to the princess."

Godric watched them walk toward the palace, leaving the horse behind with its reins trailing on the ground. He was free, and yet his heart felt more chained than ever.

"Wait!" he called. "I do not know her name."

The woman and her companion did not turn around although he was sure they heard him. The horse whinnied softly, nosing him on the shoulder.

He patted the animal, finding comfort in the warm feel of horseflesh. Of all the things he had been without over the last five years, perhaps his stallion was the thing he missed most.

What a merry chase his betrothed had led him on. Slavery, imprisonment, and now freedom. He swung carefully into the saddle, clutching his daughter.

The infant awakened and rooted into his torso, opening her mouth. A fear unlike any he had ever known settled on his heart. "Jesu, I have no breasts for milking." What would he feed her?

He rubbed the baby's face. She latched onto one of his fingers, sucking so hard her tiny cheeks drew inward. He heaved a breath of relief when her eyes drifted shut and the soft weight of her body relaxed in his hand.

Why had Nadira given him the child? He gazed at

the outlines of the two figures disappearing toward the peaks of the palace, their forms now shadowy and indistinct.

He turned his mount toward the west, his back against the rising sun. "What think you, horse? Mayhap it is the way of women not to care for anyone but themselves."

The horse snorted an agreement.

"Aye, but it is not my way." He covered his daughter's face with a piece of her blanket and snuggled her into his chest. Kneeing the horse into a trot, he determined to find nourishment for his child.

"I have land in England, daughter," he whispered, tasting the sweetness of the word "daughter" on his tongue. "It was stolen from me by an unfaithful bride, but I will take it back for you, and we will live well."

Nothing would keep him from owning what belonged to him and wreaking retribution on those responsible for his enslavement. He had been born with no future, no family. His daughter would suffer no such fate.

CHAPTER 2

Whitestone Castle, 1477

"Bloody hell!" Meiriona's father pounded his fist on the oaken tabletop as a young nobleman scurried from the great hall without a backward glance. Papers scattered onto the rushes. "Damnation, daughter! That was the third suitor this month who has left because of your shrewish tongue."

Meiriona flicked her wrist dismissively, flipping her long auburn braid over her shoulder. "His feet were too large, Father."

"God's toes!" Her father rose and paced to the window, his roar turning into a spasmodic cough. Servants scuttled out of his way, but he paid them no heed. His boots crushed the freshly herbed rushes, tingeing the hall's tense air with the scents of rosemary and mint.

Wishing she'd thought of a more plausible excuse than the size of her suitor's feet, Meiriona clenched the arms of her chair and braced herself for her father's onslaught.

"Ungrateful. Unsubmissive." He slammed his hand against the window's frame, doubtlessly watching her suitor leave the castle. "Why cannot you be more like your sweet, biddable mother?" He wheezed then gave two hacking grunts.

Meiriona slid her chair back, feeling her chest tighten with a familiar ache. "Father, please sit down. Let me fetch some of Mattie's potions for your lungs."

"You should have been married years ago!"

"Father, please."

"Ioworth—" Uncle Pierre, who was sitting at the chessboard near the hearth, palmed one of the pawns in a bony, wrinkled hand and glanced from Meiriona to her father. "Let it go, my friend."

Her father turned and glared at Uncle Pierre. "'Tis not you who has all the king's bloody taxes to pay." He strode back to the high table. Yanking up a fistful of papers, he waved them at Meiriona. "See this! More of Edward's war taxes."

Her heart sank. An endless cycle of taxes had overtaken them since the house of York had regained the throne. "If you will allow me to have Mary teach the other women to weave wool as she does, we can sell it for a fortune in London."

"Look around!" He waved his arms, indicating the bare walls of the great hall. "We need gold *now*, daughter. We haven't the time for women's foolish wool-weaving dreams."

A wave of guilt clenched her stomach as she glanced at the stark stones. The tapestries had been sold to ransom her father from prison in London six months ago. If she had been a dutiful daughter and married, their coffers would have already been refilled. But she dreaded the idea of being subject to a man. She knew—*knew*—she could find a market for Mary's weaving given a little time. Then she would not have to be sold to the highest bidder like a pig at the fair.

"Please, Father. 'Twas Mary's weaving that helped pay your way out of London. She is gifted. Our estate can prosper—"

"Bah! Wool and sheep. My daughter a tradeswoman—'tis disgraceful!"

"If you will just allow me to try, I can build our resources. I can prove I am capable—"

"Ridiculous!" he roared. "How would you get to London? You cannot even ride a horse."

A keen sense of hurt pierced her at her father's low blow. She knew how ashamed he was at what he considered her greatest weakness. But surely she could find a way to get the goods to London without actually sitting atop a mount.

"But—"

"Enough!" He snapped the papers against the table. "You have no head for trading. If you did, you would have let me die in that prison rather than pay the king's enormous ransom."

"Father! How can you say such things?"

"Winter is coming, and there will not be enough bread for the peasants."

She kicked at the rushes, her practical brown kirtle swirling around her ankles. "We shall find a way. If we use our resources wisely—"

"Everything of value has been sold. Likely as not, we'll freeze to death. Better that I had died than all our people."

Frustration settled across her shoulders as her father coughed spasmodically. If only he would let her try. He paced back across the room and spit phlegm into the fire, making it sizzle.

"I do not need to marry so hastily. We could cut back on the number of soldiers we house," Meiriona reasoned, deciding to go at the situation from a different angle.

Her father stiffened. "'Tis madness. A castle needs defending."

"But they are practically eating us out of house and home." Since returning from London's prison, he'd hired every armed man he could find. They lined the halls and kitchen and courtyard, grumpy and always impatient to be fed. "One can scarcely walk from the great hall to the kitchen without tripping over a knight."

"Depart with the soldiers? Foolishness!" He hacked loudly. "What does a woman know about defense?"

She drummed her fingernail on the chair arm. "We managed while you were locked away."

Turning, he flicked his gaze from the sparse walls to the empty cupboard, accusation written in his gaunt face. "You practically sold the keep. Even we who sit at the high table must eat on bread trenchers instead of pewter platters now."

"'Tis unfair, Father." She gritted her teeth, hating that she'd had no other way to pay for his ransom than to sell the tapestries and dishes. "If I'd had more time, I could have made Mary's wool weaving pay the full amount."

"Stubborn chit!" He stalked back to her, placing one fist on each arm of her chair and leaning down so their noses nearly touched. He glared at her for a long moment. "You won't marry because of that *bastard*, will you?"

Blood drained from her face, and she leaned against the back of the chair. "Cease! I do not wish to marry anyone, least of all him."

"You want him. I can see it in your eyes."

She shook her head, fearful he could read her secret thoughts. It had been seven years, and yet she could still hear Godric of Montgomery's voice. She heard his sweet whisperings of chivalry in daydreams and his promise of vengeance in nightmares.

"You foolish, *foolish* child! Have you any idea where your precious bastard is?" Her father's beard quivered.

She shrank back, wary of his mood.

"He is on the continent. He never thinks about you."

Conflicting thoughts swirled in her mind. While there was logic in what her father said, Godric's vow to claim her echoed in her mind.

"They call him the Dragon," her father continued, slamming his palms on her chair arms before striding back to the window. "He burns whole villages if they refuse to bend to his iron will. He drags his enemies through the street, crushing the weak and whipping any who disobey."

The news sent a streak of icy fear through her veins, leaving her feeling like a precariously perched rock.

"I do not believe—"

"You are a fool to not know."

She shivered as she saw the conviction in her father's eyes. Minstrels had bespoken the deeds of the Dragon, but she had not connected him with the handsome knight who had kissed her palm. Her world tilted. How had she not known? Had she not felt the resolve and strength in Godric as he had kissed her?

At once she saw her father's bluster for what it was: fear that the Dragon was coming and a need to protect her. She softened toward him.

"After he left here, Pierre secured him a place in the French army. He lives a silken life of luxury—fat off the land he has conquered." Her father slammed one fist into the palm of his other hand. "Bloody Yorkist bastard. He's living happy as a plump hog serving French nobility while we rot trying to find enough gold to pay the king's bloody taxes. I should have killed him when I had the chance."

"Father—" Meiriona stood, holding her hand out to him.

"I will take no more of your defiance. Turn away

one more suitor and you may as well pack your belongings. I will send you to the convent."

"Father! You cannot be serious."

He glared at her, his lack of words more potent than any lecture. Deep within his eyes, she saw the flicker of trepidation. Whitestone had the natural defense of being situated atop a steep cliff, but the castle's defenses would run low if their coffers were not refilled soon. Already some of the mercenaries had cut their losses and left.

Uncle Pierre scooted away from the chessboard, his chair scraping the floor. Grasping his cane, he hobbled onto the dais. "I say, Ioworth, perhaps *I* should marry the girl myself."

Both Meiriona and her father whirled to stare at Pierre.

"That's ridiculous," Meiriona blurted.

Ignoring her, Pierre clapped a hand on her father's shoulder. "I know you treat me as one of the family, but we are no blood kin."

Her father stroked his beard, deep in thought.

A bubble of horror rose in her throat. "Unthinkable."

"My friend, I am getting old. I have money, a title, but no land of my own. 'Twould be convenient for us to join our fortunes. I cannot believe it never occurred to me before."

Her father eyed her speculatively. "The idea has merit."

Meiriona felt her knees give way, and she grasped the edge of the table for support. Saints, she should have taken the last suitor, big feet and all. "I cannot believe you are even contemplating such a thing."

Her father, hands on hips, glared at her. "You have chased away all the *other* husbands."

"I need children." Uncle Pierre rapped his cane on the dais. "She's a strong, healthy girl."

Could one so old even produce children? The thought of his withered hands caressing her brought bile into her throat.

"This is . . ." Insane. Incestuous. Uncle Pierre, even if he wasn't *really* her uncle, was still three times her age. She loved him . . . as a *mentor*, not as a lover. Bitter betrayal that he would stoop to such a thing pierced her. "Uncle! How can you do this? You are my friend!"

"'Tis your fault we are forced to rely on old family *friends* to get us out of debt," her father interjected.

"Nay, Father!"

Pierre chortled. "Ne'er fear, Ioworth, her moods don't intimidate me like that young buck who just left. Call up a priest, and we can have your tax problems solved by nightfall."

Ioworth stroked his beard.

"We can raise a stronger army," Pierre pressed, and Meiriona saw her father's eyes light.

For a brief instant, she imagined Uncle Pierre naked, his wrinkled skin hanging from his bones like limp sackcloth on a skeleton.

"I won't do it," she said.

"You will if I say you will, daughter."

"Ioworth, I told you coddling her would lead to trouble," chimed Uncle Pierre.

She turned to Pierre, disbelieving her own ears. "You taught me to think for myself, Uncle. Now you want to marry me?"

He turned the pawn over in his hand, lips thinning. "You place an unfair burden on your father, child."

Crossing her arms, she shook her head. "Nay."

Her father stalked to the arched doorway and cupped his hands around his mouth. "Mattie!" he yelled. "Pack a small bag for Meiriona. She will be leaving within the hour."

"But Fath—"

His hand sliced through the air, cutting off her protest. "Enough. If you cannot behave like a noblewoman, then you will no longer be one."

"A disobedient woman is of no use to her lord." Pierre leaned on his cane and stood firmly beside her father.

Her heart felt like lead in her chest. "Uncle, you've oft said a woman could run a keep as well as a man."

Pierre harrumphed. "In theory, perhaps. But in truth, a woman needs a man."

Irritated at how quickly his argument changed when he was the man in question, she slid to her father and touched his arm. "You cannot mean to banish your own daughter. I am needed here to care for our people."

Ioworth shook her hand away. "You are no longer my daughter. Mayhap the convent can teach you obedience."

At that moment, the door swung open and Meiriona's half brother of ten summers stumbled inside. He wore a flamboyant purple cape and carried a dead rat skewered through the gut with an arrow. Heedless of the drama happening in the great hall, he limped over to his sister, swept his cape in a flashy bow and dropped the rat at Meiriona's feet.

"Damien!" She jumped back with a squeal just as the dogs lunged at the prize, knocking her to the floor.

Her father turned furious eyes upon him. "Weedy brat!"

Damien's jaunty grin faltered.

Picking up a goblet, her father hurled it at the hounds rummaging in the rushes. "Boy! Get your crippled arse out of here."

"Father!" Meiriona leapt to her feet, dusting straw off her skirt. "He did not mean any harm."

"I only put up with you, miscreant, on Meiriona's account, but she is no longer of any use to me." Glowering at Damien, her father motioned one of his men forward. "Take both of these ungrateful wretches outside the castle walls. I will have no more disobedience in my household." He turned his face aside, glaring out the window in the direction her last suitor had gone. "Even the convent will not accept such insolence."

A knight grasped her upper arm, but she shook him off. Holding her head high, she exited the hall while her brother limped along behind her.

"You think he means it?" Damien whispered, clutching her hand. He favored his lame leg more than usual.

Meiriona cast a dark look back at the hall, feeling the iron shackles of duty bite her soul. "Nay. Not if I agree to marry Uncle Pierre."

Dread and despair dripped down the walls of the castle's chapel a short while later as Meiriona, weak from a hurling stomach, stood next to Uncle Pierre and recited her wedding vows.

A sharp sense of remorse tortured her. Why had she been so shrewish with *every* suitor? The last one had been young and handsome. From childhood, she'd known her duty to marry. In truth, her father had allowed her more lenience than most women of her station—he had been angry when each possible husband had suddenly declined upon meeting her, but she'd never dreamed that it would come to this.

The Dragon must be a fearsome warrior indeed. She'd seen the desperation and apprehension lurking behind her father's bluster and knew he was motivated by love for her. Why did men always seem to think they knew what was best for a woman? A niggling fear pulled at her that this marriage was God's punishment for selfishly being so headstrong.

Mayhap, if she did not know how keenly her people

depended on her, she could have withstood banishment. But she could never bring that fate upon her crippled half brother. They had no place to go, no family to take them in. With winter coming, banishment was equivalent to a death sentence.

'Twas unfair her father blamed Damien for their mother's death. The Yorkist pig was responsible, not the innocent child born of her rape. 'Twas not Damien's fault he'd been born with an affliction that made him unsuitable for knight's training. 'Twas not his fault he'd been born at all.

Money had changed hands to get the priest to perform the wedding without the usual three weeks of banns being read.

'Twas woman's fate, she told herself, to marry for duty. Squeezing her eyes tightly shut, she vowed to put her childish behavior behind her and accept her lot. She would never put off doing her duty to her family again.

She glanced up at Uncle Pierre and numbness seeped into her heart. He had always been there as a friend and mentor—guiding her, loving her, teaching her how to count and read and play chess. Why would he betray her in this way?

He tipped her chin up with his weathered hand and kissed her cheek dryly. Was the service over already?

Dazed, she made her way to the great hall for whatever feast Mattie had thrown together on such short notice. Staring at her trencher, she chewed methodically, unsure if the bites she placed in her mouth were sweet cakes or pig slop.

She drank one goblet of wine, then another, and then still another, heedless of its quality—reaching only for the numbing oblivion it offered.

Her stomach churned when Mattie and other women forced her to her feet in preparation for the wedding night. She stumbled up the stairs toward her chamber.

The women, honking like a gaggle of geese, peeled clothing from her. Acrid smoke from tallow candles burned her nostrils. She gazed at Mattie, who alone of the crowd seemed unaffected by the horror that was about to occur here on her bed.

Fingers pinched her naked skin, pushing her toward the mattress. She dug her toes into the rug. The women tittered.

"Virgin modesty," one exclaimed, giggling.

Meiriona felt disconnected from her body as if the nightmare were happening to someone else. Hands gripped her arms, forcing her forward. One maid turned back the covers and shoved her onto the sheets.

Downstairs, loud clapping and cheering rang out. An image of men making lewd jokes and undressing Uncle Pierre flitted into her mind. Her stomach lurched, and she clutched her belly.

Mattie grabbed the chamber pot, thrusting it into Meiriona's hands just before she vomited.

"Be ye gone, ladies!" Mattie shooed the other women out the door. "Go on, the mistress has no further use of ye tonight. Has enough on her mind, she does."

Meiriona wiped her face on a cloth and accepted a goblet of water from her maid. "Thank you, Mattie."

Mattie watched the door until the last maid had scuttled from the solar. "Listen here, mistress. I know ye're distressed about yer wedding night but there is no need. Ol' Mattie has taken care of it all for ye." She gave Meiriona a toothless grin.

Meiriona rubbed her aching temples. "Nothing could take care of what I've got to face."

"'Tisn't true, mistress. Look ye here." Mattie yanked a cloth pouch from her apron pocket. "See this, mistress. 'Tis opium. I put a pinch in the ol' man's wine, I did."

"Mattie!"

The maid pushed the goblet of water to her mistress's lips. "Well, an ol' man like him ain't got no business marryin' the likes of ye. Raised both ye and yer mama like daughters, I did, and yer mama wouldn't want ye marryin' no ancient French count."

Meiriona rinsed her mouth and spat into the chamber pot. "I cannot believe you, Mattie."

"I gots more too, for tomorrow night and the night after as well." She plopped the pouch down on the bedside table. "See here, it only takes a pinch and 'e's out like a candle." She snapped her fingers. "It won'ts hurt him, it won'ts, I swear."

Meiriona stared at the opium pouch. For the first time since early morning she felt a ray of hope in a bleak day.

"Ye won't go a-tellin' nobody, will ye, mistress? I bes an ol' woman and gots no place to go if the master sacks me."

"Oh, Mattie!" Meiriona flung her arms around her maid. "No one will sack you as long as I have any say about it."

Mattie beamed, her snaggletoothed grin lighting her wrinkled face. "Best ye sleep naked, mistress, so as not to alert the others." She winked conspiratorially.

Quietly, the maid left the solar and Meiriona settled under the sheet, closed her eyes, and prayed for strength to reconcile herself to her new life.

Just as she drifted into sleep, a warm muscular body, too large to belong to her new husband, pressed against her.

She lurched awake and screamed. The warrior's large hand clamped over her mouth. The scent of sweat, blood, and virile male filled her senses as his powerful forearm bore her down into the feather mattress.

CHAPTER 3

Meiriona pushed at the intruder's bulk as he crowded beside her on the bed. The mattress sank under his weight, rolling her toward him. The room's lone candle had burned itself out. Struggling, she strained against the darkness to see the hulking body looming over her. She could make out naught except huge shadows cast by eerie moonlight.

"Be still," a hard, low voice said.

Sweet saints! *Godric!*

A muddle of a thousand emotions slammed into her stomach. His voice had haunted her since that time in the chapel.

She jerked upright, trying to bite his hand to get away. He twisted and locked her to the mattress with his thighs, clamping his hand even tighter. The bedsheet separating them tightened around her like a weighty cocoon.

"Do not fight me. You cannot win."

She stilled, her heart thudding against her rib cage and clammy moisture beading her upper lip. What did he want?

"Are you a virgin?" he hissed.

Saints, did he still intend to claim her? After all these years? She struggled to see into the shadows, but he was naught but a blur.

He shook her. "Answer my question."

She nodded against her feather pillow.

"Good." He leaned close, and his face scratched hers with rough stubble. She could feel sweat and dust on his skin. His body heat seeped through the sheet. "Do not scream and I will release your mouth. Do you understand?" A salty bead dripped from his face to hers.

Slowly, she nodded agreement, intending to scream the instant she could gather a deep breath.

"Be silent," he warned, lifting his palm. "Time is short."

Fear stole her voice when his hand traced its way down her chin. His fingertips left burning trails in their wake, branding her with his touch. Then strong fingers wrapped around her throat. His touch was light, the grip loose, but she understood the meaning clearly and lay very, very still.

"What are you doing here?" she whispered.

"Collecting what belongs to me." He lifted her to a sitting position, dragging her partway off the bed.

She gasped, pushing him. "Let go of me! I do not belong to you. I am newly married!"

He pulled her upright, hustling her toward the window. "That is exactly why I am here. You should not have gotten married today."

She twisted backward, wrenched free of his hold, and tumbled to the floor. A strand of her hair snaked across her cheek. She tasted rose soap as it worked its way into her panting mouth.

"Hel—" Her scream was cut off midword as his body landed atop hers, her breath crushed from her lungs.

She wiggled against him, feeling the unforgiving muscles of his chest. Jesu, she was naked!

"Release me. I do not belong to you."

"Aye, you do, you little vixen." A sliver of moonlight

shone through the window, illuminating his face. Scars slashed across his once-handsome features. He looked more monster than man.

"Sweet Mary!" Her father had assured her Godric held a high position in the French royal army. But it looked like he'd been tortured. Why would the French do that?

"What happened to you?" she breathed.

Hatred boiled in his eyes and he growled in answer, his mouth a grim slash. He glanced down, taking in her nakedness with a ravenous primal look.

Her underarms stung with the sweat of terror as a scene from her past of Yorkist men thundering after her, intent on rape, flashed into her mind's eye.

"Let me go!"

Godric chuckled low and harsh and she gulped for air, seeing in her mind her mother being dragged off her horse by vile, laughing Yorkist soldiers.

Godric's eyes glittered at her. "I intend to have you for my own." His hand twisted into her hair, and he raked his hand possessively down the column of her throat to the top curve of her breasts.

Panic overtook her. She screamed, but his hand clamped over her mouth, muffling the sound. A woman's shrill, drunken laughter floated into the chamber from the revelry in the great hall. Even if she could scream, no one would hear her over the din downstairs.

She bucked wildly, kicking and thrashing her limbs until he came unseated.

Struggling away, she slammed her fists into his torso. She landed several blows before his mighty arms crushed her to his chest. Cold metal buckles pressed and pinched her naked skin.

He rolled her onto her stomach and collapsed his weight against her back, trapping her arms and hands beneath her.

His breath tickled her ear. "Surrender, Meiriona. Fighting is futile." He held her motionless as if daring her to test his strength again.

Lying there, her cheek pressed into the rug, she saw a glimmer of moonlight dancing on the gray stones of the hearth, turning them an unnatural silver. With a sinking heart, she realized the truth of his bald statement. She was at his mercy.

After a moment, he released her mouth.

"Let me go," she bit out.

"Never. You belong to *me, Countess.*" He emphasized the last word in insult. 'Twas today's marriage that made her a countess.

She forced herself to remain motionless. Her best chance of escape was to wait until he relaxed his guard. The rug felt itchy and rough against her breasts.

"Where is your new husband?"

Oh, saints. Her husband was likely passed out on the table below. Shame that she had been grateful for Mattie's interference flooded her. If only she had been a dutiful daughter, she would not be held captive by this . . . beast.

The beast's muscular arms and legs pressed into her, solid, unrelenting. His leather garment cooled her skin, but his arms were hot and virile. Held captive as she was, his sheer size awed her.

She felt his swollen manhood through the soft, tight leather of his breeks. His hard member settled between her buttocks.

She trembled, her composure shattered. "You must not," she whispered.

"I have come to claim my own." His voice was low, demanding, that of a man accustomed to authority. Her long hair, trapped between their bodies, forced her head to an awkward angle. Godric's weight lessened, and he swept her hair aside. Cold air brushed her exposed back, sending chills racing down her spine. Gooseflesh pimpled her limbs. Gathering her hair into a fist, he anchored her to the floor.

His prickly beard tickled her cheek. "My beautiful betrayer, I had not expected you to have such fire."

Meiriona cringed and squeezed her eyes shut.

"Nay, nay," she breathed, bracing herself for what would follow. When his weight shifted and then lightened, she assumed he was unlacing his braies. She grimaced in horrid anticipation, her breath coming out in shallow spasms. It was the way of men.

She shook her head. "I beg you, do not."

Godric shoved a wad of coarse cloth into her mouth and secured it there. It tasted of lye soap and scratched her teeth and gums. Oh, sweet saints of heaven, it meant he planned to take her roughly. Her body shook, and her teeth chattered silently against the cloth. Trapped. No one would hear her screams as he pounded into her. He was large and strong. If he impaled her violently, she would die.

Meiriona knew the lot of women. She gagged, remembering the stench of red-black stains on her mother's thighs after her forceful rape. Compared to reality, nightmares were tame.

She had been wrong to think she could cross a Yorkist. They would not be satisfied until all of England was conquered. She should have known Godric would exact terrifying revenge on her body.

Oh, God, she prayed, *please let me survive.* She wanted to tell Godric if only he would be gentle, she would not fight. She garbled into the rag, but her words were unintelligible. Already her mouth was dry from the wool. She nearly choked in panic.

He held her down firmly.

An instant later, he bound her wrists together and pulled her upright. The cold floor numbed her toes. But where he gripped her arms, the flesh burned.

The contrasting sensations forced ripples of shivers through her.

Moonlight bathed him. He held her for a moment, naked before him, as if wondering what to do with her. She was too shocked at this turn of events to even blush at her nudity.

Her brow knotted in confusion. She leaned her head back, pleading for answers to her silent questions.

He only grunted in response.

The wool gag seemed to crawl down her throat. Meiriona shifted nervously from side to side. What in God's holy name was he doing?

"Where are your clothes?"

Her legs went numb with relief. He was not going to rape her after all. Had he not been holding her, she would have sunk to the floor. She could scarcely believe it.

In the dimness, she felt Godric's gaze rake over her form. It frightened her anew to be inspected in a way she could *feel* rather than see. His gaze swept down her neck, to her breasts, and on to her stomach and the vee between her thighs. He seemed to drink in her body with a deep primal thirst. Moonlight bathed her skin; heat crept up her face at his lingering perusal. Yet, at that moment, she knew she had been wrong in thinking he would rape her.

He was surveying her as a commander would a battle map, navigating the land, scoping out the hills and valleys of what he planned to take for his own.

Nay, not rape. But conquer.

As his gaze lingered on her breasts, another shiver ran through her. Her nipples puckered and rose, almost welcoming his stare. Heat flushed not only her cheeks, but her body. Meiriona would have done anything to yank her arms free to cover herself. He made her feel disconcerted and unable to think, just as he had in the chapel.

Embarrassed by her erect nipples, she lowered her eyelids.

"I grow impatient," he warned. "Show me where your clothes are or you can go naked." She jerked her head, indicating a trunk by the stone wall.

When he released her shoulders, she stumbled forward. Her breath whooshed from her lungs when she landed against his chest. His arms enclosed her, steadying her against falling.

Unbidden, Godric's leather garment touched her hard nipples. An unwelcome, overpowering sensation coursed through her. Irritated at her lack of composure, Meiriona forced herself upright. Had she not been afraid of falling, she would have jumped away from him.

The beast steadied her. He stepped back, keeping one hand on her shoulder, and reached for the trunk.

She pulled her frazzled thoughts together to escape, but her legs were like soft, limp clay. Darting her gaze about, she searched for a viable weapon.

He rummaged through the chest, found a linen chemise, and held it up to her. She backed away, her bare buttocks bumping the dressing table. When she grappled for the edge of it, her hand closed on Mattie's opium pouch.

Godric paused, his broad torso invading the air between them. "You are beautiful." In the dappled moonlight, he looked like a leopard set on devouring her, but his voice sounded gentle and oddly soothing.

She glared at him, feeling her fear slip away, replaced with something harder. Anger. Resolve. She had done naught to deserve being tied at his mercy. Although the betrothal had been broken, Godric had been living a life of luxury serving nobility on the continent. He had no right to claim ownership of her.

The hard wooden edge of the rough-hewn table sitting beside the bed bit into her exposed backside.

"You are mine. Do not forget it."

Irritation at his highhandedness coursed through her. Never, she vowed.

He shoved the linen shift over her head in one swift motion. The gown hid the opium, safely tucked in her palm. She nearly smiled. She would escape from him after all. But first she had to coax him into trusting her. If he trusted her, she would be untied. If she were untied, she could drug him. If she could drug him, she could escape.

It should be easy enough. She would feign compliance, trick him into believing that marrying Uncle Pierre was a simple mistake. Mayhap she could let him think she would annul the marriage and marry him. He had said she was beautiful. She would use that to her advantage.

"Do not panic," Godric commanded, glancing impatiently at the sinking moon. His wayward bride would need a tight rein, he decided, hustling her toward the window.

She stumbled and his arms closed around her, catching her before she fell. Gripping her slender shoulders, his palms rubbed against her arms. Soft. Warm. Feminine. Tiny ripping noises sounded as his calluses snagged the delicate fabric.

Hurry, his mind said, but he yielded to the urge to inspect his prize.

Damn, she was comely. Not like a courtier, but an odd sort of pretty. Made a man keep looking long after it had become rude to do so. Unusual. Mesmerizing.

Her eyes were overly large, her nose not quite straight. Her cheekbones were too high. But her hair—a man could get lost in her hair. It flowed around her like fire, hanging past her hips. Tendrils of it grazed her knees, the auburn a sharp contrast to her ivory skin.

Pink nipples taunted him through the linen of her shift. An animalistic jolt shot through his groin. Thank God she was still a virgin. He had only to tup her, get her with his child, and the church would annul her marriage and uphold his claim as her lord. The proof that their betrothal was illegally broken was all over his body in the ugly scars he bore.

She is mine, he thought, suddenly angry she had been waiting for another man.

Naked.

Sliding an arm around her shoulders, he pulled her forward. Her scent, like the whispery aroma of roses after a night rain, teased his nostrils. Fresh, clean. Nothing like the piss-and-sex smell of the brothel where he had last known a woman.

For the blink of an eye he felt unclean. God knew he was dirty; he had been climbing most of the night to reach her. He smelled like swine. But that was not it. She did not make him feel dirty; she made him feel *unclean.*

He half dragged, half carried her over a threadbare rug.

She wiggled and made a whimpering sound. He had not wanted to capture her like this. Snatching women out of windows like a thief went against his better judgment.

He should have collected his wayward bride when he first returned to England a few months ago, but at the time he did not have the gold to formulate a siege for a castle as magnificent as Whitestone, and he had not yet heard from the king. Stealing her in the middle of the night had been a hastily formed plan, risky at best, but he'd had no choice when he had learned of her marriage.

Releasing his prize, he pulled rope from the windowsill in a quick, practiced movement. The girl slumped against a tattered tapestry, her tense body drawing into a protective stance.

He steadied her with his arm. "Breathe slowly through your nose and the gag will be less bothersome."

She responded, taking several deep breaths.

Godric frowned, irritated that he cared about her comfort. He should *not* be concerned. Her family had not worried about *his* terror when they chained him like a dog and set him on a ship bound for a life of slavery in the East. Scalding memories of a whip across his back came unbidden to his mind.

Footsteps outside the chamber door caught his attention. Meiriona jerked backward, and he yanked her close. "Best you pray they do not enter," he warned.

She glared at him, her large eyes hurling knives, but she remained still. No doubt she would spit in his face if he removed her gag.

The footsteps passed and faded down the hall.

"Meiriona, obey me, and you have nothing to fear." He forced his voice to a whisper.

She gave him a look of pure, cold contempt. Bloody hell. He had never seen more spiteful eyes on a woman. Well, that is, if he disregarded dockside harlots when seamen did not pay them.

He grinned down at her. She would not be an easy conquest, but he would enjoy the challenge.

Oak shutters clattered against the castle wall, letting in cold night air and the scent of coming rain. She squinted as brisk wind blew a lock of hair into her face. Drunken giggling wafted up from below. He had spent too much time here already.

With a firm grip, Godric hoisted her over his shoulder.

CHAPTER 4

Hours later, Meiriona screamed into the dawn as her captor lowered her onto the soft forest-floor grass and removed the wool gag. Twigs bit into her knees. Three hundred feet below her castle, amidst the oaks and elms of Whitestone's fertile valley, she knelt before Godric, wearing only her shift.

Fear, mingled with rage, balled in her stomach and she screamed again, struggling against the bonds holding her wrists.

"No one can help you." Godric squeezed her upper arms, whether to comfort or to frighten her, she did not know.

She leaned her head back. Mercy, he was large. Using ropes and strange, clawlike iron gloves to assist him, he had carried her out her chamber window, then climbed down the wall of Whitestone and the cliff below. Such strength and stamina she had never seen.

His wide chest rose and fell with ragged huffs, biceps twitching as if they still felt the strain of the descent. If she had not just lived through the ordeal, she would not have believed a man could accomplish such a feat.

"Blackheart!" she rasped, her mouth dry from the gag. "Let me go!" Her tied hands forced her shoulders back, thrusting her breasts forward. Never in her life had she felt so helpless, so vulnerable.

In her kneeling position, his groin was a finger's width away from her face. The outline of his manhood, large and rigid, bulged through his leather breeks.

A wicked thought flitted into her mind. Damning the consequences, she squeezed her eyes shut, lowered her head and butted him between his legs.

He grunted and crumpled inward, partially deflecting the blow. "Good Christ, girl!"

Satisfaction at her ability to topple his power raced through her. "Fiend!" She surged to her feet, victorious. Her white shift flapped out around her. "Tie me, steal me, or beat me, but you will never conquer me."

Abruptly, triumph vanished.

She tumbled to the ground, her limbs numb from hip to toe. Her torso slammed into the earth, and her tied wrists bounced against her buttocks. She sprawled prone before him, his big, black boots planted on either side of her head. Sticks and rocks jabbed into her stomach.

Humiliation stung her eyes. She blinked rapidly, refusing to let her tears water the mossy earth.

Meiriona, daughter of Ioworth, never cried. Never.

Godric sank to one knee. "Easy, lady," he crooned, as if she were a colt to tame.

Arrogant man! She tried to rise, to spit in his face, but prickly needles coursed through her legs, slowly at first, like tiny raindrops, then they rushed in like an untimely downpour.

His large hands circled her waist, pulling her into his lap. "What happened?"

"My legs are asleep."

"Are you harmed?"

"Nay." Stings of agony, like a thousand wasp bites,

pierced her legs and she could not move to get away from him.

Hopelessness pinched her heart. She cringed, knowing how amused he must be at her ineptitude and pain. She could endure if he beat her, but making sport of her would be the ultimate mortification.

She squeezed her eyes closed, clenched her jaw, and determined not to cry out as she waited for his guffaw. She would die afore she showed another moment of weakness in front of this man. Godric reached for her legs. "Let me help you."

"The only help I need is for you to unloose me." She sounded stronger than she felt.

Her captor shifted her on his lap until her back pressed against his chest and the smooth leather of his jerkin slid against the linen of her shift. He reached around her, one arm on each side. His fingers massaged her thighs and relief came at once. Heat from his palms filtered through her gown.

As the pain receded, she realized her bound hands touched his breeks. Mercy! Were they touching the leather molding his manhood? She dared not wiggle her fingers. Oh, saints, what would her husband and her father say if they saw her sitting on Godric's lap all but fondling his privates and allowing him to stroke her thighs?

But his hands felt so good. His large, warm hands fascinated her. Her stomach flipped.

He was a wicked man, making her have wicked thoughts. She should struggle away, not let him touch her. She knew her duty. But this was *Godric*, whom she'd longed for during the past seven years. The only man who had ever kissed her lips.

And his hands felt so good. Calluses on his palm snagged her shift. How would they feel on her skin? Rough and terrible? Or rough and *exciting*? She turned her face aside, not daring to allow her thoughts to continue. Already, she felt uncomfortably hot. Frustration at her body's traitorous reaction to him surged through her. She felt her earlier anger slipping, and she grasped for it.

The armies of the house of York had been responsible for the rape and death of her mother, for her father's imprisonment, for a thousand wrongs against her family. This man was a Yorkist. Her enemy.

But his hands felt so good. His palm glided from her thighs to her knees in smooth, easy strokes. The barbed pain was gone. Duty prodded her to tell him to cease; his touch was no longer necessary. But for years, she had dreamed about this man and no other.

She closed her eyes, leaned against his torso, and surrendered to his hands, even as she loathed her own wantonness. His touch was a welcoming campfire in the dead of winter. His fingers left fiery trails on her legs and kindled an odd burning in her stomach.

He's a monster, he's a monster, she chanted to herself, but her body betrayed her, and heat pooled between her legs.

"Cease!"

Godric's hands stilled.

Duty to her family came first. Her pride hung in tatters. She could not consider her emotions.

Awkward as a fish flopping on the docks, she struggled from his lap until she lay beside him. She bore no delusions that she could not have done so, except that he allowed it. Her hair dragged on the earth, its long length fanning across the grass.

His hands slid from her body. He flexed them against the ground, pulled a sprig of grass, and tore it to shreds. For one unbearable heartbeat she wanted nothing more than to cradle his scarred face to her bosom and ask him what had happened.

His expression was unreadable, but his gaze smoldered, his eyes an engulfing blue flame.

For a moment her mother's voice echoed in her memory. *Do not crawl too close to the fire, sweetling. It will burn you.*

She glanced away. "Do not touch me."

"Why not?"

Because it makes me want you. "I belong to another."

Godric reached for her leg. Her skin tingled with anticipation afore his palm cupped her thigh. "Are you telling me, or convincing yourself?" His voice was husky.

Her face flushed, and she snatched her leg away. Was she transparent? How could she be so wanton? She pushed away; moss and rocks scattered as she sat on the ground. She felt more in control of herself when he was not touching her. "Get away from me. I do not belong to you."

"I have betrothal papers that prove otherwise." He leaned toward her, his gaze hot. He smelled musky, warm, a part of nature rather than civility. His presence called to her, enticing her to be free rather than dutiful.

He was too close, too overwhelming. At once she felt suffocated, as if someone had thrown her into a desert and was slowly stuffing her mouth with scorching sand.

"Let me be. The betrothal was broken."

"By force, *Countess.*"

She flinched at the use of her new title. Somehow he made "Countess" sound like "whore."

Ire bubbled inside her. "At least I am nobility. You are a titleless bastard. I would never marry you."

Leaves crackled under his boots as Godric rose unhurriedly to his feet, his softness gone. The sickle-shaped scar on his face whitened, and his eyes glittered. He wiped his hands on his breeks as if wiping the feel of her legs from them. "I will have you as my wife or as my slave. It makes little difference to me."

Fury coiled through her. She sat as straight as she could manage without toppling over. "I will *not* be your slave."

His midnight blue eyes reflected the dawn's light. A nerve twitched in his jaw. "Have no doubt, my pretty captive, King Edward will uphold my claim on you."

She shook her head, struggling to stay balanced without the use of her hands. "He will not. The papers to break our betrothal were signed and sealed by the church, and I am already married."

"You will annul this false marriage. I will not tolerate another's claim on my land."

"'Tis not *your* land." She was a noblewoman, not some milksop peasant to be intimidated by him, but she wished she felt as confident as she sounded. These days land was oft gained by sword and the king's whim. The church, rather than abide by its own laws, followed whoever threw it the most gold.

Godric breathed in a long, deep draw of air. His molten gaze cooled and his hands relaxed. His calmness reminded her of an impending storm that could surge forth at any moment. A leaf floated downward and landed on his shoulder.

"*My* lady, the land is mine, just as you are mine." His gaze was as icy as her anger was hot.

Her wrists chafed against the ropes. She spat on the grass, wishing it were his arrogant face. "Men forever take what does not belong to them."

"Mayhap. But I merely take what *does* belong to me." He tilted her chin up with long, blunt fingers. "Like you. You *are* still a virgin?"

She jerked her chin from his hold and stared into the trees, hating that her virginity had become a prize to be won in a man's revenge game. "You cannot use my virginity against me."

He cleared his throat and brushed the leaf from his shoulder. "'Tis your *lack* of virginity I plan to use." His gaze caressed her body in a long, slow look. "Soon you will be ripe with my child."

"You bastard!"

He caught her head between both palms and turned her face so she was forced to gaze directly at him. "I have killed men for less insolence."

"Do not threaten me, blackheart! If you meant to kill me you would have done so already."

Godric's face was stony, unreadable. "There are many fates worse than death, Countess."

She strained against her bonds, finding them more oppressive with each passing moment. Frustration and fear made her heedless. "Untie me, you cur!"

He stroked his index finger down her cheek. "It would serve you better to be fearful of your fate."

"Low-life bastard! Son of a whore!"

He yanked her to her feet, his face a handbreadth from hers. "Watch your tongue, girl, ere I turn you o'er my knee and give you the spanking you deserve."

Queasiness swirled in her stomach. "You would not dare."

"I stole you from your chamber on your wedding night, and you question what I would *dare*?"

Anger flowed through her. Godric had no right to threaten her.

"Apologize," he commanded, gripping her shoulders.

Like a sudden hailstorm, her anger burst into fury. He was the one who had wronged her! She'd done *nothing* to deserve being dragged out of a warm bed and held hostage.

"Beg pardon? Of you? Because you have a whore for a mother?" The instant the words fell from her lips, Meiriona realized her folly. Her words hung like a heavy icicle in early spring that could melt and smash to the ground any moment.

He blinked once, then went down on one knee, pulling her with him so quickly her breath caught. Her body pitched sideways, the earth flying up to meet her. But he guided her fall, and her stomach contacted his bent leg. She gave an unladylike grunt as the solid muscles of his thigh dug into the softness of her stomach. Her hair formed an auburn curtain in front of her face. Christ almighty, she was over his knee like a child.

"Cease! Unhand me, you brute!"

His hand cracked thrice on her upturned buttocks, hard and swift.

She screamed, tried to wiggle free, but he planted an unyielding arm across her back, anchoring her in place.

"You barbarian! Fiend!"

She sensed his arm raise once more.

"I am sorry, you damn monster!"

His hand stopped midair and he shrugged. "Call me what you will, but leave my mother out of it."

"Fine." She struggled to rise, but he held her firmly over his lap. "Let me up!"

She lay still and a long moment of silence stretched between them. It seemed even the birds stopped twittering. Saints, was there no end to the indignity she would suffer at his hand?

"Forgive me, Meiriona. There is some disrespect I cannot allow." His palm brushed her warmed buttocks and she flinched, although his touch was tender.

Her emotions whirled like a storm-tossed sea, and a terrifying wave of desire mingled with indignation crashed through her. Oh, dear, sweet, heavenly saints. Godric was much too dangerous. He *could not* make her desire him after what he had just done.

She trembled, her world thrown into shattering

madness, because she knew he could. *Dear God,* she prayed, *please do not let him know it.* Godric threatened to consume everything: her land, her people, her family, her body, *her sanity.*

"What do you want from me?" she breathed.

"Everything," he whispered, rumpling her chemise over her hips and exposing her buttocks.

CHAPTER 5

Holding her bottom up across his knee, Godric tugged Meiriona's shift to her waist.

"What are you doing?" she screamed, squirming to get away.

He slapped her bottom, lightly this time. "Be still, girl. As much as I enjoy watching you wiggle like that, I cannot untie you if you squirm."

"Oh." She stilled, her face hot, and she was thankful for her curtain of hair that shielded her face from his view.

His large palms caressed her bottom, then slid to her tied wrists.

She shivered, feeling disheveled and exposed.

Godric pulled at her bonds; Meiriona clutched the opium pouch, still hidden in her palm, and wished she could dump all of it into his food. Sweet Mary, if only she were a man! Then she could take up a sword and fight rather than waiting for a clandestine moment to use the sleeping draught.

She felt his gaze linger on her bare bottom. She set her jaw, praying that his attention on her naked arse would keep him from noticing what she hid in her hand.

The ropes slid off her wrist and Godric lowered her chemise. She said a silent prayer of relief that he had not discovered the drug.

Cold mud squished between her bare toes as he pulled her upright. Her hair fell against her back, the ends tickling the pits of her knees.

She stretched her arms, trying to ignore how her white shift, now dirty, clung to her indecently. The cool breeze caressed her nipples, making them into pebbles. Clinging by a thread to her indignation, she glared at her captor.

He towered over her. A slight breeze blew his dark hair about his shoulders. Two scars ran from his forehead to his temple and down his left cheek in a curved line like he'd been hacked with a sickle. Saints! What had happened to him? He was both terrifying and breathtaking. The marks made him fearsome, dangerous looking, but they did not detract from his masculine beauty. It was as if a master sculptor, in a fit of rage, had destroyed his most perfect work.

"Let me go!"

He grinned at her, as if amused by her impotent rage. "I will never let you go."

"My father's men will find you!"

"Even if they do, they will not get you back," he said flatly. "I have men guarding this place. We are safe here."

Like a wild, flooding river, anger coursed through her. "I hate you."

"I know." He touched her cheek with one scarred hand. "You will grow accustomed to me in time."

"Never," she vowed, clinging tightly to the pouch of drug.

Dark clouds gathered overhead, bringing damp, heavy air and the scent of rain. Sheep bleated in the pastures, echoing across the hills.

"Follow me," he commanded, turning and striding into the trees toward the sounds of a babbling brook.

Meiriona planted her feet on the soft ground, refusing to heel like a lapdog. She looked upward through the canopy of birch and oak trees.

Were her father and Uncle Pierre searching for her? Or were they still drunk and incapacitated? Climbing straight down the cliff had taken several hours, but traveling on the muddy trail to this part of the valley would take at least a day, mayhap longer with all the recent rain.

"Meiriona!" Godric called from about thirty paces away. "Come."

She stared at him defiantly. "I am not your puppy."

With an irritated huff, Godric walked back to her, holding the rope.

She turned to run, but he caught her upper arm and whirled her around, squishing more mud between her toes.

Yanking her wrists together, he tied the rope securely and pulled her forward by a tether. Leaves crunched. Her toe jabbed a pointed rock, and she limped a few steps.

Slowing his pace, he placed his hand around her shoulder and led her through the trees.

He helped her over a fallen log, as if he were a court gentleman guiding her up a set of stairs. His confident self-assurance made her want to spit in his arrogant face. She would have, too, but she still felt his handprint upon her buttocks.

Even in her anger and frustration, a grudging respect for her captor came over her. No man had ever confronted her for her sharp tongue and disrespect. Her prickly speech had lost more than a fair number of suitors, though the loss had not troubled her overmuch.

"We have only a little way to walk. Vengeance is just over the next rise."

She dug her heels into the ground, hating the involuntary lurch her stomach gave at the word "vengeance."

"What do you mean? What are your intentions?" Surely he did not plan to swive her here in the forest.

He gave her a quizzical look. "I am taking you to my home."

"Your home is over the next hill?"

He stared at her as though she were daft. "Assuredly not."

"What do you mean, 'vengeance is over the next rise'?"

His brow cleared and he laughed aloud, a deep, rich sound. "Lady, my vengeance on *you* will take longer than this short walk. Vengeance is my *horse*."

"Your . . . mount?"

He chuckled, pulled her forward. "You amuse me."

"You named your horse Vengeance?"

His smile vanished and his mouth flattened. "Revenge is all I have thought of for years."

"Oh." Meiriona swallowed, understanding. "Do you hate me so much?"

"Hate? Nay, Countess. One must have a heart to hate. I have no heart left." His low voice sounded bitter.

She shuddered and clutched the opium tighter. They neared the top of a small hill. Stumbling on a tree root, she jabbed her sole on a thorn. She lifted her foot before it could draw blood and swayed off balance, bumping into Godric. Saints, she did not want to fall at his feet again!

His arm slid around her shoulder. "You need shoes." He hoisted her into his arms, carrying her as if she weighed no more than a kitten.

Guiltily, she realized she should tell him to set her down, but to be carried was such a relief from the thorns and mud that she did not. In his arms she felt feminine and small, protected from briars and stickers.

For one small moment it was as if they were the only two people on the face of the earth, and she wished they were not enemies. His savage heat bore into her.

The leather of his jerkin carried the faint scent of a campfire.

He strode through the underbrush with long steps. "We will reach my mount soon, then you can ride."

Ride? A bubble of panic rose in her throat. For a second, she was eleven years old and hooves thundered around her head as she scrambled for safety. Her mother's scream rent the air and then she felt a large hoof knock her head and everything went black. She had not ridden a horse since that day.

Godric's brawny arms tightened around her. "You are pale. What is wrong?"

She shook the image from her mind. "'Tis nothing."

"You lie, Meiriona. What demons haunt you?"

She turned her cheek into his torso, wishing to hide from his uncanny perceptiveness. She allowed herself the guilty pleasure of inhaling his comforting scent. Her pride was already gone this day. The sooner she confessed her ignominy, the sooner the shame would be over. One more embarrassment would make little difference. "I . . . cannot ride. I am afraid of horses." There, she'd said it.

"A noblewoman afraid of horses?"

"Aye." Mortification squeezed her throat. 'Twas unnatural for a woman of her station to fear horses. She had been mistaken to think she had no pride left; her feelings were much too close to the surface. In that moment, he held her emotions in his hand. If he snickered, she would be unable to dam her tears.

"Do not laugh at me." She hated that her voice sounded small, strangled.

Stepping over a log, he peered down at her. No hint of amusement twitched his lips. Tucking a loose strand of hair behind her ear, she gave him a feeble smile.

"It does not make you weak to be afraid of something." His eyes held neither pity nor amusement, but genuine concern.

She shrugged.

"What happened?" He asked the question so matter-of-factly they could have been talking about the pending rain.

No one had ever shown empathy for her peculiar fear. It made her uneasy. *Why would he care?* "We were thrown, nearly trampled."

"Who was thrown?"

"Mother and I." She bit her lip, not wanting to remember. Godric may claim to have no heart, but she had no such luck. Remembering made her chest ache.

His gaze searched her features, probing. "'Tis common for riders to be thrown. What *else* happened?"

She turned her face aside, wishing she could cover it with her hands so he could not see inside her thoughts. There were secrets she did not wish to share with him. Or with anyone.

"Tell me, Meiriona." He hugged her tightly to his chest, until her cheek pressed against his leather jerkin.

"There were men after us. I was eleven." Her thoughts seemed disjointed, like a wooden puzzle scattered upon the floor.

Godric crested the top of a hill. The added weight of her body did not seem to slow his pace. "Is that what happened to your mother?"

"Mother died in childbirth." Slamming the door of her mind shut on her memories, she did not elaborate.

He nodded and did not ask anything more.

She wished he would stop being kind so it would be easier to hate him. He was a wicked man, a Yorkist. No different than the ones who had raped her mother. But his arms felt warm and steady against her back and knees as he carried her. Tendrils of her long hair wound around his shoulders.

"Have you been back on a horse since that time?"

Meiriona shuddered, causing more wisps of her auburn hair to catch on the fastenings of his jerkin. "Once."

"Once?"

"My father forced me to ride."

"What happened?"

Her cheeks heated as she recalled the day her father, in cold disapproval, had tried to rid her of cowardice by forcing her atop a mount while he led it behind his own horse. She had ridden in quaking silence, toes curling into a cramp until her father had released her. Later, hidden behind the stables, she had spewed fear-induced vomit on the ground.

"I did not do very well," she said finally.

"What happened?" he probed again. "Did you spew?"

Slowly, she nodded. How did he know? Had he read her mind? Frowning, she wiggled in his arms so she could see more of his expression.

"Sometimes that happens when people are very afraid."

"Truly?" She had thought her severe reaction was unnatural. "How do you know this?"

He shrugged, causing her body to shift slightly up and down. "I know much about terror."

She wished suddenly she could touch the scars on his face, soothe them with her fingers. For once, she was thankful he had tied her so she would not act on her foolish impulse. What had the French done to him?

Godric gave her a wry smile and hoisted her a little higher in his arms as he stepped over a fallen tree. Her chemise slipped against his jerkin, the white linen a sharp contrast to the black leather. "I am much relieved you only fainted and did not vomit on me last night."

Nervous laughter rose in her throat. "It did not occur to me to do so," she said cheekily.

He grinned. She smiled back.

Catching herself, she turned her face aside. He was her enemy, not some old friend to tease. What was she thinking? How had the conversation turned to this topic? The last thing on earth she wanted to do was discuss vomiting with Godric.

She frowned. He was turning her into a case for the madhouse. It seemed that his presence suffocated her. His arms were too hot, too demanding, too virile. His nearness affected her in shameful ways. She paid scarce attention to the passing trees or the direction they traveled.

Taking a deep breath, she inadvertently inhaled his musky, intoxicating scent. She coughed, hoping to expel his scent, but it did not work. His presence engulfed her, drowning her in forbidden longing.

She searched her enemy's face. He seemed to share none of her misgivings about the closeness of their bodies. There were a thousand things she did not understand about her captor. He was kind to her, yet he claimed to have been planning revenge for years. Earlier, her sharp words had reaped swift retribution. Who was he—a tender giant or a vengeful warlord?

"You do not think me a coward because I am afraid of horses?" she asked abruptly, wanting to know more of who he was.

His eyes watched her intently. Could he see her thoughts? "You are not a coward." His voice was strong and decisive. A gusting wind blew a lock of his dark hair over one of his ears.

She had never admitted her fear without shame, without judgment, without self-loathing. No one had ever seen her fright and denied she was a coward because of it.

She felt . . . liberated. Light. Like he had ripped the fetters from her feet and she could now soar in the heavens like a hawk.

She was caught in Godric's unyielding masculine arms, her hands tied. Her captor was taking her to some unbeknownst prison. And yet, for this exhilarating moment, she did not wish to be anywhere else; she had never felt so free. All because this man said she was not a coward.

"How far is your home, my lord?"

A second passed. And then another, as both of them realized what she had just said. She had just called him "lord."

Meiriona sucked in her breath, trying to suck the words back into her mouth.

Was she half-witted?

He was a bastard, not some nobleman. Exhaustion tousled her emotions like knotted yarn. She bit her lip, wishing she could pull her hands free and cover her traitorous mouth. But she did know one undeniable truth: she had never been around a man more in control of himself, one who conducted himself with such leadership. Bastard, mayhap, but his countenance demanded more deference than any nobleman she had known. Godric's inner nobleness rose above his birth circumstances.

She shook her head to cease the flow of her thoughts. She must come to her senses; she had a duty to perform. He set her on her feet. Her hair was still wound around the metal buckles of his jerkin, connecting them.

"You are not my—" she started, pulling her hair free. Her shift flapped out in the slight breeze, grazing his leather garment.

He covered her mouth with his hand, studying her

as intensely as a hawk would eye a field mouse. For an instant, she thought he would replace his hand with his mouth.

Sweet Jesu.

She gazed into his face, remembering the stolen kiss in the chapel. His lips were full, generous. They had been demanding, ruthless all those years ago. Hot. Wet. She had shamefully dreamed of them too many nights.

He had been the only man ever to kiss her on the mouth. Even at her wedding, Uncle Pierre had only tipped her chin and brushed her cheek.

What sinful thoughts Godric brought forth! He was her enemy, her family's enemy, Uncle Pierre's enemy. How could she be thinking of how his kiss tasted?

Abruptly, as if he knew her thoughts rested on his mouth, he pursed his lips and let out a low whistle.

"You have no need to fear, girl," he said. "My horse is well trained."

CHAPTER 6

So, he did not want to kiss her after all. Or did he? His enigmatic features told her nothing. How unfair it was he could read her thoughts while she could read none of his!

"Why do you care if I am afraid of horses?" she asked, searching for something, anything, to break the tension between them.

He shrugged, his hands tightening on her upper arms. "I care about all my property."

She huffed, her ire slamming to the surface. She was *not* his chattel. "Take your hands off me."

He grinned down at her. "Nay. I like my hands on you."

"You arrogant lout! I am not your property to fondle as you wish."

"Methinks you are."

She twisted, straining to get free of the ropes binding her wrists. "Uncivilized beast!"

Godric scowled and released her. "Your fear is misplaced. You would do well to fear the master rather than the horse."

Blowing a strand of auburn hair from her face, Meiriona narrowed her eyes. "I do not fear you," she lied.

Godric's large hand traced the side of her face in a slow sensual trail. It was a threat and yet not a threat.

"You should," he whispered, his breath tickling her ear.

She shivered.

His fingers continued their lazy trail down her neck and stopped when they reached the top of her breast. The muscles rippled along his arms. Fearsome. Beautiful. Seductive.

Fear swallowed her. Not fear of him, but fear of her own forbidden desires. "Please cease," she whispered.

He whistled again and released her. She was thankful the earth was solid beneath her feet to compensate for her unsteady legs.

A lad of about nine with bushy, carrot-colored hair and a face full of freckles emerged from a cove of trees, leading a large, black horse.

Meiriona stumbled backward, her shift flapping against her calves.

Godric caught her and guided her behind himself. "Fear not, my lady."

She peeked around his wide shoulders. The boy gave her an inquisitive glance.

Godric strode to the horse and took its reins. "Be off, lad. You have done good work." He tossed the boy a coin.

The lad gave a toothy grin and one more curious glance at Meiriona. He raced away, his footsteps padding across the forest floor.

Unease prickled her spine as Meiriona turned back to Godric and his huge horse. Her captor rubbed the stallion's nose and patted its neck. "Vengeance," he had called it. The horse had the dainty features of an Arabian but was much too large. Perhaps he was a crossbreed, a *bastard* like his owner. The beast's coat glistened in the filtered forest light, solid black with three white feet. How many hours had Godric brushed the steed to make him gleam so?

She suddenly felt inexplicably jealous of the bond

between men and their animals. Would a man ever care as much for his woman as he did for his horse?

"Come, Meiriona." Godric motioned her forward.

She swallowed, shook her head. Air squeezed from her lungs.

"*Now*, girl."

She had told him of her cowardice. He had pretended to understand, but he had not. Her knees quaked, and she pressed them together.

He looped the horse's reins loosely around a low branch and strode toward her, scowling.

She shrank back and a thorn scraped her heel. Bile rose in her throat. Heavens, he intended to pick her up and throw her over his mount. *Please, God, keep me from spewing.*

Feeling his body heat as he stopped in front of her, she opened one eye. "I cannot."

"You can and you will." His hand touched her shoulder. Could he feel how badly she was shaking? Oh, Jesu, she needed to make water.

Be brave, be brave, she chided herself. Tears stung her eyes, hovered, threatened to drop.

Godric wiped the moisture away, his callused hand warm and gentle. She took a deep, shuddering breath and tucked her hair behind one of her ears. He pressed his lips to her wet lashes. She closed her eyes, her emotions swirling. Why must he be kind? 'Twas better when she thought he was a monster.

"Meiriona." Godric's voice was calm, self-assured. "Can you not trust me? I swear on my life, no harm will befall you while I am your guardian."

Trust *him*? The man who stole her from her chamber on her wedding night? Her heart beat like a wild, primitive drum. A panicky giggle bubbled from her throat. "I cannot trust you."

"Meiriona." His voice was low, husky, intoxicating as sweet mead. "Just for a little while."

She shook her head.

His hand splayed across her cheek. "I kept you safe on the cliff. I will keep you safe on my horse."

Her lower lip trembled. She gazed at him. Tenderness and empathy shone in the blue of his midnight eyes.

"Trust me," he whispered. His presence beckoned more than his spoken words. It tugged on her soul. "We must ride. You cannot walk in these woods dressed as you are, and I cannot carry you the entire way."

"I am befuddled with lunacy," she muttered to herself. His words were so logical.

"I will take care of you. Do not fear." His thumb stroked her cheek. "Come." He drew her forward, holding her shoulders firmly. She glanced toward the huge stallion. Her palms sweated as they neared the horse. "Keep looking at me," he said, drawing her attention back to himself. "Can you do that?"

She knew she was probably white as mist. The horse was still, as unruffled and controlled as Godric. If it sensed her fear, the beast was not unnerved by it.

"Are you ready?"

She nodded, not daring to let her gaze fall from his, concentrating on the slashed scars of his face. Calmness seeped into her veins. Surely a man who had survived whatever nightmare had caused such marks could control his own horse.

He turned her slowly until her back was at the stallion's side. The horse nuzzled his shoulder. "I will lift you and set you on him. Keep looking at me."

Vengeance snorted and Meiriona shuddered.

"Long, deep breaths."

It seemed very important to obey her captor. She kept her gaze fixed on Godric, tamping down her rising panic. Saints, why must she be such a coward?

Something so simple should not be so difficult. She breathed in; she breathed out.

His palms cupped her waist and, all at once, she was weightless, lifted like a child into the air. Then, the warm, solid leather of the saddle slid against her bottom and she sat sideways atop his mount.

Vengeance stepped to the side, twitching his tail.

"Whoa, horse."

She waited for the familiar dread to wash over her, anticipating the battle to fight the rising bile in her throat. Her toes curled into frightened knots.

"Keep looking at me and breathe."

She stared at him, noting the tiny laugh lines around his eyes and the stubble shadowing his chin. He was beautiful. Looking at him made it easier to ignore her terror. Her toes unfurled.

He laid his arm across her thighs, grasping the front of the saddle. Stepping into the stirrup, he swung up behind her with feline grace and pulled her into his lap, surrounding her with his strong, comforting arms.

Slowly, she let out the breath she had been holding. He held her tightly with one arm as the other grasped the horse's reins.

"Are you well?"

"Aye," she answered, surprised she spoke the truth.

"You are safe."

It made no sense, yet she *did* feel safe. She shifted into a tolerable position and allowed herself to relax a little.

Godric spurred the horse forward, toward the sounds of the giggling river. Her stomach jumped, pricking her bladder. Twigs popped under the horse's hooves as it picked its way through the woods in an even rocking motion.

Her captor's thighs pressed into her body. Saints, she needed to make water! She shifted again.

They rode in silence for a time toward an unbeknownst future. Dark clouds gathered, threatening rain, and her bladder felt tighter by the moment.

She wiggled on his lap, unable to get comfortable. "What do you intend to do with me when you get me to your home?"

His arm tightened. "I intend to marry you."

She shook her head but did not contradict him aloud. One part of her wished it were true. But Godric could never be hers, and she could never be his. She had family and duty to attend to, not foolish dreams.

She wiggled her hands. "You could untie me."

He gazed down at her. "Wherefore? So you can punch me in the cods again?"

She clamped her mouth shut. Why would she want Godric? He was crude, unrefined, untamed. A wicked man.

A drop of rain landed on her shoulder, reminding her again she needed a garderobe. She transferred her weight; his thighs on her buttocks made it impossible to be at ease.

"How long will we ride?"

"Not far today."

She tried to relax again but her bladder was too full. Surely she could wait until he stopped.

She stared into the passing trees. Oh, saints, what if even after he stopped, he refused to untie her to let her relieve herself?

More rain fell. Tiny splotches of water dampened her shift and made her bladder tighten. Cold. Wet. She squirmed, rocking her weight back and forth. Something hard poked her bottom, making comfort impossible.

Godric let out an exasperated gust of air. "Confound it, girl, if you intend for me to remain honorable an instant longer, keep still."

Meiriona turned her face so he could not see the blush creeping up her cheeks. "You did not force me earlier," she reasoned.

"Nevertheless, do not count yourself safe now."

"Oh." She concentrated on remaining stationary. Now that she was forced motionless, all sensation poured into her stretched bladder. She had not relieved herself since the wedding feast. A hard bulge on the saddle prodded her backside. She gnawed her lips, feeling the wine sloshing inside her.

"How long ere we stop?"

"Soon enough." He sounded irritated.

They rode silently, the passing trees marking the edge of her property. Godric seemed oblivious to her distress.

She longed to change positions again, bring herself a measure of comfort. But she dared not move, not even flinch.

Mild rain started and stopped in small bursts. Every raindrop pounded on her bladder. If only she could have a moment of privacy.

How could she tell him of her dilemma? Noblewomen did not speak of such things. If they needed to use the garderobe, they went silently, discreetly. What should she tell him?

"Will we be at your home today?" Her voice echoed loudly through the trees.

"Nay," he said, dashing her hopes of stopping.

The ground passed beneath them for long, unbearable moments. Each sway of the horse brought on waves of urgency. She was about to burst.

"When will we stop?"

He scowled. "If you are wondering when you can attempt escape, do not even entertain the thought."

Heat rose in her cheeks. He misunderstood the question. She remained quiet for a moment, biting her lips. Sweet Mary, what if she could not contain herself and peed on his legs? The thought was too horrific to contemplate.

Oh, mercy, oh, mercy.

"I . . . I need . . ." Her voice faltered. She could not make herself form the words. What she needed was too base, too common.

"What?" his voice was terse with irritation. "Speak up, lady. I cannot hear you."

"I need . . . I mean, I must . . ."

His scowl softened. "Whoa, Vengeance." The horse halted.

Her shoulders sagged in relief. He swung down from the saddle, then reached up and lifted her off the stallion.

Oh, thank the saints.

"Gramercy," she whispered, grateful to have been spared the humiliation of asking.

A mischievous smile turned up one corner of his mouth. "I will untie your wrists if you call me 'my lord' again." His voice was deep and seductive, barely above a whisper.

"Nay."

His gaze flicked to the woods and then back to her.

Jesu, she could not possibly take care of herself with her wrists tied.

The gleam in his dark blue eyes danced with enigmatic depth. It occurred to her he was enjoying watching her struggle with her pride. Wicked, wicked man.

What if he did not allow her to relieve herself? Or—she nearly gasped—what if he helped her?

"I will allow you privacy if you say it." His voice was as seductive as a pool of sunlight in winter.

She shook her head. "I cannot." Calling him her lord was akin to betraying her family. Perhaps the urgency would fade.

"As you wish." Shrugging, he cupped her waist, and made to lift her back into the saddle.

Mercy, she would soil herself if he put her back on that horse without allowing her those moments alone.

"Prithee," she said.

He halted, looked at her expectantly. A smile played on his lips. Like a barn cat toying with a rodent.

"Nay, I will not." She lifted her chin. He had no right to make sport of her.

She felt a pang between her legs. Jesu.

Lowering her lids so she would not have to look into his alluring midnight blue eyes, she stared at the ground and tried to think about rocks, sticks, and leaves. Anything but water.

He tipped her chin up. "Look at me."

She glared at him. "My lord," she bit out, angry with her seditious body. "I hate you."

CHAPTER 7

Godric stroked his stallion's glossy mane as he awaited Meiriona. The horse stomped its hooves impatiently.

Because of his promise, he had no choice but to allow her privacy. When he had untied her, he forced her word of honor she would not run and despite his unease, he let her go.

He tapped his fingers against the bridle. Surely she would not be so irrational as to attempt escape here. Vagabonds roamed the countryside. A comely woman wearing only her undergarments would be easy prey.

He peered into the woods but could only see leaves and bushes.

A moment ticked by. Then another.

"Meiriona!"

"Be patient!" Her voice reached him from too deep in the trees for comfort, but he relaxed slightly. The girl was determined but not foolish.

"I count the time," he yelled.

He heard an oath and grinned. She was embarrassed to announce she needed to piss but swore at him like a common soldier.

What a contradictory woman. She fascinated him. Her response to him fascinated him.

Her biting tone could not cover how her breath quickened the instant his hands touched her. It had been years since a noblewoman had not shrunk away after looking at his scarred face.

The way she stared at him with curiosity rather than revulsion captivated him. He felt like a heedless, idiotic frog, pleasantly swimming in a witch's cauldron because the water felt nice and warm. Years ago, he'd had the same reaction, and the witch had cooked him and served him up to a life of degradation.

She would do anything for her own gain—including betraying a betrothal contract and marrying a man three times her age. He must remember how coldhearted she was, because her hot-blooded passion drew him like a parched man craved water.

She trembled with fear when he'd first stolen her, but she sank into his body like they were old lovers when he dragged her to his lap and stroked her legs.

Aye, she feared him, but there was more to her response than fear. Her response said she was a woman with ardor as fiery as her hair.

He heard leaves crunching through the forest and Vengeance's ears flicked at the sound. She would return shortly.

He stroked the stallion's nose.

"Countess?"

There was no answer.

Sunlight filtered through the canopy of branches illuminating Meiriona's way as she hurried through the trees. A large hawthorn, loaded with crimson berries, stood a few yards away. Its thick trunk, nearly two and a half feet across, would provide perfect cover. She raced behind it, hiked her gown over her hips, and relieved herself.

Thank the saints, she sighed.

Sweet Mary, she was glad to be free of the warrior and his overwhelming presence. Stretching her arms, she reveled in the feeling of unbound hands. A branch scraped her bare arms and the soft, late-summer grass tickled her feet.

She stared at Mattie's opium pouch. Thank God, Godric had not questioned why she clenched her hands so tightly. Now, at last, she could find a way to hide it.

Reaching down, she tore a few stitches open in the hem of her chemise. Careful not to break the tiny package, she stuffed it inside her hem, thankful she would no longer have to carry it.

She stretched her cramped fingers, the moist morning air cool against her damp palms. Snatching a low-hanging leaf, she wiped sweat from her hands and reveled in the feeling of freedom.

Now was her chance. Perhaps if she wandered far enough into the woods before her captor missed her she could escape.

Meiriona glanced at her dirty shift. Run where?

She had never been far from the keep. Her fear of horses kept her a virtual prisoner of the castle. Highwaymen and cutthroats wandered the roads. She had no weapon and would be an easy target. Still, she was duty-bound to try.

A twig snapped under her bare feet and she whimpered as it stuck into her heel. Leaning down, she pulled it out, only to catch her hair in a low shrub. When she pulled back, her shift caught on a prickly juniper branch. The linen ripped apart as she wrenched it free, exposing her hip.

She sighed in resignation. She was not equipped for escape today. She must wait a little longer.

Her decision made, she headed back toward Godric.

Seconds later, a snuffing sound issued beside her. Her eyes widened and she twisted. A large boar rooted around muddy tree bases less than a stone's throw away. She froze in place, icy fear catching in her chest.

Its dagger-sharp yellow-gray tusks dug in the dirt as it rooted for grubs. Leaves rustled around the boar. It was huge, would probably feed a small village.

She crept backward as silently as she could, determined to make her way to the safety of Godric. Once she was close to him, she could scream. He would know how to deal with the animal. Having a plan gave her confidence, and she set her jaw in determination.

She slid her foot another silent step as the pig sniffed the air again. It moved so close she saw moss hanging from its muddy tusks. Foul yellow mucus dripped from its beady eyes. The dirty nose sniffed the air and twitched in her direction.

A raindrop from the overhead branches plinked onto her arm. She jumped and bit down on her fingers to keep from crying out. The bitter taste of earth mixed with bile in her throat. She took another step, then another.

The boar sniffed the air and shuffled closer. Its eyes rolled around searching for her. Her toe kicked against a rock, and she winced in pain. Taking heart that Godric must surely be close, she licked her lips and slid back three more paces.

The boar's tiny ears flopped as if listening for her steps.

Step, wait, step, wait. Her hair tangled on the snarled prickly branches of another juniper.

"Sweet Mary," she breathed, as it caught, forcing her to halt.

The pig's ears twitched, and he paced toward her.

She pulled at her hair, but it pinned her to the branch. Oh, heavens. Not now. Not now.

She tugged at it frantically, fingers shaking, then stepped forward to gain a better grasp. Leaves crunched under her bare feet and she froze. The ugly boar looked at her, its eyes seeming to focus on hers.

"Stars above," she whispered.

The pig's cloven hooves pawed the ground, and it raised its razor tusks.

She yanked at her hair, but the sharp, twisted brambles snagged the auburn tendrils. Caught like a rabbit in a snare!

Branches popped as the wild boar charged. Its hooves tore across the ground, moving in a blur.

Meiriona screamed, waiting for the deathblow. She squeezed her eyes shut. The beast's rank stench sharpened.

Abruptly the rasp of steel being drawn from a leather sheath sounded.

"Away, Meiriona!" she heard Godric shout.

Her eyes flew open. The boar stopped, confused by the new voice.

"Run!" Godric yelled.

She reared forward, but her tangled hair held, whipping her back. Sweat stung her underarms.

At once, Godric was between her and the pig, sword raised. The boar charged, and his sword sank into its thick flesh, piercing its chest. A high-pitched squeal pierced the forest and the animal floundered to one side, red liquid streaming from the wound. It flopped on its flank and twitched for a moment, then lay unmoving on the ground. The metallic smell of blood assailed her nostrils.

Thank the saints. Meiriona let out her breath, weak with relief.

Godric strode toward her. She wanted to wrap her arms around his neck and sink into his comforting embrace. Her shoulders relaxed. For once she was thankful for his dominating presence. At this moment, he was the most beautiful man she had ever seen. His proud, scarred features looked more like a vengeful archangel than ever.

A furious archangel. Blood dripped from his upraised sword as he stalked toward her. Leaves swirled around his boots. Alarm coursed through her.

Saints, he looked ready to hack her head from her body. His lip was drawn into a snarl and his scars were an angry white.

"Cease!" she cried.

"What are you doing this far into the woods?"

"Please."

"You cannot escape. 'Twas foolish to try."

"I . . . I was not running."

"Do not lie to me!"

She shook her head. "I wa—"

He drew closer; anger sharpened his features. "You are a lot of trouble, Countess."

She tugged at her hair, trying to free it from the limb. The strands were snarled around the branch like a messy squirrel's nest. Long auburn tendrils dangled from the clump.

"I should leave you here, tied up by your hair in the woods, you little fool."

His tone pricked her ire. How dare he be angry with her! "Fool? You beef-witted—"

He reached toward her, sword upraised. "You gave your word of honor that you would not run."

Meiriona gasped, her words stuck in her throat. Her earlier thoughts of escape convicted her, and she knew guilt was written on her face.

His arm muscles bunched as he readied his sword to strike.

"Cease!" She shrank away and clawed at her caught hair. Thank the heavens she had already urinated or she would have peed on the ground now.

"I should have known a woman's word is worth less

than a pile of horse dung. At least dung feeds the crops."

"You bloody oaf! Listen to me."

He wrapped his fist around the strands of her hair that anchored her to the tree. "You cannot escape."

"I was not—"

His fist twisted fully into her hair and pulled her face to his. "You are important to me," he growled. "Do not test me again."

Pulling the limb down, he sliced the caught lock, leaving a small wad of hair wound around the juniper branch.

Her heart sank as she realized her traitorous flesh had not expected anger. Her body craved his arms around her in comfort as he had done earlier. She wanted to sink into his powerful embrace and enjoy the feeling of safety he offered. She lowered her lids to keep her thoughts to herself. She was no more to him than a prisoner for his own gain, a necessary nuisance.

He released her, turning his back on her, and stalked through the underbrush.

"Follow me," he said, not bothering to glance back to verify her compliance.

Arrogant blackheart. He expected her to heel like a lapdog.

She huffed out an exasperated breath and scooped up a handful of muddy soil.

"Wait!"

He turned at her voice, a curious look flashing across his proud features.

With all the frustration she felt, she hurled her muddy missile. It landed with a splat across his chest, breaking into a thousand dirty pieces against his jerkin.

"You dare?" he growled, but a slow gleam of amusement crept into his eyes.

"I cannot keep up with you." Rocks pinched her

bare feet as she made her way toward him. Her mouth twitched with a smile she dared not display.

He raised an amused eyebrow. "Shall I carry you, my lady?"

"Nay." She raised her hand to ward him off, but he was already striding toward her. Grinning fully into his face, she cut to the side.

Godric reached her in two steps and lifted her into his arms. He smiled at her with the same wicked amusement he had teased her with earlier. "Ungrateful wench."

For a long moment the world seemed suspended and they were the only two people alive. A tendril of longing for something that could not be wound around her heart.

She buried her face in the leather of his jerkin, inhaling his comforting scent.

"Thank you for saving me, my lord," she whispered against his chest and only blushed a little as she said it.

"Had you not tried to run from me, you would not have needed to be rescued." His voice was kind but stern.

"If you had not stolen me, none of this would have happened."

Godric laughed. A tiny scar beneath his eye puckered. "You *do* belong to me." His voice was gentle, teasing.

"Nay," she said, but the idea of belonging to him was growing more palatable by the moment.

She pulled her cheek from his chest to look up at him, bumping her head on his chin as she did so.

"I did *not* run from you."

"You will not do so again," he demanded, clearly unimpressed with her declaration.

"You vexing man." She caught her hair and twisted it into a knot on top of her head. Having no pins, she simply wound it tight. "I am a woman alone in a wood filled with wild animals and vagabonds wearing only a shift. You may be a bastard, but you *are* my protection."

"My lady—" He gave her a hard stare and a short nod. "On that point, at least, we agree."

CHAPTER 8

A gusty wind howled around them as the stallion plodded through the underbrush, leaves crackling under its hooves. Tall ferns brushed Meiriona's bare legs, but from her sideways seat on Godric's lap she was reasonably comfortable.

He smelled of leather and smoke. Hours ago he had insisted she wear his jerkin for warmth. The supple black leather cloaked her in his masculine woodsy scent, giving her a feeling of safety, but his hand splayed against her ribs made her feel antsy as a captured bird.

"Is it true they call you the Dragon?" she ventured.

"Aye. 'Tis true."

Angling her head, she studied her captor, trying to determine if he had truly done the cruel deeds the bards sang about. Midafternoon sun gave him a roguish look. Short stubble lined his cheeks and upper lip, perhaps two or three days' worth, but it was obvious he was usually clean shaven. A tiny scar, older and more faded than the others, ran below his chin. He both frightened and intrigued her.

"Did you get your scars in battle?"

He shrugged. "That could be said."

"Where are you taking me?"

"Toward my home."

Annoyed with his curt responses, she gave up on conversation.

Godric led his mount through the woods, following the river. The surety of his horsemanship allowed her to relax enough to peek beyond the muscular arm holding the reins.

The thick underbrush rustled behind them, and she felt unseen eyes watching them. Her nape prickled.

Godric turned and scanned the woods. "I heard it too."

Cocking her head, she strained her ears but heard only the wet babble of the brook and the high-pitched warble of forest wrens.

"I hear naught amiss, now," she whispered.

"Likely just a hare." He led the horse over a fallen log.

She relaxed and lay her head on Godric's shoulder, thankful to be sitting across his lap in case another boar crossed their path. They rode in silence as she continued to watch the trees.

From the corner of her eye, she saw a distinctive purplish blue cloth, the color of her brother's favorite cape, poking out from behind a tall oak about three hundred paces to one side. Her breath caught.

Godric turned his head both ways, his gaze scanning the forest. "Did you see something?"

"Nay," she answered too quickly.

Surely, she was mistaken. It could not possibly be her ten-year-old half brother. . . .

But surely Damien was the only person alive who had a cape in those awful colors. Bright purple with blue streaks. Flamboyant and unruly, like him.

A tense bolt of energy shot though her at the thought of being rescued. She scanned the trees, giddy excitement flowing through her. How many men were out there?

Godric turned abruptly, following her gaze. "What do you see?"

"Naught," she lied, her heart pounding.

Godric pulled on the reins, turning his horse in a circle to search the nearby woods. "I see naught but trees."

"'Twas a bird, my lord, naught more."

He searched her face, and she gazed directly at him to cover her lie, but his knowing eyes disquieted her.

"I fear there might be another boar." She gulped and restrained the urge to thump herself on her head. The stupidest thing one could do when telling a lie was to blurt out another one in close proximity. She saw the flicker of keenness in Godric's eyes and knew she had been caught.

As he leaned close, his stubble brushed her cheek. "You know you have naught to fear from the forest animals while I am here."

Wariness engulfed her and shivers raced through her body. Beneath the mild tone of his voice, she heard a steel resolve.

"Are you afraid of me?" he asked in a low, dangerous whisper.

"Nay," she lied, refusing to be intimidated.

"You should be."

Licking her lips, she checked the urge to chomp down on her thumbnail.

"The truth, girl. What did you see?"

"I thought I saw a man, but 'twas only a brightly colored bird."

Godric drew a dagger from his boot, a fearsome change coming over him. "If someone comes, I will kill him. His blood will be on your hands."

Her stomach sank at his merciless tone, and she saw a glimmer of the Dragon lurking just beneath his surface. The last thing she wanted was a clash of arms between Godric and her father's men. If the men attacked, no doubt Damien would jump right into the middle of the fray. If a huge wild boar was no match for him, what chance did a scrawny ten-year-old boy have?

"No one was there."

Godric gave a curt nod and wheeled the horse to the northeast, spurring the beast into a gallop. Glancing over his shoulder, she saw glimpses of the purple cape following them in the distance. Evidently the other men wore greens and browns, for she could see no one else.

Biting her lower lip, she forced herself to look straight ahead. With the instinct of a mother bear protecting its cub, Meiriona determined to protect her brother. Damien was a good rider and would no doubt outdistance any who were with him.

If he got too close she would be forced to do something to distract Godric. But what?

She thought for a moment and remembered his words in her chamber. *You are beautiful.*

She had oft seen a strong knight become besotted when a saucy serving wench cast her blinking eyes on him. Some men momentarily lost all their wits, acting like half-wits to gain the woman's attention. Could she do that to Godric? Make him lose thought of everything but her?

A surge of power went through her as she imagined Godric the warlord, Godric the Dragon, love-struck over her. Her heart beat like a wild primitive drum.

She had never used her womanly wiles afore this. What on earth would she do? The serving wenches tossed their hair, touched the knights on the cheek, and kissed the men playfully.

How would Godric respond if she kissed him? Oh, wicked, wicked thought. 'Twas unthinkable, and yet her stomach twisted with anticipation.

Cease, she told herself. These were insane imaginings! She could not possibly kiss Godric. She would have to think of something else. She looked out into the forest again. The trees were sparser in this area.

Godric slowed Vengeance.

Meiriona glanced backward.

She blinked; her brother was visible. And *alone*! Just as she suspected, he had gotten separated from whoever else was with him. Foolish child! Why could he not have stayed with the others?

She splayed her fingers on Godric's scarred cheek. He flinched as if she had burned him. "My lord?"

A twig snapped behind them. Too close behind them.

Oh, sweet Mary! She tossed her head, feeling her hair come unwound from its bun. Running her fingers through the strands, she freed it until it cascaded across her shoulders and wound around her captor's arm in a mass of auburn curls.

Godric pulled back on the reins, slowing the horse to a soft walk. Dangerous flame burned in his eyes.

She swallowed, her mouth dry.

Out of the corner of her eye she saw her brother. He was clearly trying to hide, but the underbrush had been cleared in this area. She heard his horse whinny.

Having no time to think, she clutched Godric's tunic, parted her lips, and pulled him close.

Godric jumped and his eyes flew wide open, then his lips crashed down on hers with the power of a raging storm. Heat spread through her. His tongue swept into her mouth, mating with hers in a dance as old as time. She felt dizzy, as if she'd been sucked into a gale. His tongue traced her teeth slowly, like he wanted to taste every part of her. Then he withdrew.

"Lady."

She blinked, unable to gather her scattered thoughts.

"Now is neither the time nor the place."

Her mind raced. The serving wenches smiled,

clucked their tongues, and enjoyed their feminine power after they kissed a man. They seemed so in control of themselves.

But she did not feel powerful; she felt unstable, as if his arms around her were the only thing keeping her from flying into a million pieces.

She leaned against him, heart pounding. 'Twas not supposed to work thus. He wasn't besotted and stammering for her attention. He was calm, composed. Still in control. And more frightening and dangerous than ever. He stared straight ahead as if he could not bear to look at her.

Her cheeks heated. Mayhap she had done it wrong. She had no experience in kissing men.

Saints! What had she been thinking?

She glanced over his shoulder, abruptly remembering her brother. There were only trees.

Thank God she would not have to kiss Godric again.

Less than a quarter of an hour later, her captor halted the stallion under a swinging blue sign painted with a crude picture of a bed and spoon. It creaked in the wind and threatened to clatter down upon them.

Meiriona's eyes widened. "We are stopping at an inn?"

"Aye," he stated in the same brooding air that had come over him after he pulled away from kissing her. He heaved himself off the horse and reached up for her. "We have business to finish between us."

Her heart lurched, for his eyes smoldered with blue flame. She may have had little experience with men, but there was no mistaking his lust. He had told her the forest was the wrong place. But now, he had brought her to an *inn.*

"We cannot stay hither," she protested.

Godric grinned, determination in his gaze.

Her heart threatened to beat itself out of her chest. Images of her mother running from Yorkist soldiers flitted into her mind. She closed her eyes, disallowing the vision to form, but the memory of the scent of blood on her mother's thighs assailed her. What a fool she was for tempting Godric with kisses. Men could no more control their lust than wild beasts.

Meiriona gulped. "I will fight you."

"If your kiss was any indication, I think you will not." He winked at her.

Her face heated and she glanced to the side.

His large, warm hands cupped her upper arms as she slid off the horse. As her feet touched the ground, the crisp grass wound around her bare toes.

He tucked her wayward hair behind her ear, grasped her wrist, and dragged her in his wake as he stalked toward the tavern door.

Meiriona dug her heels into the mud. "I am not your chattel."

Godric scowled down at his captive. When had he ever understood women?

At the beginning of the night, she had been righteously indignant but when he kissed her, she turned soft as butter. He knew she was exhausted and hungry. So why, as soon as he had found a bed, was she back to being mule-stubborn?

For five years, he'd had no choice about where he slept, oft in dirty cells or dank dungeons. All due to Meiriona's betrayal. He did not care what she thought of their present accommodations. Spoiled, that was what she was. Unhappy because she would not have a fluffy feather mattress.

He grabbed her waist, determined to hoist her up like a sack of grain. The wide-eyed angst across her features stopped him and understanding dawned on him.

"God's teeth, girl, if I intended to rape you, I would not have to find a tavern to do it."

Meiriona blushed. "I thought—"

"You thought wrong." He slid his arm around her shoulder.

She did not fight as he lifted her to his chest and carried her into the decrepit inn.

Her cheeks were still pink minutes later when the goodwife showed them up several flights of stairs to a sparse room. He deposited his prize on a chair by a small stone hearth. Even wearing his jerkin she looked . . . incredible. He burned to rip off her thin chemise and ravish her on the bed.

But he could not.

He wanted to; indeed, that had been part of his plan. He had papers that proved their betrothal, a contract nearly as binding as marriage. Since the betrothal had been broken by force, he felt sure both the church and the king would honor his claim on her. The only thing standing in his way was her husband. If Godric took her virginity, his claim would be stronger and the marriage would be voided. He had never forced a woman before, but to secure the future for himself and his daughter, it *was* the logical thing to do.

Meiriona drew her knees to her chest, cocked her head, and looked at him.

She was beyond beautiful. In truth, he wanted nothing more than to see his petite captive spread naked on the bed. She was small; she would not be able to stop him if he forced her. So, why, then, did he not?

She bestowed a little smile upon him, and Godric knew exactly why he did not wish to rush her. She was the first woman in years who looked at his scarred face without revulsion. She had been angry, scared, embarrassed, haughty, but not once had she looked on him as if he was anything less than a man.

Rushing her might snuff the flame of desire. He wanted to fan the flame, build it to an inferno. He wanted her eyes to glaze over with hunger for him.

"Why are you looking at me thus?" she asked.

"Pardon?"

"As if you are trying to read what is written on my soul."

He smiled. "I want to know the best way to seduce you." His heart warmed when her cheeks pinkened; he could see the thinly veiled desire behind her embarrassment. "I am going to get us food and other provisions. I will be back in an hour or so. Try to sleep."

Closing the door to the room, he locked her inside, shaking his head at his own weakness. So many men depended on him securing the Whitestone property. He was risking the futures of his loyal, trustworthy men for the chance to win the heart of a fickle, betraying woman.

He was taking the fool's path in hoping he could open her to her own passionate nature rather than swiving her here and now.

But he did not want merely to claim her, he wanted her to *want* to belong to him. Selfish. Selfish. Selfish.

The heavy oak door slammed and the lock clicked into place. Meiriona sank further into the tattered cushion and drew her knees into her chest in a comforting gesture from childhood.

What a dismal place. Aside from her chair, the bare room contained only a lumpy bed, a rickety table, and a rusted chamber pot. The rushes smelled musty with age. The inn was as bleak as her thoughts. A sliver of evening sun shone through the narrow window. She stood, rubbed her sore legs, and followed the ray of light.

Bracing her hands against the splintered windowsill, she studied the window. Could she climb out of it and reach her father's men? She poked her head and one shoulder through the hole. A story below, the cluttered courtyard bustled with activity. She shoved her shoulders against the sill, but the opening was too small. She sighed and looked down. The building had no balcony or even a ledge upon which she could climb. Even if she fit through the window, she would have been unable to reach the ground.

Oh, vexation!

Horses peeked out stall doors; two dogs and a fat hog roamed in the busy yard. Chickens scattered about clucking indignantly when a purple and blue caped rider reined in at the barn.

Damien! Meiriona gripped the window sill and gasped. She scanned the courtyard, looking for Godric, but saw only animals and a few servants.

"Damien!" she called in a loud whisper. "Psst! Damien!"

The rider pushed back his hood, and an unruly mass of black hair tumbled forth. He glanced upward. The fading light revealed the same high cheekbones and flashing green eyes as Meiriona's, but his raven hair belonged to their mother's rapist.

"Damien!" she hissed. "Over hither."

Her brother caught her gaze, and his face broke into a lopsided grin.

"I knew I would find you!" He waved back frantically.

"Lower your voice, Damien!" She looked back and forth across the courtyard, praying Godric was not there. "Where are father and his men?"

Damien cocked his head to one side and shrugged. "No one here but me."

Coldness settled in the bottom of her stomach. "You are *alone*?"

He nodded. "I've been searching for you all night. Why did you run off after the wedding?"

"Saints! I did not run away. I was stolen!"

His eyes rounded with intrigue. "Stolen? You mean *captured*? By that man you were riding with?"

The tips of her fingers felt cold and she wiped her clammy palms on her skirt. "Holy saints above, Damien! Are you telling me that Father does not even know where I am?"

Damien's horse pranced to the side, and he pulled back on the reins. His purple cape fluttered around him. "Were you captured by that big man you were *kissing*?"

"Heavens, Damien, I kissed him to hide *you*." Her cheeks heated and her agitation rose. He was acting like he had all the time in the world. "Begone afore he sees you. Go and tell Father where I am."

"Leave?" Her brother pulled his horse up until it reared back. Her heart nearly dropped out of her chest. "If you are captured, then I must rescue you."

"Damien," she hissed, "be sensible. You are only a boy. He is a warrior. For the love of St. Jude, go find someone who can help me!"

Damien shrugged. He walked the horse forward a few steps, then threw aside his flamboyant cape, revealing a lumpy bundle perched across his knees. "I brought Grandpa's sword."

Meiriona gasped. "Be careful! You are not big enough to lift that thing. You will poke an eye out."

"Aye!" he agreed. "I will poke your captor's eye out."

"Damien!" She pushed away from the window, ran to the door, and pulled on the handle. The door rattled, but it did not budge. She scurried back to the window, her heart pounding with worry. "Do not dare challenge him!"

Damien pulled the long broadsword from its scabbard. "I will show you!" The blade wobbled unsteadily as he held it above his head with a scrawny arm. He puffed out his chest, his face awash with triumph.

Meiriona held her breath.

A gust of wind caught the sword and the sharp steel swung in a wide curve that gained speed at the bottom of the arc. Meiriona stared in horror as the blade sliced into his leg. Damien's wrist twisted at an awkward angle; he yelped and the weapon clattered to the ground. The mare danced beneath him, and he clutched her mane to keep from tumbling.

"Damien!"

The horse calmed, and Damien looked up sheepishly and shrugged. He held his bleeding leg. "'Tis only a scratch."

"Saints!"

He straightened his shoulders, sending ripples down his cape. "I can still ride a horse, and you can't."

Meiriona closed her eyes and grasped the edge of the window. Fear and frustration boiled in her stomach. "Damien, you fool, go get help!"

Her brother swung down from the pony and picked up the fallen weapon. He replaced it in the long scabbard and limped to the window. A red stain marred his hose.

Meiriona strained her hand out the window, wishing she could touch him for a moment to assure herself he was well.

"Sweet Mary, your leg—How deep is the cut?"

"'Tis barely grazed. My leg is stiff from riding."

Her heart caught in her throat. Damien had been crippled in one leg since birth, but he never complained. Not even when her father raged at him and blamed him for Mother's death. Truthfully, he was more son than brother to her. She was the only one to comfort and shelter him from the harshness of life.

"You treat me as though I am still a baby. I'm eleven summers now, you know."

"Too young to be traipsing all over the countryside alone," she muttered. She had never used his disability against him, had always treated him like a normal boy. But 'twas time for him to face facts. "You are a cripple, Damien. You cannot save me from Godric."

He lifted his chin, indignant anger gleaming in his eyes. "I will show you. I will fight him."

The door hinges rattled, and Meiriona's heart thumped in alarm. "Godric arrives! For the love of God, hide yourself," she whispered, slamming the shutters.

CHAPTER 9

Godric sucked all the air from the tiny room when he ducked under the narrow doorway, holding bread trenchers laden with food. The smell of fresh bread and spicy stew wafted around them, causing Meiriona's knotted stomach to feel queasy.

He eyed her keenly. "To whom were you talking?"

Meiriona edged away from the window and composed her face. "The stable groom," she lied, her gaze locking with his.

His deep blue eyes clouded with suspicion. "What were you talking about?"

Meiriona's mind raced, finally settling on a half-truth. "About escaping."

Godric moved closer, towering over her. "You cannot escape."

She raised her chin, and they glared at each other in a wordless stalemate. She *would* escape, but arguing about it would not help. He no longer intimidated her. If he wanted to hurt her, he would have done so already.

"Here," he said at last, shoving a trencher toward her.

She raised an eyebrow and accepted the food. "Gramercy." Her stomach churned, but her voice was calm and steady.

Godric stepped so close their bodies brushed and

she could smell his spicy, woodland scent. Leaning around her, he pushed the shutters open.

She flinched as he grasped the windowsill and scanned the courtyard. *Please, God, keep Damien away from Godric.*

Holding the trencher aside, she bent sideways to gaze out the window, but the strong line of Godric's back blocked the opening.

"I do not see anyone." He stepped back and scowled.

Rocking onto her heels, she steadied her breathing and smiled, relieved her brother had disappeared.

There was a pregnant pause.

"You need food," he stated flatly, taking two steps back and sitting on the bed. Propped there, his big booted feet wide apart, he looked just like a lion toying with a mouse.

He needed her to accomplish his goal of gaining her land, she reasoned to herself. But Damien? Would Godric consider her brother expendable?

Her captor tore a hunk of bread off his trencher with one huge, scarred hand. Power radiated from him, at once dreadful and compelling. Saints, if Damien attacked, Godric might kill him without a second thought. Meiriona turned and closed the shutters.

Godric raised an eyebrow. "What are you hiding?"

"I am cold." She made a point of shivering. Stew sloshed from her trencher into the rushes.

"You are lying." His gaze pinned her. "'Tis not cold in here. Who are you hiding?"

Meiriona held her trencher in front of her face to hide her features from his probing eyes. "No one."

Godric shrugged, dipped bread into his stew, and took another bite. "You will not escape."

Meiriona braced herself, fully expecting him to insist she reopen the shutters.

When he seemed more interested in his meal, she

let out a long breath. *Please, God,* she prayed silently, *Damien's a hardheaded urchin sometimes, but please make him go back home where he is safe.*

"We have been riding hard. Sit and eat," Godric said, motioning toward a chair.

She scooted around him. Her shift swirled about her ankles and stew slopped over the side of her trencher as she crossed the room. Plunking down in the tattered chair, she stared at her food.

Godric frowned, his spoon stopping halfway to his lips. "Verily, if you are cold, I will make a fire, but do not entertain the idea of escape. I will hunt you down anywhere you go."

She stuck her lip out in what she hoped looked like an indignant pout. 'Twas better if he thought she was miffed about escaping than for him to guess the real reason for her edginess.

"I do not need a fire right now."

"Then eat."

She gave him a defiant stare, brandishing her spoon like a drawn sword.

He scowled, but his lips twitched with what might be amusement.

As he ate, she stole glances at him through lowered lids. She expected him to feed himself like a barbarian, tearing his food in great hunks and shoving it into his mouth. But instead he ate with the manners of one of the king's court, each bite carefully selected and fully chewed before taking another.

What an enigma he was, this barbarian gentleman.

His hair was wildly tangled, his scars fearsome, and he had an untamed power about him, but at times he was more chivalrous and kind than any courtier she had known. He made her feel like a child's top that would not spin straight. She had felt more emotions in the past twelve hours than she had in the previous twelve years.

When he had kissed her, she had felt it all the way to her core. Whatever else happened, she would never regret the kiss.

He stared at her, his dark blue eyes burning into her like blue coals. "You stare at me as if you have ne'er seen me afore."

She pushed rushes around with her foot, trying to think of a plausible answer. She damned well would not tell him she had been imagining his lips on hers.

She settled again on a half-truth. After all, half-truths were the easiest type of lie to get away with.

"I am concerned about my virtue."

Godric scowled. A tiny scar beneath his lip flinched. "Virtue?"

Meiriona nodded, watching him intently.

"A woman who breaks an honest betrothal contract by marriage to another could easily be called an adulteress."

"I am no adulteress."

Godric's gaze flicked to her breasts. "Not yet."

She drew in a sharp breath, disliking the intensity of his gaze and the abrupt change in the room's air. "Is that why you brought me to the inn?"

He chuckled. "On my honor, as tempting a prize as you are, I will not tup you tonight."

"What do you mean," she demanded, "*not tonight*?"

"Damnation, girl, when I take you I will be damn sure you enjoy it."

Heat crept up her cheeks, and an unbidden wave of rippling desire spun though her. Dipping her bread into the stew, she forced a tiny bite and chewed carefully to avoid choking.

Her captor watched her with avid interest and the food turned to bland mush in her mouth. She did not dare speak. Sweet Mary, there was no telling what he would say next.

A second later, a knock sounded at the door. The

hinges screeched, and the door opened with a bang. Her brother, clad in peasant's garb and a large, floppy hat, entered struggling with a bulky empty tub.

Her breath left her body.

He flashed her a wink and bowed awkwardly to Godric. "Here is your bathing tub, milord."

Meiriona stared at her brother in wide-eyed shock. She choked back the urge to scream. What in the devil did he think he was doing?

Godric stood, glancing curiously at Damien and then at Meiriona. "I did not order a bath," he said gruffly.

"Courtesy of the inn, milord."

Go away, Meiriona mouthed at Damien, laying her trencher on the nearby table.

Damien gave her a nod and did not budge. He stood in the doorway, holding the heavy tub.

Godric stood between them, an unmoving wall of muscle. His dark gaze moved over her brother's face and then back to her.

Meiriona twirled her fingers around the ends of her hair fretfully.

Damien prattled on unabashed, drawing Godric's attention back to himself. "Me mistress says if our Lord Jesus could wash his disciple's feet then surely our guests can be given a bath."

"I have ne'er known an innkeeper to spend more time or coin than necessary on their guests," Godric said flatly.

Damien's mask of cheeriness faltered.

"I would like a bath," Meiriona blurted.

Godric's burning blue gaze cut to her before giving Damien a hard perusal. Her brother shuffled his feet, and she could feel his composure slipping.

"Prithee, my lord." She covered her nervousness with a slight smile. "I would love to soak in the tub."

Godric's eyes danced. His gaze burned a trail from

her breasts to her hips. For a moment she feared he would rip off her shift and throw her into the bath himself.

She would be willing, if it meant Damien would be safe.

Her brother lurched as if his leg had given out and the tub was dropping. "Please, milord, I am just a lame beggar boy trying to please my mistress."

Meiriona wheeled on him. Beggar boy indeed! She could not remember the last time Damien had tried to please anyone. If only he would leave!

Godric kicked at the rushes with his booted foot. A large puff of dust rose. "It seems that the innkeeper is fond of *cleanliness.*"

Meiriona sneezed.

Damien flashed her a brief grin when Godric took the tub and lowered it to the only bare spot on the floor.

Thank the saints. *Go,* she mouthed at Damien. *Please, go!* Her insides twisted.

"Thank ye, milord, me leg pains me from time to time," he said when Godric straightened to his full height.

Sweet Mary, he was laying it on thick. She checked the urge to snatch his arm and shake him.

Godric stared at her brother, and Damien pulled his hat brim lower.

"The water is at the bottom of the stairs. Be right back." He stomped down the short flight of stairs with loud bouncing steps.

Leaning by the window, Godric folded his arms over his chest and propped one leg negligently against the wall. A coiled prowler waiting to strike. He examined her face as if he were trying to remember something.

Her toes curled on the rushes and she drew her hand to her throat, lest he see the pounding erratic pulse of her heartbeat.

Her brother trudged up the steps carrying two buckets of steaming water. He dragged his lame leg to the point where she did not know if his act was real or simply part of his wild stint. Water sloshed on her hem and into the rushes as he poured it into the tub.

Her legs seemed leaden and her fingers quivered no matter how tightly she held them. What the devil did Damien think he was doing? She wanted to kick him. *Get out of here, you fool!*

Her tongue felt thick in her mouth. She could not think of one thing to say to distract Godric, who leaned unmoving against the wall, glancing keenly from her to her brother.

Damien stomped down again, hoisted two more buckets, and climbed back up, slopping water onto the stairs and the floor. She hoped it was not as obvious to Godric as it was to her that he was no manservant.

When water overflowed the top of the tub, Damien looked at her.

Leave! Leave!

Only Godric's eyes moved. A leopard waiting to pounce.

Hurry, you fool! Leave! He suspects!

Damien shuffled backward as if debating whether to stay or go. He turned and crossed the threshold.

Godric's arm shot out, grasping her brother by the shoulder. Meiriona's stomach lurched. "With strong arms like that, you would make a fine bowman."

Damien beamed, staring at her captor with moon-faced awe.

"I . . . I would?"

Oh, please. She nearly groaned.

"Aye, if you were one of my men, I would start you in training right away."

"Honest?" Damien straightened his shoulders.

Godric nodded.

Meiriona scowled at him. What a stupid idea. The

last thing Damien needed was some fool notion in his head about being a bowman.

Leave, you little brat!

Godric does not know who Damien is, she told herself, biting her tongue to keep from screaming.

"Thank you for the water. You may go now," she said pointedly.

Damien blinked, ignored her, and grinned at Godric.

You fool! Can you not see that he suspects? He does not want to make you a bowman; he wants to capture you for use as a hostage.

"Come hither, Meiriona," Godric commanded, snatching her upper arm in a tight grasp.

She flinched. Wariness ran through her as her toes slid across the rushes. Godric now held them both. He looked at her expectantly.

"This boy has fine, strong arms, does he not?" He pulled her closer to her brother. Dust motes swirled in the air.

She shook her head, not bothering to look at Damien. "Nay, I do not think so."

Godric peered at her. Her hand went protectively to her throat.

"He does."

Her gaze flicked to Damien, who suddenly seemed uneasy. Jesu, why could he not have seen the danger ten minutes ago? Damien pulled aside, his hand reaching for the doorway, but Godric's hand tightened on his shoulder and forced him back.

Meiriona gritted out a smile; she could feel her lips wobbling. "You are correct, my lord. He has nice, strong arms. Perchance we should let him go about his duty."

"You have the same nose," Godric said.

"Pardon?"

"I said, you and the servant boy have the same nose. And the same eyes as well."

Meiriona's stomach flipped. "Many people have green eyes, sir."

Damien stepped back, sliding into the hallway, but Godric pulled him forward. "Who are you, boy?"

Damien's eyes went round with terror. He squeaked something unintelligible.

Saints! Just wrench free and run!

"Your . . ." Godric's gaze cut from her to Damien. "Brother?"

"Aye, milord," her brother said, nodding frantically.

Meiriona lurched forward. "Holy Saints, Damien! Hush!" Damien might dare some wild schemes, but when caught, he could not lie to save his life. If he had kept his mouth shut she might have been able to talk their way out of this. "Run, you fool!"

Godric's hand tightened like an iron manacle on her arm. His knuckles were white on Damien's shoulder, clamping him into place.

She jerked backward. Godric released her, and she fell unceremoniously onto the bed. He spun Damien around and slammed the door shut, blocking it with his body.

Damien stared at him as if he were some mythical god.

Godric's gaze turned to her. "I did not know you had a brother."

"Half brother," squeaked Damien. "I'm a well-kept secret. Her father's ashamed of me, sir."

Bouncing off the bed, Meiriona sprang between Godric and Damien. Her long hair flew about her face. "If you hurt him, I will kill you, I swear it."

Damien peeked around her. "I *would* make a nice bowman, milord, if you would give me the chance."

"Damien! You fool! He said that to get us close together. You cannot be a bowman."

Her brother hung his head and shut his mouth.

Godric leaned against the door, propping one foot against it. "What will I do with both of you?"

"If you harm one hair on his head—" Meiriona warned, her angry gaze meeting Godric's like a mother bear whose cub was being threatened.

Thumbing his jaw, Godric glanced at Damien. "Your brother is safe, as long as he obeys me."

Oh, sweet Mary! Her nerves stretched like a tight bowstring. Damien rarely followed *anyone's* orders.

Damien nodded like the village idiot, and she wanted to kick him.

"Our plan has changed. Lady Meiriona, you have one hour to bathe and refresh yourself afore we leave." He pushed her toward the steaming tub and took a firm grip on Damien's arm, guiding the boy to the door. "You, boy, will come with me."

CHAPTER 10

Exactly one hour later, Meiriona sat before a small fire combing her hair with her fingers to dry it. The last rays of light glimmered through the tiny window, and specks of dust danced in the fading sunbeams. Her stomach churned fretfully. If Godric harmed one hair of Damien's head, she would kill him.

The rasp of a key sounded in the old lock, and the heavy door swung inward, revealing Godric and Damien. Meiriona jumped up, shift swirling, and ran to her brother. He had changed back into his own clothes: a too-small gray tunic, black woolen hose, and the familiar purple and blue cloak. He grinned at her.

She grabbed his chin like he was a small child although he was nearly as tall as her.

"Did he hurt you?" She turned her brother's face this way and that, inspecting him for signs of abuse. She did not see any discernable bruises.

Damien pulled back his head and rolled his eyes. "He fed me."

"You ate with him?" she hissed. "This is not some party with the queen."

"Well, you kissed him, sister."

Irritation shot through her. "He is our enemy, Damien!"

Godric, still standing in the door frame, cleared his throat. "That will be enough, lady."

"What did you tell him?" Her voice came high and fast. She ignored Godric, although she felt his gaze boring into her.

Damien shrugged. "Naught."

She wheeled on her captor, then stopped and blinked. He was clean shaven, his strong jaw and aristocratic cheekbones exposed. His dark hair was slicked away from his face, revealing the midnight blue of his piercing eyes. The damp ends of his locks curled around his collar and dripped onto strong, wide shoulders. The scars and his countenance implied danger, but his sensuous mouth hinted at unspoken erotic promises.

He was clad in black. A clean tunic pulled across the width of his chest. The muscles of his thighs strained against his breeks, every fiber discernable through the leather. The dust had been knocked off his tall boots. A dark midnight angel.

Her mouth went dry, and for a moment she could not speak. She blinked several times before realizing her grandfather's sword hung at Godric's hip.

She balled her fists on her hips. "That is our sword."

"And 'tis in better hands with me."

She narrowed her eyes, frustrated with his highhandedness. "You cannot steal our things."

Godric scowled. "I steal nothing. I take what is mine."

Anger grew inside her, like a brewing storm. "That is not yours. Damien is not yours. I am not yours."

Her captor's brow darkened even further, and he stepped close, his large boots crushing the rushes. "My patience wears thin, lady."

She scooted back, away from the hearth. Bumping her calves on the chair, she sat down with a plop. "You will not get away with this."

"Mayhap. Mayhap no." He extended a hand to help her rise.

Looking disdainfully at his hand, she rose unassisted and dusted her palms on her chemise as if she could wipe him off as easily.

Shrugging, Godric handed her a small ragged bundle. "Put this on."

"What is it?" She eyed him warily and shook out the fabric, stirring up the dancing dust particles. It was a huge, ugly tunic. Long rips rent the tattered garment. Three of the tears had been poorly repaired while the others gaped open, strings hanging. The original color was hard to discern through the many black, green, and red stains.

"You want me to wear this?"

Godric's jaw hardened. "'Tis what the serving wench had."

She wrinkled her nose. "'Tis disgusting."

He shrugged again. "Put it on or go naked, it matters naught to me."

Meiriona clamped her lips and pulled the garment on over her head. She sniffed it suspiciously, but the odor would be easier to tolerate than traipsing around the countryside wearing only her shift.

"It don' fit." Damien smirked. "Hangs off of ye like a dishrag."

"It scratches too." Meiriona gave her brother a hard look before turning to Godric. "I suppose I should thank you, but I will not."

Godric's sensuous mouth turned up in a slight smile. He dug into a pouch swinging from his great leather belt.

"Mayhap this will amend for it." He held out a small wooden box, tiny in his large palm. His voice seemed to gain an edge of vulnerability.

She searched his handsome, scarred face, but he scowled. She was obviously mistaken to assume he had any feelings. Taking the gift, she ran her fingers over it. The wood felt cool and inviting. It was plain, smooth, made of exotic teak and well crafted. She would have loved to throw it in his face, but curiosity stopped her. An awkward pause grew between them as he waited expectantly in silence.

Pulling back and forth, she pried the tight lid from the box then opened it slowly, as if there might be a spider inside waiting to bite her fingers.

Green jewels enthroned on a scrap of white silk twinkled at her, and she gasped. Reaching inside, she pulled out an ornate hair comb. Four large tines with gilding sparkled in the firelight. The handle, encrusted with large emeralds and tiny diamonds, caught the firelight and bounced their reflection around the room in a dappled glow.

Her fingers fondled the bauble with guilty longing. Its price would fetch a goodly meal for her people. Mayhap even pay for her ideas about taking Mary's wool to market. Just holding it made her feel spoiled.

"Where did you get this?"

Godric cleared his throat. "I brought it with me."

"You did?" What sort of man brought a present to someone he planned to abduct?

"Aye," he said, his voice sharp and curt. He looked distinctly uncomfortable, his large shoulders hunched, and he glowered in a way that made her wonder if he had ne'er afore given a woman a gift.

Her nails, ragged and ripped, looked altogether out of place against the shining hair bauble as she turned it over and over again in her hand.

"'Tis beautiful."

"I remembered your hair." He fidgeted with the hilt of her grandfather's sword as if preparing for battle.

She smiled, her heart melting somewhat. "Are you *courting* me?" she blurted out.

A dark scowl crossed his scarred features. "You belong to me. I have no need to court you."

Meiriona shot him an exasperated look.

Pulling her hair back, she pushed the hair comb

into it and tamped down the vain longing for a looking glass. She would have to sell the bauble to buy food for her people as soon as she escaped. Still, her hands itched for a mirror to see how the emeralds looked against her auburn hair.

Surely it was not such a great sin to enjoy wearing it for just a little while.

"We found shoes, too," squeaked Damien.

Meiriona swiveled toward her brother. Sweet saints, she had forgotten he was there! He held out a pair of well-worn, plain leather shoes. He seemed completely unaware of the crackling air between Godric and her.

She took the shoes in a daze and bent to slip them on, heedless that they were scarcely better than the nasty tunic. She wiggled her toes against the thin leather, reveling in the feeling of having something between her soles and the dirty floor.

Godric handed her a strip of rope, and she tied it around her waist as a belt.

"Gramercy."

He leaned his hip against the bed, waiting. "Are you ready?"

She nodded, feeling bewildered.

"Come." He motioned her forward. "Our time of rest is gone."

They traipsed down the short flight of stairs and past the inn's common room, making their way toward the courtyard.

Being clean from her bath and having a new jewel made her feel like one of the queen's ladies. Tamping down her guilt over wearing something beautiful while her people neared starvation, she adjusted the hair comb so it felt secure.

She followed Godric and Damien across the courtyard through a clucking labyrinth of chickens. Suppertime neared and several servants labored with their chores. A boy mucking out the stables stopped and leaned on his shovel. He raised an eyebrow as she passed, his gaze flicking from her hair to the splotchy tunic.

She lifted her chin and he smirked. Cringing, she felt her composure slip. She hesitated in her step, and one of her overlarge shoes flopped on the dirt. Feeling like a fool, she readjusted her footwear and stared at Godric's back as he paced across the grounds. The fog cleared from her mind with every step he took.

She watched, disgusted, as Damien followed their captor like a dog. Godric ruffled the boy's hair, much like one would a pet's. It felt like she observed a mirror: had she not been following Godric as well? Snatching the comb, she shoved it into the belt of her tunic. She, too, had been behaving like a lapdog with a pretty collar.

Lingering behind, she dragged her feet. Godric was dangerous. Her own behavior, like a bitch in heat, appalled her. If he continued to cast his spell, she would in truth be crawling at his feet.

That vile thought brought her sharply to her senses and she remembered her vow to never again put off her duty. Had she not already learned what disobedience and willfulness brought into her life? If she'd been a more dutiful woman, a better person, she'd likely now be married to a sweetly handsome man who would have protected her from men like the Dragon.

She sucked in a deep, calming breath. A man who dragged her from bed like a wild beast to feed his revenge was not a man to be toyed with. If she did not get free from his hold, she might lead all her people to destruction.

She now had shoes, a dress, and the means to purchase food. Surely those things were a sign from God that she should flee. Better to face the dangers of the woods than the dangers to her soul. She would flee back to her father and her husband. God would protect her because she was doing her righteous duty. Damien would follow if she broke away.

Searching for an opening, she noted that the yard was well fenced. Horses watched them from their stalls and a pig snorted at his feeding trough. She swung her gaze to and fro and spotted an unlatched gate on the far side of the yard. She lingered farther and farther behind, knowing she needed a good head start to outrun Godric. With luck, they could lose him in the woods. She prepared mentally, waiting for the moment Godric would duck inside the stables.

The instant he stepped inside, she surged forward, feeling vigor pump into her limbs. The gate was within easy reach. Glancing over her shoulder, she saw Damien had not budged. She pushed the gate wide and slowed, but he still had not seen her.

"Run, Damien," she was forced to yell, then sprinted into the woods, confident Godric would follow her first, giving her brother a moment to catch up.

The trees passed in a blur as she raced through the woods. Hiking up her skirts, she sprinted faster when she heard Damien behind her. Now, they just had to find a place to hide.

Hot breath fell upon her neck, then Godric snatched her upper arm and swung her around. Her skirt flew up and one of her shoes flopped.

"Do not think you can get away." The crescent scar on his cheek was white with checked anger.

She balled her hands into fists, her helplessness fueling her own fury. "Release me!"

He held her rooted in place. "Confound you, lady, you will behave." He turned and dragged her in his wake back through the gate, across the yard to the barn. "I will not spend the journey home chasing you."

In the stable yard, Damien waited, holding Vengeance's reins. Her ire rose when she saw her brother acting like a servant. "So that is where we are going? Your hovel?" she spat out. "So you can dress us in ridiculous clothes to be your slaves?"

Godric marched her to the horse. A tic formed in his jaw as he dragged rope from the saddle's bag and held it up to her.

"Give me your wrists."

"I will not."

Damien slid beside her, touching her arm. "Sister," he said softly. "We cannot outrun him."

Anger burned in her heart. "You jolthead! What has come over you?"

"Your brother has some sense about him," Godric growled.

Damien beamed at the praise.

She shook away from Godric and caught Damien's tunic in her fists. "If you had run we could have gotten away! At least one of us!"

Damien pulled back, leaving her holding empty air. "Do not be a fool, sister."

"Damien!" she yelled at his back.

The boy wheeled, grabbed her sleeve, and yanked her close so he could whisper in her ear. "He said he would train me to be a bowman. We can get away after—"

"He poisons your mind," she hissed.

Godric pulled the boy from her, his jaw hard and determined. "Do not conspire together. Now, give me your wrists," he said to Meiriona.

She looked from her captor to her brother, both of whom were rooted to the spot. She tossed her hair back. "There is no need. I will not leave without my brother."

Godric raised an eyebrow. "You are right." He turned to Damien. "Here, boy, give me your arm." He snatched Damien's wrist before the boy could proffer it, wound the rope around it, then tied it to his own waist, leaving a long trail between them. A puppy on a leash.

He clapped Damien on the shoulder. "My apologies, boy, this is a precaution for your sister's good."

Meiriona could have kicked Damien, who shot her a hard look before turning his starry-eyed puppy gaze back to Godric. "I understand, sir."

Godric clasped Meiriona on the shoulder. "'Twill bode ill for your brother should you try to escape."

"How dare you." Her insides twisted. "You would put Damien on a leash like a dog?"

"If it means you will behave, then aye." He let her go, dusting his hands on his leather-clad thighs.

Her hands balled into fists in impotent rage. "Blackheart!"

Godric grinned sardonically. "I have been called worse."

She grabbed her brother's tunic sleeve. "See what you have done."

"What *I* have done?" Damien's purple cape whipped around him as he held up a bound wrist. "'Tis your fault I wear this. Had you kept your mouth shut I would still be free."

"He is poisoning your mind. We could have run!" She turned to Godric. "I will not ride with you."

Godric heaved a deep breath. "I grow tired of arguing. If you do not wish to ride, then you can walk."

"Fine. She crossed her arms over her chest. "I would rather ride with a pig."

"So be it," Godric answered.

CHAPTER 11

The full moon shimmered high in the sky by the time Godric stopped for the night. Meiriona had the distinct impression he would have pressed onward except her legs had grown so weary she stumbled.

She walked beside the horses, hurling angry glances at Godric and her brother. Damien, still tied to Godric by the long tether, returned her irate glares from atop his dapple-gray mare. Godric sat stoically on Vengeance, watching only the river and the path that closely followed it. He held his reins in one fist and Damien's in the other.

They had not spoken, nor had she made a single sigh of complaint since leaving the inn. She refused to whimper even when sticks cut through the thin soles of her shabby shoes or when brambles scratched her legs. Despite her new dress and the blessed lack of rain, Meiriona felt chilled and miserable.

Godric dismounted, indicating an area of level ground. "We make camp here."

An owl hooted above them and frogs chirped into the night. A small brook gurgled over rocks a few steps away and trees provided an enormous leafy canopy shielding the stars. 'Twas a peaceful place. She might have enjoyed it under different circumstances.

Their captor untied Damien so he could dismount.

"You are a good rider, boy. Many men would come unbalanced with no reins and a tied hand, even at the slow speed we traveled."

Meiriona cast her brother a dark look when he smiled up at Godric. Little traitor!

Damien pulled his pony to a patch of late summer grass illuminated by moonlight. "How much farther is the journey?"

"If the bridge has not washed out with last week's rain, we will be there in two days."

"Where are you taking us?" Meiriona asked, breaking her self-imposed silence.

"My *cave.*" Godric raised his brow in a teasing gesture.

Meiriona ground her teeth in irritation. *Condescending lout.*

"Do you really live in a cave?" Damien looked intrigued.

"Nay." Godric chuckled and clapped the boy on the shoulder.

Annoyed, Meiriona tapped her foot against the rich forest earth.

"We ride to Montgomery," Godric said.

"Is that a castle?"

"Aye, boy, a fine castle. Enough questions. Go gather firewood. Be back shortly, and do not go far."

Damien nodded eagerly, whistling as he bounced away from the two of them.

Irritation burned inside her, and she scowled at her brother's back, wishing he were home. She glared at Godric.

"You put fool ideas in his head. Talking to him about being a bowman."

Godric knelt to fill his drinking bladder with water from the brook. "'Tis clear you love the boy. Let him make his own decisions."

"He is a child!"

Leaves swirled about the forest floor as Godric

walked toward her. "He seems intelligent enough. I was about his age when my father took me into his house to become a knight."

"Your father? You mean the Earl of Blackhawk?"

"Aye."

Tipping his head back, he took a long draw of water, then lowered the vessel and handed it to her.

She glanced at the drinking bladder, hesitating. Would the rim still be warm from his lips? Drinking from it seemed too intimate, yet her parched throat longed for refreshment.

"Go on," he said. "My lips did not kill you afore."

Meiriona blushed. Could he see into her thoughts?

"It matters little to me what your lips do." She gave him an indignant look and gulped a mouthful to belabor the point.

The rim was not warm, as she had feared, and the water was so cool and delicious she had to resist closing her eyes in pure pleasure.

Vowing to hide her thoughts better, she thrust the vessel at him curtly. Water spilled onto his tunic, making the linen cling to the muscles of his stomach.

He grinned rakishly at her rudeness and stared at her lips with a sultry gaze that made her cheeks heat. She knew she had not fooled him at all.

"We were talking about Damien," she said haughtily.

Godric cleared his throat. "There are many things a boy can learn—even one with no previous training."

"He is a cripple," she said softly.

"Do not judge him by his leg."

She pursed her lips. "Do you propose to know what is best for *my* brother?"

"If the choice is between being cloistered away or learning a trade that can benefit him, then aye."

"I do not cloister my brother. I keep him from harm."

"You keep him from life."

"I do *not* keep my brother from life." She picked at a twig and snapped it in two with restless fingers.

Leaves rustled behind them, and she watched Damien return, his arms laden with small branches, sticks, and a couple of larger logs.

Frustration ate at her. Why did men always seem to think they knew what was best for those around them? She looked from her brother to Godric, more determined than ever they would escape. "My men will find us."

"Your brother told me he came alone to look for you."

Meiriona's jaw dropped. "I do not believe you."

Godric shrugged. "Nevertheless, 'tis true."

Her throat constricted. "When did he tell you that?"

"While we ate at the inn."

She turned to her brother. "Is it true?"

Damien set his load on the ground in the middle of the small clearing. "There was a commotion in the village. The bells sounded and most of the men went, but I saw something moving on the cliff below your window. I took the secret passage from your father's chamber to make it outside the castle walls quickly. 'Twas only luck that I found you at all."

Her heart sank. "You mean they are not even looking for me?"

Damien shrugged apologetically. "I do not know. I left right away. I thought you'd run because of having to marry Uncle Pierre."

Godric glanced from her to her brother. "If you had married me, I would never let someone steal you. What sort of weakling is your new husband?"

"Just because he does not steal brides in the night does not mean he is weak," she said irritably.

Godric shrugged. "I do what I must to keep what is mine."

She sank sullenly onto a fallen limb, smoothed her

skirt across her knees in long-born habit, and turned her shoulder to Godric.

"Build a fire, boy." Godric tossed Damien a flint and tinderbox.

She cut Godric a look over her shoulder. "He does not—"

Damien's glare stopped the words in her throat. Heavens, he was already angry enough with her.

She could feel her brother's awkwardness as he shuffled his feet for a moment then knelt, favoring his lame leg. He piled the two logs atop each other and put the small branches in a haphazard stack on top.

Meiriona watched him, unease growing, as he fumbled with the flint. After several attempts, it flashed, but the spark burned out before lighting anything on fire.

She slid partway off the log, but Damien gave her a look that said he would never forgive her if she interfered.

Sparks flashed in the night but burned out cold. Damien's face paled in the moonlight and beads of sweat formed on his upper lip. She saw Godric watching from the corner of his eye as he tended to the horses.

She grasped the log she sat upon so tightly the bark splintered under her nails. The forest seemed as tense as she. Silence grew as Damien struggled with the fire. Even the owl stopped hooting. Godric finished his chores and frowned at her brother.

"Who taught you to build a fire?"

Meiriona flinched at Godric's disapproval. "He is not a servant," she hissed.

Damien's composure crumbled under Godric's harsh gaze. His lip trembled, and a deep blush crept up his face.

"No one, sir," he said, his face downcast. Twigs cracked with his fidgeting as he stared at the ground. "I have ne'er afore built a fire."

Godric shot a look at Meiriona. "You do not know how to build a fire?"

Damien's blush deepened.

She tapped her foot. "There is no need for you to be building fires, Damien. There was no need at home, and there is not now."

"Do *you* ever build fires?" Godric gave her a pointed look.

She shrugged, refusing to answer. She knew a way to make one fast and hot.

Damien shuffled his feet. "Meiriona said I might fall in on account of my bad leg."

Godric's countenance softened. "Mayhap 'twas true when you were a child around your nanny's skirts, but you are more than a child now."

Biting his lower lip, Damien stared at the ground. Her heart went out to him. She was ready to screech at Godric like a fishwife but had the impression it would only embarrass her brother further.

Godric booted over the haphazard pile. It felt like he kicked her in the stomach.

"Look at me, boy," he said, kneeling beside Damien.

Her brother blinked rapidly before complying.

"No one can expect you to know how to do something you have ne'er done afore, you understand?"

Damien nodded, still biting his lower lip.

Meiriona clenched her fists. It irritated her that Godric would pretend he cared about an eleven-year-old's pride when 'twas obvious he was a blackheart. Why could Damien not see through him?

"First, pile up dry leaves and tiny sticks that burn easily," Godric said gently, scooping some into his large palms and making a little pile.

Meiriona folded her arms across her chest. Godric should know fire was dangerous for children. Her brother could slip and fall in any second. She longed to say so, but Damien looked so relieved her heart would not allow her.

"Take some of the smaller sticks and pile them around thus." Godric made a little tent of sticks around the dry leaves.

Her brother laid a few twigs on the pile.

"Do not stack them too tight, boy, the fire has to breathe. Now give me the flint."

Their two heads bent close together, focused on their task. She saw tension leave Damien's shoulders. His response to Godric's gentle teaching style felt like a slap in the face.

Godric struck the flint, and the pile burst into flame. Cupping his hands near his mouth, he blew until the wood caught hold.

"Add more leaves, if needs be, but get the small sticks burning first."

Once the fire was glowing, Godric began adding larger sticks and then finally the two logs.

As she watched, Damien seemed to grow before her eyes. He was no longer the awkward child who constantly got too close to the fire and had to be rescued from falling in. She blinked back tears. Where had the time gone?

Godric clapped Damien on the shoulder. "Tomorrow you will practice doing it by yourself."

Her brother stared at their captor as if he were the Messiah come back to earth.

Meiriona turned her back on them, her feelings jumbled.

Damien piled some leaves up for a cushion and then lay upon his purple cloak watching the fire.

Their captor dusted his hands on his breeks and fished in the saddlebags that lay on the ground beside the camp. He handed her a block of cheese and dry bread. "Eat. Tomorrow we ride early."

She took the food and chewed methodically, lost in

thoughts of how to escape. Her brow furrowed as she watched Damien and Godric talk softly by the fire. Running had not worked. He was too fast, too strong for her to best on her own. She would be forced to use the opium tied in her hem. But how much should one use on someone his size? Too much would kill him. Too little would anger him.

Surely Montgomery Castle would have a healer and she could find an answer to her question. And then Damien and she would flee for home.

Once she formulated a plan, the dried food tasted much better, and she was able to choke down most of it. But why did her heart tug for the impossible?

Damien rolled onto his back and closed his eyes.

Godric rose, walked to her, and sat down uninvited. He was so close she could smell the lingering scent of the campfire. Scooting to the end of the log, she leaned away.

"Give me your feet," he said without preamble.

She looked at him quizzically. "Pardon?"

"I want to inspect them."

Tucking her feet under her skirts, she glared at him. "I am not a horse to be inspected."

Godric sucked in a breath of air and blew it out in a long breath. "Save my stepmother, you are the most exasperating woman I have ever met. Now give me your feet!"

Meiriona frowned and plunked her foot into his lap with a hard thrust that made him groan and adjust himself.

He glowered at her, and she smiled, feigning innocence.

Muttering something about the treachery of women, he drew her foot up to look at it. She held onto the edge of the log to keep from toppling.

He slipped off the worn peasant shoes that now had three holes in the sole. Her flesh was beginning to bubble into blisters.

"Why did you not tell me?"

"Better to be blistered than to ride with a bastard," she said sweetly.

He poked at one of the blisters, and she winced.

"You think I am an ogre?"

"Well, are you not? Capturing women at midnight, climbing down a castle wall, forcing a woman to walk while you ride."

Godric looked at her for a long moment, his hair gilded in the fire's glow. "'Tis true, I did those things and have done much worse."

She sniffed haughtily. "So you do not deny it, and in fact say you have done even more."

He lowered her foot and slid so close their body heat mingled. "I did not force you to walk, as well you know." His voice was a soft caress.

Meiriona looked out into the gently swaying leaves lit with the soft glow of the campfire. She breathed in a deep, long-suffering breath.

"So this is my fault?"

He brushed her hair behind her ear, and her scalp tingled from his touch. "We do not need to argue over the past. Let us start a new day together as husband and wife of Whitestone."

"I am already married, sir." Her voice was so shaky she was afraid it would crack any moment.

"So you are."

The leather of his breeks strained against his thighs as he rose, picked up the length of rope, and held it out to her as if it were a dark, snakelike gift. He looked like a gorgeous avenging archangel sent to judge the unfaithful.

"Time for sleep." His voice was flat and unyielding.

Her heart beat a hollow drum in her chest. She was to be tied like an animal. She glanced at the trees, longing to run, but knew Godric was too fast and powerful. *And* he still had Damien.

Godric cleared his throat, telling her his patience ran thin. Lines of exhaustion crinkled around his eyes.

She rose with all the dignity she could muster, walked the two steps between them, and thrust out her hands in silent surrender.

He gripped her wrists and pulled her toward him, catching her waist in a powerful embrace. "Someday you will come willingly," he whispered. His voice stroked her thoughts the way his hands had stroked her thighs when they were at the bottom of the cliff. Warm, commanding, full of erotic promise.

Never, her mind screamed, but she was too breathless to say the word.

He took both of her hands in his, and his fingers lingered on the insides of her wrists, drawing deliberate sensuous circles with his thumbs. A thrill of fear and fascination bolted through her.

Placing her wrists one against the other, he wound the rope around them like a slow, coiling snake. She watched, morbidly captivated, as he slipped the cord's ends into the space between her hands, then tied it at the base of her wrists, out of reach of her fingers. Sliding his finger between the rope and her wrist, he checked for tightness as one would a dog's collar. The binds were snug but not hurtful.

Helping her to the ground, he laid his cloak upon the earth as a pallet. "You sleep here."

She lay down, exhaustion stealing her strength. Damien already dozed. The fire's glow flickered across his boyish cheeks.

Godric leaned against a nearby tree. His long legs stretched beside her, one crossed over the other. He was so close she could touch them if she uncurled her hands.

She rose on one elbow to scoot back, but he placed an uncompromising hand on her shoulder and pressed her to her pallet. For all his strength he seemed weary, and she feared she had tested the bounds of his patience.

Slowly, his hand slid from her shoulder, and he wound his fingers into her hair, wrapping the strands around his fist in a possessive gesture. She wished she could insist he remove his claiming hand, but his heat comforted her, and she had no will left to fight. Spreading her skirt over her bruised feet, she listened to frogs and crickets chirp until sleep claimed her in its drugging embrace.

Cold crept in around them, and she dreamed odd, lush dreams of passion. She shivered and vaguely registered Godric's strong arm around her. Allowing him to pull her close, she snuggled into his torso.

Mere minutes seemed to pass when Godric lurched, and the sound of tromping horses awakened her.

"What have we here? Lovebirds fast asleep?"

Her eyes flew open. A huge hairy man towered over them, holding a long sword to Godric's throat.

CHAPTER 12

The sword poised at Godric's throat glinted in the hazy morning sun and wavered a handbreadth from Meiriona's nose. She grasped Godric's tunic, the linen slick against her fingers. Sometime in the night, she had climbed nearly atop him, using his massive chest as a living pillow. He held her close, his hand entangled in her hair, overly familiar, yet comforting.

She smelled musty earth and uprooted plants. Men on horseback stomped around them scattering mist and foliage from the forest floor. Holy Mary, she could see the nails in the horses' shoes. Apprehension seized her stomach and brought bile to her throat.

The weapon's sharp point wobbled toward her.

Squeezing her eyes shut, she pressed her cheek into the nook between Godric's torso and shoulder.

He laughed, and she sucked in a sharp breath. How in heaven's name could he be laughing?

"Byron, you dog." Godric nudged the pointed tip aside. "You will give the fair lady a bout of dropsy waking her thus."

Meiriona gulped and frowned. He knew these men?

The shaggy man looked disheartened at Godric's bellow. He was a bear of a man with a huge, round gut and a bushy carrot-colored mustache and beard. Where his left arm should have been, the hem of his sleeve was neatly sewed to the shoulder of his tunic. Godric leapt up, and the one-armed man's empty sleeve flapped like the wing of a flying squirrel. For all his girth, the bear moved quickly, and Meiriona had the impression the lack of a limb was not much of a hindrance for him.

She tried to sit up, but the ends of her hair were caught under Godric's boots. From the ground, she watched, amazed, as they pounded each other on the back like enormous wild beasts.

"I have ne'er seen ye sleep so soundly, master. What happened to ye?"

She tugged at her caught locks. Godric, evidently heedless of her, stepped back. She scooted away. The other four men, laughing and boasting, dismounted and filed into the clearing beside them, but the bear was the only one as tall as her captor.

Godric brushed leaves and dew from his breeks and tunic. "In truth, Byron, I slept like the dead."

"I've never been able to sneak up on ye afore, although God knows I've tried."

"I am glad 'twas you, old friend." Godric heaved deep breaths of air as if he were drinking the morning in gulps. He shook his head with an uncivilized shudder, and Meiriona had the impression of a leopard awakening after a long afternoon nap.

"We were to meet at the inn," said Byron.

Godric shrugged. "We were waylaid."

The one-armed man did not seem to mind that Godric brushed off his unspoken question. He bent toward Meiriona, squinting. "Is this the prize? She doesn't look big enough to cause all the trouble ye say."

The corners of Godric's sensuous mouth turned upward. "Do not be deceived by her small stature."

Byron's gaze flicked over her ripped tunic. "She hardly looks like a grand lady."

Meiriona wished she had a blanket to pull around herself. Her heart was still pounding from the shock of waking with a sword in her face.

"And two captives instead of one."

She glanced at her brother, still lying on the other side of the fire. He gazed at the men wide-eyed, blinking rapidly in the steamy dawn light.

"You are Byron, the one-armed swordsman!" Her brother's voice was high with excitement. He leapt from his blanket and hurried toward the bear. "The one the bard sang about."

"I knew I should have made you go to bed last time the traveling minstrels came," Meiriona muttered, giving her brother a hard look.

The bear ignored her, focusing on her brother now standing beside him. "And who might you be, squirt?"

"I'm Damien."

The man let out a low laugh that was more of a snort. He took a step forward, nearly placing one of his huge feet in the ashes of the campfire. "Well, then, nice to meet ye, Damien. Me name is Byron, but most folks call me Bear."

Well, that fits, Meiriona thought crossly.

Godric stomped out the smoldering ashes. "How went the raid on Whitestone?"

"Raid?" Meiriona gasped. "What raid?" Her face flushed as the six men turned and stared at her. Heavens, she was still sprawled on the ground with her wrists tied. Ignoring Godric's outstretched hand, she rose as gracefully as possible, meeting their stares with a defiant one of her own.

She nodded at their attire, and Bear clicked his thumbnail against a loose ring encircling his index finger. The other men wore cloaks that had familiar markings woven into the wool.

She pulled at her wrist bindings, feeling ire rise in

her chest. "Those are from my village. Mary weaves wool thus."

"Aye, milady." Bear nodded vigorously, continuing to pluck his shiny ring. "The plundering was good."

Fury burned low in her stomach, and she narrowed her eyes at Godric. "How dare you let your monsters loose on my village!"

"'Tis your own fault for not honoring our betrothal."

"Men forever blame women for their own acts of war."

"You brought this on your people."

Rage erupted, flowing though her veins. Swinging her hands like a club, she smacked Godric in the chest. He looked at her impassively. She might as well have hit solid rock.

"I see what you mean," Bear cut in, "about not being deceived by her size."

Godric snatched the ropes on her wrists so quickly she gasped. "My men raided the village as a distraction. They were under orders not to harm any of the people." He pulled her toward him until their body heat mingled. "If it pleases you, I will repay the villagers for their losses when I am Baron of Whitestone."

She blinked at him, caught between belief and wariness.

He ran his finger under her bonds. Her skin tingled at his touch. "Do your hands ache?"

The rope was soft, tight but not biting, and her hands did not hurt, except where she had clubbed him. "Nay."

Godric gave his men a dark gaze. "Byron, get food to break our fast. Damien, gather more firewood. The rest of you dogs, cease staring like you have never seen a woman and get us ready to move out."

The men turned aside slowly.

"*Now!*" Godric ordered.

They jumped into action.

Godric untied her hands. She pulled them away, but he caught her wrists and tugged them back, forcing her to let him inspect them. Rope tracks circled her wrists. His rough thumbs pressed the pink skin very gently before releasing it. He nodded, satisfied.

His concern stunned her. Saints, what a vexing man!

She moved to rub her wrist, but he stopped her, holding her small hand in his larger one.

"Do not rub directly across the tracks; the skin is tender and easily broken. Let it come back naturally."

She stretched her hands, and he massaged her forefinger from the base to the tip several times. Then moving to the next digit, he slid his palm up and down the length of her middle finger.

"That feels good," she whispered.

He grinned at her, one corner of his mouth lifting higher than the other. Heat crept into her face. She had not meant to speak aloud.

His hands moved in a slow, even rhythm, his blunt-tipped fingers sliding down the length of her smaller, tapered ones. He rubbed her ring finger, then her smallest digit.

Abruptly, he turned to the side. "Get to your chores," he barked to the men who had stopped to watch their exchange.

Grinning, the men turned to prepare their horses. Her earlier haughtiness evaporated, and she wished the forest floor would open so she could sink inside. She had been so focused on Godric's hands, she had not even noticed them watching. He addled her wits.

"They cannot resist looking at a comely lady." Godric brushed her hair behind her ear.

Feeling the urge to do something, anything, to put distance between them, she took the hair comb from her belt and shoved it into her locks. Her fingers came away with mud and dirt on them.

She could feel her pulse beating in her throat. What a mess she must look in the tattered tunic, her hair wild and dirty. "You think I am comely?" she asked self-consciously.

"Nay," he answered curtly.

Her heart dropped, though she knew he only spoke the truth. She spared a downward glance at her ragged dress, felt her hair hanging in limp waves around her face and down her back. Patting the hair comb, she came away with more sticks, brambles, and dried mud. It would take a month to get all the tangles out.

Godric's mouth turned up at the corners. "You are not comely. You are exquisite."

Meiriona blinked. "Oh."

Abruptly, he dropped her hand. The loss of connection felt like a pinch. "You have a short time of privacy. Linger, and I will hunt you down."

She scowled at him, ire bubbling to the surface at his high-handedness.

"Remember, I have your brother."

Huffing an irritated sigh, she turned abruptly and marched into the forest.

Godric leaned against a tree, watching the sway of Meiriona's hips. He frowned. The last time he let her wander off, he had to chase her down and rescue her.

Byron slid beside him. "You think allowing her to be alone was wise?"

"Nay." Godric put his hands on his hips. "But she does not need any more reasons to think I am some demon out of hell."

"Did you take her just as you planned?"

Godric felt his jaw tighten. "Capture her—aye; swive her—nay."

Byron's bushy red beard quivered. "She is still a *virgin*?"

Godric scowled. "Aye."

"You were supposed to be taking care of her virginity while we were taking care of the village. That is why you stopped at the inn."

Godric leaned forward, peering into the forest after her. "I had no stomach to do it."

"But she's beautiful, and she's *yers.*" Byron huffed and flailed his arm in frustration. "Taking her is what ye've planned for years."

Godric shrugged.

"The king, the church, all will stand behind your claim."

Thumbing his jaw, Godric stared into the trees.

Byron narrowed his eyes. "Have ye gone soft?" He glanced at the empty sleeve where his arm should be. "Have ye forgotten what prison was like? That little bitch sold ye into slavery."

Wheeling in a blur of motion, Godric's fingers closed on his friend's throat. "You will address her properly. She is to be my wife."

Byron stumbled back and Godric released him.

"Aye, master, and ye will have more claim if ye take her virginity."

"I know. I will seduce her."

Bear rubbed his throat with his hairy paw. "The time for seduction is gone. Her husband could show up tonight, and all our work and planning will be for naught."

Godric drummed his fingers against his sword hilt for a long moment. It was not the ideal way, but Bear had a point. "Old friend, you speak truth."

"Just be done with it. She does not deserve yer mercy." Byron clapped Godric on the shoulder. "King Edward will be pleased to know ye can handle a wayward woman. Besides, ye can be gentle. Ye learned many ways to ease a woman's pain the first time."

Godric stroked his chin, weighing his friend's words.

"Seduce her the *second* time, and she will forgive ye for insisting the first," Bear continued.

"Aye, I should."

"Did her capture go as ye planned?"

"Aye, 'twas easier than expected. Shame, though, that the husband was not there. I would have welcomed a fight."

Scratching his shaggy head, Bryon watched the men milling around the horses. "Odd. And on his wedding night."

"He is an old man."

Byron pumped his hips back and forth. "Mayhap 'e's not able to . . . unsheathe his dagger."

Godric glowered at his friend, who hid his laugh behind a cough. "Cease! Or I will hack off your other arm."

Byron laughed aloud, his red mustache puffing about his lips. "Ye cannot. Yer daughter would miss me."

Grinning, Godric shook his head. "She would not miss your hairy face for long."

Byron fingered his sword hilt, his expression serious. "Ye should have killed Meiriona's husband, foined her, and been done with it."

Godric took in an exasperated breath. "Did you not see enough bloodshed fighting our way back to England?"

"What difference would one more make?"

Gazing into the trees, Godric watched squirrels scamper for acorns. A thousand battles blurred through his mind. He snapped a twig off a sapling. "A man cannot slay all his enemies, Byron."

"'Tis only one more."

"I swore when we escaped that hellhole I would have peace and the home I never had. I am not likely to get it if I kill the husband she is fond of."

"Ye will not get yer peace as long as she has a husband either."

In the distance, Godric saw Meiriona's hair glinting

in the daybreak through the trees. She ambled toward them at a snail's pace, each slow movement emphasizing her hips. Heat tightened his groin. Byron was right. He would carry her directly to his chamber once they arrived at Montgomery Castle.

Shuffling his feet, Byron stared at the ground. "Speaking of peace, there's something ye need to know."

Godric blinked, reluctant to turn back from gazing at the hypnotic sway of Meiriona's hips, but he could feel Byron's unease.

"What?"

"'Tis about Owain."

Godric balled his hands. "Did you two have a row again?"

"Nay, but I did not want to say in front of the lady."

"She is nearly here. Spit it out, man."

Byron scratched his bushy red mustache. "He went berserk during the raid. Caught a village wench and—"

Godric felt his jaw tighten. "He harmed someone?"

Byron took a half step back, crushing leaves into the musty forest floor. "We had to pull him off her. She was screaming like a fishwife, and blood was all over him. I don' know if it was his blood or hers. She ran afore we could check her."

A tic pulsed in Godric's jaw. He could feel rage boiling up inside. "My orders about not harming any of the people were clear. I will deal with him."

Stepping back, Byron nearly stumbled on a tree root. "Remember, 'e's barely a man. Still feeling his oats."

Godric clenched a low-hanging branch. "Old enough to follow orders. And old enough to know the difference between right and wrong."

"Ye're not planning to kill him, are ye?"

Godric cut his gaze toward Byron. "I might."

"'E's a good fighter."

"He is no use if he cannot obey orders. No one in my ranks breaks my rules. No one." Godric stared hard at his friend.

Byron opened his mouth as if to say something, but Godric put his hand up and turned his shoulder. He searched his men until he saw Owain sitting on a log finishing a loaf of bread.

"Owain, come."

The young man, lanky and handsome, looked as if he had just been caught with his thumb in a blackberry tart. He turned a furious gaze at Byron. "Why did y' have to tell him?" he whined.

"'E is yer master and mine. If I did not tell him and he found out—"

"You would be punished right along with him," Godric finished, looking pointedly at Byron.

Owain spat at the ground. "You are a coward, Bear. Following in his steps like a trained dog."

Byron turned his back on the whining young man. "Ye beat some sense into him. I already tried."

From the corner of his eye, Godric saw Meiriona coming closer. She neared the edge of the clearing. He jerked his head toward her. "Keep her out of this. And for God's sake, do not tell her what Owain did to that girl. She already thinks we are monsters."

As if reading his mind, Byron gave a short nod and stepped between Godric and Meiriona to shield her from what was about to occur. Godric had no doubt his second in command would take her back into the forest until he was done with Owain. He took two steps and grasped the boy by his throat.

Owain gurgled and clawed at Godric's hand. "She was just a village wench."

"And your orders were to not harm the people—*my* people." Anger burned through Godric's veins.

Owain's skin paled. "'Tisn't as if they belong to y' yet."

Fury surged inside Godric. All he would have to do was squeeze. "The orders were to not harm the people. You were to create a distraction so I could take my wayward betrothed, nothing more."

"She was a peasant." Owain looked like a scared turtle, but his eyes were defiant.

Godric gave the boy a little shake. "She was one of mine."

"What is the difference between me taking a woman and you taking a woman?" Owain spat on the ground, his face full of contempt.

Wild bloodlust surged through Godric's veins, and his fingers tightened around Owain's neck. "'Tis a knight's duty to protect those weaker than himself."

The boy jerked, and Godric caught himself before cutting off Owain's air completely. He thrust the young man to the ground. "Nicholas. Gareth. Hold this boy and bring me a whip."

Owain's features turned from insolence to terror. His eyes rounded until the white could be seen all around the iris. He began to shake as Godric uncoiled a leather bullwhip.

"Count yourself lucky, boy. Had you spat on me rather than the ground, there would not be enough left of you to whip."

Meiriona sidestepped Bear's hulking form just as Godric shook out a long, snakelike whip over a boy's body. She gasped and broke into a run.

"Damien!"

Saints, what had Godric done to him? Bear gripped her shoulder as she ran past, pushing her behind him.

"'Tis not yer brother, milady." His big hand held her rooted to the spot. "Do not interfere."

Meiriona peered around him, her heart in her

throat. She blinked and breathed a silent prayer of relief.

The lanky boy was caught between two burly soldiers. He was nearly the same build as Damien, but it was *not* her brother, thank heavens. He was stripped to the waist, and his tanned, smooth skin was beaded with sweat. He shook, apparently terrified, but his jaw was stubborn. What was Godric about?

"I do not deserve this," the boy said.

Meiriona drew her knuckle to her mouth to keep from crying out. "Do something," she whispered to Bear.

"I am doing something, milady. I am stopping ye from meddling."

"Next time you will obey me." Godric's voice was thunderous.

Straining against Bear's hold, Meiriona felt her legs go numb with fear. Sweet Mary! Was this what would happen to her or Damien?

Bear placed his hairy hand on her shoulder and stepped in front of her. "Do not watch, milady. 'Tis men's work."

She scuttled to the side, trying to see around Bear's girth. "What crime did that boy commit?"

Bear looked distinctly uncomfortable; he shuffled his feet and his empty sleeve flopped against his tunic. "No crime was done, milady."

"No . . . crime?"

Bear cleared his throat, his face flushing red. "He disobeyed Godric."

"This"—the whip cracked through the air and Meiriona cringed—"for merely disobeying him?" The brute!

Byron's bushy brows pinched together. He gave a short nod and turned to watch the scene, refusing to meet her gaze. The empty sleeve seemed to give silent testimony. Her father's words came to her. *He drags his enemies through the street, crushing the weak and whipping any who disobey.* She shivered. Next time it could be her . . . or Damien.

Bear shielded her eyes with his hand, but she ducked under it. Even from this distance, she could see Godric's eyes glowing like merciless blue coals.

"This is monstrous," she breathed. She had to stop him.

Bear's wooly hand grasped her shoulder like a ship's anchor. "I have orders, milady. Ye are not to interfere."

She halted, realizing that he would allow her to get no closer. She closed her eyes, then, unable to resist, opened them again, watching the scene in wide-eyed, morbid fascination.

Godric drew back his hand to strike; the muscles of his forearm rippled with the effort. They played beneath his tanned skin in a violent dance. He crouched into a warrior's stance, one leg slightly behind the other. His movements were controlled, calculated, and utterly terrifying in their precision. His face was calm, as if he were merely eating a pleasant meal instead of about to scourge a man.

The boy strained against the soldiers to get free. Sweat glistened on the skin of his back. He twisted wildly, but they held him tight. From the back, he looked exactly like Damien.

There was a sharp crack, and a bloodcurdling scream echoed into the forest.

Meiriona jumped, remembering what her father had said about the Dragon whipping those who crossed him. Saints! What sort of monster was Godric? She looked frantically about for her brother. He leaned casually against a nearby tree, staring at their captor as if he were a pagan god. The little fool! Could he not see the danger? Next time it could be him.

Turning her face, she squeezed her eyes shut.

There was another crack. And another scream. And then another.

She peeked through her fingers. Blood oozed from three red stripes crisscrossing the young man's back. The whip's tip lifted high in the air. Godric flicked his wrist, and the whip cut down again. The boy jerked against the men holding him, pain contorting his face. Another angry welt slashed his back.

Godric's muscled arm raised, his features detached and unemotional. Merciless. Just as it had been when he had stolen her from her chamber.

The whip sliced the air and struck with a heavy snap. The boy squealed, his voice high and inhuman as a pig facing the butcher's ax. Meiriona saw his knees quivering. She could almost smell his fear and feel his stomach spasming.

Unable to turn aside, she watched Godric uncurl his fingers and take a firmer grip on the handle. She knew instantly he had just been warming up and now he planned to strike harder on the next set of lashes.

"Nay," she whispered.

Godric's cold eyes flicked to hers, commanding her not to interfere. Her legs gave and she sank to the ground.

He cocked his arm back; the whip snaked through the air.

A wet stain formed on the inside thigh of the boy's breeches. Moisture dripped into the dewy earth, and the stench of urine assailed her nostrils.

"Goddamn bloody hell!" Godric hurled the whip to the forest floor. It landed in a puff of leaves.

His soldiers lowered the man to the musty ground.

"Tend his wounds and ready the horses." He stalked toward her, larger and more dreadful than ever. His scars slashed across his tanned face, all signs of softness erased. No wonder they called him the Dragon.

She shrank back, wishing she could disappear into

the earth like a worm. Her mouth opened but no sound came forth.

"Hurry and break your fast. Get bread and cheese from Byron. You will ride today." His voice lacked the warmth she had become accustomed to.

She shivered. "I will walk," she whispered.

"Nay, you will not." His tone left no room for argument. "The sooner we arrive at Montgomery, the quicker I can guarantee you will remain mine."

Meiriona had no doubt what that meant. Would he beat her if she fought him? She set her jaw, determined to show dignity. But she did not feel dignified. She felt panicked.

The small company formed ranks hastily after breaking their fast.

"Move out, men," Godric commanded.

CHAPTER 13

A dark, uneasy truce settled between Meiriona and her captor as they rode toward his home. Sunlight flickered through the oaks in a dismal glow. Low gray clouds shadowed their party and rain drizzled in dreary drops. Sitting sideways on his lap, she was sheltered by his broad back and remained relatively dry, but Damien looked as wet and miserable as a stray cat.

At hedge breaks, she saw a large keep atop a hill a league or two away. It protruded from the craggy land with the dominating presence of an unholy prison. Lofty dark turrets were buried in dank fog. "Is that castle our destination?"

"Aye. Montgomery."

She bumped her head on Godric's chin as she squinted up at the keep. A sense of awe and dread came over her. She had not expected Godric's home to be grand—or even modest. But Montgomery was twice the size of Whitestone. Once they entered it, she and Damien would be completely at his mercy. Her chest squeezed at the lack of control of her life.

She indicated the looming castle. "The king rewarded you well."

Godric leaned close by her ear. "You are my reward, not Montgomery."

She gestured toward sheep dotting fields in the valley below the castle. "This land is not yours?"

"Nay, 'tis my family's land."

"I thought you were a bastard and had no family."

Godric growled deep in his throat and spurred the horse onward. "So I am."

She twisted to look at him. "I meant no insult. I thought your parents were unmarried, yet you speak of family."

His direct gaze made her shift her eyes to stare at the pocked road under Vengeance's hooves.

"My mother was a serf," he said. "She died when I was twelve, and I came to live with my father."

"You were fortunate he acknowledged you."

Godric's hands tightened on the reins.

Meiriona grimaced, realizing how spoiled she must sound to him. He told her his mother had died, and she replied he was lucky. She glanced back at him.

"Forgive me," she said softly, not wishing to break their fragile peace. "I did not mean that how it sounded."

He nodded, silent acknowledgement of her apology.

"*Were* you legitimized?" she blurted.

"Nay, my stepmother views me as a threat to her son." His voice was hard.

"Oh." Meiriona did not know how to answer, so she turned to watch the passing hedgerows. Each break between them gave her another glance at the dreary castle. It seemed no closer than before, although the men had finished a long round of singing. Vengeance sniffed the air and sped up, making her breath catch. The beast was as eager to enter the massive walls as she was to avoid them. Godric pulled back on the reins. The stallion's muscles bunched beneath them, and the horse pranced sideways. Like his master, their mount was filled with pent-up energy held in close check.

A flighty thought pricked her mind. Mayhap she could tame Godric the way he had tamed Vengeance. Mayhap she could soothe away the desire for revenge burning within him. She could agree to stay with him willingly if he would let go of the need to own her lands.

She glanced at the brawny arm imprisoning her waist. Even if she could, her father and husband would declare war anyway, and it would mean death for her people. She felt like a pawn on a chessboard, easily sacrificed for a higher-ranking piece's gain. If only she were a man and could choose her own destiny!

"Tell me about your family," she said after a time.

Godric cleared his throat. "My father allowed himself to be led like a puppet by his foolish, spoiled wife."

"But is that not what men have been doing to women for centuries?"

"'Tis the natural order for a woman to obey her lord."

Irritation shot through her. "Is your father still alive?"

"Nay," he said tersely.

"Was his manner like yours?"

Godric grew grave, wary. "We were similar."

She turned her face, tilted her head and looked directly into his eyes. "Did she poison him?"

A flicker of amusement flamed in Godric's eyes. "Ho, lady. Remind me to keep you tied at night should there ever come a day that I think I might trust you."

She smiled. "What makes you think I would not be able to get free of the ropes?"

"I shall keep my hand twisted into your hair and I will bind you very tightly to my bed." He said the words with mock seriousness, his tone husky and pleasure burning in his eyes.

Her heart fluttered. The thought of being tied to Godric's bed, his large warm body holding her, was not nearly as unpleasant as it should have been.

She turned away, heat creeping up her cheeks.

A lone hawk circled overhead. An omen? The predatory bird added to her unease, for she felt very much like a mouse caught in a hawk's talons.

"Who *is* lord of the castle?" she asked, turning their conversation back to safer ground.

Godric's arms tightened around her. Tension exuded from him as if he were facing some huge demon. She tamped down an irrational urge to pat the tight muscles of his neck in the same manner he had done when he calmed Vengeance.

"My worthless young half brother." His husky voice was stiff and choppy.

"Oh," said Meiriona, suddenly understanding. Godric was the eldest son of an earl. The *illegitimate* son. So, while he could live in the castle, be educated in the castle, even govern the castle, he would never inherit it or its land.

It had never occurred to her what being unwanted and resented must feel like. She had been the heir of Whitestone all her life. Because Damien was not her father's child, even the birth of a brother had not abolished her birthright.

"Your father cheated you," she blurted.

Godric pulled back on the reins, slowing Vengeance. His ice blue gaze pierced her. "Although I was not legitimized, my father provided for me. I have land of my own," he said gruffly.

"But you live here?"

"Aye."

"Wherefore?"

He leaned down unexpectedly and she flinched. His breath stroked her ear, making the hair on her neck rise. "The one I was to marry betrayed me." His voice held undercurrents of emotion.

She had stolen his birthright.

Guilt smashed her heart.

A long, awkward moment passed before he straightened in the saddle. She looked up at the castle—her new prison. They would reach it within the hour.

"My brother James, the heir, is a drunkard. He allows his keep to be overrun by women."

Her guilt vanished, and she crossed her arms over her chest. "Women can run a castle, you know. They are not stupid."

"The church teaches otherwise."

Meiriona squared her shoulders. "Then the church is wrong." She pronounced each word with a distinct clip, heedless that she had just spoken heresy.

He laughed aloud and patted Vengeance. "My mother would have agreed with you completely."

"You were teasing me," she accused, tilting her chin down.

Godric grinned. His white teeth flashed in the morning mist, and his whole face transformed. He was beautiful. "Women are *treacherously* intelligent." He matched her clipped pronunciation, but his voice held an erotic undertone she knew she could never copy.

Meiriona lifted an eyebrow. Was he courting her or mocking her? She swatted at a tiny fly buzzing around her head. "If your stepmother is so horrid, how are you and your men allowed shelter at the castle?"

"My brother is a puking drunkard, but he is not a fool."

Meiriona started to ask what he meant, but two armor-clad sentries interrupted them. One was a paunchy, weather-bitten man, the other a wiry boy, but they both wore their armor well.

She was sorry for the intrusion. It was the first conversation that gave her some clue of her captor's life.

The castle was close enough that village huts poked through the oaks, and she surmised these were the outermost patrols. Both guards looked at her curiously.

The noon sun hung just above the tops of the trees. It glinted off the helmet of the heavyset man as he greeted Godric. He shifted his gaze away from her, but the thin guard continued to gape. His gaze flitted from her ripped, dirty tunic to the impressive hair comb.

Her gaze followed his to her filthy dress. Her chemise peeked through the faded tunic. Her hair hung in a thick, unkempt braid. She must look ridiculous. She snatched the emerald comb and thrust it back into her belt.

Godric's arm went around her just as it had each night when he lifted her off the steed. She flinched. Vengeance stamped his hooves impatiently. One of the guards helped as he set her on her feet beside the horse.

"What are you about?" She looked from Godric to the guards, who nodded their approval. Sticks poked her soles as her toes sank into the earth.

Her father's words rang in her ears. *He drags his enemies through the street.*

Saints, he intended to display her as a prisoner of war! She should have anticipated this, but somehow she had not. Her father had done the same many times to his captives. He claimed it broke their spirits. They were heckled and laughed at. Rotten fruits were thrown at them. If they tripped, they were dragged behind the horse.

Tilting her head back, she glared up at Godric.

His face was unreadable.

She had felt a kinship to the blackheart just a moment ago, had thought him to be a reasonable man. Fool! Glancing at Damien, she saw her brother huddled, shivering, under a thin blanket. Like a raging river, anger overtook her.

"How dare you!" Yanking the hair comb from her belt, she jabbed it into Godric's thigh.

Godric bellowed and grasped his bleeding leg. "Damnation, girl, what the devil was that for?"

She stepped back, shocked at her own actions. Merciful heavens, he would kill her. And then who would protect her brother? The hair comb dropped to the forest floor from limp fingers. She backed away.

Damien stared at her in openmouthed astonishment.

Godric swung off Vengeance and stalked toward her. "I should take a switch to your pretty little rump for that."

Her back thumped the base of an oak and her heart lurched. Strands of her hair caught on the tree's bark, pulling and stinging her scalp. There was nowhere to run. Planting her feet, she thrust out her jaw. "Do your worst, beast. I will never cow down to you."

He strode toward her. "Shall we test that?" His voice was as icy as his eyes and his hands clenched.

Abruptly, he changed direction, laid hold on Damien's upper arm, dragging him from his mount. Leaves crackled. Damien's eyes went wide as Godric pulled him across the ground toward Meiriona.

"Since you have no care for your own body, mayhap 'tis your brother who should pay for your transgressions." Godric's gaze flicked to Bear's. "Bring me the whip."

"Nay!" Her knees felt numb with terror. Memories of the horrible sound of the whip slicing Owain's back and the smell of blood flooded her mind.

Godric closed the distance between them, dragging Damien in his wake. "What say you?"

"Nay! Nay!" Tears stung her eyes. "My brother is innocent."

Leaning close, Godric traced her jawline with his thumb. "Aye, but you are not."

Bear held out the whip, but Godric ignored it and Bear backed away.

"Sister—" her brother started, but Godric cut him short with a quelling glare.

Her pride vanished, and she knew she would do whatever it took to keep her brother safe. She hated Godric for it.

"What do you want?" she whispered.

The ice in his eyes melted. Blue flame took its place. He took her chin between his thumb and forefinger, forcing her gaze to his. A choked cry lodged in the back of her throat. Godric's clean masculine scent filled all her senses, making it impossible to breathe.

Several heartbeats passed.

Damien gaped at them.

Godric's hot breath caressed her ear. "I want you to cease fighting me. I want you willing in my bed."

Fear erupted into fury. "So that is it? You violate either my body or my brother's? You devil! You lewdster!"

He released Damien at once. The boy stumbled backward and ran to his mount with an awkward limping gait. Her heart twisted.

Godric grabbed her shoulders, wrath burning in his eyes. "It would not be thus, and you know it."

"How would it be?" she snapped.

Bending down, he retrieved the hair comb from the ground with a slow precise movement. His jaw was set harshly when he straightened. He held the comb in front of her face. A smear of red blood darkened the gold tines. His blood.

"Choose, or I will choose for you."

She swallowed, horrified.

He rested his hands on the tree behind her, forming a prison of muscle around her. His body enveloped hers so she could not see anything but him, could not smell anything but him.

Godric leaned forward until his chest grazed her nipples. White-hot lightning sensation skittered through her.

"It would not be thus at all," he whispered, brushing her forehead with his lips.

He kissed her temple, her eyebrow, the crest of her nose. "Because I feel how your skin responds to my touch. I feel your heartbeat."

"'Tis anger and fear."

His hands traced a slow trail down her shoulder. She shivered, her nipples puckered against his chest. Leaning back, he allowed enough room between their bodies to rake his fingernail softly across her breast. Sensation arced from her nipple to her woman's core.

"This, my lady, is neither anger nor fear," he murmured.

Although her dress and shift were between them, she felt naked. She gasped and pushed him back, not wanting to experience the desire curling in her stomach.

He took a tendril of her hair between his fingers and rubbed it. "Your passion matches your hair."

"Everyone knows red hair is unlucky," she whispered.

"Bah. Men make their own luck by following their passion. And yours awakens each time I touch you."

She turned her face away, not wanting to hear.

His lips brushed her temple. "The passion was between us years ago." He kissed her brow bone. "'Twas there when I took you from your room. And 'tis here now, despite your fear, despite your anger, and despite your loathing that I am claiming you thus."

She covered her ears with her hands. But she could still see him, still sense him, still smell him.

Still want him.

"I cannot."

"Surrender, Meiriona. 'Tis a fight you cannot win."

"My father—my husband—"

"Are not here." His lips touched hers. "There is only you and me. Let me show you all the pleasure your body will allow."

All the pleasure my body will allow. His voice echoed in the recesses of her mind. Her world tilted out of control.

"Aye or nay?" Godric's voice was a whisper of gossamer silk.

She shook her head, trying to clear the fog from her mind. With him so close, she could not think. She could only feel.

His shoulders straightened. Stepping aside, he yanked the whip from Bear's hands and pointed to her brother. "As you wish."

"Wait! I was but trying to clear my head. I—"

"Aye or nay? Choose now, Meiriona. My patience is gone." His voice and manner were harsh, his eyes cold. The beckoning lover was gone and the Dragon was in his place. Leaning near, he shook her shoulders slightly.

"Submit, Meiriona."

A strangled noise came from her throat. She heard herself say "aye."

His lips claimed hers. His tongue swept inside to explore and dominate her senses. Her fingers wound hesitantly around his neck, stroking the soft hairs of his nape. The hard, claiming kiss softened when she did not fight him. Time whirled around her.

Tentatively, she met his tongue with her own. A dance. A taste of all the pleasure her body would allow.

He pushed her back, held her at arm's length, a look of victory in his eyes.

She clung to him to keep from falling.

"Say aye so we both can hear it."

"Aye," she whispered.

"Louder."

"Aye, you coxcomb."

"Coxcomb?" He grinned at her. "Now that is something I have never been called afore."

"Lewdster."

He laughed, his harshness gone. "Do I have your word that you will not bolt if I give you a few moments tc refresh yourself?" He spoke in such a soft, sensuous tone she almost missed the words.

Meiriona blinked. "What?"

"We have been traveling hard. You may wish to wash the dirt from your face."

"Dirt?"

Godric chuckled, a light glowed in his eyes, and she had the impression her face was covered with streaks of filth.

She self-consciously wiped at her nose. He looked devastating while she probably resembled something that had been dragged headfirst across the English countryside.

"Well?" he asked. "Do I have your promise?"

She frowned. "Did you set me off your horse so I could cleanse myself?"

A look of complete bafflement crossed his face. "Aye."

"You never intended to parade Damien and me through your town like war prisoners?"

He cocked an eyebrow and seemed genuinely taken aback. "Assuredly not. Why would you think that?"

"The guards—you setting me down—oh, saints!" Her cheeks felt aflame. She pushed his chest, although he did not budge. "I am not keeping some promise I made under duress."

"Methinks you *will* keep your promise." Leaning down, he kissed her nose. His body grazed hers and her emotions whipped like a banner in the strong wind. Desire. Fear. Anger.

"Oh, you dark devil."

"Hurry," he insisted, rubbing her cheek with his thumb. "I count the time." He chuckled and left her staring at his broad back as he swaggered toward the others, a stone's throw away.

Bear slapped his thigh. Four slow mocking claps bit the air. She cringed, realizing that most of the men had been watching them.

"Cease," Godric growled.

Bear grinned.

Meiriona balled her fists, her chest tight with indignity. *Damn men who think of women as nothing more than another conquest to be won!*

Stretching his long legs, Godric took the water vessel from his saddle and tossed it to her. His lips lifted in a knowing smile, crinkling the skin around his crescent-shaped scar.

Blackheart!

But his eyes seemed to speak. *All the pleasure your body will allow.*

Jerking her gaze from his, she turned to her task of making herself presentable. She washed her face with the last of the drinking bladder's contents and rebraided her frizzy hair. It was so tangled, she braided most of the knots back into it. At least it was not as frazzled as it had been. Although she could not say the same for her emotions.

She wiped the blood off the hair comb with her skirt before shoving it back into her hair. She still looked ridiculous, but 'twas as good as she could do at the moment. "I am ready."

"On to Montgomery, then."

Moments later, Godric's strong hands clamped around her waist as he lifted her atop Vengeance and swung up behind her.

Bear walked his horse nearby. With his one arm, he thrust a fat blue bundle at his lord. Godric smiled and shook out a wool sleeping blanket that smelled of lye and fresh grass. He draped it around her shoulders, hiding the ugly tunic.

She should have thanked him for the chivalrous gesture but felt too churlish to do so. Her stomach hurt with the mixture of emotions that swirled inside it.

All the pleasure my body will allow. She wished she could get that thought out of her mind. With any luck he would lock her in a solitary room once they reached the keep, and she would have time to think sensibly about her plight.

The road widened enough for two carts to pass as they neared the castle. The ruts were deep and ancient. She rubbed the tight muscles of her neck as they pressed toward the two round towers marking the entrance of Montgomery.

The set of Godric's massive shoulders echoed her tension. He seemed more edgy and commanding with each passing step until none of the seductive lover was left. The blue veins on his forearms throbbed as he flexed and unflexed his hand against the rein in an angular and severe manner.

It was as if a stranger held her. She shifted slightly, but his hand around her waist did not tighten. She was acutely aware the muscles of his forearm pressed against the underside of her breast, but he did not seem to notice. He focused on the looming castle.

The withdrawal of his attention made her feel more exposed than his unwanted advances. While she was reeling from his declaration that he could give her all the pleasure her body would allow, he seemed not to be affected at all.

She studied his home. White well-kept mortar gleamed in the sun. The river was routed so clean water surrounded the castle in a deep moat. Rounded towers, pocked with arrow slits, squatted along the thick walls. This would be a formidable keep to siege.

As the horses clattered across the drawbridge and entered through the gatehouse, she spared a glance at her captor. The lines around his mouth were taut.

Two guards met them at the entrance and motioned them under the portcullis. She could see eyes gleaming down from the murder holes above them.

They turned abruptly to the left once they reached the wide courtyard of the dark castle. The smell of crowded people mingled with the yeasty scent of fresh bread. The grass was trampled and worn. Bare dirt trails led to various towers and buildings. The pathways were eerily vacant and looked like dried skeletal bones. Peasants hid in shadows and peeked around corners as the men filed in. Where her castle was lively, this one seemed gloomy and dead.

Although the men were returning from a triumphant raid, no victory banners waved, thank the saints. To see others rejoicing over her people's defeat was too vulgar to think of.

Meiriona caught the wide gaze of a serf hiding behind a water cistern. The woman pulled her cap down and slipped into the shadows. "Your people seem terrified of you."

"'Tis because I brought you here."

"Why are they afraid of that?" she asked.

Godric didn't answer, he peered over her head across the courtyard.

A little elf of a girl ran toward them, pumping her arms hard. She was olive skinned with dark hair and huge midnight blue eyes. Her blue velvet skirts flew around her in a flurry of motion. "Papa, Papa!"

CHAPTER 14

Godric had a *child*?

Astonishment washed over Meiriona. It had never occurred to her that a man so fearsome would have a child. Well, mayhap a bastard or two strung around the countryside, but not a pixie of a girl who would run to him and call him "Papa."

Numbness overtook Meiriona's limbs. From her sideways position on her captor's lap, she could only stare in bewilderment at the youngster.

The elf stopped beside the tall stallion and reached skinny brown arms up to him, impish and demanding. Her hands were small, delicate, but the nails were snagged. Dirt clung to her palms. Vengeance swished his tail and nosed the little girl on top of the head. She did not flinch away but lifted her hands higher.

"Carry me, Papa."

Godric leaned down, his muscled arm stretched toward the child.

"Heavens, there is not room atop a horse for three people!" Fear made Meiriona's voice high. Vengeance could bolt and crush them all.

The child giggled and wrapped her grubby hands around Godric's forearm. He lifted her with one brawny arm, her tiny feet rising from the ground as though she were caught in a magical wind.

Godric gathered his child to his chest. She squirmed

like a wild animal trapped in a hunting bag. Meiriona hunkered forward to avoid the girl's flailing legs. The elf's foot smashed into Meiriona's temple.

"Saints." Meiriona gasped, toppling backward and grabbing Godric to keep her balance. The blanket around her shoulders glided to the grass.

The elf sniggered. Vengeance snorted and pranced sideways.

"Ho! Be still, you two!"

Meiriona righted herself, clinging to Godric's thighs. "I was not the one moving," she fussed.

The girl's heart-shaped face was devoid of expression. She had a sweet little-girl smell—grass and wildflowers. Staring at Meiriona with wide, almond-shaped eyes, she whispered, "Who is she?"

Godric's eyes gleamed with unspoken love. "This will be your new mama."

"What?" both Meiriona and the child exclaimed at the same time.

The girl cut her blue eyes toward Meiriona. They were the same shade as Godric's. "I don' like her." Her beautiful pixie face twisted into a look that said what she did not like, her papa did not force on her.

"I am *not* going to take the place of your mama." Meiriona tried to sound reassuring. Swiveling her head, she frowned at Godric. "I plan to leave as soon as your papa will allow me."

"Nay, you will not," Godric stated.

Vengeance skittered sideways again and snorted, his tail swishing. Meiriona felt her stomach drop.

"I *don'* like her," the little girl persisted, her tiny hand tracing the outline of the scar running from his eye to his jaw.

Godric cocked his head as if this possibility had not occurred to him. "I expect you will learn to get along."

The child's eyes widened, and Meiriona had the impression he had never contradicted her afore. "I don' want to get along."

Vengeance snorted again and pranced to the side, adding his piece into the argument.

"Your horse wants us to dismount," Meiriona said.

Pulling back on the reins, Godric brought Vengeance to a halt. He leaned over and set his daughter on the ground, leaving Meiriona clinging for dear life to his legs, her fingernails digging into his thighs.

"I wish you would not do that!" While he might feel perfectly comfortable leaning over the side of the stallion, it made her queasy.

From below, the elf propped her hands on her hips and stuck out her bottom lip. "I don' like her, Papa."

Godric dismounted, then helped Meiriona off the stallion. He kissed his daughter's forehead. "Now, puss, none of that."

The beautiful child shook her head, dark curls bouncing. "Take her back."

Meiriona looked from her captor to the elfin child. "Aye, sirrah, your daughter has a brilliant idea. Take me back."

Godric scowled, his fatherly softness gone. "None from you either."

He gestured to one of the men to tend to Vengeance. Meiriona watched the mount being led across the courtyard and through a gate into another walled section of the huge castle. The vastness of the bailey made her realize the futility of her father laying siege here to gain her back. Mayhap she could slip out unnoticed, she mused, scratching her chin. But not without Damien.

She searched for her brother and saw him talking to Bear. He seemed content with his captivity. Thinking of Godric's threat of the whip, she shuddered.

Godric's men were scattered around the courtyard in various stages of dismount. Castlefolk emerged from shaded doorways and people began filling the courtyard. The smell of horses mingled with the scent of fresh bread. In the distance, the metallic clang of a blacksmith's hammer beat a steady rhythm.

"Come," Godric said, laying his hand on her shoulder and picking up his daughter. The little girl stared at her from Godric's arms with wide, unblinking eyes.

"How old are you, child?" Meiriona asked amicably as Godric led them toward an open archway.

The little girl curled her lip up and tossed her head. "I don' want to talk to *her.*"

"Now, puss, be courteous." Godric smoothed the child's dark hair. "She is two," he explained. "And a little shy."

Spoiled is more like it, Meiriona thought grumpily.

With grubby fingers, the child pulled his ear close to her bowlike mouth. "She dresses funny," she said in a loud whisper.

"Your papa picked these clothes for me." Meiriona spread the large ugly tunic as if it were a court gown and gave a mock curtsy. "He got one just like it for you!"

The elf stared at her, her wide eyes so suspicious Meiriona laughed. It was hard to blame a child for manners that obviously came from her father.

"What is your name, child?"

"Go on, tell her," Godric prompted.

"I don' want to tell her," she said, hiding her face in his tunic. Her skinny leg kicked Meiriona in the process.

"Ouch!" Meiriona rubbed her throbbing shoulder.

Godric kissed his daughter atop her head. "Her name is Amelina."

A loud masculine voice rang into the courtyard from deep inside a darkened room. "So, Godric, brother, you've arrived." The voice was slurred as if its owner was far into his cups.

Meiriona peered at the archway, curious to see who

had spoken. But they were at least twenty paces away, too far to see inside. The doorway, pitch black, looked like the entrance to a dark cavern.

"Well, come on, let me ssshe the woman—your prize."

"Does everyone here think I am some prize to be won?"

"My brother is drunk again," Godric muttered, ignoring her question and taking her elbow. He steered her toward the arch where the voice had come from.

A servant emerged as they approached. She raised her arms to the little girl. "Come here, Amelina. Your clothes need to be changed for tonight's feast."

Amelina slid into the woman's arms, giggling. "Can I wear my green dress? Papa says I look pretty in it."

"Aye, child."

"I will send for you anon," he said.

Godric kissed his daughter atop her head, and Meiriona found herself wondering what sort of father he was. The servant carried the child, who waved furiously at her papa, to a tower and mounted steps that led into the castle.

Turning, Godric led Meiriona toward the archway and she decided her musings were best left for another time. A handsome woman clad in a rose-colored gown rushed toward them. Her silver hair was plaited in a tall upsweep and covered with a gossamer veil that highlighted dark, angry eyes. She might have been slightly older or younger than Godric but was so striking in her beauty it was hard to tell which. The tightness in the alabaster skin of her face bespoke displeasure. Her gaze flicked from Meiriona's tangled hair to the stained tunic before giving her a dismissive glance and glaring at Godric.

"Welcome home," she sniffed. It was clearly not a welcome. Her voice, like claws screeching across rocks, startled Meiriona. "The feast is not yet prepared."

"Fine," said Godric.

The woman stood between him and the doorway. "Perchance you would like to clean yourself afore going into the great hall." She gave Meiriona a pointed look.

Meiriona stiffened, but remained silent.

"Nay." Godric climbed the steps. "Stand aside."

The woman relented with a heavy sigh. "Aye, sir." The words were right, but her aura was one of an angry conquered foe.

Turning, the woman stalked to the water cistern, giving a look of undiluted hatred at Godric when he was not looking.

The lines around Godric's eyes tightened with tension, making one tiny scar pucker slightly.

"She dislikes you," Meiriona whispered.

"Aye." Godric steered Meiriona up the steps, his hand warm against the small of her back.

"Who is—"

"My family's problems are not your concern." Godric's mouth was a grim slash, and his stance did not invite argument. Taking her elbow, Godric guided Meiriona through the stone archway. She blinked as her eyes adjusted to the dim light of the great hall of Montgomery.

The stench was staggering. The room reeked of stale wine, trampled rushes, rotting food, and vomit. She held her nose to keep from gagging. Did pigs live in the great hall?

Trestle tables were set with pewter trenchers but were barren of food and empty of guests. Dogs rooted in the rushes. Heavy wine-colored velvet curtains covered the windows, leaving the room dark, cold, and austere. No candles burned, no fire glowed in the hearth, and no tapestries lined the walls.

Servants scurried hither and yon carrying pitchers and platters to a young man slumped in a large chair at the center of the great table upon the dais. In contrast to the lower tables, eels, pork, venison, and vegetables threatened to fall from high-piled platters.

The young lord was a copy of Godric, wild dark hair and high cheekbones. Only he was younger and unmarked. Where Godric had grooves in his forehead from scowling, this one's face was boyish and unlined.

Chains of civility seemed to slide from Godric as he walked into the room. His jaw hardened. His eyes narrowed. His black tunic strained across his shoulders as if the fabric could scarcely contain him. She shivered at his transformation.

James watched Godric with shifty, unfocused, bloodshot eyes. He looked to be tottering on the edge of unconsciousness. A toppled goblet formed a pool on the wooden table before him and liquid dripped into the rushes. Although his shoulders were nearly as wide, he seemed pathetic compared to Godric.

A serving wench brought a tankard of ale to Godric, then scurried from him like a frightened mouse.

Godric stalked across the length of the hall, leaving Meiriona openmouthed by the door.

"You drunken sot," he boomed, slamming his fist upon the table.

Meiriona jumped at the intensity of his voice, and the slumped lord gave a mindless lurch. His lips turned upward into a stupid boyish grin. "So my bashtard brother is home," he slurred. He sat up straighter, but his head weaved.

Godric's fingers fisted in his brother's tunic, and he hauled him up by the shirt. "You damn fool."

Shuddering, Meiriona glanced at the door. Godric's men, including Bear and her brother, filed into the room, blocking her escape. She had no choice but to witness what was about to occur. She prayed there would be no repeat of the scene with Owain.

"G'day, men," the drunken man said. "Have a good raid?"

Godric shook him, the veins in the backs of his hands jumping with tension. The man's gray tunic quivered. "Do not play games," said Godric. He swept his gaze around the chamber. "I leave the castle for one week and this pigsty is what I find on my return?"

The dogs tucked their tails and crawled under the benches. Meiriona sucked in her breath. The foul air caught in her throat and she choked. Clamping her hand over her mouth and nose, she breathed only when absolutely necessary.

Several of Godric's men, she noted, held their noses as well.

The drunkard shoved against Godric, but his movement was ineffectual. "'Tis my castle. I can do what I please."

Jesu, Meiriona thought, being nobility meant duty before pleasure. Godric had been right about his brother; he did not deserve the earlship.

Abruptly, Godric released his brother and the young lord staggered backward, falling into his chair. "Nay, you may *not* do as you please if it means starving the peasants and living in filth."

Godric's brother waved a drunken arm around and stood, swaying unsteadily. "Nobody's shtarving."

Godric caught him with one fist in his embroidered tunic before he fell back to his seat.

"They will be, if the lord does not learn to control his ale." Godric spat out the word "lord" as if it galled him.

"I only tasted the ale." The man patted Godric's shoulder awkwardly. His fingers shook.

Godric cocked his arm back, his skin tight across his muscles.

The pale woman rushed into the room, pushing aside Bear and the others. Her pink skirt swirled around her in a frenzy.

"Let go of him!" she shrieked, her high-pitched voice bouncing off the bare walls.

"If you would control him while I was gone, I would not have to pound sense into him while I am home." Godric lowered his fist and shoved his brother back into his chair.

The woman shook her head, whipping her veil back and forth like a wind-torn banner. "He cannot help himself. Can you not see he is ill?"

Godric thrust the young man's chair away from the table with his booted foot. The drunkard fell backward; only the arms of the chair kept him from sinking to the floor.

Meiriona cringed, feeling the tension gather in the air like an impending storm.

"He is not ill," Godric said.

"His stomach is weak, unable to hold down food," the woman pleaded, her eyes wide with an appeal for Godric to understand. "I have been nursing him all week."

Godric's lip turned up in disgust. "He is drunk."

The man staggered to his feet and raised his fist at Godric. "Now, lishen here—"

Godric pressed him into the chair and wheeled on the woman. "You protect him from me. Why do you not protect him from himself?"

The woman quivered like a rabbit and began to cry. Her voice became higher and higher with mounting fretfulness. "I have been nursing him," she repeated. "He just needs a little sleep."

A tight tic pulsed in Godric's jaw, and he clenched his fist.

The woman seemed to shrink in stature. Her head sank into her neck, and she turned her face as if expecting a blow.

From the corner of her eye, Meiriona saw Damien cringe.

Picking up the hem of her tunic, she ran and leapt between Godric and the woman. "Leave her be."

The other men became so still the tiniest whisper could have been heard. Godric took a deep breath, the stench of the room evidently not affecting him. He flexed his hands.

"You dare interfere." He reached for her.

She jerked away, and his hand caught the end of her braid. She gasped, pulling back. He wound the braid slowly around his fist, reeling her in like a caught fish until their noses nearly touched.

"You have no rights here," he whispered, his generous lips flattening to a hard, thin line. He seemed dangerous and unpredictable as a black, stormy sea.

She shook her head, struggling to get away. Her scalp stung where his hand captured her hair.

"Be careful, my pretty captive. I know many ways to tame a woman, and not all of them are pleasant."

Godric pressed a harsh, punishing kiss to her lips. His short stubble scraped her cheeks. She felt anger and violence boiling under his thin façade of civility. Despite this, heat spread through her limbs and moisture gathered in her woman's core. What a traitorous body she had. He held a power over her that had nothing to do with brute strength. He released her lips, but his hand still held her in place.

The kiss was meant to be a warning. She knew that. A proof that she was nothing more than chattel to him. Nothing more than a whore, if that was his will. Dread and desire pooled inside her, warring with each other and making her stomach cramp.

One of the men coughed, and her cheeks heated. She pulled against Godric's hold, but his fist held her tight.

Her outrage burned into anger. "Release me."

Godric motioned to Bear standing beside the door. "Take my unruly pet to my chamber. Lock her in."

Bear stepped forward, reaching for her with his burly hand.

Meiriona gritted her teeth in frustration. She fought the urge to kick Godric in the shins. Only the knowledge that he would no doubt kiss her again kept her from doing so.

Her cheeks felt aflame.

With measured twists of his wrist, Godric released her hair. He did it slowly and deliberately, his gaze boring into her, daring her to move. She rooted herself to the spot, determined not to let him see how shaken she was.

The long braid bounced near her hips when he released it. She leaned back, putting an arm's distance between them.

The drunken man lifted his goblet in a toast. "So you got the prizhe you went for." He took a deep swallow of wine. "Sheesh a beauty but needs taming."

Godric turned an eye back to his brother. "'Tis exactly what I intend to do with her."

Trepidation pierced Meiriona's stomach. All around her were strangers. She was at Godric's mercy. He could feed her, starve her, beat her, or lock her in the dungeon. Or he could bed her.

She looked fervently at the pale woman who had caused this uproar. Mayhap she could find a friend there. But the woman shrank into the shadows, biting her lips and wringing her hands.

Meiriona folded her arms, determined that no matter the outcome, Godric would not have an easy victory. "I will not sleep in your chamber."

One of the men coughed as if to hide a snicker.

Godric turned to the woman. "Find my captive clothes to wear."

The woman sniffed and nodded with a strained jerk.

"How dare you cow that woman so!" Meiriona exclaimed.

Raising an eyebrow at Bear, Godric pointed at the door. "Go. I will be there anon."

Bear tugged her arm. "Please, milady. I do not wish to be punished, even for your sake."

Meiriona narrowed her eyes at Godric, feeling like a cornered wolf. "I am not your whore!"

"Take her to my chamber!" Godric roared.

Jumping into action as if he had been shot in the arse with an arrow, Bear bowed to Meiriona with a low, exaggerated dip. "Please, milady, follow me. I will take you to—" He cut his words off awkwardly as if he hated treating a lady in such a way.

"Now!"

Bear half dragged, half carried Meiriona from the great hall. With a swish of skirts, the rose-clad woman exited the hall after them.

Meiriona felt like a saint wrongfully condemned to an eternity of hell.

CHAPTER 15

Meiriona's feet dragged on the worn flagstones leading up the steps and along the narrow hallway toward Godric's chamber. Trepidation and frustration pierced her heart like poisoned arrows.

Since their arrival at Montgomery, Godric had become a stranger. His gentleness was gone, replaced by something harsh, curt, and demanding. Tremors ran along her spine as she wondered what would happen to her now. She clenched her fingers into tight fists, refusing to give in to her fear.

The woman beside her sniffed, adding to Meiriona's agitation. If the woman had handled Godric better, they would not be on the way to his chamber like sheep to slaughter.

Smoke from tallow candles stung her eyes; she blinked in the ominous yellow and orange flicker. Bear tugged gently on her elbow, directing her down the castle's corridors. He led them past several archways before stopping in front of an oaken door at the end of the long hall. A burly guard, short with an ugly, pocked face and one eye missing, sat in a chair beside the door. He cradled a war ax in his lap.

Mercy, Godric must not feel comfortable in his own home if he needed a chamber guard during times of peace.

"Master Godric ordered me to deposit this lady

hither," Bear said, indicating the chamber with his one arm.

The guard grunted, the corner of his mouth drawn into a snarl.

"Mayhap ye should lock the door." Bear eyed her warily and clicked his thumb against his stolen ring. "'Twas a lot of trouble to get her, and the master has business to complete with her."

Meiriona balled her hands, her anger and exasperation growing as she dwelled on the way Godric and his men treated her like a piece of property.

Holding the war ax steady in one hand, the guard opened the door and stepped to the side. He motioned her toward the room. "I will care for the lady," he said, his voice thick and gravelly.

Casting him an irritated glance, Meiriona threw her shoulders back and walked through the door like a queen. She heard the woman slide in behind her.

Meiriona's breath caught when she crossed the threshold. The chamber was enormous, an extension of the man who occupied it. It smelled of leather, sandalwood, and Godric.

Decorated in burgundy and midnight blue, with dark, heavy furniture, the room was as lush as a sultan's bedchamber. It was daunting and overpowering but consoling and beckoning at the same time. Being here made her feel like Godric's arms surrounded her. Alarm and desire spiraled together, settling as a hard knot in her stomach.

"You cannot leave me here," she whispered. "Please take me somewhere else so I may change clothes."

Bear gave a short chivalrous nod that caused his red beard to quiver before slamming from the room without a word. The lock clicked into place.

Meiriona blinked and glanced around, feeling more frustrated than ever at her captivity.

Light from six-paned windows reflected across the

room. The sunshine glimmered across a small table topped with white marble. *Godric's family must be very wealthy to afford that much glass for the solar,* she mused. Thick Arabian rugs graced the polished plank floor.

An enormous four-poster bed with heavy carved legs and a dark ornate headboard stood against the east wall. Carved flames topped its columns.

She turned her gaze aside. The bed brought up all her feelings of frustration, vulnerability, and longing. It jutted so far into the heart of the chamber that erotic images formed in her mind. It made her want to beat the door and scream for Bear to take her back, but it also made her wonder how it would feel to lie beneath Godric while he kissed her again.

She heard footsteps clomp down the hall away from them. The pale woman sniffed loudly and let out a high-pitched whine.

Meiriona glared at her. All her crying and sniffing was bloody irritating. Completely unbecoming for a lady of her station.

Seemingly oblivious to Meiriona's glower, the woman gave an exaggerated sigh and crossed the room. For all the stiffness in her face and spine, she walked with grace and poise. Her slippers trod silently across the luxurious Oriental carpet. She sat in the only chair in the room—a massive throne.

The chair swallowed her. It was a heavy structure, as prominent and indecent as the bed. Her silver-blond hair contrasted sharply with its dark cushions. Openmouthed lion heads were carved into the sides of its broad arms and the pinnacles of its tall, upholstered back. For a second, Meiriona imagined Godric's huge black boots sinking into the sheepskin rug that lay beneath it.

The lady gazed at Meiriona with a sort of half-witted wonder. Her eyes seemed haunted, and Meiriona could not help but feel a little sorry for her.

"He cannot truly mean I am to sleep here," Meiriona said at last, breaking the awkward silence.

The woman's face was a brittle mask of resentment. "Have you not discovered that Godric does whatever he wants?"

"Who are you?"

"I am," she paused, as if about to make some grand proclamation, "the evil stepmother."

Meiriona frowned, taking in the woman's youthful appearance. "You are Godric's . . . stepmother?"

The lady nodded, her white-blond hair slipping against the chair's dark cushion.

"But you are the same age as him." Meiriona pursed her lips, trying to understand the relationship.

"I am six years older than he." The woman smiled, a brilliant, shining gesture. Her face transformed from beautiful to stunning. "The women in my family age well."

Of a truth, Meiriona thought. "I am confused. You were married to Godric's father?" Was this stunning creature the woman who Godric claimed to be the stupid, jealous scourge of his youth?

"Aye, I was given in marriage to the late lord of Montgomery, God bless him, when I was fifteen. I had a son, and we lived a peaceful existence for several happy years. Then Godric changed all that."

"Go on," Meiriona prompted, eager to learn more about her captor.

Grimacing, the lady clutched the arms of the chair. "My husband, God bless him, knew he was dying and saw the tough, scrappy boy as a way to repent for his past sins."

"What do you mean?" Meiriona leaned against the door.

"My lord husband wanted to turn the boy into a nobleman. Can you imagine that? I mean, Godric is a bastard, the get of a village whore."

"His mother was *not* a whore." Meiriona crossed her arms, unsure why she felt the urge to defend a man as exasperating as Godric.

The woman sniffed haughtily. "Any woman who gets herself with child outside of wedlock is no better than a whore, if you ask me."

"'Tis best you not let Godric hear you speak thus," Meiriona admonished.

The stepmother tsked. "I swear, my husband, God bless him, would have legitimized the bastard if my father had not objected so fervently."

Her high-pitched voice irritated Meiriona. *The way she blesses her husband every time she speaks his name, you would think the man was a veritable saint,* Meiriona thought crossly.

"Godric was twelve when he showed up on our doorstep. From the moment he arrived, *he* acted as though he should be the lord hither instead of James."

"And your son is the man below?" *The one living like swine?* Meiriona added to herself.

"Aye, he is the true lord of Montgomery."

He acts like a drunkard, not a lord.

The woman's face saddened, and she crossed and uncrossed her legs. "My son is not well."

She looked so sad, pity replaced Meiriona's irritation. "Mayhap your son needs guidance."

The woman's composure crumbled and two giant tears ran down her white cheeks. "Let us . . . Let us not talk of such things."

Meiriona rubbed her hands together as if to warm them. This conversation made her very uneasy. "What is your name?" she asked, steering their talk to less complicated territory.

Propping her head upon her hand, the woman rested her elbow on the arm of the throne. "I used to be Lady Silvia Vaughn, Countess of Montgomery, but now I am nothing."

The dejection in her voice made Meiriona wish she could help her somehow. "Wherefore do you say such things?"

"Once Godric arrived, my husband, God bless him, changed. He ignored James and me. He spent hours and hours training his bastard son. He oft claimed, 'The boy's got natural talent as a warrior.'" She sighed. "I suppose 'tis true—Godric is a feared knight in Edward's army." She gave a short, heartbreaking laugh.

"Your husband is gone. Can you not remove Godric now?"

The woman's mouth flattened and she leaned her head against the back of the thronelike chair. "Have *you* had any luck removing him?"

Glancing around the solar, Meiriona shook her head, feeling as if she were wrapped in some bizarre nightmare. Abruptly, as if remembering something, Lady Montgomery slid from the chair, crossed the room, and pounded on the locked door. "We need a maid hither," she yelled.

Screaming in that awful voice is not likely to get you one, Meiriona thought peevishly.

The guard outside the door grunted, but no footsteps followed.

For a countess, the lady did not seem to have much authority. Where had she been fostered?

Lady Montgomery rattled the door handle. "Bring this girl one of my gowns." She pounded on the oak. "Did you hear me?" she shrieked.

Saints! The whole castle heard you.

Shoulders rounded, she turned from the door, looking more defeated than ever.

Mercy, it is no wonder her son does not behave like a proper lord, Meiriona thought. She plucked at one of the stains on her tunic and bit her tongue to keep herself from saying so.

"Lazy swine. You cannot make them work," Lady Montgomery muttered in that same squawky voice.

"You cannot shriek at a guard in that manner and expect obedience."

"And I suppose you are much better at getting Godric's men to do your bidding, eh?"

Meiriona sighed, smoothing a section of her wayward hair. "I take your point. I am as caught in this as you." A few moments of strained silence came between them.

"Godric took my keys," Lady Montgomery offered, indicating her empty girdle.

"Oh."

"What did you do to warrant this treatment from Godric? Did you breathe too loudly?"

"I was sleeping," Meiriona started to explain.

Lady Montgomery's dark eyes widened. "A crime of direst consequences."

"Nay." Meiriona ran her finger along the hem of her sleeve, trying to find comfort in the rough fabric. "That is not all." Bitter edges of guilt nipped at her heart. "I betrayed him."

"Betrayed him?" Lady Montgomery's oval face showed keen interest. "How did you do that?"

"I was to marry him," Meiriona answered warily, unsure how much she should explain. "But my father did not wish it."

"Ah." The lady's lips turned up, but her smile was not brilliant this time. It was as pale and strange as the rest of her. "Then I should be thanking you. It was you who gave James and me years of peace."

Meiriona rubbed her forehead. She was having a hard time following the conversation. "Prithee, I do not understand."

Lady Montgomery drummed idly on the arm of the throne, her face dreamy. "It was so quiet and peaceful here when Godric was locked away."

Meiriona's fingers stilled on her tattered skirt. "Locked away? Godric has been in France, at court."

"Godric the bastard at a French court? Who told you that tale?"

"My . . . father." Meiriona's heart squeezed and her hands went suddenly numb. She shook her head to clear the niggling of doubt creeping into her mind. "I do not believe you. Godric's been in France."

"My dear, can you honestly imagine Godric at a French court?"

Meiriona tried to imagine Godric's muscular body clad in the prissy lace and gaudy silks men wore on the continent.

The image did not form. All she could see was Godric, strong and fearsome, dressed in armor, wielding a long, bloodied broadsword, a war cry on his lips.

Her throat constricted. "Lady Montgomery," she whispered. "How did Godric get his scars?"

The lady stared at Meiriona, her dark eyes wide. "Do you not know?"

The room swam before Meiriona in a slurry of reds and blues. She felt she was in the corner, merely watching Lady Montgomery and herself converse. "Nay. How?" she heard herself say, her voice sounding very far away to her own ears.

Lady Montgomery giggled, her pale cheeks wobbling. "Child, you sold him into slavery on a ship to the East."

The image of Godric in battle evaporated like mist and was replaced with one of Godric in chains, his huge body covered with sweat while a whip cracked across the handsome features of his face. The walls closed in around Meiriona, and her heart seemed to tumble from her chest onto the floor.

"'Tis impossible," she whispered, but she could see the satisfied, catlike smirk on the woman's features.

CHAPTER 16

"Oh, sweet saints. I must sit." Meiriona stumbled to the huge bed, brushed aside its velvet curtains, and sank into the fur coverlet. Her heart felt as though it had fallen into a quarry and been covered with weighty limestone bricks. Bricks of guilt.

Godric's scars—her fault.

"Child, you look pale. Are you well?" Lady Montgomery stood, crossed the room, and poured water from an earthenware pitcher onto a cloth. Her sniffing disappeared as she carried the rag in a copper bowl across the Arabian carpet. Sliding next to Meiriona, she pressed the cloth to her forehead.

Numbness overtook Meiriona, and she scarcely felt the damp rag. "Th—thank you."

"Did he abuse you badly?" The lady's eyes glowed with genuine concern.

Meiriona glanced at her wrists, running a finger around their circumference. Godric had tied her, but he had been so careful with her bonds she had no bruises, not even a trace of a red mark. He had slept with his hand buried in her hair, but even then, he had been careful not to pull it.

"Nay, he has not harmed me." Mercy, she had thought him rough when he abducted her, but, in truth, he had shown more honor than she.

Lady Montgomery wrung the rag into the bowl and

crossed the carpet to retrieve a flagon. Pouring wine into a goblet, she handed it to Meiriona. "Drink."

Meiriona cupped the vessel with both hands to hold it steady. The wine, dark as blood, sloshed over the rim. "How long was Godric in sl—sl—" She could not say the word. That she had sold a man into a life of pain was unthinkable. Oh, Holy Mary, why had she gone along with her father on that day? She could have warned Godric, or run off with him. Anything.

"Five years." Lady Montgomery retrieved the cloth from the copper bowl and pressed the cooling rag against Meiriona's forehead.

"He must hate me," Meiriona whispered, her voice strained.

The lady patted Meiriona's arm. "He cannot hate you. He is a beast without any emotion."

Drawing in a sharp breath, Meiriona recalled the impassive look on Godric's face as he whipped Owain. A tingle of fear crept up her spine. "What will he do with me?"

"He plots revenge. The men have been preparing for war since Godric's return. He has obtained weapons that hurl fire to burn whole villages."

"Oh, saints."

Lady Montgomery gave her a sympathetic look. "He is not a merciful man. When he took Beacon for the king, he dismantled the whole castle brick by brick. He ravaged the village, although the people begged and pleaded."

"I do not believe—"

A knock at the door gave Meiriona a little start. The key scraped in the lock, and Bear stuck his wooly head in.

"The master requests both of you downstairs for a feast immediately."

Lady Montgomery uttered a small unladylike curse and flicked invisible dust off her rose dress.

"Master," she scoffed. "They all call him Master when it is my son who is lord. He is a bastard, not nobility. I will sup in my chamber, thank you."

Bear shook his head, his wild red locks flying out around him. "Nay, the master has requested both of you."

"A moment, please," Meiriona said, a sudden desperation to find a safe hiding place for the opium coming over her. She stood and fled behind the dressing screen. "Allow me to smooth my hair."

Bear nodded, still glaring at Lady Montgomery.

Snatching the pouch from her hem, Meiriona stuffed it into a small crack in the wall's mortar behind the dressing table, then snatched an ivory comb and flattened down the front of her hair as best she could. Her heart pounded as she emerged from behind the screen and headed toward Bear.

Lady Montgomery sniffed but did not resist as the giant took her arm and led her to the door. Meiriona followed, treading carefully. Squaring her shoulders, she determined to bravely face whatever awaited her.

Bear guided the ladies through a stone torchlit walkway and down a narrow stone staircase, fawning over them like a mother hen. "Watch yer step, ladies, the stones are worn and slick."

Godric waited at the bottom of the tower, looking so unbelievably handsome Meiriona blinked several times. He had changed into hose and wore a fresh tunic. His clothes, all black, were plain but of fine material and well stitched. Did the man ne'er wear clothing with color?

A wave of guilt washed over her as she thought of him bound and shackled. She imagined he would have stood proud and tall on a slaver's block in some unbeknownst port.

What could she tell him? I am sorry? The words lodged in her throat. One said, "I am sorry," when one bumped into someone accidentally, not when one sold someone into a life of pain.

Godric's sickle-shaped scar was stark against his tanned skin. She wound the end of her braid around her fingers to quell the urge to smooth it away. Had someone carved him there on purpose?

Oh, Jesu. Meiriona remembered how his unmarked face had smiled at her in the chapel, how he'd looked at her with hope.

He scowled at Lady Montgomery. "You were to find a gown for my prisoner."

"We were locked in your chamber." Lady Montgomery pushed out her lower lip. "How were we to accomplish that?"

"You could have asked the guard," Godric said logically.

Lady Montgomery huffed like a perturbed child. "They do not listen to me."

Godric laid his hand on the stone wall, as if he were grabbing on to his patience.

Meiriona stepped between them. There had been enough discord without arguing over petty things like her appearance. "My gown is fine."

Godric glowered at her and gave her a long, slow perusal.

Her betraying nipples tightened at his leer. She crossed her arms over her chest.

Finally, he shrugged. "As I said afore, it makes little difference to me what you wear."

She narrowed her eyes in silent retort.

He offered his arm as if the row had not occurred. Lady Montgomery turned away coldly, but Meiriona accepted. The linen of his tunic slipped against his firm biceps.

Laughter and loud talking floated toward them as they walked down the corridor. The floor's stones were cold and damp through the worn places of her ragged shoes.

They neared the great hall, and Meiriona's grip on Godric's arm tightened. She took quick steps to keep up as he crossed the threshold and led her toward the head table.

The room had changed from her earlier impression. Hundreds of white and yellow candles gave the hall a festive air. Pewter trenchers were set at the high table and wood ones at the trestles. The floor had been swept clean. The stench of stale wine was gone, replaced by the aroma of fresh bread and roasting meat. Soldiers and women milled about in beautiful clothing, chattering excitedly. Children chased large dogs that ran under the trestle tables and between legs, knocking over goblets with their huge wagging tails.

There was no pause in the clatter as Godric led her to the large table at the far end of the room. It was situated on a raised dais under the only decoration in the hall, an engraved carving set into the stone wall with the Montgomery family crest—a hawk sitting on the back of a dragon.

There were no tapestries, which was odd. All great halls had tapestries, except for Whitestone, or so Meiriona thought.

Godric pulled out the lord's seat. It was a majestic carved mahogany chair, ornate, but not nearly as savage as the one in his solar.

"Where is my son?" Lady Montgomery demanded.

Godric drummed his fingers on the wooden table, the skin around his eyes tightening with irritation. "No doubt sleeping off his ale."

Lady Montgomery's jaw worked up and down, but she did not deny the accusation.

Meiriona released Godric's arm. "Leave her be."

She laid a comforting hand on the lady's shoulder. "Surely, he will be well by morning."

Godric grabbed Meiriona's hand and pulled her into the chair beside him. He sat and leaned close to her ear. "I have been lenient with you. Do not defy me in front of my people."

All her earlier guilt evaporated. Meiriona jerked back her hand.

Godric caught her chin between his thumb and finger. "I shall thrash you soundly if you disobey me." His flashing blue eyes told her he did not lie, and her retort died on her lips. This Godric was a stranger. "Tell me you understand."

"Aye, my lord," she hissed.

He motioned Lady Montgomery to the chair on his other side. She sat, but turned her back to him like a petulant adolescent.

He frowned but said nothing.

A dog yelped and Godric's child scurried from under a table holding the hound's ear. The little girl tugged it and the dog scooted away with a mournful whine. Scrambling to Godric, she kissed his cheek and sneered at Meiriona.

Meiriona shot a disapproving look at Godric's back, the only part of him turned toward her.

The toddler, evidently perturbed by the lack of reaction, wagged her tongue at her.

Meiriona clamped her lips together, determining to find a way to make peace with the child.

"Go on," Godric said to his impish daughter. "Take your seat."

The two-year-old bounced into the chair beside Lady Montgomery, her tiny elfin face barely showing over the oak tabletop. Bear sprawled onto the seat beside Meiriona. His hairy hand reached for a wine goblet, and his chair groaned under his weight.

Soldiers and other castlefolk took seats on benches in front of the low tables.

Once everyone was settled, Godric stood and clapped. "We return with a great prize." His voice boomed across the hall. "May I present the honorable Lady Meiriona of Whitestone."

Meiriona's mouth dropped open. He took her hand and lifted her to her feet. Her cheeks heated as the guests stared at her. Why in the name of the saints had she told him the dress was fine? She tightened her grip on Godric's fingers, seeing the questions in the crowd's eyes. One lady whispered behind her hand to the woman next to her and they both snickered. Meiriona's spine went rod straight. She squared her shoulders and glared at the two women until they looked away.

Godric cleared his throat, and the people clapped politely. "I insist you treat her as an honored guest until arrangements are made for us to marry."

"I am already—" The words choked in her throat as his gaze cut to hers. His grip tightened, and she felt as if his fingers were around her neck rather than merely on her hand. How bloody irritating to be naught more than a prize to be won.

He smiled, but his eyes were ice cold. Her neck prickled, and she remembered what he had said about not defying him.

She touched her face; her cheeks weighed ten pounds each. Her lips quivered under their heaviness as she pasted on a smile. "I am all ready."

"Ah." He turned back to the throng. "We have been on a long journey and our guest is starving. Let the feast begin."

A trumpet sounded, and a page carried an aquamanile shaped like a mounted knight to the high table. He poured water from it to wash their hands. Servants flowed into the hall carrying great platters of venison, pork, and eel. The entire scene was a bit disorderly, as if the servants had no clear mistress in the kitchen.

The soft blather of muted voices sounded like a funeral. No musicians enriched the hall with song or dance. No jesters or acrobats lightened the mood.

Heaps of meat lined the tables, but the food was bland and tasteless. Godric ate heartily as if he did not notice how terribly the food was prepared.

Meiriona peered around him at Lady Montgomery, who seemed on the verge of tears. Her lips turned into a pout, and she put food into her mouth the way a sullen spoiled child would.

"I thought ye told her to get yer prize some decent clothing," Bear said, talking over Meiriona's head as if she were absent.

Godric paused midbite to scowl at Lady Montgomery. "I will see to it myself."

Meiriona knifed a piece of tasteless pork. The tension in the household had more taste than the food.

A side curtain opened, and Damien entered the hall wearing clean, pressed garments and grinning from ear to ear.

Meiriona's knife stopped halfway to her mouth.

Her brother crossed the room in giddy strides bearing a platter of blackberry tarts. He walked straight, barely favoring his lame leg. Bowing low to Godric, he set the tarts on the high table ceremoniously.

"You have made my brother a servant?"

"A page," Godric corrected, bringing his goblet to his lips. "'Tis a suitable profession for a boy of his age."

Meiriona stabbed her meat violently. "He is *not* your page."

Godric stroked his chin, his long, callused fingers running over his generous lips. "You are wrong."

She narrowed her eyes, exasperated Godric seemed to think he knew what was best for her and her brother. "How dare you."

Godric's child snickered. "He walks funny, Papa."

Meiriona jumped to her feet, knocking her wine goblet over in the process. "My brother walks perfectly well. And I will challenge anyone who speaks differently."

Silence permeated the hall, and a hundred pairs of eyes turned, gawking at her.

Bear plunked his goblet on the table. "Milady," he whispered. "I am begging yer pardon, but she is only a child. She means nothing by her talk."

Damien shrank from the high table, his face flaming. He stumbled toward the door, catching himself on one of the tables.

"See?" Amelina giggled.

Disgusted with the child's behavior, Meiriona gave Godric a pointed look.

"Be kind, Amelina." Godric patted his child on the head.

Sticking out her lower lip, the toddler grabbed a tart.

Godric's hand shot to Meiriona's shoulder. With an unyielding grip, he pulled her to her seat. She slumped, her face hot and her eyes fixed on the trencher. "You are so bloody good at controlling everyone, you should control your child."

Godric halted one of the servants. "Take our new page back to the kitchens. He will not serve at the tables until his sister learns to contain herself."

Meiriona went livid as Damien cast her a dark look and dragged his feet on the way to the kitchens. She rose partway off her chair, but Godric's grip on her shoulder tightened painfully, forcing her back down. She glared at him mutinously. If she could have, she would have dumped the entire contents of the opium pouch in Godric's wine at that moment.

He banged his goblet on the table. "Go back to eating," he commanded the crowd, his voice tight.

The hundred pairs of eyes shifted downward to gaze mutely at their trenchers.

Godric took a long slow drag of wine. "The boy needs to fend for himself, Meiriona. Defending him does him no good."

"Of course it does him good. I have kept him safe all this time," she hissed, folding her hands in her lap.

Godric leaned close. His large hand covered her smaller ones. "Safe, nay; you have only kept him sheltered."

Glancing up, she noticed the guests peering at them beneath lowered lids. None met her gaze. She turned her shoulder to Godric, and they finished the meal in excruciating silence.

No one talked. No one moved. Not even after their bellies were full. Not even Amelina.

Meiriona placed her eating dagger on the table beside her trencher and stared into the silent crowd.

Bear scooted his chair back, startling her. He stalked to a table by the window and came huffing back, balancing a large worn chess set with his one arm.

"Chess?" he asked, breaking the silence of the somber hall.

"Aye." Godric rose, bowed to her curtly, and followed Bear to the hearth.

Once the two of them settled in large chairs by the fire, a collective sigh of relief filled the hall. The guests began to talk quietly. Some rose and left, including Lady Montgomery and Amelina.

A young squire, tall and lanky with an odd burn scar under one eye, hoisted a small table and set it near Godric.

Meiriona swept her gaze around the room. No one paid her any attention. Heart pounding, she snatched her eating dagger and stuffed it into the sleeve of her stained tunic.

The squire walked back toward her, and Meiriona smiled widely, hoping she looked innocent.

He blinked several times as if taken aback. He was only a few years older than Damien with blondish brown hair and large hazel eyes that dominated his boyish face. He would have been handsome if not for the bumpy, purplish scar under his eye. His skinny arms stuck out from his plain homespun tunic. "Milady—"

Meiriona let out her breath, positive he had not seen her steal the dagger.

"Would you care to watch the chess game with me while the servants prepare for the night?"

Meiriona nodded. Watching chess was as good a distraction as any. She doubted Godric would give her leave to wander the halls of Montgomery alone, and she certainly was in no hurry to be taken back to his chamber.

Rising, she allowed the squire to escort her near the enormous lip of the huge hearth where Godric and Bear sorted out the chess pieces. Servants clattered about, breaking down the tables and rolling out blankets and cots to sleep on.

"What is your name?" she asked the squire as they settled into a couple of chairs. The fire warmed her back.

"Eric, milady." He smiled, showing two dimples.

Bear waggled a shaggy red eyebrow at her and grinned at Godric. "I vow, I hear a win coming."

Godric's lips twitched as if he were just about to smile, but he did not. "Black or white?"

"White." Bear scratched his unkempt beard. "I'm no' too proud to admit wanting the advantage of the first play."

Godric motioned a page to refill their goblets. "So I am black."

Meiriona leaned toward the squire. "I am surprised he puts himself at a disadvantage by going second."

"Shh," whispered Eric. "You have not seen him play."

Meiriona cocked a brow at the boy.

"All deathblows and no mercy. He is keen and logical. Makes each move without emotion." There was a fair bit of hero worship in the squire's voice.

"Truly?"

Eric nodded. "He likes to capture the opponent's queen first off. He sets out with a frenzy to do so."

Meiriona blanched and leaned closer to watch the board. Surely the squire was only talking about chess.

Sparing her a glance, Godric thumbed his jaw slowly. "'Tis not always a disadvantage to be patient and wait to see your opponent's move, my lady."

Marble clicked against marble as Bear started with his knight jumping to queen's bishop three. Godric countered, moving his pawn to queen's pawn three, and before long the two of them were locked in an intense game of wits.

Meiriona watched the board with growing trepidation. If Godric played half as bloody on the battlefield as he did on the chessboard, her castle did not stand a chance.

Bear's queen sat on king four and, without a blink, Godric captured her. It meant the death of his own queen by a mere pawn, but that did not seem to faze him. The move clearly agitated Bear, who had not expected such an exchange.

"Does he always play so heartlessly?" she whispered to Eric.

"Always." The squire grinned, eyes lighting up. "'No mercy' is his cry in chess *and* on the battlefield."

Meiriona cringed.

Godric forced Bear's pieces farther and farther into the corner of the board while he dominated the middle. After a long pause, he exchanged a rook for a bishop. "Check."

Bear slid his king one space, his composure crumbling.

Eric's words haunted her as Godric followed Bear's king with his rook. "Check."

Propping his head on his shaggy knuckles, Bear leaned over the board. There were only two spaces for his king to move.

Meiriona felt queasy. She could see the trap. If Bear took the space that looked the most open, the game was lost.

Godric leaned back and stroked his chin, waiting. He peered at the board, confidence radiating from him.

"Eric, can you take me to . . ." Her voice trailed off and her cheeks heated. "To where I am to sleep."

For the first time, Godric looked up from the board. "Nay, I shall escort you to my chamber myself."

Bear's jaw dropped. "But the game," he protested.

Godric scrutinized Meiriona; his gaze seemed to linger just beneath her clothing. "I forfeit."

Meiriona felt her throat constrict. "You should finish your game," she choked out.

"Ye never forfeit," Bear said sullenly.

Rising, Godric extended a hand. Eric scampered off his seat as if he feared sitting beside her had displeased Godric.

"Come, my lady." Godric's voice gave no room for argument.

The eating dagger inside her sleeve tickled her forearm.

CHAPTER 17

From her seat, Meiriona could see the tight muscles of Godric's thighs bulging through his hose as he stood before her, waiting. The tiny hairs on the back of his beckoning hand concealed neither his strength nor his gentleness. For a wicked, terrifying moment her mouth went dry, and she wanted nothing more than to allow him to lead her to his solar with its obscene bed. Mayhap he would hold her through the night with his hand twisted around her hair as he had done in the forest.

She pricked her finger on the point of the hidden eating dagger to bring herself back to her senses. She could not betray her family or her people by giving in to her wicked inner desires. Such thoughts must come from the devil himself.

Bear gaped at Godric, evidently miffed about not getting the chance to lose the chess game.

Eric slid into the vacated chair. "I will finish Master Godric's game."

Bear's shaggy eyebrows rounded, and he gave a short laugh. "Mayhap I have a chance yet." Eyes alight, he moved his one remaining white rook to block the impending checkmate.

Clearing his throat, Godric cocked an eyebrow at Meiriona. "You claimed a desire to go to bed, my lady."

"Not with you," she whispered, her food feeling like a leaden mass in the pit of her stomach.

Godric's hand traced a lazy line across her collarbone. "Come."

She shivered, wishing she could ignore the warmth of his finger pads.

From the corner of her eye, she saw a woman wiping tables give them a curious glance. She sighed; she had made enough of a spectacle of herself tonight and longed to escape to a private place. Standing, she took Godric's proffered hand. Her chin lifted at the raised eyebrows of the servants as they crossed the hall.

"Gramercy," Godric said, once they reached the corridor. "I feared I would have to carry you across my shoulder kicking and screaming."

She gave him a coy smile. "Would you have done so?"

"Assuredly." He pulled her forward. "We have many things to do that I would prefer to do in private."

His tone gave her pause, and she wished she could grasp the dagger in her sleeve to bolster her confidence that some of those "things" would not occur.

Lady Montgomery rushed toward them from a side room as they made their way down the hall. "Lady Whitestone—"

Godric stopped her with a quelling glare. "Go back to your chamber."

Lady Montgomery turned aside and allowed them to pass. Godric grasped Meiriona's wrist and strode down the hall.

"That was rude," Meiriona chided.

"You will not become friends with that woman."

Meiriona felt anger boil from the pit of her stomach. "You cannot determine my friends."

"Aye, as your master, I can. And I will."

Meiriona jabbed a finger at him. "You will never be my master."

"I already am." Godric's hand wrapped around

her upper arm, forcing her to follow in his wake. She took the steps leading upward as if her feet were made of iron.

They reached the oak door to his chamber, and the burly one-eyed guard stepped aside without a single inquisitive glance in her direction. She surmised that he had seen it all and was no longer surprised at whatever odd thing his master did.

Godric thrust her into his chamber unceremoniously. The door closed with a heavy thud and she pressed her back against it. The coldness of the wood seeped into her body.

A fire glowed in the fireplace, and several candles had been lit as if a servant had anticipated their arrival. The scent of beeswax and smoke tinged the air. The chamber, luxurious as a sultan's palace, was neither heaven nor hell but some lonely interim between the two extremes.

Godric crossed the Oriental carpet, walked to the hearth, and placed one hand on the back of the ornate throne. The fire silhouetted him in its winking light. Her gaze lingered on the strong line of his back. Powerful. Beautiful. A fallen angel.

"Do you plan to linger by the door all night?"

"Mayhap. What are your plans?"

His gaze turned warm as hot, spiced mead. "Whatever pleases me."

Meiriona glowered at him. "I am not your whore."

Godric chuckled.

"I will fight you."

"I have no doubt about that."

She shoved her hand into her sleeve and took a firm grip on the hilt of her eating dagger. "You think I cannot win?"

"Meiriona." His voice was husky and his gaze direct. "We both know I could easily force you to my will. But I brought you here to talk."

"Talk?"

He nodded. "Just talk."

Releasing the knife, she peeled her back from the door.

"You can honor your promises anon," he said.

She started, then realized his eyes glowed with amusement. He was teasing her! The scoundrel.

"You devil." Oh, the man was outrageous. "Why do you say such things?"

One side of his mouth turned up in a knowing smile. "I like to watch you blush."

Her stomach did a lazy flop.

"Come, Meiriona."

She eyed him suspiciously, her hands still flattened against the door. Long seconds ticked by. The firelight flickered over his face, and he beckoned her with his mysterious eyes.

"Let us declare a truce." He held out a hand, palm up. A gesture of peace. But her wits felt as scattered and splintered as a woodcarver's shop. She would have no peace as long as Godric was around. He lived in a gulf between heaven and hell, and he would pull her there, too.

And yet . . . She released the door, part of her soul already lost. *I am a fool,* she thought. For this insane moment she wanted nothing more than to sit on the ledge of the hearth and be alone with him. She stepped toward him, her feet sinking into the exotic rug.

Godric peered at her with the same look he'd given her years ago in the chapel. Only they were not in the chapel. They were in his chamber. She hesitated. 'Twas as if he saw right through her clothing.

Lush, exotic scents teased her nostrils. Amber, myrrh, and others she could not discern.

The bulge of his manhood strained against his hose. Large. Hungry.

"You risk eternal damnation for lusting after a married woman," she warned.

He withdrew his proffered hand, tucked his thumb into his belt, and gazed at her, his eyes changing from blue flame to blue ice. "God threw me away a long time ago."

Shuddering, she dug her toes into the Oriental carpet. His voice sounded haunted. Guilt crashed against her heart, and suddenly, she wanted to weep for him. She knew how heinous and frustrating it was to be considered mere property for the whims of others, yet that was the sort of life she had sent him into. What had he suffered those long years in slavery?

"I am sorry," she whispered, unable to keep the words locked inside, no matter how inadequate they were. "I did not know what happened to you."

He squatted, turning his back to her, and she was unsure if he had heard her. He poked around the embers with an iron rod and set another log on the fire. The scent of smoke wafted in her direction. After several moments he stood.

"Come, sit by the fire so we may talk. You owe me that."

Meiriona felt her insides knot.

He took a pillow from the bed and placed it on the ledge of the fireplace, then sat in the carved throne, peered at her, and stroked his chin. The chair had overwhelmed Lady Montgomery, but it fit him perfectly. His black leather boots sank into the fluffy sheepskin exactly as she had imagined. He waved her forward, and she slid beside him to sit on the pillow, the fire crackling behind her.

Godric's piercing stare made her uneasy. She crossed her arms and rubbed them.

"Are you cold?"

"Nay."

He studied her with the interest of a steward examining faulty ledgers. She took a long, shuddering breath. The silence between them wracked her nerves more than any argument they'd had over the past days.

The firelight caressed his face, alternately concealing and revealing the scars. Scars she had given him.

Her lower lip trembled. "I did not know."

"Exactly what did you not know?" His voice was mild, but she saw his interest in the intensity of his gaze.

Squirming against the pillow, she gathered her nerve. "My father deceived me. I was not aware you had been imprisoned." There, she had said it.

"I was not only imprisoned, my lady. I was *enslaved.*"

She opened her mouth to speak, but guilt constricted her throat.

Leaning toward her, he placed his hand on her knee. An old, well-healed scar ran the length of his thumb. "What were you told?"

"Oh, sweet Mary, I was told you had a place in the king's court on the continent. That you were a captain in the army."

"I see." His expression was unreadable.

"Oh, saints." Reaching forward, she traced his raised crescent-shaped wound. Then she ran her fingertip down the length of the smaller scar under his eye, feeling its bumpy ridge. If only she could smooth away his disfigurement as easily as he had smoothed away her fear of horses. "Do they hurt?"

His large hand covered hers, pressing her fingers against his cheek until she could feel his uneven skin against her palm. He slid her hand down his neck to his chest until she felt the thump of his heartbeat. "It only hurts in here, my lady."

His voice was strong, but she heard its disguised agony. Guilt threatened to swallow her. "Forgive me. I did not know what my father planned."

"And if you had, would you have married me?"

Meiriona swallowed. Would she have? "I . . . I . . . Nay, I could not have."

"Why, Meiriona? Even at our first meeting I saw desire in your eyes."

She averted her eyes. How could he, a bastard, understand the trappings of duty?

He turned her face back so she was forced to look at him. "I understand your reluctance now, but I was not always an ugly beast."

"Ugly? Saints, you are the most beautiful man I have ever known." She gasped and covered her mouth. She had not meant to blurt out such a private thought.

Godric stared at the enigmatic woman seated afore him on the hearth. Why, he almost believed she spoke the truth. If he had never seen his own image in a looking glass or seen the revulsion in women's eyes, he could have believed her.

He tilted her chin up. "Wherefore do you speak thus?"

She shrugged and a pleasant blush lined her cheeks. "I do not know."

"Do you believe it?"

She swallowed and her lower lip trembled, but she nodded.

"Meiriona." He kissed her cheek. She was soft and feminine; the firelight licked her skin, making her exotic beauty even more pronounced. "Why do you fight me? When I come near you, I can see the longing, the passion within you, and yet I also see fear. Why?"

She shivered, but met his gaze. "When I was a little girl, men invaded Whitestone." Her voice took on a faraway quality, like she was distancing herself from her memories.

"Soldiers?"

"Aye, from the Yorkist army. Mother and I hid in the keep for days. When it was overrun, we made our way out the secret tunnel. A few of our men found us, but they were in bad shape by that time. We had a horse and ran, trying to make it to Tintern Abbey. We thought we had gotten away."

She was looking at him, but not looking at him. Behind her, a log fell and the fire snapped, but she did not flinch. He took her hand in his, admiring the smallness of it. He had bathed, and she had not, so her palms were grubby while his were clean. Even so, there was a softness about her fingers that contrasted sharply with his own. Doubtless, she had never killed anyone with her bare hands.

There was that feeling again: the feeling of being *unclean.* The same way he had felt when he'd stolen her from her chamber. He had blamed her for something she knew nothing about. Mayhap her hands were dirty, but her soul was clean, unlike his own.

"So you got away?" he asked.

Her eyes focused on his again. "Nay, the Yorks found us in the forest. Mother and I were thrown from our mount. We scrambled through the brush but, oh, dear Jesu, I can still hear my mother scream. A huge, dirty man ripped her dress and fell atop her. I ran for her, but I must have tripped." Meiriona's voice broke. She pressed her lips together and blinked. No tears marred her cheeks. "I do not remember anything else."

Godric slid one arm around her shoulders and the other under her knees, wishing he could somehow protect her from the past. She felt limp and fragile as he picked her up and placed her on his lap. "You are safe here."

She laid her head on his shoulder, curled her legs like a child, and stared into the fire.

"What happened next?"

"I was told that I tripped on a rock and was knocked unconscious. The men thought I was dead so they left me alone. When I awoke, Mum was huddled into a ball with blood all over her thighs."

"Christ! How old were you?"

"Eleven."

"Where was your father?"

"He was at war, marching with the Lancastrian army." Meiriona clutched his tunic, and Godric shifted in the chair so they would both be more comfortable. "'Twas terrible. I think in some ways 'twould have been better had she died right then. Is that selfish of me to think so?"

Godric stroked her hair, anger burning in his stomach. He knew how awful the sins of war were, but he had never heard it explained from a woman's point of view. Bloody monsters! If he had heard this story before Bear told him about Owain's tryst with the village wench, he would have killed the young whelp instead of merely whipping him until he wet his breeches.

"What happened to your mother?"

"I cleaned her up, and we managed to make our way to safety. She died nine months later."

"Damien?"

"Aye. When you stole me from my chamber, I thought—"

"Meiriona—" He kissed the top of her head. "I will not deny my desire for you, but it will not be thus between us." He nuzzled her ear and kissed her neck. She shivered and caught her breath sharply. "We both know I would have no need to force you."

In an instant, she jumped from his lap. Her heartbeat pulsed in a vein on her neck. "Nay, nay, nay. My father never recovered. He blamed God and himself and Damien when Mother died. He is nigh his deathbed. If I betray him, I will kill my own father. I must do my duty to my family."

"Calm yourself, pretty lady. We will discuss your duty at a different time."

Abruptly, a knock sounded on the oaken door.

"Enter."

A short servant with a shaggy black mustache and a stump of an arm stepped into the solar wrestling a large tub. He had only one hand, so the tub wobbled precariously before he set it down with a thump near the bed. Several more servants entered and poured steaming water into it.

"Will that be all, me lord?"

"Have Cook send up wine and see what happened to that fool woman who was supposed to be bringing my captive a gown."

The servants gave short, deferential dips, and Godric dismissed them with a wave. Turning back to Meiriona, he motioned her toward the water. "Go on, you must feel filthy from the journey."

Outrage stormed her expression. "Surely you cannot mean to sit there in that chair while I *bathe*!"

He winked at her and slowly rose from his chair. "Nay, my lady, of course not. I intend to bathe you myself."

Her eyes widened, but he saw them dilate. "You cannot."

He laughed. "There are many things I will give you choice about, but this is *not* one of them."

She shook her head, but he saw hesitation, mayhap even yearning in her eyes.

"Have you forgotten your promise to come willingly to my bed?"

"'Twas made under duress with false knowledge."

"Mayhap. So let us compromise." Lifting a brow, he stepped toward her. She did not move away, although their bodies nearly touched—a good sign, he surmised.

"Compromise?" Tilting her head back, she licked her lips.

Christ, if she knew how thin his veil of civility was,

she would not do that. She stirred his blood more than any woman he had ever known.

He held his hand out to her, as if merely asking for a dance. "I will not hold you to your promise tonight. In exchange you will allow me to bathe you."

She watched him for several heartbeats, her eyes searching his face.

For the love of God, he was entirely too tempted. She had the innocence of a saint and the passion of a harlot. If she did not say yes willingly, he would strip her clothes off and plop her in the tub anyway just to see her naked again. He was much, much too tired of pretending to be a gentleman.

He began counting silently, determined to give her until one hundred to make a decision. On the count of ninety-three, she placed her hand in his. He let out his breath.

"Verily, I am bedeviled," she whispered.

CHAPTER 18

She would allow him to bathe her, no more. Oh, she was wicked to let him touch her intimately, and yet her skin had already warmed, anticipating his touch.

Firelight danced around the opulent chamber as Godric led her to the bathing tub, his hand engulfing her own. Steam drifted upward in lazy tendrils from the hot water.

If only she could blame her wickedness on her need to bathe. But in her heart she knew the desire to be clean paled next to her desire to belong to the man who held her captive.

She stopped, her toes digging into the carpet.

"Are you afraid, Meiriona?"

"Nay," she said, tilting her head back to look at him.

"You need not fear me. I will hold to our bargain."

She shivered. "I do not fear you." Mayhap her lack of fear was the most dangerous thing of all.

Godric pulled her forward until they stood between the bed and the tub. He sat at the foot of the bed, drawing her between his legs until her breasts pressed against his torso. The flickering light played across his skin.

"I want you," he said simply.

She closed her eyes, wishing his frank statement didn't tug at her heart. She should not want to be touched by him. She had her duty to her family to think about.

His callused palms cupped her cheeks, and he brought her face close to his. He kissed the bridge of her nose and then each of her eyebrows.

The devil take him, it was not supposed to be thus. If he were rough or forceful, she could fight him, but she had no defenses against his tenderness. Why could he not stay the beast she had built him up to be in her mind?

She drew back and glanced at the chamber door a few steps behind her. Mayhap 'twas not locked. Even if she could not escape, he would stop being kind so he would not tempt her.

"Will you dishonor our bargain already, Meiriona?" His thighs locked her between them. "Would it be easier to surrender if I said you have no choice?" His voice was low and erotic.

Her gaze snapped to his. Mercy, she had made a bargain with the devil, and her soul was already lost.

"Let me caress you. Let me pour hot water over your skin and wash away all the years and hurt that stand between us."

Lost in his words, she touched the crescent scar marring his cheek and nodded.

His mouth slanted over hers. *I will not fall in love with him,* she determined. Mayhap he *could* give her all the pleasure her body would allow, but he would *never* claim her heart.

His tongue licked her lower lip, and she surrendered to his kiss. The air felt cold around her legs and ankles as his hands bunched her dress, hiking the fabric to her thighs. He kneaded her buttocks, pressing her groin against the hard bulge in his hose. Lightninglike pleasure arced through her. Oh, heavens. It was *not* supposed to be thus.

She pulled away, pushing her hands against his

shoulders. Leaning back, she tried to put space between them, but he held her trapped within the prison of his body. His scent was warm, masculine.

"'Tis not right between us," she whispered.

His hand splayed across her cheek. "You need not fear the private desires between a man and a woman, Meiriona."

"You spoke the same words when we first met."

He bunched the fabric of her dress higher until the night air licked the skin of her hips and stomach, exposing her groin. "And 'tis still true."

In one motion, he yanked her dress and chemise upward. They slid against her skin and over her face.

She gasped, unprepared for the swirl of emotions spinning in her stomach. Desire. Passion. Hunger. Godric made her into a mad fool, unable to know her own heart.

Grinning, he flung her garments to the floor. The eating dagger slid from the tunic's sleeve and skittered across the floor.

Meiriona gulped, her hand going protectively to her throat.

Godric thumbed his jaw for a long moment, then bent and scooped it up.

"You lost this," he drawled, holding it out to her hilt first.

She glanced from his face to the sharp point of the knife and back again. The puny weapon seemed foolish. She could not use it to fight against his tenderness.

"'Tis the wrong sort of weapon," she whispered.

Quirking a brow, Godric slid his fingers to the end of the blade, cocked his arm back and hurled it at the dressing screen. It stuck in the wood with a heavy thud. His arms went around her and he kissed her tenderly.

She melted into his embrace. "'Tis not supposed to be thus," she breathed.

"How is it supposed to be between us?"

She swallowed. "You are supposed to be terrifying and mean and demanding."

"I am demanding." His voice was a low rumble.

"Aye, but you are neither terrifying nor mean." Her hands slid over the curve of his shoulders. His tunic was damp where water from his freshly washed hair had dripped onto the fabric.

He blinked once, then scowled at her, but his eyes sparkled in the dim light and amusement twitched his lips. "You do not think I am terrifying? Mayhap I should try harder."

A giggle welled inside her. She bit her lower lip to suppress it. 'Twas dreadful enough her wicked body desired him, but to laugh with her enemy? Oh, saints, what other sins would she commit?

"*You* are a blackheart."

He chuckled, the sound sensual and husky. "Aye, so I have been told." He nibbled the lobe of her ear. "Meiriona, wrap your arms around my neck."

Logic demanded she refuse. *Remember your duty, remember your duty*, she chanted to herself, but her fingers itched to run through his dark, curling hair.

"Now, girl," he commanded in a low whisper.

She obeyed, unable to resist. The junction between her thighs felt wet and hot. Slipping her arms around his neck, she caressed his hair. She twirled her index finger, enjoying the soft, springy texture of his locks. The scent of sandalwood soap lingered on his skin, filling her nose and lungs with his masculine presence.

Her home, her father, her husband were far, far away. Godric was here, now. Although it was a sin, just for tonight, she would enjoy the comfort of his arms.

He smiled. One of his hands caressed her shoulder, the other slid down her hip to the back of her knees. Lifting her as easily as a child, he stood and carried her to the tub. Her long hair trailed across the carpet.

Slowly, he sank to one knee and lowered her into the warm, enveloping water.

A sigh of pleasure escaped her throat. The water lapped around her shoulders, sloshing onto the floor. Godric's hands slipped from under her, and her buttocks bumped the bottom of the tub. She closed her eyes and leaned against the edge, gifting herself with the pure bliss of the moment.

His hands slid across her stomach and between her breasts. He held one palm softly on her neck. She felt his body stretch to the side, disturbing the water and splashing more of it out of the tub. The heady scent of myrrh and amber wafted toward her. Fluttering her eyes open, she saw he held a cake of perfumed soap.

"You are very beautiful," he whispered, "but 'tis not your beauty that interests me."

She swallowed, her mouth dry.

He knelt behind the tub, and she felt his tunic brush against her back. Massaging soap into the tops of her shoulders, he dragged his large palms across her skin in slow, decadent strokes. "You have beautiful shoulders, Meiriona, but many women have beautiful shoulders." His voice was low, unhurried.

Reaching around her on either side, he broke the cake into two pieces, releasing more of its luxurious scent. He held a piece of soap in each hand and slid the slippery cakes down each of her arms. "You have fine, slender arms, Meiriona, but many women have slender arms."

Her skin tingled. His voice made her dizzy, as if she were a child who had spun in circles too many times and the earth now whirled before her.

He bent her arms so her elbows rested on the sides of the tub. Starting with her pinkies, he took each finger and rubbed it, cleaning dirt from her cuticles and knuckles.

"You have delicate hands, Meiriona, but many

women have delicate hands." His fingers moved leisurely, touching each part of her hands as if the world had passed away and only their bodies remained.

She sighed.

His fingers slid to her shoulders, down her rib cage to her stomach, and back up the space between her breasts. Her nipples puckered although he did not touch them. In slow circles, he traced the path twice more. Three times. Four. Then five.

She relaxed, letting her arms sink into the tub and float atop the water. Surrendering to his touch, she allowed him to smooth away the past until she focused only on the present moment.

His hand slid outward, across the top of her bosom, somewhat closer to her nipples, but still not touching them. Blood rushed into the peaks of her breasts, stinging her with tiny hot prickles. Oh, sweet Mary.

His hands caressed down her rib cage again, moving only half a finger's width with every heartbeat. Slow. Slow. Oh, Jesu, it was too slow.

Her nipples tingled. His thumbs must be less than half a finger's length from them. Surely he would touch them this time.

His palm pressed up her sternum, his fingers on the inner curve of her breasts, and yet, not quite stroking the tips. Saints! Mayhap if she were just a little to the left, his hands would brush her nipples, quell the stinging need for them to be touched. She shifted slightly to one side.

He kissed the top of her head. His hands moved over the upper curve of her breast once again and worked their way down her side, one agonizing rib at a time. Moisture trickled from her core.

Through lowered eyelashes, she glanced down. The distance between Godric's little finger and her nipple was less than the flat of an eating dagger.

He had been bold until now. Why was he not touching her *there*? At the peaks! Where the skin itched and stung and ached for his touch.

She squirmed, wiggling to the side, but his fingers remained that maddening distance away from where she needed him.

"Meiriona," he whispered, sliding his hand betwixt her breasts and closer to her burning nipples. But *still* not touching them. Vexing man! "Do you know what interests me?"

Her mind felt drugged as if it floated beyond reality, but she shook her head.

Abruptly, Godric pinched her swollen nipples. Meiriona gasped at the lightning arc of pleasure pain, liquid seeped from her queynt, and a wave of ecstasy slammed her body.

"Dear God," she breathed, her eyes flying open.

Godric's hands cupped her breasts gently. "There are thousands of beautiful women in the world. 'Tis your *passion* that interests me."

CHAPTER 19

Godric's already swollen member tightened as Meirіona sighed and her arms went limp. He rounded the side of the bathing tub. Misty tendrils drifted off the surface of the water, filling his chamber with the scent of myrrh and amber. Reaching into the warm water, he slid his hands beneath her, enjoying the soft silk of her skin. Straightening, he pulled her from the tub, pleased she did not resist.

"My lord," she murmured, snuggling into his torso.

Relief that he had not had to force her compliance flowed through him. Thank God she would not fight as he took her virginity. Kicking aside her tunic and chemise, he carried her across the Oriental carpet, then laid her on the bed's soft fur coverlet.

"You are the most passionate woman I have ever known."

She turned toward him, her gaze glazed with desire. Candlelight danced across her skin.

Flicking his fingers across the springy auburn hair of her pubic mound, he heard her sharp intake of breath.

"You promised we would just talk," she protested weakly, her voice a murmur.

Realizing he had moved too quickly, he sank onto the fur coverlet, his palm caressing her hip. His hand looked huge and monstrous against her alabaster limbs and he thought of their earlier conversation. She'd seen only the horror of rape, not the beauty of passion. He would have to lead her slowly to trust him.

"This is wrong," she whispered.

"Shh," he admonished, knowing her protest was but a feeble effort to relieve herself of the guilt of wanting him.

He kissed her, his tongue sweeping inside her mouth to dominate her senses.

She sighed and melted against his tunic, just as he expected, but the feeling of being unclean nagged at him.

He pushed the pesky emotion aside; too many lives hung in the balance, depending on him to claim Meiriona. He *must* take her virginity. He must get her with child.

He thumbed his jaw, contemplating how best to seduce her into compliance. He was well versed in the ways to give pleasure to a woman. If he heightened her anticipation, as he had in the tub, he could ease her journey, make her hungry for him. Already her protests were given without heat.

He kissed her shoulder, enjoying the spicy scent of amber that lingered from the exotic soap he had used. Running his hand across her stomach, he smiled when her eyelids fluttered closed.

He kissed the tops of her breasts, enjoying watching her nipples pucker. Slowly, he drew tiny circles around her pink areolas. Gooseflesh rose on her limbs.

Pleased, he pressed his advantage and gently sucked one of her breasts. She sighed, and more blood flowed into his engorged member.

He took a deep breath to calm himself. Long ago he'd learned the skill of forcing his attention away from his own wants so he could focus on pleasing the woman before him. 'Twas a skill Nadira had taught him well. His thoughts lingered for a moment on the numerous virgins Nadira had insisted he swive for her own perverted pleasure. From behind a secret veil, the princess loved to watch him overcome a woman's modest virginal protests and set her aflame with passion.

A feeling of uncleanness, sharp and bitter, pierced him.

He pushed his mind back to the task at hand.

Kneeling above Meiriona, he ran his tongue down the length of her hip. She sighed, her legs going slack so that he could now see the pink, dewy nether lips of her sex. He gently pushed her knees apart. She stiffened but did not protest, and he knew with disgust, it would be as with the other women: she would be willing for anything he insisted so long as the spell between them was not broken. Tomorrow, she would hate him, knowing that she had been duped by his sexual skills.

Bed ropes creaked as he sat up, yanked his tunic over his head, and flung it onto the floor.

"Godric . . ." She reached for him.

He rubbed the muscles of his neck absently, then rolled her onto her side, spooning her with his body and letting their passion quell.

Of a truth, he could make her body willing—but selfishly, he wanted her mind willing as well.

"Meiriona, tell me you want this as much as I do," he whispered, knowing his request was selfish. He should allow her the delusion that he was forcing the issue so he could spare her the guilt of going against her family. Instead, he wanted her to admit her desire.

She turned toward him blinking, as if trying to focus. "My lord . . . I . . . uh," she said as if she could not find the words. A pregnant pause stretched the air.

He set his jaw, knowing that if he kissed her again, she would kiss him back passionately. It was as with the other women: so long as they did not *think* about what they did, they would sigh and moan and float in the sensations. Without the fog of passion clouding their vision, they saw the folly of their desire.

'Twas no wonder that since his time in slavery, he had only taken a woman when he did not have to concern himself with her wants beyond how much money he paid her.

Meiriona licked her lips, and he saw debate in her features. "We should not," she murmured faintly.

Owain's words came back to him, convicting him. *What is the difference between me taking a woman and you taking a woman?*

Disgusted with himself, he rose from the bed. The mattress ropes moaned.

"My lord?" Meiriona sat up, confusion on her features.

"Ah, girl . . . Sleep."

She reached for him and he slid back beside her, determined to wait until he possessed her mind as well as her body.

CHAPTER 20

Morning sunlight slanted through the glass windowpanes as Meiriona, disconcerted, dangled her feet from Godric's large four-poster bed and gathered the sheet around her naked shoulders. She could scarcely believe she was yet a virgin.

Sweet saints, Godric had made her body frenzied with waves of pleasure. But after the bath, he had not taken her. He had held her silently here on the feather bedding, cuddled like a favored pet, until finally, shaken from the fever he had created in her, she slept.

Wiping sleep from her eyes, she blinked and glanced around the huge solar.

Godric, Godric, Godric. Every part of this room bespoke Godric. The smell, the decadence, the size. If she stuck out her tongue, she could probably taste him.

Rainbows from the glass-paned windows bounced off the whitewashed walls, the marble-topped table, and the massive throne. Never had she seen so much luxury in one place. Surely, not even the cathedral at Tintern Abbey was so richly arrayed.

Sliding from the mattress, she stood on the chill floor and rubbed her arms and shoulders. Last night was a warm, delicious dream, but today's frigid air was a nasty splash of reality.

She fingered her nipples, already erect from the

cold. They puckered harder under her thumbs. Saints, what had Godric done to her? Surely she was no different than last night; he had *not* taken her virginity.

She ran her palm across the top curve of her breasts and down the sides to her belly, tracing the path his callused hands had traveled last night.

Nay, she was not the same. Mayhap her body was unchanged, her virginity intact, but Godric had done much worse than claim her *body*. He touched her mind, her emotions, her soul. That was far, far more intimate than merely taking her body.

She padded to one of the windows, dragging the sheet across the floor with her, grateful Godric was not here now addling her thoughts even further. Leaning on the windowsill, she watched men practicing in the field below. Their swords flashed in the sun as they parried and thrust in mock battle.

Cursing her evil, lustful heart, she searched the field for her captor. For the love of God, she was a fool. She was married to another man. She could never belong to Godric, and Godric could never belong to her.

Still, she wanted to know what he had done to her to make her feel so weak last night. Reaching her hand under the sheet, she pinched her nipple between her thumb and forefinger as he had done. It felt . . . pleasant, but there was no lightning strike of sensation as there had been when *he* had done it, no waves of ecstasy that caused womanly fluid to flow from her sex.

Mayhap it was because he had pinched her nipples much harder. Sliding the sheet down, she clamped her fingers together and gasped. Nay! It hurt when she did that—it did not feel at all the way it had when it had been *his* hands.

She glanced up, and her hand flew to her throat,

yanking the sheet with it. Godric, shirtless atop Vengeance, stared at her from the practice field, a roguish half-smile pasted across his features.

Oh, sweet Mary! She jumped backward, away from the window, pressing her back against a nearby tapestry. Had he seen her touching herself? Playing with her nipple like a whore teasing a customer? Her insides quivered; surely her cheeks were as crimson as the thread of the carpet.

For the love of Saint Jude, Godric was turning her into a madwoman. He made her want things she must not want. Surely Montgomery had a chapel and a priest. She would go straight there and confess her sins. Mayhap spend the whole day in prayer prone afore the altar.

She swallowed, gathered her courage, and peeked around the side of the window. Could she move about without being seen?

Oh, Jesu! He was still there! His muscled thighs gripped the stallion's flanks as he sat tall and proud atop Vengeance. Even at this distance, she could feel his gaze upon her skin. Her rebellious nipples tightened under the sheet. At once, he gave her a cocky salute, wheeled his mount, and tossed his practice sword to one of the squires. Oh, dear Christ, even from this height she had seen the smolder of his eyes. His intent was clear. He was coming. Here. Now.

And she was naked!

Racing to the bed, she ripped down the fur coverlet and slid her hand across the mattress in search of her shift and tunic. She would go straightway to the chapel before he could make his way to the solar.

Tossing pillows, furs, and bed linens to the carpet, Meiriona patted the bed with desperation. The bedsheets were still warm from their bodies.

By all that was holy, where were her clothes?

What was she thinking? To stand in the window

and fondle herself! Straightening, she tossed her hair behind her shoulders, scanning the room with frantic eyes.

Pulling the sheet tightly across her chest, she rounded the bed. Surely her clothes were by the tub at the foot of the bed. The evil, evil tub where he had made her lust for him. She knelt, searching under and around the bed and tub.

Were those his footsteps on the planks of the hallway outside? Desperation pounded in her chest.

He was coming because, like Eve with her fruit, she had tempted him with her womanly nature. She was naked as Eve too.

Oh, sweet saints! Holding her hair from her eyes, she peered anxiously under the bed. *Holy Mary*, she prayed, *if only you will give me clothing before he enters, I'll cut my hair, the symbol of womanhood, as penance.*

Relief flowed through her like warm honey when she saw a wad of white cloth by the chamber pot under the center of the bed. She offered up another silent prayer, this one of thanksgiving. Godric must have kicked her shift there when he undressed her.

Reaching for the linen prize, her hand grasped empty air. She crouched lower, forcing her shoulders under the bed. She could almost reach it, almost.

Almost.

She stretched farther; the sheet she'd wrapped around herself for modesty slipped off her backside and cool air caressed her bottom.

The chamber door banged open and heavy footsteps clomped into the room. Scrambling backward, she snatched for the fallen sheet, banging her head on the bottom board of the bed.

"Oh," she said, suddenly very aware her naked buttocks wagged in the air while she rooted under the bed for her damn shift.

A deep masculine chuckle echoed through the

room, and for one heart-stopping moment, she contemplated flattening and crawling the rest of the way underneath the big bed.

He cleared his throat. "Shall we try that position on top of the mattress rather than under it, my lady?"

Yanking the sheet over her buttocks, she abandoned her cursed chemise to its place next to the chamber pot and pushed her shoulders and head from under the bed. Scrambling to her feet and clutching the sheet tightly around her nude body, she found that Godric stood much, much too close. He smelled of leather and horses and maleness. She could feel the warmth of his skin.

"Saints! You are not supposed to be here!"

He gave her a lopsided grin. "Had I known you were crawling around on the floor wiggling your sweet bottom in the air, I assure you I would have climbed the very walls again to reach you faster."

Mortified, she lifted her chin, stalked to the large throne, and sat, tucking the sheet as best she could around her naked thighs. She stared at the embers, too embarrassed to move. Surely even the backs of her knees were blushing.

His boots were noiseless on the rug, but she felt him coming closer like a silent brooding storm. He reached her in long, lazy strides and tilted her chin toward him, but she could not meet his gaze.

"Lady, you are exquisite and passionate. Never hide that."

If possible, she would melt into the chair and disappear forever. Exquisite and passionate?

"Wanton and whorish," she said, her voice sounding dejected, defeated even to her own ears.

"Never that." He kissed her temple, and she could smell his warm outdoorsman scent.

"Sir, the church frowns upon passion in a woman."

"I am not interested in what the church thinks."

Her gaze roved over his tall, muscular figure. He had just come from the practice field and wore no shirt. Against a crucifix of dark hair, scars crisscrossed the tanned muscles of his chest. Some were raised and others flat, darker, older.

A fallen angel.

And he pulled her down to hell with him. He had come here to swive her. To make good on what he started last night. She should fight him. But could she?

His thigh brushed hers, and she jumped. His manhood stretched the leather of his breeks tightly across his hips.

Memories of his hands on the lower curve of her breasts popped unbidden into her mind. A trickle of moisture seeped onto her inner thigh. Oh, evil, soulless man.

Why had he not just taken her virginity last night, had his man-pleasure and been done with her? He could force the union between them.

Mayhap she wanted him to. Dear Jesu. She pushed the wicked thought aside.

"Why did you not . . . I mean, last night . . ." She stumbled over the words.

He waited.

She slapped her hands on her thighs, disgusted with her embarrassment. She was not some blushing milksop, ignorant of the ways between a man and a woman. A man pumped his rigid member into a woman's sex until a fluid was spilled. It was messy and undignified.

She looked pointedly at his crotch. "Well, 'tis obvious you want me."

"Do you think that is all there is to the act?"

"Well, isn't it?" But she knew from last night that with Godric, it would be much, much more.

He laughed. "Assuredly not. Do you want to know why I did not take you when I want you so much?"

She nodded.

He leaned close, his breath caressing her cheek. "Because I want you as hungry for me as I am for you."

Abruptly, she turned her face away. She *had* been hungry for him last night. She was hungry for him now. Her fingers itched to caress the long scar that ran from his shoulder to his sternum.

"Do you want me?" he asked.

Startled, she stiffened. "Nay, of course not," she lied. "I am a married woman."

"These are lame lies, Meiriona. But they stand between us."

"'Tis no lie that I am married."

He took a long, deep breath and stepped backward. Sitting on the hearth, he took her small hand into his large one. "I want you. You want me. Annul your marriage and become my wife in truth."

He looked at her so earnestly, she dared not answer. For she knew if she opened her mouth, she was as likely to say aye as nay.

A moment passed. Then another. Then yet another.

He smiled. "I see this matter will not be settled today. Come, walk with me."

"Walk?"

"Aye, clouds roll in from the north, but the sun is shining now. I brought you fresh garments."

She quirked an eyebrow. The last clothing he had brought her was a splattered and stained tunic.

Leaning back, he propped one foot over the opposite knee and shrugged. "If the gown I brought is not to your liking, you may stay as you are. I burned the other one."

She sucked in her breath. She definitely did not want to be naked for the remainder of her time here. "Whatever you brought will be lovely."

"Good." His gaze flicked to the bed. "'Tis on the mattress."

On the sheet, she saw a heap of emerald green cloth. It shimmered in the morning sun, luxurious and decadent. Fine silk, no doubt. She could almost feel its delicious smoothness against her skin. Her skin was chafed from the rough homespun tunic, and the lush silk would feel wonderful.

"Thank you." She rose, but Godric caught the hem of her sheet.

"The gown is there for your pleasure. The sheet stays hither for mine."

Indignation flowed through her. She snatched at the sheet, but he twisted it around his fist. She glared at him.

He smiled blandly, looking like a satisfied cat that was about to make a huge meal out of a barn mouse.

CHAPTER 21

Meiriona glanced from the shimmering scrap of fabric on the bed to the huge man sitting on the hearth.

He was serious, she realized abruptly. Of all the lowlife, swag-bellied things to do. Her anger rose and she wanted to slap the smirk from his handsome face.

"I will not prance around naked for you."

Another half-smile. "Consider it the price for clothing."

"And if I refuse?"

"You will not."

He should be cast into the darkest dungeon and eaten by fleas . . . slowly. How dare he.

He drummed his fingers on the hearthstone. "Come, Meiriona. Be reasonable."

"Reasonable!" If she would have been holding something, she would have thrown it at him. "You want me to parade across the room for you and you expect me to be reasonable?"

Godric shrugged, the tanned skin of his shoulders dancing with the movement. "As you wish." He stood, his large body coming to life like a stalking panther.

She thought he would reach for her, but he merely brushed her with his gaze.

He walked toward the door in long, graceful strides. His hard warrior thighs stretched the leather of his breeks. She smiled. She had called his bluff and won. A woman needed only to stand up to a man every now and again.

Pausing slightly, he turned toward the bed and picked up the dress. Shaking out the fabric, he revealed a stunning emerald green gown that matched the haircomb he had given her earlier. "Last chance."

She shook her head. She'd rather spend eternity wrapped in a bedsheet than give in to his arrogance.

Shrugging, he picked up her shift from the floor and flipped both it and the gown casually over one of his tanned, muscled shoulders. He left the chamber, whistling. The door slammed behind him.

It took Meiriona a moment to realize what he had just done. *Curse the man's dark heart.* Indignant pride bubbled to the surface. She reached for the jewel-encrusted goblet that she'd drunk wine from last night and hurled it at the oaken door.

It clattered to the floor with a satisfying thud.

She heard a masculine chuckle from the other side. The same sound as when he'd entered the room and she had been bottom up, crawling around on the floor.

Well, Godric of Montgomery, you will not win this time.

Two hours later she was still sitting by the hearth. Still naked. A maid had come and stoked a nice warm fire. She had tried to talk to her, but the girl was either deaf and mute or had been given strict orders not to speak.

The fire had taken the chill from the room. She looked around at her decadent prison with its exotic trappings: the rich glass windows, the down bedding, and the luscious tapestries and carpets. It would have been a lovely solar if she were not a naked hostage.

How dare he.

* * *

Another hour passed. *Curse the man.*

She had expected him to be back by now. She glanced out the window again but dared not get too close, considering how it had turned out last time she'd done so.

Another servant brought a platter of bread and cheese and warm spiced mead.

"Good day," Meiriona tried, but the servant rushed from the room, not even glancing her way.

Death by fleas? Ha! 'Twas too merciful a death for one such as Godric.

Indignant anger boiled in her chest. And still no one came to bring her clothing. Servants' gossip spread faster than a whore's legs. 'Twas likely the whole castle was alert by now to how she, a lady, was naked at Godric's disposal.

She banged at the door. "Bring me clothing."

The guard outside grunted. "I am not allowed. Master's orders."

She tried the handle and the door swung open easily.

Godric's ugly guard rose to his feet, heaving his huge ax over one shoulder. With his smashed nose, patched eye, and bull-like shoulders, he looked like a nightmarish goblin. He stared at her with his one good eye. "Where go ye, mistress?"

She clutched her sheet around her. "I am leaving my prison."

He gripped the war ax closer, blocking her way. "I cannot allow you to do that, mistress."

She lifted her chin, determined not to be cowed. "Why not?" she demanded.

He looked positively ashamed, his ugly mug turning bright red up to his eyebrows. "Master's orders," he muttered.

"Exactly what can you not allow me to do, sirrah?"

"I am not allowed to let you leave this room wearing anything but what Godric brought you."

"I cannot pass?"

He shuffled his feet uncomfortably. "Mistress, you may pass freely. It is the, er, uh—"

"Well, what is it, man? Spit it out."

"'Tis the sheet." He looked down at this boots, his ears glowing. "The sheet must stay here."

"Absolutely not!"

His gaze snapped to hers, and she had the impression all his loyalty had come charging to the surface. "I'll not be disobeying my orders, mistress." Devotion to Godric burned in his one bright eye.

His allegiance took her aback. The gleam in his eye told her she would get no help from him.

She turned, marched back into Godric's chamber, and slammed the door. Wrapping the sheet tightly across her chest, she walked to the window and laid her forearms across the sill.

Men were below, riding horses and practicing their fighting skills. Bear spared with Owain and Eric was showing Damien his longbow.

Godric was among them, riding Vengeance over a series of hurdles. Unlike before, he did not look at the window. Somehow this drove a stake into her heart. She pushed the thought aside. She should not care that he did not notice her.

Two days later, Godric still had not come. Maids came and went, emptying the chamber pot and bringing fresh food and spiced mead.

But Godric did not bring clothing. Anger boiled deep inside Meiriona's blood.

On the third day another tub of warm water was brought, along with exotically spiced oils for her skin and perfumed soap for her hair.

Anger clouded her vision as she sank into the tub of

hot water. Fury flowed from the pit of her stomach and pulsed through her veins.

She was a noblewoman. The daughter of Ioworth the warrior. But she felt like a caged bear. How dare Godric treat her like some child's doll he could dress and undress at will.

Her arms floated atop the tub of water. She glared at her naked limbs. By all that was holy, the bastard of Montgomery could not keep her a prisoner of her own skin.

She scrubbed her arms and legs, her rage growing with every stroke the rough cloth made against her body.

A mousy maid with a pert nose and a linen muffin cap scampered into the chamber carrying a tray laden with cheese and bread. She scurried to the bed and laid the food there. Turning, she hurried toward the door.

"Halt!"

The maid stopped and eyed her warily.

Meiriona rose from the bathing tub, strong and angry. Her long hair clung to her knees and soap bubbles skittered down her body. For three days she had cowered here in his chamber. But no longer. She felt like the Lady of the Lake rising from the mist. Godric the bastard would not intimidate her with her own skin. If Godric wanted her to walk to him naked as the day she was born, then so be it.

"Can you dress hair?" she asked the maid, who was staring at her as if she were a vision.

"Aye, mistress." She lowered her eyes and hurried toward the chamber door.

Meiriona was faster. Blocking the door, she clutched the maid's arm. "You will comb my hair, then."

She could feel the girl trembling. "Nay, mistress. We have orders not to speak to you."

Meiriona tossed her hair behind her shoulders and gave her best queen imitation. It was hardly fair to intimidate such a mousy servant, but she needed her help.

"Then do not talk to me. Just attend me."

Meiriona saw debate in the maid's gaze.

"Master Godric will not mind if you help me comb my hair. See—" she pressed, pointing toward the table by the window. "He gave me a nice hair bauble to wear."

The girl glanced at the table, clearly relieved to have somewhere to look besides Meiriona's naked body.

"His orders have been for no one to talk to me, and I am not to leave this chamber wearing aught but what he has given me. If this is his command, then I will follow it." She added a friendly smile to hurry the maid's decision. "Help me dry and dress my hair. I intend to find your bloody master and demand he give me clothing."

The maid swallowed. "'Tisn't a good plan to test the master, mistress."

Meiriona glared at her. The girl crossed herself and retrieved the hairbrush from the dressing table.

"Methinks the master has not been tested nearly enough," Meiriona muttered.

The midday church bells marking sext rang several hours later. Meiriona stood, took a deep, steadying breath, and studied her image in the polished silver mirror. Her hair hung to her knees in fiery red waves. The maid had brushed and twirled it until it crackled and shone like fire. It flowed around her curves, covering the peaks of her breasts and the juncture betwixt her thighs. Her shoulders and the sides of her hips peeked out from its fiery curtain, but the hair was artfully arranged to cover her somewhat.

Her bare feet slid silently against the lush carpet as

she crossed to the oaken door. Her hand hovered above the door handle. *Dear holy saints, I cannot do this.*

She shoved the thought aside and adjusted the emerald hair comb. She *would* do this.

Like Lady Godiva.

Only she was not Lady Godiva, she was Meiriona of Whitestone, daughter of Ioworth, and the townsfolk would be watching. There would be hundreds of peeping Toms here. She was not marching through the castle naked to save her people from some wicked ruler. She was doing it to prove to Godric once and for all he could *not* cow her.

She ran her fingers through her locks to arrange them to cover more of her skin. Setting her jaw, she gathered all the fury and anger that had been boiling in the pit of her stomach over the last few days. Her fingers grasped the door handle, firm and determined, and she pulled the heavy door open. If Godric wanted her wearing only her hair, then so be it. She would *not* abandon her plan now.

Godric's ugly guard jumped when she strode into the hallway. He lurched to his feet, frowning at her furiously. "Where go ye, mistress?"

"To see your master." She dismissed him with a look and breezed past him.

"Wait, mistress." He rounded on her, standing in front of her holding the war ax. "I cannot let you go *thus.*"

They were nearly the same height, so she stared directly into his one good eye. "You have made it perfectly clear what Godric's orders were, and I am not breaking any of them. Now, step aside."

"But, mis—"

She pushed around him. Strands of her hair caught on the handle of his war ax, but she did not stop even when she felt the hair sting, pull against her scalp, and break loose. Naught would stop her. If every strand of her hair was pulled out and she was naked as Eve, she would face Godric.

And she would win.

Godric's guard tromped after her. "I'll guard your back," he grumbled.

"Good," she said, striding down the hallway. The breeze cooled the skin on her arms, her hips, her thighs, and a thousand other unnamed places.

Oddly, she did not feel embarrassed. She felt feminine and powerful.

The castle's corridors became deafeningly quiet as she crossed under archways and passed rooms filled with servants going about their daily chores. With each person whose mouth fell open to gape at her, she felt stronger. Wool spinners hung in doorways, their looms abandoned; sewing women left their needles to trail down the corridor after her. Even the old hermit under the staircase ambled out to take a gander as Meiriona passed, her head up and shoulders thrown back victoriously.

She felt a moment's hesitation as she reached the door, knowing she had to cross the courtyard to reach the practice field where Godric would be. But she had come too far to become a coward now. Godric had started this, but she would finish it.

One of the servants held the door open for her. Meiriona blinked in the bright afternoon sun. She could hear the clash of metal against metal as the men practiced on the other side of the hill. The menagerie of castlefolk followed her out the door and across the courtyard.

The stable boy dropped his shovel when he saw her and howled as it landed on his foot. Then there was silence once more except for the sound of swords in mock battle over the rise.

Grass and mud squelched between her bare toes as she crested the hill and looked across the practice field. The clash of metal grew fainter as knights and squires paused in their sparring and stared at her.

Godric, dark and forbidding, was crouched in a warrior's pose, circling Eric.

Seeing him spurred her determination, and Meiriona quickened her pace.

"By all that's holy!" Eric cried. He lowered his sword and gaped at her.

Intent on the fight, Godric gave the squire a ringing blow on his helmet, then turned, the muscles of his chest straining against his black tunic.

Sweet victory flowed through her veins at his expression. Surprise. Incredulity. Astonishment. His sword twisted in his hand and fell to the ground, landing on his foot. He yelped and jumped back.

She laughed. That she could reduce the Dragon's reaction to the same as the stable boy's made her feel amazingly superior to him. She had done it. She had defeated Godric the Dragon, and they both knew it.

His jaw worked up and down for a moment and then a glower settled across his features. "Dear sweet holy God, what the bloody hell are you doing here?" he yelled.

She lifted a brow. "Obeying your orders." It was all she could do not to swipe her hair aside and expose more of her body just to see if it would make him clumsy again.

Someone from the crowd snickered. Servants and knights murmured, making a collective roar that filled the courtyard.

"Aye, she's got one up on him."

"Ne'er did understand women."

"She'll make 'im come to heel."

"Needs a rod to her backside is what she needs."

"Serves him right for treating her thus."

Godric reached Meiriona in two strides, his hands clamping onto her upper arms. She heard the crowd draw in a collective breath, but she no longer feared the Dragon. Hot fire burned in his eyes as she appraised him coolly.

"I walked to you, just as you demanded, and now I would like some clothing." She kept her voice deliberately mild but was unable to keep the smirk off her lips.

"You, my lady, are a fool."

"And you, my lord, need to keep your promise and bring me something to wear."

He released her at once and yanked his tunic from his body. In one motion, he jerked it over her head.

She smiled, recognizing his move for the parry it was. The garment hung nearly to her knees and enclosed her in his scent, causing her stomach to have a little frisson of excitement.

She tossed her hair and turned boldly to the watching crowd. Raising her arms, she twirled as if she were before the seamstress getting a new gown to meet the king rather than wearing a man's dusty tunic. The horde of castlefolk whistled and applauded loudly, reveling in her victory as much as she.

"Behave!" Latching his hand about her wrist, Godric whirled her around and began marching back toward the castle, dragging her in his wake.

But victory was too sweet, and she laughed.

CHAPTER 22

"Give her a firm hand, he will. Just you look and see," one man called out from the gawking crowd.

Godric's foot throbbed as he pulled Meiriona in his wake through the throng of castlefolk toward the keep. Ne'er in his life had he been so clumsy as to drop a sword on his own foot. The woman was a witch. A witch without mercy. She made him daft.

What had she been thinking? He had determined he would seduce her, not force her. Indeed, he had left her alone for three days and exercised his body to its limits because the thought of Meiriona naked in his chamber ate at him. He took the steps in long strides, daring not to even look at her. By God's holy toes, if he glanced at her, he would yank his tunic off her and ravage her here in the courtyard.

The image of her lush, naked skin, half covered, half exposed by her blazing cloud of hair, tormented him. And her laugh? Her taunting laugh. She knew he would not force her, and, merciful Christ, she was a water nymph sent to destroy every dram of sanity he possessed.

He swung open the keep's door, blood pulsing through his veins. "You vex me, lady."

"As you do me."

They were alone; the castlefolk were outside where they had followed her into the courtyard to watch the hurly-burly. Godric pushed her against the inner wall of the corridor with his body, intending to intimidate her and show her the error of testing him.

She did not cower as he expected. Instead, her green eyes glowed, and he knew at once she wanted him as much as he wanted her. His effort to intimidate had only aroused her.

"You are not afraid of me, but you would be if you knew the way I want you." He rocked his erection into the softness of her stomach. Sliding his hands down her sides, he bunched up the tunic and cupped her buttocks, relishing the feel of her soft, feminine skin against his rough palms. She made a half-moan, half-whimper sound that called to every animalist urge buried inside him. He lifted her slightly, and his groin contacted the soft womanly juncture betwixt her legs. Even through his breeks, he could feel her wetness. Her eyes were dilated, wide with desire.

His cock throbbed harder. By God, he was sickened by ladies who shrank, afraid of his scars, and repulsed by the ones who found him a fearsome plaything to be toyed with. But Meiriona saw him as neither toy nor monster, but as a man. A man!

She slipped her hand between them and splayed it against his cheek, stroking the scar beneath his eye with the pad of her thumb. Torchlight flickered a red-orange glow over her skin.

"Be mine, Meiriona. Say you will belong to me."

She swallowed, uncertainty crossing her features.

He eased away until their bodies barely touched. Why would she not acknowledge the passion between them?

"I can pleasure you in ways you can only imagine." For once in his life, he was thrilled about the knowledge he'd gained in the princess's clutches. "I know ways to make your skin so sensitive that the slightest caress will cause you to scream with pleasure."

He saw hunger in her eyes. Pressing his advantage,

he scratched his fingernail very lightly from her hairline down the length of her nose to her chin. Her eyelids closed as if she was soaking up the sensation. Aye, she would be a very apt pupil for passion indeed.

Sweat beaded his brow. It took all his willpower not to throw her over his shoulder, carry her to his chamber, and teach her the disciplines of pleasure.

And why not? Why should he not? 'Twould solve so many problems.

Her hand curled around his nape, tugging him closer, and he knew exactly why he must not. He would not break the bond between them by rushing.

He turned abruptly, not trusting himself to be so near her. He had to get clothes on her as quickly as possible.

"Come, girl."

Meiriona blinked, feeling dazed as if waking from a dream. Godric took her hand, pulling her gently toward the heart of the castle. She followed, unresisting. His rough hand felt delicious on hers as he led her up several worn sets of stairs. Disconcerted, she knew whatever he planned, she would be unable to refuse.

A few moments later, he drew her into a chamber crammed with disorderly bolts of wool, velvet, and silk. A small flock of women, chattering excitedly like squawking hens, ceased their clucking and stared at them.

Stunned, she stared back, feeling very much like a grasshopper whose legs were about to be pulled off. She turned to Godric. "Are we not heading to . . ." Her voice trailed off. What was she thinking? Surely she did not want him to bed her.

He pulled her into the room. "Make my prize some clothing."

Fog cleared from her mind as he said the word "prize."

The head seamstress, a plump woman with soft,

grandmotherly eyes and gnarled hands, cleared her throat and laid aside her needle and the square of fabric she had been stitching. "Yea, Master Godric."

"Use fabric from the new shipment."

The seamstress glanced from Godric to Meiriona. "She would look stunning in green."

"See to it, then."

Meiriona pulled a lock of hair through her fingers, feeling her earlier confidence crash to the floor.

Godric glanced around the untidy room. "I left a green gown here three days ago. Tailor it to fit her, then work on a new wardrobe that befits her station."

Meiriona flinched, too stunned to think of anything to say.

The seamstress nodded to a couple of the women, then crossed the room and dug around in a drawer. The ladies closed in around Meiriona, thrusting Godric aside. They yanked his tunic over her head so she was naked once more.

She tried to grasp at the anger and indignation she had cloaked herself in when she'd stormed to the practice field. But those emotions slipped through her fingers now, and she felt exposed and suddenly shy.

Godric smiled at her, blue fire blazing in his eyes and clothing her with his warmth and desire. Oddly, she felt vulnerable, shy, exposed, and a thousand other things, but she did not feel embarrassed. The hens flocked around her, pushing Godric farther away. A dozen hands touched her, measuring and pinching the length and breadth of her body.

"The light green," clucked one hen.

"Nay, the dark," squawked another.

"Methinks the blue silk to match his eyes. What a pair they would make."

"A matching tunic for Master Godric."

Godric was thrust from the room by the horde.

Meiriona heard him chuckle and his heavy boots tread down the castle corridor.

Did she love him or hate him? She took a deep breath, allowing the women to drape her with various lengths of fabric. How could she bear a passionless marriage after knowing the fervor she could share with Godric? The thought of Uncle Pierre caressing her intimately turned her stomach.

Mercy, Godric was an obsession. What should she do? Even if she were willing, Uncle Pierre and her father would never agree to an annulment, not even if the king demanded it. They would resist and there would be war. Even now, she imagined them preparing for battle, just as Godric and his men had been doing every day since her arrival at Montgomery.

Frustrated with her thoughts, she turned her mind back to the flock of women now measuring the length of her arms. She smiled at the nearest seamstress, a middle-aged woman whose beauty would have rivaled the most stunning courtier except a long white gash marred her cheek and most of her left ear was missing. The woman touched her ear self-consciously, and Meiriona averted her eyes, wishing she could think of something comforting to say.

"M'lady," the head seamstress said. "Does this color please ye?"

Meiriona turned her attention back to the task at hand. Lifting her arms, she allowed the women to pull the emerald-colored gown over her head. She cared naught what color or style of gown they chose so long as she no longer had to bide her time at Godric's home naked.

A woman lifted her hair and ran the strands through her fingers. "The master is taken with you, m'lady."

Another woman brought a polished silver mirror. "You are very lovely, m'lady."

She gasped, glimpsing the miracle the hens had worked. She looked—stunning. Sweet saints, she would rival a princess. The emerald gown hugged her bosom and caressed her hips, fitting her perfectly. They had sewed gold-embroidered trim to the edges of the sleeves and neckline.

When the king had demanded more taxes and ransom for her father, she had sold every beautiful gown she owned to come up with the gold. It had been more than a year since she'd been dressed in anything of quality.

"Does the gown meet yer approval, m'lady?"

"Oh, aye." Meiriona glanced around the room at the hens. "Thank you, good women."

"Give us a few days and you shall be spruced like a princess."

"The master will approve of you, no doubt about that."

"'E already cannot take his eyes from ye."

Unable to resist the urge toward time-old female vanity, Meiriona turned sideways to better observe her image in the looking glass. "Truly?"

"Aye. 'Tis true, mistress. I 'ave not seen the master look on a woman the way he looks at ye. 'E's been in a foul mood since ye arrived. Wants ye, he does."

Could she make him want her enough to not battle her father?

She studied her image. Feminine wiles were a time-honored weapon. She smiled, recalling the memory of Godric dropping his sword on his foot. Ah, yes, she could tame the Dragon and avoid war. And she knew exactly how.

She would offer herself.

A tremble of anticipation ran through her.

Turning back to the plump head seamstress, Meiriona asked, "Can you direct me back to Godric's chamber?"

The head hen clucked her tongue and nodded approvingly. "This way, m'lady."

Meiriona felt a great lightness of spirit as they passed through the door, slowly making their way down the hallway. *I love him,* she thought, elation soaring inside her. *I will give myself to him, and mayhap we will go to the continent to live quiet lives.* I will have Godric and Godric will have me.

Lady Montgomery stood in the hallway as they passed, lovely and cold in blue velvet. Under her sharp perusal, Meiriona felt her confidence falter.

"Did he tire of your nakedness? Sending you home already?"

Meiriona cringed and set her jaw, seeing the jealousy and bitterness in the lady's eyes. "I am not leaving. I wish to stay with Godric."

The seamstress pulled her down the hall. "Pay no attention, m'lady."

"You are already married," Lady Montgomery accused.

Guilt spun its way through Meiriona's heart like dark rain clouds. "Aye."

Lady Montgomery eyed her slyly. "What is this about? Tell me."

I love him.

"I must prevent war."

"Ah." Lady Montgomery crossed herself. "You would become a bastard's whore?"

Meiriona grimaced. Her notion to stay with Godric against outside logic had sounded so romantic earlier, surrounded by Godric's clucking hens. But echoed back in such a cold way, it seemed idle-headed. Her hasty plan threatened to unravel.

"He will not accept you." Lady Montgomery sniffed.

"He will," Meiriona said with more confidence than she felt.

"Yea, 'e will," chimed the seamstress. "Come, m'lady, this way."

Lady Montgomery gave her a placating smile. "'Tis not you he wants, but your land. Do you think your new dress will make any difference in that?"

Furious at her pointed tone, Meiriona faced her directly. "Nay, I have seen desire in his eyes."

"Mayhap. He wants to rut as much as any man, I suppose. 'Tis your land he wants. He will take your castle just as he's taken ours."

Glaring at Lady Montgomery, the seamstress took a firm hold of Meiriona. "Come, m'lady, I take ye to yer chamber."

Meiriona turned. "Aye, my chamber, please."

"'Tis not *your* chamber, Godric's whore," Lady Montgomery hissed. "'Tis his."

CHAPTER 23

Meiriona sat on the bed in Godric's solar, stomach churning, staring at her burgundy and blue surroundings. Doubt crept into her mind as she thought of the exchange between her and Lady Montgomery. What if the lady was correct and Godric only wanted her land?

Glancing around, Meiriona scrutinized the expensive glass windows and the lush tapestries and carpets.

Nay, the lady was wrong. Wrong. She *had* to be wrong.

Godric had a good life here. He did not need her land. He did not need her gold. If Godric's desire for her were merely physical, he would have forced her long ago. And if he merely wanted her castle, he could have overtaken it with his men.

What he wanted was revenge. He wanted her as his captive, plain and simple, to amend for the years he had been a captive. 'Twas men's pride—a pissing contest she would allow him to win to prevent war.

Pushing away her lingering doubts, she rose, crossed the chamber to the dressing table, and stared at herself in the looking glass. The hens had done magnificent work. She looked every bit like a captured princess.

Godric would accept her. Taking her from her

home would satisfy his male pride and prevent him from slaying her father.

'Twas a worthy plan. Taking a book from a shelf, she trod to the hearth and sat in the thronelike chair to wait for him.

"By the rood," Godric breathed as he entered his chamber several hours later. "You are stunning."

Meiriona laid her book aside and smiled. Rising from her seat, she held her hands out to him. "Come, my lord. We have much to discuss."

He took her hands, turned them palm up, and planted a feather-light kiss on each one.

A tremble of desire flowed through her. All remaining doubts about her plan to offer herself to him fell away. He wanted her; she wanted him. It was a simple, mutual exchange.

She drew him toward the fire, and he settled himself on the huge chair, crossing one foot over the opposite knee.

"My lord—" she began again, then stopped and sat on the ledge of the hearth. The desire between them was palpable, but how was she supposed to go about explaining she wanted to become his paramour?

Godric stared at her, his gaze intense and enigmatic. Unnerving.

She faltered in her purpose. Mayhap this was madness after all. Rising, she poured two goblets of wine, and handed one to her soon-to-be lover. "I wish to prevent war."

Godric cocked a brow. "I have no desire for war either."

Relief flowed through her, and she took a sip of her wine. "Then I will stay with you."

"Of course."

Elation made her feel like a giggly youngster. Impulsively, she leaned down and kissed his temple.

He stiffened. "Meiriona—" He snagged her upper arms and tugged her gently toward him. "Come sit with me."

She smiled and sat on his lap, reveling in the largeness of his body and how it cocooned her in warmth and his woodsy campfire scent. Sitting on his lap, she felt that everything in the world was right.

"Tell me about your marriage to Pierre."

Meiriona sighed, feeling safe and comforted in Godric's arms. "He is my friend, but I am not in love with him." *I am in love with you.* She wished she had the courage to speak her inner thoughts aloud.

"Why did you marry him?" he asked mildly.

She swept her arm out, indicating his opulent chamber. "I had no choice. I have not your wealth. Many of our possessions were sold to pay the king's taxes."

"I see."

"My people were starving." The conversation's tone had somehow turned, and she leaned back to better see his face.

He watched her keenly, but his thoughts were hidden behind the blue fire of his eyes. One of his hands made slow trails up and down her back. "If you had married me, your people would not be starving."

"Mayhap." She traced her finger along the sickle-shaped scar across his cheek. "I am very sorry. Tell me what happened after you left the chapel all those years ago."

"Your father's men attacked me. I fought, but I was armed with only a dagger, and the odds were too great." He blew out a breath. "I was a fool to leave my sword with my mount. The letter your father sent was very cordial, and I was greeted warmly at the front gate. When one of the servants told me your priest frowned heavily upon weapons in the sanctuary, I did not question it."

"Why were you alone?"

He shrugged. "No one has time to follow a bastard to his wedding."

"But your father—"

"Was busy with his own affairs."

His jaw hardened, and she kissed it to smooth away his hurt. "What happened next?"

"I was bound and placed on a ship. After several months of travel, I was sold on the block in a slave auction. I was young, strong, and angry. I fought every chance I could." He paused and stared into the fire. "I was beaten many times in the beginning."

Meiriona's heart squeezed. "How did you ever survive?"

He tipped her chin up. "I learned when to fight and when to submit. A lesson you would do well to learn."

"Mayhap," she said cheekily.

"The slavers seemed to think I was a great prize despite my rebelliousness, and I was given to the sultan as a gift. I did grueling labor, more workhorse than man, until my talent for numbers and accounts was recognized. After that, my lot improved considerably. My cell was opulent, even more so than this chamber. I was still a slave, but the sultan trusted me as his steward."

That thought alleviated a small portion of her guilt. Leave it up to a man such as Godric to not merely survive but to *thrive* in a place where a weaker man would have been crushed.

"What happened?"

"The sultan's daughter found me fascinating. She oft sent secret messengers to rouse me from my chamber in the dead of night. God help me, I had the sultan's trust, but I betrayed it."

Meiriona felt a twinge of jealousy over the exotic

princess he had known in a foreign land. "Did you love her?"

"Love?" An intense fire burned in his blue eyes, hotter than the fire in the hearth. "Nay. I was lonely, bored. And it had been a long time since I buried myself betwixt a woman's thighs."

Meiriona blushed at his frank speech, but she felt the pain in his voice. "You were a stranger, sold into a strange land. No one can blame you for taking what pleasure you could."

Save for the crackling fire, there was quietness for several heartbeats. "No one but Amelina."

Awkward silence stretched like a too-tight bowstring. Guilt threatened to break Meiriona's heart. The child was innocent of the circumstances of her birth. The path of life was hard for bastard-born children.

Sweet saints, the wrong she had done to Godric went on and on.

"I was a selfish, rutting swine," he said at long last, his voice laced with pain.

She splayed her hand against his cheek. "Nay, my lord. Nay. The fault be mine. I should have gone against my father's wishes. I should have warned you—"

"*Warned* me?" His eyes grew dark, stormy.

"Aye." The words tripped off her tongue. "I am sorry for my failure. Please, my lord, let us begin anew." She took a deep breath, fortifying herself. Giving herself to Godric was the only thing that would prevent war between him and her father. She would not become a coward now. "I will stay willingly with you, be your captive as you have been a captive."

There. She had said it. She let out the breath she'd been holding.

His jaw clenched and anger flashed in his eyes. "You sell yourself to me to correct your father's wrong?"

She blanched, unprepared for anger. "Aye."

"Is that truly what you wish? To be my slave?" His voice was hard.

She nodded, willing him to understand the sacrifice she was making to prevent war. "I will stay with you. Amend for the years you have suffered."

Godric stood her on her feet abruptly, making her feel dizzy. The loss of the warmth and comfort of his arms chilled her.

"Strip," he commanded.

Her eyes flew open, and she felt as if he'd dunked her into an icy lake. "What?"

"Strip," he repeated, his voice soft and ominous.

She shivered, wary. A frightening change had come over him, and she did not know why.

"Obedience is required of slaves. Do you wish to be my slave or no?"

Saints! He was testing her. She'd made this bargain and he was testing to see her seriousness. She squeezed her eyes shut. She had not expected this, but if this was the price of peace, then so be it. He had already seen her naked. His entire castle had seen her naked. Once more would matter naught, and she knew full well that once he snapped from his present mood, he would be a considerate and caring lover. She had naught to lose.

Untying the laces of her gown, she allowed it to slither over her hips and pool on the floor.

"Your shift also."

Reaching for her hem, she noticed her fingers were shaking. She glanced at him, but his face was unreadable. Yanking the shift quickly over her head to avoid further dilemma, she hurled it at his feet. "If the price of your peace is to embarrass me, I accept."

"Good," he said, stroking his chin. "Lie on the floor, on your back, here at my feet."

Nervously, she tucked her hair behind her ear. "Surely you are not serious."

He lifted a brow. "You claim you wish to stay with me as my captive. Obey my request. 'Tis the price of *peace* you agreed to pay."

Disquiet rose in her chest at his dangerous tone. Would he hurt her? Nay, she knew he would not. 'Twas all merely a test of her resolve. She sank to her knees and then lay down upon the rug, her naked back sinking into the soft sheepskin.

Jesu, why did he not touch her? He seemed intent on making her feel uncomfortable.

From this angle, she could see the huge bulge of his manhood in his breeks, frightening and thrilling at the same time.

"Open your legs wide."

His mannerism unnerved her. She sat up and frowned, disliking this change in him. "Why are you acting thus?"

"A woman, a captive, is not allowed to question her lord. Open your legs."

"Nay."

"Nay? A slave has no choice to say nay. Think you that I was able to say nay to each indignity I was forced to endure?"

Meiriona gulped, realizing exactly what her bargain was. She had asked to be his whore, but she wished to be treated as his wife.

Slowly, she sank back to the floor. He would not harm her, of this she was sure. This change was merely male pride to amend for the indignities he had suffered. Squeezing her eyes shut, she opened her legs.

"Wider. And raise your legs up."

She complied, her face hot as she felt cool air breeze upon her privates.

"How do you feel?"

"Embarrassed. Exposed." She lowered her legs and drew them together. "Prithee do not do this."

"Think you that a slave has any choice in how she is taken? Think you that I had a choice?"

She grimaced.

"Nay," he continued, "none at all. If her master wishes her to lay naked at his feet and spread her legs, then she obeys."

Meiriona swallowed, hot tears stinging her eyes.

Godric sank from the chair to the floor, kneeling beside her on the sheepskin rug. He kissed her cheek and both eyelids. "I want you as my *wife*, Meiriona. Not my slave. Not my whore." His touch was tender, but his voice was angry, bitter. "Do not think you can appease my revenge by merely offering your body."

Her stomach flipped and she raised her arms to twine around his neck, longing for more of his tender touch, but he pulled away and stood, towering over her.

"Get up."

She blinked and rose awkwardly to her feet, disconcerted.

He yanked her into his arms. "Listen to me, you little fool. I may want you in exactly the same position that you were just in, but I want you there because you want to be there. Whitestone is mine because it is mine.

"You cannot offer yourself on the altar of sacrifice to appease the beast and keep your family safe. You will have to come up with a better offer."

Her chest ached and she felt a tear slide down her cheek. "I have only myself—naught better to offer."

"Meiriona—" He thumbed her tear away. "In the chapel years ago, you should not have warned me. You should have *married* me."

His lips crashed down on hers in a demanding kiss, then he released her at once and stalked from the room. The dam of tears broke and she flung herself onto the bed with a thick, heart-wrenching sob. Rolling her nude body in the bedsheet, she cried herself to sleep.

CHAPTER 24

The next day, an insistent hand shook Meiriona's shoulders. "Wake up, girl."

She opened one eye. Godric, wearing a soft, black tunic, sat on the bed beside her, his large body pressing the feathers down and making the mattress groan against its ropes.

He shook her shoulders again, and she glared at him crossly. "Begone."

He grinned, not the least bit put off by her morning grumpiness.

They had not spoken since the disaster of yesterday's "bargain." All night she'd dreamed of being married to him—the Lord and Lady of Whitestone together. Somehow, some way, she would get her marriage to Uncle Pierre annulled.

Leaning back, Godric opened the heavy curtains from the nearby windows. The sun burned brightly into the chamber, gilding his shoulders. Meiriona blinked and shielded her eyes with her hand.

"Saints, what time is it?"

"Nearly midmorning," he answered cheerfully, earning him another scowl from her.

She sat up at once, pulling her linen chemise onto her shoulders. "I do naught but sleep and eat here," she grumbled. "Have you heard from my father?"

"Nay, Meiriona, I have not. I am concerned about

that. I sent a messenger to bargain with him when we first arrived at Montgomery." Godric caressed her arm gently with his fingertips, sending fiery trails across her skin.

"Think you that he has not received the message?"

Godric shook his head. "I do not know. I sent another envoy at sunrise today."

Unease tickled Meiriona's spine. What if her father planned attack rather than negotiating for her return? She laid her hand on Godric's forearm. "Promise me no matter what happens you will not harm my father or Pierre."

Godric's eyes darkened to a deadly midnight blue. "Do not harbor any thoughts of returning to your husband. Despite the fact that we did not come to a conclusive bargain, you are well and truly mine."

Meiriona splayed her fingers against his cheek. "My lord, I—"

Dear sweet heavenly saints! What should she tell him?

Godric had told her once he wanted everything from her, and sweet Mary, she wanted to give it to him. Saints help her, she could not deny her heart. As wife or captive—it mattered naught to her—she wanted to belong to Godric. But she could not bear it if her selfishness cost her father and uncle their lives.

"Please, my lord. Promise me you will not harm my family. Pierre is . . . I mean . . . Pierre . . ." She glanced away, ashamed of her unfaithfulness to Uncle Pierre. "I do not want Pierre as husband, but I do not want him dead either."

"Meiriona—" Godric covered her hand with his, pressing her palm to his cheek. "I received a message from King Edward yesterday."

Meiriona's stomach clenched. "Foul monarch," she muttered under her breath.

"Careful, my lady. Verily, castle walls breathe and

talk on their own. I will not have my future wife accused of treason."

Her gaze fluttered to the numerous tapestries hanging on the chamber's walls.

"King Edward's spies claim Whitestone harbors Lancastrian rebels."

Meiriona felt blood drain from her face. "'Tis untrue."

Godric looked at her intently, and nervous butterflies flittered in her stomach.

"What is it, my lord? What do you know that you are not telling?"

"Your father is wanted for questioning in London."

"Nay! Edward will kill him. Last time Father was in London, he was held prisoner for months. I paid a king's ransom to have him released." Meiriona felt her world whirl around her. "Why does the king want him?"

"Meiriona—" Godric took a deep breath. An eternity passed. "The king was not amused when he discovered your father sold me into slavery. Nor was he happy your father married off his daughter to a French count who is known for his Lancastrian sympathies. Edward ordered me to arrest him and bring him to London."

Her hands twisted in the linen sheet. "He is an old man. Why can the king not allow him to live out his days in peace?"

Godric grasped her shoulders. "Listen to me, girl. Edward will convict your father of treason for certes. If your father is to live, he *must* cooperate with me. Your marriage to Pierre must be annulled posthaste. With you as my wife and Whitestone firmly in my hand, I can ask for a boon that the king spare your father."

"Dear Jesu." Meiriona stared at Godric, her stomach so knotted it ached. "My father will never agree to it. He's got an old man's pride and stubbornness. He will die afore he accepts help from a Yorkist bastard." She flinched, suddenly realizing what she had just said. "Forgive me, my lord. I meant no offense."

"None taken, my lady. He leaned forward and kissed her cheek. "I am indeed both a bastard and a Yorkist."

Meiriona's insides melted. Godric's kiss was so gentle, so soft. She had to make her father and Uncle Pierre see reason. "Let me go home, my lord."

Abruptly, Godric pulled away as if he'd been struck with an arrow. "Nay."

"Please—"

"Nay."

"I can parley with my father. Explain."

"Nay."

"He will listen to me—"

"Nay."

"But—"

The bed ropes creaked as Godric stood, his eyes stormy. "Do not speak of this again, *captive.* 'Tis men's business."

"Men's business? 'Tis *my* family. *My* home."

Godric's shoulders were tense, determined. "You will not leave. Do not ask me again." He walked to the window and stared into the courtyard, leaving her cold and alone on the bed. After a moment, he returned to the mattress's edge and offered her his hand. "Come. No more talk of you leaving."

Meiriona placed her hand in his palm, allowing him to draw her from the bed.

Why must men be so obstinate? If only she could speak with her father and Pierre.

"Get dressed. We have much to do today."

She sighed. Arguing with Godric would do her no good. Snatching one of the new gowns the ladies had delivered whilst she slept, she pulled it on. It was a simple blue with lovely long sleeves and a fancy embroidered hem. She glanced at her reflection and smiled, feeling as spoiled as a princess.

"Where are we going?"

"To the stables."

She cocked an eyebrow at him. "Have you changed your mind already about taking me home?"

"Assuredly not." He stepped toward her, took her hand, and tugged her gently forward. "Turn around and I will lace your dress."

Meiriona obeyed, and Godric straightened the laces running up the back of her gown. She closed her eyes. His hands were warm and sensuous. Her breasts and nipples tingled. Her body craved his touch the same as it had when he had bathed her. Saints, the man made her clay-brained.

He pulled the laces tight and tied them, but it felt more like her heartstrings were being tightened and knotted. His hands slid along the gown's fabric until they spanned her waist, then he turned her around to face him.

He leaned down until only a hairbreadth was between them.

She leaned back, but he followed the sway of her body with his own. He waited for what seemed like an eternity. She smiled up at him coyly, enjoying their play, and stepped back. He stalked her until her back pushed against the tapestry.

She grinned as he placed his arms on each side of her head, trapping her. The rabbit caught by the leopard.

He was so close she would only have to lick her lips to touch his. He smelled of sandalwood and leather and smoke. His lips turned up, one of his lopsided smiles, but he did not close the distance between them.

Saints, he was not touching her, but her skin felt

alive and sensitive as if straining for his caress. She forced herself motionless, waiting for him to touch her. His lips hovered above hers. Her hands itched to draw him closer—yet it seemed so forward of her to take such a liberty.

Annoyance crept over her. "Do you plan to kiss me?" she asked abruptly.

His lips twitched. "Do you want me to?"

She glared at him. "Of a truth."

Godric smiled. "Ah, at last the lady admits the truth."

Her cheeks, her whole body felt overwarm. The parchment width between their bodies felt like miles.

"I—" She wiggled forward, and her breasts touched his chest, closing the distance between their bodies. Heat shot betwixt her thighs, making her sex feel slick, and she sighed.

Godric brushed her cheek with his rough knuckles. "You are trembling."

"I am not."

"Now you are lying."

She opened her mouth to protest, but his lips silenced her. His tongue brushed her teeth and gums. Soft. Gentle. Coaxing. It stroked hers, mating it in a primitive ecstatic dance. It occurred to her vaguely this was the first kiss they had shared simply for the pure pleasure of kissing. He'd kissed her to defy her father in the chapel, she'd kissed him to hide Damien, and he'd kissed her to claim ownership. But this kiss was a kiss of exotic delight and sensual enjoyment. His body pressed her to the wall, her nipples tightened, and she felt the thump, thump, thump of her heartbeat.

"Godric," she murmured.

Abruptly he pulled away. "Say it again," he demanded.

Her breath came out in gasps. "Say what?"

"My name."

She blinked. "Godric."

His fingertips stroked her collarbone. "Nay, say it in that husky tone like you want me to go on kissing you forever."

Her cheeks heated. "I did not—"

His mouth lowered onto hers, his tongue pressing inside. She trembled and clung to his shoulders. He lingered with his kiss, and she melted against him. When he pulled away, she opened her mouth to whisper his name.

"Shh." He laid his index finger on her lips. "Do not say it now or, verily, we shall not make it to the stables at all."

Meiriona saw his hands quivering against the tapestry as if he longed to rip it from the wall.

"Sweet Mary, you are trembling too."

"Aye," he said curtly. "Come now."

He glanced once at the bed but grasped her wrist and dragged her in his wake out the door.

Meiriona frowned at his back, feeling both humbled and powerful. The kiss had made him shiver just as it had her.

Oh, saints, Godric *was* correct—this was right between them. Somehow she would get her father to understand. A pox on both King Henry and King Edward for this war between the Lancasters and the Yorks.

Godric led her down the narrow stairs into the courtyard. The sounds of steel clashing, men shouting, and blacksmiths hammering rang in the air as they passed the practice field.

Unease washed over her as they neared the stables. She had ridden with him from Whitestone to Montgomery, but something about the determined set of Godric's shoulders made her suspect he planned something today that was not to her liking. "Where are we going? Are we leaving Montgomery?"

He did not pause to answer but headed, single-mindedly, toward the stables. "You must get over your fear of horses."

Meiriona dug in her heels. "What do you mean? What do you plan?"

"This fear keeps you caged. 'Tis time you overcame it."

"I am fine without riding, thank you."

"Nay, you are not." He tugged her wrist to get her to step forward.

Anger shot through her. "I have managed quite well, sirrah."

He slanted her a sidelong glance. "You were frightened out of your wits when Vengeance first arrived."

"And, to my chagrin, I still managed to make it here."

"Aye, because you were with me. You must learn to ride alone. 'Tis only right for a woman of your station."

Saints above! He would force her, as her father had, to ride by herself. Shame and fury balled together as she remembered her father's look of disapproval. Her feet felt ice cold.

She wrenched her wrist from his grasp. "I will not!"

Godric turned with infinite slowness, a look of gentle but firm determination across his features. "Meiriona, today will not be a repeat of that day with your father."

She ducked her head, all the feelings of shame bubbled to the surface. Her father's voice boomed in her head. *Fool girl! How dare a child of mine be afraid to ride a horse!*

Godric traced her collarbone with his thumb, and Meiriona felt warmth skitter through her. He caught her in an embrace. "Meiriona, you are safe here. There will be you and I. No one watching and no one forcing you." He cupped her cheek. "Let me tell you a story about the slave ship."

She nodded.

"I had bested two of the guards, broken one's nose. Other guards caught me between them. Shoving a gag into my mouth, they wrestled me down, ripping my clothing and hitting and kicking me as they went."

Meiriona recoiled in horror, but Godric gripped her shoulders, not allowing her to move back.

"I kicked and screamed, but they were too strong and too many. They forced me into a tight, foul-smelling wooden box. Only I was not alone—a corpse on a journey to its final resting place was there with me. Mayhap if I had been fully of a sound mind, I could have borne it, but hungry, exhausted, angry, I began to scream and then to cry. I lost control of all feeling except my own panic. I curled into a ball like a baby and wept, chewing my own thumb for comfort."

Meiriona watched him, imagining this proud warrior reduced to an infant. A lump of guilt rose in her throat as she thought of the horrors Godric had suffered.

"Nay, Meiriona, do not look so stricken. Look at me." He turned her face up so their gazes met. "For many years I reviled myself for being weak and pathetic. Then the day came they put me in the catacombs and beat me. On that day I realized that they could not defeat me. By God's wounds, it was hell and I hated them for it, but they could hurt me, kill me, scar me, but they could not defeat me. If I screamed, if I cried, aye, even if I sucked my thumb again, they could not hurt *me*." He paused; his hand cupped her cheek gently. "Do you understand?"

She took in a long draw of air, her heart aching for him.

"Meiriona, once I accepted my fear as a natural part of myself, it had much less power over me. I never,

ever had to act like a baby again, and I suffered much worse indignities than that box."

"Oh, Godric."

"Even if your body betrays you and you lose control, what you are inside is more than that. You are safe here with me. Can you trust me for just a little while? I will not force you to ride alone."

Trust him? He had carried her safely down a cliff, rescued her from a wild boar, fed her, clothed her, and cared for her brother. If he said he would not force her to ride alone, then he would not. She nodded. His story of the slave ship somehow diminished her embarrassment about spewing in front of her father and his men. Godric had suffered great indignity and yet he was strong, mighty. What had he told her once? That courage was action in the face of fear. Mayhap he spoke the truth.

"I trust you," she said simply.

"Gramercy." He kissed her on the forehead and led her to a stall at the end of the stables.

The smell of fresh hay and barnyard droppings assailed her, making her dizzy and apprehensive. Godric gripped her arm, granting her some of his strength. A swayback dapple-gray mare leaned against the wall, dozing. Godric whistled softly and the old mare opened her eyes and gazed at them with distinct disinterest. Although her stall was piled with hay, she was skinny with bony hips and sunken-in places above her eyes.

"I want to introduce you to Blue Thunder."

More like Last Thunder, Meiriona thought sharply. She turned to Godric. "This is a terrible plan."

Ignoring her, he pulled an apple from a pouch at his waist. Blue Thunder perked up. The old mare shuffled toward them, arthritic knees clicking.

Godric stroked the mare's nose. Several white whiskers twitched against his hand.

Meiriona swallowed a lump of fear. She'd ridden with Godric atop a huge stallion. 'Twas milk-livered to be fearful of a gentle swayback mare.

As if sensing her rising panic, Godric stroked Meiriona's shoulder. He leaned close to her ear. "Meiriona, if you feel fearful, just think about me sucking my thumb."

Suddenly, her apprehension turned into a nervous giggle. What had seemed horrible just moments earlier now struck her as hilarious. Cocking an eyebrow, he stuck his thumb out and opened his mouth. "Shall I demonstrate?"

Meiriona blinked and looked at him, dumbfounded. Godric grinned and laughed aloud. He was being silly! Silly! So that her fears would have no power over her.

He thumbed her lower lip, the tip of his finger lingering on her mouth. "Mayhap you should try it." His voice turned husky.

Caught in a wave of emotion, Meiriona flung herself into his arms.

Laughing, he captured her in his embrace. His mouth crashed down on hers, bending her body backward against the stable wall. When his lips left hers, she felt dizzy.

"Oh, saints, my lord. You must let me go and talk to my father."

Godric, grinning, slapped her lightly on the bottom. "I have already said nay to you leaving, impertinent wench."

"But—"

"No argument, Meiriona. You will trust me in this. Now come, we will finish your riding lesson."

Meiriona turned back to the swayback mare. Arguing with Godric was pointless, and she did not want to break their fragile peace. She would simply have to find a way to return to her father on her own. "How old is the horse?"

"Nineteen or twenty. We are unsure."

"Very old."

Godric nodded and patted the old mare's neck. "She has been well cared for." He plucked another apple slice from his pouch and Blue Thunder bit into it with flat, yellowed teeth, then rooted his hand for more.

"She looks to be on her last leg."

"Do not let her fool you. She used to be the queen of the stable. She may be old, but she is still very strong. She needs someone to show her off again." Godric lifted Meiriona's hand gently to the horse. "Feel how soft her nose is."

Blue Thunder leaned into her, searching for a treat. The mare's breath was hot against her hand and the velvet nose soft and warm. Amazingly, Meiriona felt no fear.

"See, she likes that."

Meiriona moved her hand slowly, caressing the soft hair beneath her fingertips. Her heart gave a little lurch when Blue Thunder rolled her eyes as if to say, "Well, where is it? You were supposed to bring me a treat."

Meiriona smiled.

Godric leaned around her, his big body pressing hers. "All right, 'tis finished. Lesson over."

She twisted to look at him. "But we did not even ride."

Godric chuckled, his eyes dancing. "There is plenty of time to learn to ride, girl." His voice was soothing and low, ripe with erotic promise.

CHAPTER 25

Nearly a fortnight later, laughter and loud talking floated around them as Meiriona walked with Godric into Montgomery's great hall. She was still a prisoner, but Godric had allowed her some freedom and they had made a delicate peace. Servants were setting up trestle tables and arranging trenchers, preparing for a feast. A huge fire burned in the fireplace, casting beautiful mottled shapes around the room.

Lady Montgomery paused in her stitching and glared at Godric from her seat by the window. "Where is my son?"

Godric shrugged. "Probably spewing into the garderobe."

Lady Montgomery jabbed her needle fiercely into her fabric.

Meiriona laid her hand on Godric's forearm. "Leave her be," she said quietly. *Why must he goad Lady Montgomery?*

Godric scowled. "Mind yourself, lady."

"You would do better to secure a friend rather than make an enemy," she whispered.

Godric's scowl deepened, but he did not answer. She sighed. He rubbed salt into old wounds by making no effort to mend the bad blood between himself and Lady Montgomery. It would likely be the same with her family. She cringed inwardly, feeling once more her desperation to speak with her father and Uncle Pierre.

Godric turned his back to Lady Montgomery and signaled for one of the servants to bring a table and chairs. "Do you play chess, Meiriona?"

"Of course."

They settled into sorting the pieces, a disturbing silence between them. A servant brought goblets of spiced wine and a platter of blackberry tarts, sweetmeats, and bread with honey.

"My lord—"

"Nay, Meiriona. Do not mention it. You may *not* go home." His voice allowed no room for argument.

Sighing, she sank into her chair. "How is my brother?" She had not been allowed to talk to him, but she'd caught glances of him from her window and he seemed content.

Godric shifted into his chair. "He does well. He has been serving in the stables."

Meiriona smiled, a feeling of relief coming over her. "He is good with horses. When he rides, 'tis as if he isn't lame."

"He has a certain way with horses. Likely someday he will be a master horseman."

At that moment, a dog yelped loudly and the outside door swung open. Amelina rushed inside, holding a hound by the scruff of its neck. She let go, and the dog scooted away with a whine. Scuttling to her father, she glowered at Meiriona.

"Papa, why is *she* still here?" The child flailed her arms, knocking two pawns and a rook onto the floor. A maid scurried to replace them.

Godric frowned.

The little girl grabbed a fistful of blackberry tart and stuffed it into her mouth, puffing her cheeks out like an overfilled water bladder. Lady Montgomery and Meiriona exchanged a disapproving look. Snatching a hunk of buttered bread, she jumped from Godric's lap and hurried off.

Godric said nothing, his face enigmatic.

Of all the men she'd seen, his table manners were impeccable, yet his training in such matters did not seem to extend to his child.

Bear, sitting beside her, stretched his legs and leaned toward Meiriona. "Needs a mother, she does."

She glanced at Godric, but he was concentrating on the chessboard.

"The child has no need of another parent. She needs discipline from the one she has."

Lifting a brow, Godric moved one of his bishops.

Bear harrumphed.

A curtain opened, and Damien entered the hall, grinning from ear to ear.

Meiriona nearly dropped the tart she was holding.

Her brother crossed the room in giddy strides, carrying a training bow, a quiver of arrows slung over his shoulder. He walked straight, barely favoring his lame leg.

Her heart swelled with pride as he reached their table and bowed low to Godric. "I hit the bulls-eye with the last three arrows. Bear wants me in charge of the horses while your men are gone."

Godric clapped him on the shoulder. "No doubt you will do a fine job, boy."

She felt her lips quiver with happiness. Godric would see to Damien's training. She no longer had to fear for his future. 'Twas a bigger gift than either the emerald hair comb or her new clothing.

She smiled at him. "Thank you, my lord. Thank you."

Godric's child ran from the window seat, snatched a blackberry tart, and sneered at Damien. "He walks like a sick old man."

Damien's smile faltered.

Meiriona shot a look at Godric, waiting for him to correct his child. Paying no heed to his daughter's behavior, he gulped a drink of ale and jumped his knight to the middle of the chessboard.

Damien looked from Godric to his daughter. She could feel his need for Godric to contradict the little girl's verdict. When he did not, Damien limped awkwardly away from the hearth.

Meiriona watched the servants bustling about. No one paid the child any attention. In fact, they all seemed intent on ignoring the little girl. She turned to Godric.

"Amelina needs discipline."

Godric looked up abruptly, just as the child sat down on the hearth and popped a second tart into her mouth. She looked . . . adorable. The blue ruffles of her dress frothed around her, and her dark hair curled around her elfish face framing her huge blue eyes. A perfect picture of innocence.

Godric shrugged.

"She terrorizes the dogs."

Godric glanced around. Several hounds lay on the rushes, chomping contentedly on bones. "All seems in order."

"She insulted my brother."

"Nay, she spoke the truth with a child's innocence, not with malice."

Meiriona crossed her arms. "If you keep explaining away her actions, her behavior will only become worse."

At that moment, Amelina hurled the remainder of her tart at Damien. "I don' want you here."

The tart splattered across his quiver, dripping blackberries into the arrow chamber.

"Ho!" Damien screamed, lunging for her.

The elf jumped from the hearth and dove under a trestle table, scrambling the hounds.

Serving maids squealed as the dogs bounced around the room. Two servants collided trying to sidestep the hurly-burly. Trays of roasted ham crashed to the rushes. Women shrieked, men yelled, and dogs barked. The curs scrambled into the fray to snatch their share of the bounty while servants tried to shoo them away to collect any salvageable pieces.

Meiriona turned back to Godric.

He scowled.

She lifted an eyebrow.

Slowly, Godric took a deep breath and stood. "Amelina!"

At once all shouting and barking ceased. Quiet as death. A spoon fell to the rushes, sounding unnaturally loud in the silence.

Bear and Lady Montgomery shot Meiriona a look, whether of triumph or dread, she was unsure.

"You—" Godric pointed at his child. "You come with me."

The girl crossed her arms. "Nay."

Godric stalked toward her and swung the child into his arms. She screamed and kicked, bowing her back to get loose, but her father carried her from the room.

Meiriona turned to Bear. Amelina, spoiled as she was, was a tiny child, and Godric was a warrior. "He will not harm her, will he?" she whispered.

Bear shook his head. "Milady, the master would give his own life rather than harm one of his own."

Meiriona bit her lip, thinking of the scene in the forest with Owain. Of the whip cracking across the young man's bared back.

"What about Owain?" she asked suddenly.

Bear looked at her as if she had grown a second nose. He harrumphed. "A wife should not question her husband's judgment."

"But I am not his wife."

Bear shrugged. "Ye will be."

CHAPTER 26

"Ho," a man's voice slurred from a side room as Meiriona walked toward the sewing room a few days later so she could thank the seamstresses for all her new clothing. Today she wore a burgundy surcoat shot through with gold threads. Gratitude welled in her heart for all the women had done.

"Ho!" he called again.

Pausing, she peered inside the chamber where the voice came from. Dark hair curled around the wide shoulders of a man sitting in a richly carved chair afore a roaring fire. For a second, she thought it was Godric, but seeing this man's boyish, unlined face, she realized it was Godric's brother. What was his name again? An unstoppered flagon of wine, an empty goblet, and a haphazard stack of books sat on a side table near him. He held one book open on his lap.

She placed her hand on the door frame. "You called me?"

He motioned her toward his chair's twin. "Have a seat. I would like to speak with my brother's prize."

Meiriona huffed. "I am no prize to be won, sirrah."

The young lord chuckled, sobering somewhat. "Forgive me, milady. Come," he beckoned. "I wish to speak with you about Godric."

Curiosity drew her closer. "What about him?"

Godric's brother snapped his book closed and laid it atop the pile with the others. "Just things."

Grasping the door frame, Meiriona debated.

He lifted a brow, making him look exactly like Godric. "I shan't bite. Sit and drink with me."

Crossing the threshold, Meiriona eyed the empty goblet. "You, sirrah, have already had quite enough."

He threw back his head and laughed. "So, the tales about your prickly tongue are true."

Walking across the room, she felt as though she were being drawn into a wolf's den. The scent of burning wood permeated the chamber. She pushed up her sleeves as the heat waves from the huge fire hit her.

"Saints, 'tis a furnace in here."

Shrugging, he leaned back in his chair. "The hotter it is, the easier it is to talk women into parting with their garments."

Meiriona scowled at him and turned to leave. She had better things to do than deal with a drunkard.

He leapt up and grabbed her arm. "Forgive me. The wine makes me forget my manners." Releasing her arm, he looked sincerely ashamed. "Prithee, stay. Only for a moment."

"All right," she agreed, "only for a moment."

He held out his hand. "We have never been properly introduced, milady. I am James Vaughn, Earl of Montgomery."

She took his hand and he bent, kissing it politely, then straightened and showed her to one of the chairs.

He took a seat and she studied him. Although he was into his cups, he was much more sober than he had been the first time she'd seen him.

"Godric's not a bad man," he said without preamble. "Mum thinks differently."

Meiriona leaned forward in her chair. "So I have gathered."

James tipped the flagon, but only a few drops plunked into his goblet. "Damn."

Tapping her foot, Meiriona wondered if she should have left. "You planned to tell me about Godric," she said pointedly.

James slurped the drops of wine from his vessel, then stared at her intently. "He wants you. His smoke is worse than his flame."

"Meaning?"

"If you treat him well, you can conquer the Dragon."

"Oh." Leaning back in her chair, she awaited more explanation.

"He's never had anyone to love him," James continued. "His mother died, Father was not much on love, and my mum hates him."

Meiriona was taken aback. "You sound like you care."

James waved his hand dismissively. "He is demanding, overbearing, and stubborn. What is not to love?"

Meiriona laughed. The fire popped as a log shifted. "Verily, you are correct. But sometimes he is kind."

James smiled. "He needs love."

Irritated with the direction of the conversation, Meiriona smirked. "Of a truth?"

"Aye, I know so."

Meiriona crossed her legs. "What know you about love?"

She would have sworn the room got colder, even though that was impossible given the vastness of the fire. James rose, crossed the room, and retrieved another flagon of wine from a cabinet. "I was in love once," he said bitterly.

Her heart went out to him and curiosity tugged at her. "What happened?"

Holding his new wine flagon, he looked up at her, startled. "Truly, you wish to know?"

She nodded.

"She was only a peasant girl. I took her to France for the trip of her life." His voice sounded haunted.

"Go on," she prompted, settling into her chair's cushion.

"She did not want to go. She begged me not to take her, but I was heedless and forced her to go along anyway." He poured wine into his goblet. It sloshed over the rim and landed on the flagstone.

He turned to the fire and threw another log on, even though it was already sweltering in the chamber. Perspiration dripped down her back.

"She died," he said flatly.

"Died?"

"Aye, just so. I should not have taken her. I killed her by forcing her to go."

Meiriona rose and walked to the hearth to stand beside him. Unsure of what to say, she patted him awkwardly on the arm.

Turning, he took Meiriona by the hand. "Never have I told anyone about this."

"You . . . You haven't?" she asked, surprised that he would share such a deep secret with a stranger. "What about Lady Montgomery?"

"Least of all her. My mother values rank above something stupid like love." He thumbed his jaw in a movement that reminded her of Godric. "Godric loves you. Do not waste the time you have together."

Startled, she mumbled a reply.

His handsome, boyish face looked troubled. "May I tell you the entire story?"

"Of course," she said, relieved not to have to think about Godric loving her.

He led her back to her seat, poured her a goblet of red wine, and handed it to her. Silence drew between them as she awaited him to begin.

"She hated the cold," he began, settling into his

chair and twirling his goblet round and round in his long fingers.

An hour later, Meiriona perched on her seat, fascinated with the story of James's love affair with a peasant woman and her tragic end as he took her to France to marry her.

Tears shimmered in his eyes. He wiped them away with his tunic sleeve.

Meiriona stood and walked to him, her soles slapping softly against the flags. Putting her arm around his shoulder, she squeezed him tightly. "Have you ever grieved for her?"

"I ache inside, if that is what you mean."

She hugged him. "Nay, I mean really grieved for her. Allowed yourself to cry?"

He crumpled, leaning against her. "Men do not cry."

"Oh, James," she said, cradling his head to her bosom as if he were a child to be comforted.

"I loved her," he sniffed. "I loved her and I killed her." His shoulders shook and she patted him motherly on the back.

"Now, now," she crooned.

The doorway darkened and a large shadow flooded the room. "By God's rood," Godric cursed, striding inside.

Meiriona jumped and began to straighten. "My lord."

He reached her in two strides. Yanking her from his brother, he slammed his fist into James's nose.

"Godric," she yelled, grabbing his arm. "'Tisn't what you think."

James held his nose. Blood dripped down his tunic and onto the flags. "G'day, brother," he said sarcastically.

Godric cocked his arm back.

"Cease!" Meiriona yelled, jumping between the two

men and trying to push Godric back. "Do not be daft!"

Scooping her up in one arm, he flung her over his shoulder. She made an unladylike "ooph" as the air whooshed from her lungs.

Godric pointed at his brother. "I will deal with you anon."

"Put me down, beast!" Meiriona screamed.

With long strides, Godric exited the chamber.

"What the bloody hell did you think you were doing?" Godric yelled, depositing her onto his bed. "Are two men not enough?"

Bed ropes creaking, Meiriona scrambled from the mattress and pointed her finger at him. "You jolthead, why would I need him when I have you?"

"Exactly my point."

"Your brother was telling me about his love affair with a peasant woman."

"So you decided to push his face into your breasts?"

Meiriona's eyes turned mutinous. "How dare you! I was *not* pushing his face into my breasts!"

Fury pulsed through his veins. "What the hell do you call it then, vixen?"

"Comforting him."

"Some kind of bloody comfort!" Godric boomed, not wanting to feel the jealousy and hurt floating on the edges of his anger.

Meiriona stalked to the dressing screen and yanked out the eating dagger he had thrown there days ago. "How dare you think I would even want another man after what you do to me."

If she were not so furious, he would have questioned her sincerity. He stilled, flexing his hands.

She pointed the eating dagger at his heart. "Do you

even know why your brother drinks himself into a stupor every day?"

Godric shrugged. "Because he is an irresponsible lewdster."

"Nay, nay, nay." Meiriona scowled at him. "Why not take time to listen to him instead of assuming the worst?"

"What good would come of that?"

"He had big dreams to travel the world, but when the woman of his life died on one such adventure, he gave up hope and returned home, drowning his sorrow in ale."

Crossing his arms, Godric leaned against the back of the throne. "He told you that."

"Of a sort. He told me about the woman."

"And the rest."

"I surmised the rest."

"'Tis a big assumption."

Meiriona set the knife on the bedside table and glanced over her shoulder at Godric. "Was he thus afore you, er, um . . ."

"Afore I was sold into slavery," he finished.

"Aye, afore that."

A wave of hope for his brother rolled through his mind and he thumbed his jaw, quiet for a long moment. "Nay."

Meiriona cocked a brow. "Well?"

Blowing out a deep breath, he walked to Meiriona. "Truly, that is what the scene was about?"

"Aye." Winding her arms around his waist, she hugged him.

For a long moment, he thought about what he had seen in James's chamber. The look on Meiriona's face had been one of pity, not passion. It hit him abruptly that he was wrong.

Feeling awkward, he hugged her back and realized

he'd have to think of a way to amend for his lapse in judgment.

Deciding the best gift he could give her was to help her learn to ride, he took her hand and led her out the door toward the stables.

CHAPTER 27

Lady Montgomery, carrying a trencher of food, crossed the path as Meiriona again made her way toward the seamstresses' room a few days later.

"Help! Help!" a small, high-pitched voice called from above them.

They both turned. Stew from Lady Montgomery's trencher slopped onto the rushes.

"Help! Up hither!" Looking up, they saw Godric's child atop a very long, steep staircase. Tears streamed down the elf's face as she clung onto a broken rail for support.

There was clearly no immediate danger to the two-year-old, but every time she looked down, her face became panic-stricken.

"How did you get up there?" Meiriona called.

"I climbeded," Amelina wailed pitifully.

"Well, then, you can bloody well climb down," Lady Montgomery said, hurrying off with her platter of food.

Sighing, Meiriona walked to the bottom of the stairs. The seamstresses would have to wait a little longer to receive the thanks they deserved. "You cannot climb down?"

"Nay! Nay!" the child cried, another panicked look crossing her features.

"All right. Just stay put. I am coming." Meiriona mounted the steps.

Gasping for breath, Amelina watched her climb with wide blue eyes. "I'm going to fall!" she screamed.

"Nay, love, you will not fall," Meiriona soothed, keeping up her steady pace of climbing the steps. "Hold tightly to the rail."

"What if it breaks?" the child wailed.

"I shall catch you." Huffing and puffing, Meiriona realized she was only halfway to the top. No wonder the child was terrified. "You climbed all this way?"

A pitiful moan came from Amelina. "I'm scared."

Panting, Meiriona reached the top. "Goodness, 'tis quite a climb, love."

Amelina flung herself at Meiriona, burying her face in Meiriona's shoulder. Sobs echoed off the stones as the child wept in relief.

Meiriona patted her on the back, glad the little girl was no longer fussing about how much she did not want her there. "How long have you been hither?"

"Days and days and days."

Meiriona stifled a chuckle. No doubt it seemed like days and days to the little girl.

"Papa told me not to climb up here," the child whispered. "Are you gonna tell him?"

Meiriona playfully poked the little girl's nose, glad she was no longer screaming about how she hated her. Mayhap this was a chance for them to become friends. "I tell you what. If you promise ne'er to climb hither again, we can keep it our secret."

Biting her trembling lower lip, the girl nodded. Big tears leaked out of her eyes. "I thought nobody would ever come."

"How about we go see if we can find a sweetmeat in the kitchens?" Meiriona asked, tucking a strand of wayward dark hair behind Amelina's ear.

The girl sniffed. "Perchance a tart?" she asked hopefully.

Meiriona smiled. "Definitely a tart. But you have to promise not to throw it at anyone."

"I promise, I promise."

Amelina hugged Meiriona so tight Meiriona made a strangling sound. The elf giggled and loosened her hold.

Clutching the child, Meiriona climbed down what seemed like a thousand steps. At the bottom, she set Amelina on her feet and stretched her back. "Whew."

Amelina glanced back up the long stairway. "I was way up there?" she asked, her eyes rounding with amazement.

Taking Amelina by the hand, Meiriona led her down the hallway. "Aye, love. Let us find the kitchens."

The servants bustled with disorganized activity when Meiriona and Amelina entered the kitchens.

A plump maid wearing a muffin cap ran to them. "Amelina! Where have you been, child? I 'ave looked everywhere!"

"Eleanor, Eleanor!" Amelina hugged the servant. "I climbeded the stairs Papa told me not to."

"For shame, child," Eleanor scolded.

The little girl looked conspiratorially at Meiriona. "Meiriona promised she wouldn't tell."

Eleanor squeezed the child. "You are the 'ardest little imp to keep up with."

Amelina giggled. "Not a imp."

"Come on." Sighing wearily, Eleanor led the child toward a chamber where people performed various tasks around rough-hewn tables. "You too," she called over her shoulder at Meiriona.

Servants scrambled about pouring flour into big bowls, chopping vegetables, and cutting meat. They hopped from task to task haphazardly. Pans lined the tables, some clattering on the floor as the servants moved about.

"Where's my pat of butter?" one yelled.

"I 'ad a trencher of food hither. Who took my trencher?" another screamed.

Meiriona slid between two maids carrying pitchers of mead. In all her life, she'd never seen such an undisciplined kitchen.

"Who is in charge?" she asked Eleanor when they reached a quieter nook.

"That would be Master Godric," Eleanor said, sitting down at a small table and running her pudgy fingers across its edge.

"Godric?" Meiriona exclaimed. "What does Godric know about running a kitchen?"

Eleanor harrumphed, her cap quivering. "You should 'ave seen it afore he arrived." She held up her left hand, which was missing the middle finger. "'Twas so higgledy-piggledy, the bloody butcher cut my finger off by accident. So I'll not 'ave you talking bad about the master, I won't."

Laying a hand on Eleanor's meaty arm, Meiriona sat beside her. "Sorry, dear, no offense. 'Tis just that Godric is a warrior, not a kitchen maid."

"Eleanor," Amelina wailed, hopping on one foot. Her skirts flounced up and down. "Meiriona promised me a tart!"

Meiriona glanced at the child, then back at Eleanor and shrugged. "I did."

Eleanor rumpled the two-year-old's already mussed hair and whirled her so that she faced a shelf on the far side of the kitchen. "Yon on the bottom shelf," she directed, giving the girl a light swat on the bottom to get her moving.

Amelina ran off, screaming "Gramercy" over her shoulder.

Sighing, Eleanor patted the table. "An active child."

"Indeed." Meiriona watched Amelina dodge between servants who carried plates of roasted pork. The jumbled confusion pricked Meiriona's sensibility as lady of the keep. "Now what is this about Godric running the kitchens? How on earth can he run a kitchen from the practice field?"

"He can't." Eleanor hitched up her leather girdle making her wide stomach jiggle. She glanced around to make sure no one was listening. Pots and pans clanged. "Lady Montgomery leaves us in a muddle," she whispered. "Master Godric is the only one we can depend on for direction."

"Harrumph." Meiriona mulled over this new piece of information. 'Twas no wonder the food here was so terrible.

Two servants scurried by, carrying platters of leeks and onions. When they nearly collided, Meiriona itched to correct their paths so that the servants coming into the kitchen weren't overrunning the ones who were leaving.

"We ain't got nobody to care over us, mistress." Eleanor eyed Meiriona scrupulously. "You don' seem much like the type that would just lie abed all the day." She didn't finish her sentence with "like Lady Montgomery," but Meiriona heard it anyway.

"No tarts left," Amelina moaned pitifully, coming back to them with large tears in her eyes.

Eleanor sat the little girl on her knee and hollered at a maid to bring the child some bread and honey. Amelina sniffed, but hushed.

After a moment, a young lady with large brown eyes and soft cheeks brought a platter. "Amelina, do you want to pick flowers with me?" she asked.

Amelina bounced off Eleanor's lap. "Hooray!"

The young woman tickled Amelina on the tummy

and the little girl giggled. They scrambled from the kitchen hand in hand.

Glancing around, Meiriona noted the shelves piled high with haphazard cooking pots, tangled wooden spoons, and pottery jars. 'Twas a wonder anyone could find anything.

As if reading her thoughts, Eleanor said, "'Twould give you something to do, mistress. I can't take care of the little imp and see to the kitchens too. Master's too busy to offer much guidance." Propping a fist on one of her wide hips, Eleanor stood. "I'll show you around."

A loud crash sounded from the main section of the kitchen followed by a scream of outrage.

"Get your bloody coneys off my cabinet," a stout woman who was kneading dough yelled at a man carrying a fistful of freshly slain rabbits.

"Well, where the 'ell do ye want me to put these, then?" he hollered back.

"See what I mean?" Eleanor whispered, traipsing across the crowded room. "'Tain't got no organization."

Undoubtedly, they needed her help. Her decision made, Meiriona stood. "Aye, show me around," she directed. "I *am* weary of being a slugabed."

"Come then." Eleanor led her out the room and motioned her toward a closed door. "Here's where the spices are kept. I'll send someone to fetch the key." She snapped orders to a skinny, beady-eyed woman wearing a dull greasy apron. Meiriona observed the rowdy kitchen, thinking of improvements until the woman returned with Bear in tow holding a ring of keys.

The skinny woman pointed him toward Eleanor and Meiriona.

"Why did Bear come?"

Eleanor shrugged. "Somebody's got to take the keys back to Master Godric."

Meiriona frowned. If Godric controlled the keys to the spice pantry, 'twas no wonder the food was so bland.

"Why does he not give the keys to a storekeeper?"

"'E can't trust them not to give the keys back to Lady Montgomery. The servants are all afraid of 'er," Eleanor whispered conspiratorially. "She sold off all our food and we nearly starved ere Master Godric arrived to care for us."

"Oh," Meiriona said, shocked at this tidbit of information.

Jangling the keys, Bear slid one into the lock. The monstrous lock undid with a snap and the door swung inward.

A heady mixture of scents wafted toward them, and Meiriona gasped. Bags, stuffed with spices, piled on the floor and shelves. Cinnamon, cardamom, cloves, nutmeg, and other indiscernible aromas swirled around them.

"Sweet Mary, this must be worth a fortune."

"Godric is a spice trader, m'lady," Eleanor chattered as if Meiriona was daft.

"Goodness," was all Meiriona could think to say. She'd never seen so many spices in her life. She had known Godric was wealthy, but this was beyond anything she'd ever imagined.

"Impressive, 'tisn't it," Bear muttered.

"Why does the cook not use them in the food?" Meiriona asked. "With so much stored, the food need not taste so bland."

Bear shrugged.

Eleanor gave her a pointed look. "'Tis a lot of trouble running back and forth to the practice field for a spice, m'lady."

"Hmm," Meiriona mused, her mind ticking with possibilities. If Godric was a trader, mayhap he'd be interested in Mary's weaving. She would definitely find a way to ask him about the wool trade—*after* she dealt with the kitchens.

"And Cook refuses to arise afore sext," Eleanor continued.

"Ah." Laziness in the servants irritated Meiriona's sense of duty and insulted her training as a lady of the keep. She itched to put things in order. "Bear, give me the keys, and we shall have decent food tonight."

He rubbed his shaggy beard. "Don' know if that's a good idea."

"Fine," she said, taking command. "Then you will stay here and help. Godric may be a fine swordsman, but he's an inept lady of the keep. Eleanor, show me to Cook."

Bear raised a brow, but remained silent.

Eleanor beamed. "This way, m'lady. But don' expect 'er to be happy."

"Fine."

Heading back into the chopping room, Meiriona felt a flush of excitement over having a goal instead of spending her days wandering aimlessly about waiting for Godric to finish his work so he could take her riding.

Eleanor led her to a short, round woman in a dirty apron who sat on a stool drinking a cup of milk.

"Cook," Meiriona said, "I understand you make wonderful blackberry tarts that are best served hot."

Cook turned, her wide bottom hanging off the sides of the stool. She looked suspiciously at Meiriona. "The best in the shire, mistress."

"Wonderful. I expect breakfast in the morning no later than an hour after sunup, and I would like to sample the tarts tonight after we eat."

Cook's piggy features took on a look of astonishment. She gazed from Meiriona to Bear to Eleanor then back again. "'Twill not be possible."

Meiriona lowered her voice to her most no-nonsense tone. "Why not?"

Cook glowered at her. "I am not making tarts today."

"But I have heard they are delicious."

Cook frowned, but Meiriona could see the lines around her lips softening with the flattery. "You have?"

"Aye, I have heard that no other cook in the world can make them as you can."

Cook's lips twitched and her eyes lit up. "'Tis a secret family recipe, m'lady."

"Excellent." Meiriona drew herself up to her full stature, keeping her voice authoritarian. "I shall sample one tonight."

Cook slapped one of her fat legs, her face a mask of irritation. "I cook tarts the second Tuesday of the month. 'Tis not my day for tarts."

Meiriona changed tactics. The flattery was not working. "Master Godric has put me in charge of the kitchens. You will make tarts, or you will go and tell him of your refusal yourself."

Frowning, Cook pursed her lips.

"I suggest you have some ready for him after sunrise in the morning with fresh hen's eggs or you may find yourself outside the walls come morning."

Standing, Cook flailed her arms around. "Everyone wants my tarts," she muttered. "They will stop at no cost to force me to make them." She walked toward the huge open oven, her wide rear lurching as she went. "How would the master like his eggs?" she grumbled over her shoulder.

A few moments later, as Meiriona, Bear, and Eleanor walked into the great hall, Bear slapped Meiriona on the back. "Ho, I'll take ye on my command team anytime." He waggled his fuzzy eyebrows. "That is, if ye'll secure me one of those tarts."

She smiled, feeling a flush of pleasure.

Rubbing his gut, he handed her the keys. "If Master Godric has a problem with ye having them, he can take it up with me."

Godric's boots thumped on the flagstone as he made his way toward his brother's reading chamber.

Crossing the threshold, he noted the blazing fire in the huge hearth. "Still hot as the Sahara in here, James."

The figure sitting in the huge chair was slumped over and snoring. Papers littered the floor at his feet.

"Drunk again." Disgusted, Godric turned to leave.

"Wait," he heard James call.

Turning, Godric saw his brother, hair mussed and eyes ringed with red, standing straight and unwavering in front of his chair. He waved Godric inside. James's eyes, despite the redness, were unclouded with drink. Mayhap since Meiriona had spoken with him, he had finally released his anger and grief over the peasant woman.

"Brother." Godric walked back to the hearth, feeling hopeful.

James nodded, and they sat in the chairs and stared at each other awkwardly for a moment.

"You were a good fighter," Godric offered, unsure what one was supposed to say in this sort of situation or how to amend for busting his brother's nose unfairly. "Father could not see it."

Crossing a foot over the opposite knee, James thumbed his jaw. "Ne'er as good as you."

"Do you remember that day we were wrestling and you smacked me on the temple?"

Smiling, James got a faraway look in his eyes. "You were knocked out for an hour."

"You were only half my size then, runt."

They both laughed.

Turning toward the blazing hearth, Godric noted that the usual flagons of spiced mead weren't heating by the fire. He indicated the papers scattered over the floor and side table. "What do you study?"

James glanced from Godric to the fire and back again. He blew out a long breath. "Astronomy and the workings of ships."

Interested, Godric leaned forward in his chair and gazed at the papers, trying to decipher some of the scribblings. "You have been studying for quite a while," he surmised.

"Do you ever think the church is wrong?" James asked, abruptly changing the subject.

Godric shrugged. "Oft. What does that have to do with astronomy and ships?"

"Do you think the world might be round?" His eyes, normally dull with alcohol, were wide with excitement.

Godric chewed his tongue to keep himself from blurting how daft the idea of the world being round was. But 'twas the first time since he'd arrived home that James wasn't buried in ale, and he did not want to curb his brother's newfound enjoyment for life. "'Tis possible," Godric lied.

Picking up a stack of papers, James leaned toward Godric. "I met a man on one of my adventures, and we have been in correspondence about such a theory. Look at this," he said, pointing to a star chart. "Christopher is convinced a ship will not fall off the earth if it sails west," he began.

Over the next two hours, Godric slowly became less convinced that his brother's theory was completely outlandish, although it still sounded too fantastical to be true.

After a long, rambling discussion, James sat back in his chair. "So, brother?"

"Mayhap," Godric said.

James punched Godric on the shoulder. "You shall see."

"Mayhap," Godric said again.

A comfortable silence grew between the brothers as they both stared into the fire, which had grown much dimmer as they talked.

"Your lady is quite a woman," James said, changing the focus of the conversation without preamble.

Balling his fists, Godric felt his jaw tighten. "Do not even think about making her one of your conquests."

James rubbed his bruised nose. "What you saw was not what you thought."

Godric unflexed his hands. "I know. She explained."

Laughing, James stood. "I owe you a good beating, brother. Let us go to the practice field and see if I can lay you flat again."

Grinning, Godric clapped his brother on the shoulder. "Not bloody likely, runt."

CHAPTER 28

Meiriona leaned against a trestle table and surveyed the work the servants had accomplished in a short span of time. Satisfaction burned in her heart, and she could hardly wait for Godric to come in from the practice field to sample the feast she had prepared. Would he appreciate all her work?

Fresh rushes, mingled with mint, lined the floor. Candles burned in sconces on the wall. The trestles were laid with wooden trenchers and the high table with pewter ones. Good French wine had been brought from the cellars, and servants bustled to place freshly roasted vegetables on the tables.

As a maid strode by with a platter of seasoned lamb, Meiriona snatched a bite. "Perfect," she said, nodding her approval.

The maid smiled and hurried off to deposit her load.

Meiriona watched the servants work, correcting their pathways as she saw fit, to keep the steady stream of workers from running haphazardly around. Liveliness buzzed around the great hall as if it were the first time in ages that the servants were proud and excited about their labor.

Her eyes widened as Godric and James ambled into the hall, laughing like old friends. Godric felt James's sword arm. "Not bad, runt, for someone who has been drinking himself into a stupor for years."

Chuckling, James snatched a cup of water. "Three more weeks and I will have you pinned to the ground, brother."

Beaming at them, Meiriona smoothed her green silk gown over her hips and patted her emerald hair comb as she felt Godric's gaze drawn to her.

"Good God, woman. Bear said you were helping in the kitchens, but are we expecting the bloody king?"

She felt her smile falter. "That's some kind of greeting," she said sourly.

He crossed toward her. Taking her hand, he bent and kissed her knuckles. "Forgive me, my lady. I am overwhelmed and forget my behavior."

When he straightened, she saw pleasure gleaming in his eyes. And something more—perchance hope.

"Verily, you do not," she said cheekily.

His eyes twinkled. "Mayhap 'tis better to misbehave sometimes."

She tucked her chin and looked up at him. "My lord," she admonished.

Smiling, he led her to the high table.

Lady Montgomery entered the hall. She said nothing, but took a trencher of food and exited.

From the corner of her eye, she saw James hesitate.

Godric nodded toward the lord's chair at the center. "Go on," he said to his brother. "'Twas ne'er your place I wanted, but for the castle to prosper."

James sat and Meiriona could have sworn she saw his eyes water. He snatched her hand. "Gramercy," he whispered.

"'Twas your own doing, not mine."

"Nevertheless."

She beamed at him as Godric took a seat beside her.

The roasted pork, venison, and lamb tasted even better than she had imagined. Godric glanced at her from time to time as if to make sure she was not an apparition that could vanish like mist. Lively musicians and a knife juggler entertained them between courses.

Bear let out a loud burp at the end of the meal and patted his belly contentedly. "Best meal since leaving France," he announced.

Meiriona felt a lump of happiness swell in her throat as one by one the men lined up to thank her for preparing something so wonderful.

A fortnight later, pride welled in Godric's chest as he watched Meiriona, red hair flowing, ride across the courtyard astride Blue Thunder. Blue Thunder was as frisky as a colt and Meiriona's color was high.

God, she was exquisite.

He had been correct to assume with gentle guidance and patience she would be able to ride again.

These last weeks had been heaven. Meiriona had altered the entire mood of the castle. The great hall was now a festive resting place. The food had improved significantly; it felt like a home. James and he practiced together daily, getting James ready for his grand, dubious adventure of finding his friend Christopher and testing his wings. Mayhap best of all, Amelina's behavior had changed so much it seemed she was a different child.

At night he'd entwined his fingers in Meiriona's hair and kept her close to him. He kissed her, he teased her, he tickled her, he stroked her skin until both of them were hot and needy. But he had *not* taken her. Tonight he could wait no longer.

Pulling the horse to a halt in front of him, she swung down from her mount. "My lord."

"'Twas the best you have done since we began our daily treks to the stables."

She smiled up at him, her eyes glowing. "I can scarcely believe it! I am riding again!" Standing on tiptoes, she kissed his cheek. He felt blood rush to his groin.

That she no longer hid her affection pleased him greatly but also made him apprehensive, for he knew she might withdraw it soon. He still had not answered the king's summons to arrest her father, and the time drew short. The men had trained hard to prepare for the siege of Whitestone and he planned to leave on the morrow. Furthermore, he must consummate their relationship before he left to meet her father.

He took the reins from her, and they walked the breadth of the courtyard to cool down the mare.

"I never doubted you would be able to ride again on your own."

"'Twas positively wicked of you to insist I ride astride," she said, slipping her hand into his.

He squeezed her hand and a wave of possession gripped him. She belonged to him, and he would ne'er let her go. "This new fashion of noblewomen riding with both legs dangling off one side is daft. One cannot expect to stay balanced thus."

She stopped and turned toward him, face alight with giddy pleasure. Twisting her hand into his tunic, she tugged him close and kissed him. He smiled. If this was the welcome he received when she went riding, he would buy her dozens of ponies.

Blue Thunder nosed her on the head and she pulled away, laughing. Patting the mare's chest, she hugged her neck. "You may have a treat as soon as you cool down, you greedy hound."

"Meiriona"—Godric tugged both her and the horse toward the stables—"you were magnificent."

She laughed, her voice filling him with joy. "When I was young, I loved to ride. Blue Thunder and I make quite a pair, do we not?"

"Have you any lingering fear?"

"I doubt I will join any racing team in London, but for now, nay."

"Good." He smiled to himself. His patience had been rewarded. And tonight his patience in other areas would be rewarded as well. Swiving the lady could wait no longer. Leading the mare into the stables, he tossed Blue Thunder's reins to a groom. "Walk her a few more moments, then brush her well," he instructed. "Tell Bear I am taking the lady for a walk on the wall afore we sup."

Meiriona quirked an eyebrow at him but said nothing. He grasped her hand and led her from the stable and across the courtyard.

They walked silently, hand in hand, toward the keep. The morning's rain had cleared and the day was sunny but crisp, full of the smells of the coming winter.

"Have you heard from my father?" Meiriona asked abruptly as they reached the stairs leading to the top of the castle wall.

"Nay." Godric inclined his head toward her. "I bade him to meet with me four times but have received no answer." He took a deep breath, steeling himself against losing Meiriona's affection. "I cannot stave off the king any longer. I must answer his demands that I take Whitestone and bring your father to justice."

Meiriona pulled her hand free of his and climbed the remaining stairs without assistance. It felt like a knife scraping across his heart. "My father will never willingly grant Whitestone to you."

"He has no choice." He wanted to grab her, force her to give back the affection she had just withdrawn, but he knew that he would have to force her soon enough. Because willing or no, he could wait no longer. "Meiriona—" He paused, unsure how to tell her. "I am riding to Whitestone tomorrow to negotiate with your father."

She glanced down over the wall at the training field. Men loaded carts of weapons, siege engines, and supplies.

"Negotiate? With weapons of war?"

"There will be no war if your father will be reasonable."

Meiriona felt her heart sink. No matter how much Godric was a man of honor, no matter how many riches he had accumulated, her father would never willingly grant Whitestone to a Yorkist bastard. "'Tis impossible, my lord. If you will not allow me to parley with my father, let us go elsewhere. We can start life anew."

He did not answer her plea but drew her forward along the wall. As they walked, her heart sank further and further. All around them men were packing, preparing for battle. Bear, with his one arm, directed progress. They climbed down a short set of stairs into an alcove, passing an old humpbacked woman sweeping the floor with a straw broom. "G'day, Master Godric," she said cheerily.

He patted the ugly woman on the shoulder as they passed. When they had crossed another castle landing, he grabbed Meiriona's elbow, yanking her close to him. "Did you see her?"

She looked back down the corridor at its austere stone walls and flagstone floor. "You mean the old woman?"

"Aye."

"Her husband is dead, her eyes are near blind, and she has no beauty about her. Think you that we cannot find younger, more able women to sweep the floors?"

Meiriona nodded, unsure what he alluded to.

"Her body is old, but her spirit is willing to work.

Have you not noticed how many of that sort abide here? If I could, I would gladly take you to France, purchase a small chateau and forever live a quiet life." He ducked under an archway. "'Tis impossible, Meiriona. Surely you can see why."

A downpour of emotions flooded Meiriona. Why had she not seen it before? Every castle had its share of odd members, but here there were many. Bear with only one arm, the ugly guard, the woman with the missing ear, the blind humpbacked woman. She had seen others but somehow had not seen them. "You *keep* them," she said suddenly, unable to hide the amazement from her voice. "You do not need Whitestone merely for revenge. You need land to keep your menagerie of people."

She stared at the man walking next to her, new respect forming inside her. His white scars slashed his cheeks. What had he said? *It only hurts on the inside.* How much unfairness had he known because of his appearance? His face had been so fair, so sweet, years ago. She had always thought of him as strong, tough. Yet he had admitted how afraid he'd been of the box. Mayhap he had a softer heart than she. Did he feel it every time someone looked upon his scars with revulsion?

"I give them a home, Meiriona."

"Nay, 'tis not all," she said, thinking of Bear being a soldier, the guard being a guard. These were people others might allow to live as beggars but here, under Godric's guidance, they were not outcasts but useful members. "You give them hope."

He inclined his head slightly toward her but did not answer. As they made their way to the great hall, Eric rushed up to them. "Master Godric! Master Godric! Come quickly. A load's fallen off one of the wagons, damaging the extra swords."

Heaving an exasperated breath, Godric kissed

Meiriona on the cheek. "I shall return within the hour." He and Eric rushed to the bailey.

As Meiriona made her way alone toward the great hall, a mixture of longing and dread pierced her heart. 'Twas late, and the soldiers scurried with last-minute preparations to attack her castle. Her father would never reason with Godric or surrender their lands. Her people's only chance for survival lay in her getting to Whitestone ahead of Godric and parleying with her father.

Lost in her thoughts, Meiriona started when she nearly walked into Lady Montgomery.

"I am sorry about the other day," Lady Montgomery ventured. "'Tis not safe for you to stay hither." She turned and stared out into the bailey, indicating the carts laden with trebuchets. "Godric will destroy your home."

Noticing the sheer number of weapons, Meiriona wondered if the lady spoke the truth.

"He rules with an iron hand. All except for his child. I thank you greatly for forcing him to see his daughter's misbehavior."

Meiriona turned and looked at Godric's stepmother. "Your castle prospers under Godric's hand."

Lady Montgomery gave one of her sad smiles. "Come and walk with me."

Meiriona drew her short cape around her shoulders as they made their way across the castle grounds and up several flights of stairs.

She watched the men loading carts with heavy trunks. Bear was among them, barking orders. Voices rose to them on the wind, but she could not understand any of the conversations. Trepidation grew inside her as she watched swords, spears, and bows being loaded.

"Make no mistake, child. Godric *will* destroy your home."

Meiriona took a deep breath. "I must reach Whitestone afore Godric's army does. Only then will I have a chance to prevent war. If I am able to speak with my father, I can make him see the desperation of the situation."

Lady Montgomery eyed her warily. "Mayhap I could help you."

"You?" Unease crept up Meiriona's spine. Had this been the reason for Lady Montgomery's sudden kind overtures? "How?"

Leaning closer, the lady placed a hand on Meiriona's arm. "For a price, I could secure you a guide and a guard."

Meiriona swallowed, torn by this development. "I have no gold," she said at last.

"Your hair comb would fetch a goodly price." Lady Montgomery's gaze rested on the emerald bauble gleaming from Meiriona's tresses.

"Nay," Meiriona said, patting her hair self-consciously. "The comb is precious to me."

The lady was quiet for a long moment, then shrugged. "Mayhap the price of peace is too high."

The price of peace. The words echoed in Meiriona's mind like sheep bleating across the hills. Desperation welled inside her. If only she could speak to her father, all would be well.

Hating herself, Meiriona dug the emerald bauble from her hair. She swallowed a bubble of selfishness. If the comb could buy peace, then she could not allow sentiment to keep her from paying the price.

"Prithee, find me a way home." Handing it to Lady Montgomery, Meiriona flinched at the coldness of the lady's hands.

"Stay here," Lady Montgomery commanded, turning the hair comb over in her hand. "I will send someone." Turning, she marched down the stairs.

A feeling of wrongness slammed into Meiriona's heart as Lady Montgomery's footsteps faded.

"Dear Mary," she breathed, shaking her head to clear her mind. She patted her naked hair. "Lady Montgomery! Wait!"

CHAPTER 29

Meiriona rushed down the stairs to a landing where the corridor headed in two separate directions. "Lady Montgomery!" She looked down the right-hand steps, then the left, but saw only stone, mortar, unlit torches, and cobwebs. The lady had disappeared.

Heart lurching, she picked the right-hand stairs, which seemed to lead back the way they had come. Hopelessness weighed heavy on her heart. She had no horse and now no jewels to secure an escort to Whitestone. What had she been thinking to trust the bitter Lady Montgomery with her hair bauble? Balling her fists in frustration, she determined to have her jewel back. Already, she missed its weight in her hair.

At the bottom of the stairs, the hallways led in three different directions. She wrung her fingers for a moment, then chose the one on the far left.

Cobwebs hung from the low ceiling as if the maids had not touched it in years. She was unfamiliar at best with the castle, but she recognized nothing in this wing at all. She moved downward, knowing that eventually she'd reach the lower level. The tapping of her slippers against the flagstone was the only sound in the deserted corridor. The hall seemed to go on forever. *Why would an entire wing of the castle be unused?* Turning another corner, she noted that footprints were pressed into the musty rushes. Mayhap the castle recluse lived here. She reached the end of the corridor, where two sets of heavy wooden doors blocked the path.

She felt eyes watching her. A trickle of fear slid into her. Shaking off her unease, she tried both sets of doors. Locked. Saints! Turning, she made her way back down the long hallway determined to find her way to the great hall.

She passed under a low arch, searching for the stairs that had gotten her onto this level. She reached another door and a passageway. Now, which way had she gone before? Left or right? Searching her memory, she realized she could not recall. Both directions seemed hauntingly familiar. She chose left and made her way down another flight of stairs and then another long, deserted hallway.

At the end, two more sets of huge locked doors blocked her path. Her wariness returned as she once again imagined eyes watching her.

Turning back, she made it back to the landing. Was it the same landing? Studying a cobweb, she tried to determine if it was the same one she'd seen before. Sighing, she realized there was no way to tell. She turned, determined to go up the stairs and regain her bearings. She had wondered around in circles so long she'd lost her sense of direction completely.

Mounting a steep set of worn stone steps, she heard footsteps and saw a flash of red above her.

"Ho!" She heard scrambling and rushed toward the noise. "Ho! I need help getting back to the great hall." Even old hermits should be willing to show her the way back down.

The scrambling stopped and there was dead silence.

"Lady Meiriona?" a soft voice called.

"Aye!"

A man, runty and bald, stepped from behind a platform. He doffed his hat and gave her a low, courtly bow. "M'lady!"

"William!" Relief flowed through her as she recognized the blacksmith from Whitestone. "What do you hither?"

He rose to his full height, barely inches taller than her. Wide and short, William was nearly shaped like one of the castle's building blocks. "I arrived days ago."

"Are you alone?"

"Aye. The kind Lady Montgomery's been hiding me, bringing me food."

"Lady Montgomery . . ."

William winked. "Pretty thing, ain't she? Why, if I were a younger man . . ."

Meiriona frowned, choosing not to respond to his comment about Lady Montgomery. "You have been here several days?"

"Aye, m'lady. I've come to rescue ye."

Irritation spun through Meiriona at the lady's trickery. She had not needed the hair comb to secure passage to Whitestone!

"M'lady, ye look troubled."

Meiriona sighed and turned her attention to William. "I have someone to get even with, but it will have to wait until better times."

William nodded. "Whatever business ye have 'ere must wait, m'lady. Your father is in danger."

"Aye, I know. Godric leaves tomorrow to siege Whitestone."

"Nay, m'lady. 'Tisn't Godric 'e is in danger from. His cough has returned. 'E lies abed, nigh to death. Ye must return immediately." William pressed his wool cap back onto his bald head.

"Oh, sweet Jesu."

"Can ye get past the guards, m'lady?"

"I . . ."

"Meiriona!" Godric's voice boomed out toward them.

She jumped.

"Meet me at the postern gate afore dawn," William whispered.

"Saints! I—"

William turned tail and huffed down the hall, not waiting for her to finish.

"Meiriona!" Godric boomed again.

She took a deep breath to still her rapid heartbeat. "Here, my lord!"

He rounded a corner and seized her upper arms. "What do you here, girl?"

"I was lost." She kissed him on the cheek, feeling a tingle of excitement from being in his arms. "Thank the saints you are here."

He held her at arm's length. "I swear, Meiriona, I shall chain you to my bed should you attempt escape. I have been patient, but time is short. I leave for Whitestone tomorrow to bargain with your father. I will have your word that you will not run while I am gone."

Meiriona blinked.

"Swear to me, Meiriona."

"Godric, my lord, I swear I will not attempt escape while you are away." Her heart jumped in her chest although she spoke the truth. She intended to leave tonight whilst he was still here.

He nodded, apparently satisfied with her oath. Guilt welled inside her. Would he hate her on the morrow when he awoke and she was gone?

He kissed her hotly, pushing her against the cool stone wall. She smiled, kissing him back with all the passion and desperation she felt. Somehow she would make him understand that it was her need to be with him that was driving her to escape and face her father. Somehow she would make her father understand that

Godric was the best choice for Whitestone. Somehow she would make Uncle Pierre understand she could not stay married to him. Somehow. Somehow. Somehow. She offered a silent prayer to God. She could not fail.

"Meiriona," Godric said, his voice husky. "I cannot be patient any longer."

She snaked her arm around his neck. "Then be patient no longer, my lord. For I want you as much as you want me."

Fire burned in his eyes. "Truly, Meiriona?"

"Truly, my lord. Truly."

He lifted her, cradling her in his arms, and she sighed in surrender. She would be his tonight with nothing between them.

Holding tightly to his neck, she allowed him to carry her to his chamber. He crossed the threshold, passion blazing in his eyes.

Out of the corner of her eye, she saw the opium's hiding place behind the dressing screen. Shifting her gaze, she determined she would only look at Godric tonight.

He laid her across the coverlet of the bed and sat beside her. Rolling her toward him, he pulled her hair from beneath her back and splayed it around her like a giant fan.

"Godric?"

"Aye?" His voice was husky.

"May I touch you?"

The fire in his eyes burned into an inferno. He smiled a soft, secretive smile at her. "Aye."

She reached for him, but he seized her hand inches away from his chest. She lifted an eyebrow, questioning him. Still holding her hand, he withdrew from the bed and stood before her. Dangerous, powerful, and gentle.

"What are you doing?"

His gaze locked on hers. Saints, he was beautiful!

Amusement gleamed in his eyes. "You want to touch me?"

Her fingers itched to explore his body. "Aye."

He took a step back and grasped the hem of his tunic. Slowly, measure by measure, he lifted his shirt. His skin looked like soft velvet stretched too tightly over steel. His crucifix of dark hair, slashed with white scars, added to his dangerous beauty. Her mouth went dry. Two scars ran across one of his shoulders and another ran down his arm.

Sitting on the edge of the bed, he removed his boots, the muscles of his torso rippling with contained power.

Liquid fire coursed through her veins.

His callused hands slid to the ties on his breeks. The leather molded the outline of a large, unmistakable bulge. Heat and curiosity pooled inside her. With deliberate slowness, he pulled one of the strings, peeled the leather down his legs, and stood before her wearing only his braies.

Godric felt heat soar though him as he watched Meiriona watch him. Not once in the two years since he returned from slavery had he felt proud or even grateful for the erotic lessons he had learned in the princess's clutches. Suddenly, he found himself glad for his knowledge and glad he'd waited so that Meiriona's anticipation ran high.

Her eyes dilated. He could see her passionate hunger, and he intended to fan her desire. Her fingers quivered, and he basked in the knowledge that she wanted to touch him. He turned toward a chest that was pushed against the tapestry.

"Where are you go—"

"Shh. Trust me," he whispered.

She relaxed against the pillows, her face awash with curiosity.

He paced to the chest, opened it, and stared at the contents: instruments of pleasure he had purchased while traveling. There were many sorts of textured objects: silk, velvet, soft rabbit fur, both smooth and rough scraps of leather. Things designed to enhance pleasure when rubbed on highly sensitized skin.

Toward the bottom of the chest were more exotic items: a set of Oriental love balls, ceramic beads on a knotted string, and two carved stones shaped like a man's member, one of jade, one of alabaster.

He had ne'er used the items in his trunk, and a thrill went through him as he realized why. In some part of his wits, even through the years of planning revenge, he must have clung to the hope that he would someday love a woman. For what other reason would he have even bought such items? It took trust to use such toys, and he had not swived the same woman twice since leaving slavery. Certainly their joys would be lost on a harlot.

Gathering some of the items in his arms, he turned toward the bed. Catching Meiriona's heated gaze, he walked toward her.

An image from the past floated into his mind: freshly bathed and oiled, with his chest hair removed, he strode naked toward the princess and her ladies. Nadira, ever spoiled, had been displeased with his prideful walk. At the flick of her hand, her eunuch guards prodded him with spears, forcing him to his knees to crawl toward her instead. Shame burned inside him, not because he had been forced to endure one more indignity, but because his young, overeager body had been so long without release that he had not cared. The princess and her ladies had taken great pleasure in his ability to suffer humiliations and still perform. He had learned to detach himself from the indignities of the moment but never from his underlying pride.

Reaching the bed, he held out his hand to Meiriona. She placed her palm in his, a simple gesture of trust. He smiled. Meiriona would never toy with him for her own selfish reasons.

Laying his instruments of pleasure on the coverlet, he sat beside her and pulled her into his arms. "I love you."

She kissed his cheek, eyes glazed with desire. "You do?"

"Aye."

She stiffened but did not echo his declaration. He had always been good at reading her, but her gaze this time was guarded.

In a swift movement, he pulled the clothing from her body and let it slide to the floor, determined to have nothing between them.

"Meiriona, you are exquisite."

She bit her lower lip and smiled shyly. "So are you."

Running his fingertip slowly down one of her arms, he watched a new wave of longing wash over her features.

Her gaze flicked to the pile of items where a long peacock feather rested on top. "What are those?"

"I will explore every tiny spot on your body and learn exactly how and where you like to be touched."

She gazed up at him in a way that made him grateful for every humiliating thing the princess had ever made him suffer.

Taking her hand, he placed it on the strings of his braies. "Have you ever seen a man's member?"

A fetching blush crept up her cheeks. "Nay."

"Undress me, Meiriona. Touch me as oft and as much as you desire so that we can learn each other's bodies."

Her breath quickened. Pride swelled in Godric's chest as he saw the heat in her eyes. He would never tire of how she looked at him. Her fingers flicked across his groin, tugging and pulling to unloosen the ties. His cock tightened, pulsing with every stroke of his heartbeat.

With hesitant fingers, she nudged aside the cloth, and his member sprang free. He sucked in a breath through clenched teeth. She would kill him.

"Did I hurt you?"

"Nay." Wrapping his fist around her hair, he tugged her close. Passion flamed in her eyes as he brought her lips down to his. His tongue explored her mouth, tasting her sweet, soft surrender.

He broke the kiss, took a deep, calming breath, and relaxed against the pillows, locking his hands behind his head with interlaced fingers to keep himself from ravishing her. Self-control was one of the many lessons he'd learned. Likely, he would need every ounce of it.

She pushed his braies down his hips and he lifted so she could remove them. A look of distress crossed her features as her gaze lingered on his cock. "It will not fit. We are too different in size."

Godric growled.

"My lord—" She shook her head. "I think we have made a mistake."

He grasped her upper arm and rolled her onto the bed beside him. "Meiriona . . .my love . . . I *will* fit inside you."

Her brow furrowed. "You are very large."

"I know ways to make the first time easier."

She shivered, her eyes unfocusing as if she were watching something inside her mind. "Will there be a lot of blood?"

He stroked her cheek with his thumb. "There will be some blood when I take your virginity, but it will not be like your mother's rape."

She gazed at him with such trust, he felt humbled. "I believe you."

With the pad of his finger, he traced a line from her shoulder to her hip, closely watching her reaction.

She sighed and closed her eyes.

"Which feels better, Meiriona?" He traced another line, this time using his fingernail. Gooseflesh popped up on her skin and she gasped. He chuckled.

Her eyelids fluttered open. "Are you laughing at me?"

Splaying his hand across her belly, he kissed her softly. "Assuredly not. You delight me. A man and woman *should* take pleasure in each other's responses."

"Oh." She glanced at the red mark his nail had caused, then her eyes closed and she relaxed, rolling onto her back and allowing him more access to her skin.

Oh, God. If this was her response to something so simple, how would she respond to the more exotic ways of pleasure? How would she respond blindfolded, with her skin more sensitized?

Picking a feather from his pile of erotic items, he flicked it down her body, then followed its path with a scrap of smooth silk and then rough leather.

"Ooh," she cried softly.

"Which is better?" he asked, first running a warm fuzzy rabbit skin across her breasts and then a flat metallic object.

"Aye." Her speech was slurred.

"Aye?"

"Aye, they are both better."

Not wanting to ruin her enjoyment of the sensations, he bit his tongue to keep from chuckling. Thank God he had waited to take her. If he had swived her the first night, they would have never been able to reach the level of trust needed to fully explore their body's sensations.

He laid his items of pleasure aside and fluttered his fingers down the column of her throat to the peaks of her breasts. He loved the way her body lifted, reaching for his hand. Her nipples puckered. Drawing lazy circles around the pink rosebuds at her breast's tips, he watched the pulse quicken in her neck.

He pinched one of her nipples, softly at first and then much harder.

She drew in a sharp breath. "Dear Mary."

He smiled. "What did you feel?"

Licking her lips, she gazed up at him, her eyes glassy with desire. "Lightning. A bolt of magic shot from my breasts to—" A blush stained her cheeks and she closed her mouth.

He traced his hand over her stomach, down to the junction betwixt her thighs. "Open your legs, Meiriona."

With a sigh, she obeyed, her eyes fluttering closed.

His cock throbbed as he slid one finger down the side of her queynt, then lifted the finger to his mouth and relished her taste on his tongue.

"Bend your knees, love. I want to spread your sex and look at you."

All at once, she clamped her legs together and sat up, her face flushed with a beguiling combination of passion and embarrassment. "Nay. 'Tis shameful."

Gathering her in his arms, he kissed her cheek, her ear, and her neck. She smelled like soft summer rain. "Meiriona, do not fear the private desires between a man and a woman," he whispered. "You are safe here. And I want to look at you."

She looked at him, a dazed expression in her eyes, then slowly lowered herself to the mattress and opened her legs.

Sliding his palms from the inside of her knees to her thighs, he opened her legs farther. Springy auburn hair curled between his fingers as he grazed her sex with his palm. Her outer nether lips were swollen, puffy with desire. Gently tugging them apart, he spread her queynt. Her dewy inner lips glistened with womanly moisture, and her folds reminded him of sweet pink rose petals. "You are beautiful, love."

She reached for him. "Godric . . . I feel so hot."

He growled, her gesture taxing the thread of his control. Shifting upward, his lips crashed upon hers, and he felt her woman's core, wet and inviting, open on the tip of his cock. He gripped the sheet on either side of her head, desperately holding himself back so he wouldn't hurt her or break the trust between them.

"You are trembling," she whispered.

"Aye. I want—"

"Please, my lord, now. I do not want to wait any longer. Show me more of your collection anon. Right now, I only want to belong to you."

With a cry, Godric drove into her.

She screamed in pain.

"Oh, God," he said, going perfectly still. "Forgive me, Meiriona."

A tear trailed from the corner of her eye to her ear. Softly, he kissed it away.

"I am so sorry. I should have been slower."

She wiggled her hips beneath him, a look of wonderment on her face. "I feel so . . . full."

"I know." He shifted slightly, then pushed back into her, feeling the muscles of her sex tighten around him. "Do you want me to withdraw?"

She lifted her hips, rocking them from side to side. "It doesn't hurt now . . . at least not much."

"'Tis only the first time that there is pain."

Her finger traced the sickle-shaped scar beneath his eye, and he saw something deeper than passion burning in her eyes. He withdrew a little, then pushed himself back inside her.

"Mmm," she said, closing her eyes.

Moving his hips in slow, tight circles, he felt her relax beneath him and knew her pain had subsided. His hands moved to caress her breasts and thumb the puckered skin of her nipples. In long, unhurried strokes he rekindled the flame of passion, enjoying her every sigh and moan. His fingers trembled against the bed.

After a time, she gasped and her queynt contracted around him in a series of short ripples. "Oh, oh, Godric!"

Satisfaction coursed through him at both her orgasm and her cry. He wrapped his arms tightly around her.

She made a little mewing sound, then wound her legs around his waist. "Possess me, Godric. Hard. I want to be yours."

Godric grasped the sheet so hard, a section of it ripped. He drove into her, losing the last thread of his control. God, she was soft and feminine. Their bodies molded together. He'd wanted her for years, and now she was his.

For long moments, time was suspended as their bodies became one. With long, slow strokes he moved in and out of her. She stroked his back, amazed at the sensations he created in her.

At last, he groaned his own release and collapsed atop her. "Meiriona, my love." Lifting himself onto his elbows, he kissed her possessively. "You are mine."

Meiriona smiled up at Godric, her heart soaring. "Aye, Godric. I am." Saints, how she loved him, her beautiful, dangerous captor. Wrapped in his embrace, she clung to him for long, silent moments.

After some time, he moved from atop her. She whimpered at the loss. What she would give to forever belong to him!

Her fingers traced a scar running down his chin and steel determination shot through her nerves.

Whitestone *would* belong to him. She *would* correct the mistakes of her past. Her father *would* see reason. She *would* prevent war.

"Are you sore, love? You have an odd expression."

She shook her head. "Nay, my lord." Glancing down, she saw blood staining her thighs. She grasped his shoulders, willing him to understand the desperation that was driving her to do what she must do. "I love you."

He smiled, a satisfied expression on his face, and leaned contently against the pillows.

She sat and swung her legs from the bed, hating herself for what she must do next.

His hand snatched her wrist. "Where do you go?"

"To clean myself." She feared for a second he had read her mind, but he released her arm.

Slipping behind the dressing screen, she poured water into a copper dish and cleansed her thighs with a rag. Her heart quickened as she fished the opium pouch from its hiding place and poured mead into two goblets. Her fingers trembled as she dumped the drug into the spiced drink. *Please, God, let Godric understand when he awakens.*

Slowly, she emerged from behind the screen and crossed the Oriental carpet.

He reminded her of a reclining leopard: beautiful and deadly. She gripped the goblet tightly to bolster her resolve.

Reaching the bedside, she gave him what she hoped was a coy smile. "Drink, my lord. Surely such rutting saps a man's strength."

He laughed. "Such saucy language from one who is suddenly not a virgin."

She touched his cheek, her heart breaking that she had to leave him so very soon. Her fingers grazed his crescent scar.

"To our future together," she said and downed her goblet.

He followed suit, gulping his wine in one long swig.

Guilt threatened to overwhelm her, but it was too late to turn from her path now. She watched him warily, wondering how long it would be before the opium took effect. He seemed to suffer no ill effects.

Setting her goblet aside, she kissed a scar in his eyebrow, wishing she could spend the night with him. "My lord," she said, "I fear you will hate me on the morrow."

He gathered her into his arms, kissing her. "I could ne'er hate you."

She turned and took the wine flagon, praying he did not notice how her finger shook. "More mead, my lord?"

He reached toward her, his hand unsteady, the expression on his face changed from seductive lover to disbelief. "Meiriona! Christ, girl, what have you done? What is wrong with me?"

She kissed him softly. "I love you, Godric." He tried to grab her with drug-heavy arms, and she slipped free.

"I will beat you, Countess," he growled, the words coming out slow and heavy, then he sank to the bed in a drugged slumber.

CHAPTER 30

Bang! Bang! Bang!

Sunlight streamed through the window, smashing pain into Godric's eye sockets. When he sat up, his stomach gave a heave, and he lunged for the chamber pot.

Bang! Bang! Bang!

"Saint Peter's toes," he growled, mopping cold sweat from his forehead and wiping his mouth. What the bloody hell was all that banging about?

Bang! Bang! Bang!

"Cease!" he roared, realizing that a heavy fist was pounding on the chamber's door. Stumbling from the bed, he lunged to the entrance and yanked open the door.

Eric stood outside with panicky eyes, breathing hard. "She is gone, master! Gone!"

Pain pierced Godric's skull at the lad's shout, and he hoisted the young man up by the tunic. "What do you mean, gone?"

Swallowing, Eric grasped Godric's shoulders. "She left with the man pretending to be a merchant. We 'ave been banging on your door since sunrise, sir."

"She who? Breathe! You are not making sense."

"Meiriona, master. Meiriona is gone."

Agony stronger than his pounding head snaked its way into Godric's stomach. "Nay!" He turned to the bed. Red virgin blood stained the sheets and the scent of sex permeated the room. "It cannot be."

But his heart felt numb. How could she do this? Had their lovemaking been nothing but a ruse? She'd used him, used his lust to trick him into believing he could trust her. Lusty evil wench. Had he not learned anything in his life about women?

"'Tis true, master," Eric said, but Godric barely heard him.

What had she said? "I love you." How had he forgotten that women did not love? Women took. Love was not something women could understand or feel.

Numbness gathered in his chest as he felt his foolish hopes of a peaceful home and a loving wife shatter. What a simpleton he had been. Waiting, playing the part of an onion-eyed coxcomb when she had been stringing him along, waiting for the perfect moment to betray him.

"Master?" Eric's voice cut through his thoughts, and he realized he still had his hand wrapped around the boy's tunic. He thrust the lad away, feeling the numbness slide away as fury poured though him.

"Do not call me master! I am a fool!" Godric whirled, bellowing as he picked up the nearest marble table and hurled it across the floor. Goblets shattered and the white marble made a sickening snap as it broke into two pieces.

Eric shrank back, stumbling into the hallway beyond the solar. "I'll ready the horses, sir."

Rage boiled, but Godric caught himself before he picked up the table's twin. Destroying his solar would accomplish naught. Ripping the stained bedsheet from the mattress, he turned very slowly to Eric. "Thank you, Eric. Tell Bear we ride immediately," he said, flinging the bloodstained linen at the squire. "Use this as our standard."

Eric nodded and clattered down the stairs, clutching the sheet.

"I shall beat her," Godric muttered to himself. He flexed and unflexed his hands, feeling more in control of the burning fury rippling through him. "Nay, I will collar her and chain her to the bed."

With her back at Whitestone, all hope of negotiation was gone. There was no option but to storm the castle by force. He donned his leather breeks with intentional slowness, forcing himself to move deliberately and not give in to the raging storm boiling inside. As he buckled on his sword, his hands itched for the coming battle. He glared at the bed where she had tricked him and felt another wave of fury crash upon him. He pulled on his boots, fighting the urge to slash the mattress to ribbons with his sword.

He exited the room, making his way toward the stables. As he crossed the threshold of the keep's door, his stepmother snarled at him. "She hates you, you know. She told me that herself."

He gave her a curt nod.

"She wanted naught you had to give her." She hurled a green target at him.

It bounced off his chain mail and landed in the rushes: the hair comb he'd given Meiriona. Pain ripped across his heart, deeper than any flesh wound he had ever gotten.

Crushing the emerald bauble under his boot, he stalked into the courtyard.

He had given her opportunity for a gentle surrender, but now he burned to conquer by force.

The king had demanded him to take Whitestone. And, by God's teeth, he would do it. He would root out every traitorous Lancastrian rebel and haul them to London. There would be no quarter, no second chances for Meiriona or her father or her husband.

He would burn a trail straight to the heart of her castle.

CHAPTER 31

Cold rain spattered Meiriona's cheeks as she raced her mare across Whitestone's drawbridge, relief pouring through her. Thank the heavens she would soon be out of her sodden clothing and she could at last be able to reason with her father about the castle's future.

A bell tolled from the tower. "The mistress is home! The mistress is home!"

William gave a toothy grin, shook water from his hat, and slowed his mount. "Home, m'lady, thank the stars. We would have never made it if you had not overcome your fear of horses."

Meiriona blinked against the raindrops, guilt tamping down her excitement at being home. The escape had been easy because no one had suspected when she made her way across the bailey to the postern gate where William had waited with the horses. That she'd won the trust of Godric and his people intensified her gnawing guilt. Godric had taught her to ride, and she'd used the knowledge to betray him.

The past nights had been cold without his warm arms around her. Saints, she even missed him entwining his fingers into her hair! Truly she must love him for such a dominating gesture to have become one of reassurance.

Dismounting, she glanced at the gray sky. Where

was Godric now? Would she have time to convince her father that he must peacefully surrender Whitestone before Godric arrived? She handed the reins to William. "I must speak with my father and Pierre at once. With luck, the rain has rutted the road so Godric's war engines cannot pass."

"Ho! Mistress! Praise be to God!" Dozens of children, heedless of the mud and rain, poured into the bailey.

"Meiriona!"

"Meweeona!"

"Meiriona!"

They ran to her, hugging her and twisting their hands into her sodden skirt. "Ooh," she said, coming off balance with their overeager greeting. Slipping in the mud, the children pulled her to the ground by the weight of their tiny hands. She laughed. "I will get you for that." Gathering a fistful of mud, she threw it at one of her oppressors.

"Can't catch me!"

"Chase me!"

Meiriona pushed her hands into the muck and rose to her knees. The children danced around her like a flock of rowdy ducks splashing in puddles. Laughing, she snagged the nearest one by the leg, and the squealing boy landed in the mud beside her. "You are on my side now," she announced.

Shrieks of giggling erupted as two more children slid into the mire, one landing atop her, covering the remaining clean spots of her dress.

"Meiriona!" a man's voice bellowed out. Abruptly the laughter stopped and the children scrambled from the sludge and fled across the bailey with a slosh, slosh, slosh. Meiriona pushed her mud-caked hair from her eyes.

Uncle Pierre, tall and dignified, leaned heavily on his cane, staring at her with disapproving eyes. "So my *wife* has finally tired of being the bastard's whore." He sneered at her. "Your clothes are as soiled as your virtue."

Meiriona froze, feeling like a seven-year-old who had accidentally set fire to the horse barn.

Pierre tapped his foot, just as he'd done many times while teaching her to play chess. "Have you naught to say?"

Meiriona swallowed. She had come here to explain matters like a woman, but she felt like a naughty child. An image of Godric flashed in her mind, and she latched onto it for courage. Taking a deep breath, she rose. "I cannot be married to you." There. She had said it.

Pierre cleared his throat. "I *am* married to you." He rapped his cane on the ground impatiently. "Come with me now, *wife.*"

Slowly, with all the dignity Meiriona could muster, she squared her shoulders. "*Uncle* Pierre," she said firmly, "we must annul our marriage. 'Tis wrong."

Pierre's spine stiffened, and his fingers whitened upon his wooden cane. "Whilst you have been playing the whore, your father is dying," he said, ignoring her request just as he had done when, as a child, she had wanted something he was not prepared to give. His voice was clipped and overly polite.

"Truly, uncle, we cannot remain married."

"Silence, *wife*, or I shall send you to your room without supper!" His mouth curled down in displeasure, making his mustache droop. He turned, shuffling back toward the keep, and she imagined he expected her to follow him.

Meiriona looked around for support. Several of the castlefolk watched their exchange from behind trees and barrels, but none interfered. One peasant shrugged his shoulders.

What had she expected?

She turned her face upward and let the rain rinse mud from her cheeks.

Pierre stopped and rapped his cane upon the ground. "Child . . ." His voice trailed off, and he softened all at once. "While we stand hither fighting, your father needs you."

Meiriona stared at Pierre, and she saw him as she had when she was a little girl. He had been tall, dignified, with a sort of timeless grace about him. He had awed her with his knowledge of foreign languages and chess and art. But she saw something else now: she saw his love for her father.

"Come with me."

She nodded, her heart sinking, and followed him into the keep.

Dark curtains had been drawn over the deathbed and the room smelled of decay and the flowery stench of death, as if her father had already died. He lay in the middle of the bed, several quilts piled atop him, looking pale, feeble and ghostlike. Her chest felt hollow every time he coughed.

"Papa?" She clung to her father's hand. Although the room was stuffy and warm, his fingers were cold. They felt fragile, as if the palm was made merely of loose flesh, stretched to hold the bones together. A candle flickered beside his bed.

His eyelids fluttered open. "My child . . . You came back." His voice was thin, and he labored to talk.

"Papa, I have so much to tell you." How could she begin to tell him about Godric? *Should* she?

"Meiriona . . ." He coughed and she pressed a damp cloth to his forehead. "There is no time."

"Papa, do not say such things."

He squeezed her hand weakly. "Shh, child." He

sank back into the mattress and closed his eyes, still wheezing.

"Papa?" She barely resisted the urge to shake him awake. "You will *not* die."

His thin eyelids fluttered open. "Bah! Denying death does not make it any less powerful." His breath was labored, and he spat phlegm into a bucket.

She blinked away tears, a feeling of helplessness settling on her. She needed him to convince Uncle Pierre of the need to annul their marriage, she needed him to be the papa he'd once been. She needed a thousand things she could not ask for.

With great effort her father hoisted himself up and began, slowly, to wiggle the signet ring from his finger.

"Nay, Papa. This will pass, as it has afore."

"I am dying, daughter," he declared. "Be strong."

"I will not let you die." She rose and yanked open the dark curtains, letting outside light into the dismal solar. "I did not let you die when you came home from London, and I will not let you die now!"

Her father chuckled at her passionate speech, as if her declaration amused him. Then his laughter turned to spasms of hacking and he spat out more phlegm. She crept over and sat beside him, very still, unwilling resignation washing over her. There was naught she could do to halt his death.

"Daughter," he said when the coughing was once more under control. "Give me your hand."

His hand felt cold and dry when she placed hers in it. Weakly, he patted her hand, then dropped his signet ring into it. "You have been a better daughter to me than many sons . . . but you are not a son. This ring gives you ownership, but a woman cannot guard a castle herself. Pierre will take care of you for now, but he is an old man." He wheezed spasmodically. "Meiriona, you must give this ring to a man who is strong and able."

She held her emotions tightly. She wanted so much to tell him about Godric and all that had passed between them, but she found that she could not.

He hacked again, this time harder, and his breathing sounded wet and bubbly. "Seek wise acquaintances, and stay away from the Yorks."

All at once, as if the speech had drained him, he sank to the bed, his body limp.

"Papa? Papa? Oh, saints. Papa!" She shook his shoulders, and his body rocked lifelessly from side to side. Her chest ached as if someone had jabbed her in the heart with a dagger.

Slowly, Meiriona sank to her knees. *Our Father which art in heaven,* she prayed, *hallowed be Thy name.* Tears welled in her eyes, and she choked back the rest of the ritualistic Lord's Prayer. *Oh, God,* she started again, *I am in a terrible fix that I don't know how to get out of. I've been an adulteress, Papa is dead, Uncle Pierre wants to be married to me, and the man I love will burn my castle down if I don't figure out a way to stop him. Can you help me, God, Jesus? I don't know what to do.*

Meiriona rose, unsure if God listened to women who refused their wedding beds and cuckolded their husbands. Mayhap God threw her away, just as Godric had claimed had happened to him. Her father's dying words were for her to stay away from the Yorks, but she wanted nothing more than to annul her marriage and give her castle to Godric. Guilt threatened to close her throat. Her mother had been a great Christian woman: submissive, gentle and biddable. Why could she not have any of her mother's traits?

Somehow, some way, she must convince Pierre to give up their marriage before Godric came.

There was a scrape in the hallway and the door swung open. Pierre.

"Uncle Pierre—" she started, sounding stronger than she felt. "My father is . . ."

"What have you done to him, mademoiselle?" He hobbled across the planks to her father's bedside. "Mon Dieu, you have killed him!" The words choked her as he glared at her, accusation written across his features.

She stepped back, fearing for a moment he would strike her with his stick.

"Mon Dieu, mon Dieu, I knew he was dying, but it should not have come so quickly! What did you say? Did you tell him about your lover and how you fouled our vows?" Pierre threw himself across the body of her father. "Oh, Ioworth, oh, Ioworth. My friend, my friend."

She watched Pierre with morbid fascination as he hugged and shook her father's lifeless form.

"Uncle—" Never had he been anything less than proper and dignified, and it pained her to see him distraught.

"You killed him! You killed him!" he wailed. Then his laments turned to curses.

Abruptly the door swung open and a messenger, huffing and red faced, raced into the room. "Mistress! An army is coming. They carry the banner of the king, a banner with a dragon and something that looks like a bloodstained sheet."

Oh, dear sweet Mary. Godric! She nodded, feeling numb.

The messenger looked from her father's lifeless body to her lamenting husband to her.

Pierre's sobbing increased and, at once, Meiriona felt the iron grip of duty seize her, clearing away her emotions and allowing her to function mechanically.

"Close the gate and bar the doors. Have the men prepare for siege. I will send a message to parley with Godric."

The messenger nodded. "What should I tell the people about your father?"

"Tell them . . ." Meiriona weighed her words. Telling the men of her father's passing would cause discord in a time when they needed a steady hand. Facing the Dragon would be difficult enough without men breaking rank and disobeying her orders.

"Send Mattie. I can trust her to care for my father's body and keep this matter secret until I have a chance to address the men properly. I will go and prepare to lead the defense and plan my words for when Godric arrives."

"Aye, mistress."

With a loud sob, Pierre lunged from the bedside, moving faster than she would have thought possible. "Unfeeling whore! Your father is dead and you flick him off your hands without so much as a tear so you can meet your lover!" He latched her wrist in a surprisingly strong grip. "You will not get away with this!"

He turned to the messenger. "Tell the men, Ioworth is dead. Send for a priest to bless my friend's flight to heaven."

Meiriona felt blood drain from her face. Likely the whole castle could hear him shouting. It would not be long ere the people were scrambling like panicked cats and chaos would reign.

"Nay! Listen to me, uncle, 'tis unwise."

The messenger backed away, confusion erupting on his face.

"Do it, boy! I am lord here now!"

"Nay!" she shouted. "Nay!" Curious onlookers stole glances into the room and, with a sinking heart, she knew it was too late.

A gray-haired woman with a tight-lipped expression rushed into the room and scurried to the bedside. "The lord is dead," she declared, looking down on Meiriona's father's body. "Send for a priest." She flicked her gaze suspiciously over Meiriona and crossed herself.

Meiriona blew out an exasperated breath. Controlling the men would be much harder now. Likely as not, any mercenaries in the ranks would be climbing the walls to join the army of Edward's mighty Dragon. If that occurred, her chances of a peaceful settlement with Godric was lost.

"'Twas foolish, Uncle." Turning to the messenger, she gripped a nearby chair for courage. She would use everything her father had taught her about defense and everything Godric had taught her about being a woman to bring down the Dragon. "Shore up the defenses. Tell the kitchen crew to start heating oil and the bowmen to prepare themselves. Our time is short. Raise a white banner. We will sue for peace and pray for the best."

"Mon Dieu!" Pierre shouted. "You are a traitor to your own people! Sue for peace, indeed. We all know where your true loyalties lie."

Anger bolted to the surface. "Listen, Uncle! You have no idea what befalls us. Godric will not stop until the entire castle is in ruins if you do not—"

Pierre latched onto her upper arm. "Lock this traitorous harlot in her room!"

"Nay!" Panic began to rise within her. "You old fool! He has king's orders! It is time to bend to the king's will."

"Bend to the king's will? Ha! 'Tis more likely you want to bend over the bastard's bed!"

"How dare you!" Stabbing pain burst in her chest. "I came home out of concern for my people, for you and my father!"

He sneered at her. "A whore with a heart. How novel." He thrust her at the messenger. "Lock her away, then bring me a goblet of wine so that we may contemplate the castle's defenses."

Meiriona lunged away, bolted past the messenger, and fled.

"Catch her!" she heard Pierre shout. "I am lord here, now. Catch her, you knaves!"

Heavy footsteps echoed behind her and Meiriona was pulled up short by several pairs of burly hands.

"Nay!" She twisted to get free, but the hands dragged her down the hall, toward her solar.

CHAPTER 32

The acrid odor of burning wood hung in the air. Panic worked its way into Meiriona's throat as she watched a pillar of smoke rise from Whitestone Village and knew Godric was coming.

She longed to go to him, soothe the angry Dragon, but she was locked in her chamber.

The last two days had been a tapestry of frantic worry. Back and forth she paced from her courtyard window to the valley window and back again. She'd yelled until she was hoarse and had beat on the door until her hands bled, but no one came to rescue her.

Of the mixed voices in the courtyard, one hysterical warning was repeated o'er and o'er: "An army is coming! An army is coming!"

Guilt and a heavy feeling of helplessness weighed her down. If only she had handled Pierre better. If only she had secured a blessing from her father. If only she had not left Godric. If only she were not locked in her chamber.

She beat her hands on the door. "Let me out!"

All the if only's in the world did not change the present.

She heard men shouting, securing passageways, and preparing for battle. Godric carved a fiery path straight to her castle. Scads of peasants made their way into the safety of the castle walls, running from the Dragon.

Hurrying back to the window overlooking the valley, she watched the plume of smoke with rising desperation. Godric had not set out to merely conquer Whitestone—he was making a point. He wasn't just coming for her land. He was coming for *her.* Saints, he had not understood at all. She had left so war could be avoided, so they could live together peacefully. She had known he would be angry, but she'd intended to send word to him posthaste and soothe his male pride. Being locked in her chamber had thwarted all her plans. What had he thought when he awakened to find himself drugged and her gone? Did he hate her?

She hurried to the courtyard window. "Somebody listen! I must speak with him! Let me out!"

Saints! Men shouting orders and instructions ran hither and yon across the grounds, intent on preparing for the forthcoming siege. *Please, God, send someone to release me.*

Crossing the chamber again, she watched the smoke wax thicker. No doubt Godric would arrive before nightfall.

And then what?

She shook her fist at the smoke. "You madman, I left because I love you! Do you hear me, Godric? All men can think is war, war, war. Why do you ne'er tire of it and try other tactics?"

Her anger spent, she slowly sank to the floor and hugged her knees. Oh, saints, what a mess she'd made of everything. If the rising smoke was any indication, Godric hated her and her home was doomed.

"Meweeona?" A tiny voice came from the other side of the door.

Meiriona choked back tears and ventured to the chamber entrance. "Yea?"

"Meweeona! I founded you!"

Meiriona's heart lurched. It was Cook's three-year-old son. "Justin!"

"Mama says bad men are coming and I'm scawed. Mama says I can't be in the kitchen 'cause they're cooking hot oil for the bad men. If they are bad men, why is Mama cooking for them?"

"Justin, love, I will explain about the oil anon." She felt a ray of hope. "Is there a key hanging on the wall?"

There was a long pause, and Meiriona pressed her ear to the door.

"Can you pway with me, Meweeona? Mama says I gotta stay out of the way."

"Aye, love, I will play with you, but first I have to get out of this room. Can you look on the wall for a key?"

"I don't see one."

Her heart sank. "Nowhere? Can you look some more, love?"

"Why don't you come out of your room and pway with me?"

A hysterical giggle welled in Meiriona's throat. She felt like laughing and crying at the same time. How could she possibly explain to the child that her husband had locked her up and the man she loved was coming to burn her home down?

"Justin, I am locked in. If you find a key, I can come out and play with you. So look all over the walls."

There was a long pause, and she imagined the toddler scanning the stone walls. "Here, Meweeona!" A shadow blocked the light coming from under the door, and a scraping sound issued across the planks. Pudgy little fingers pushed the object into view. A rock. "Pretend this is a key."

"Argh!" she exclaimed, expressing her pent-up frustration. "Oh, Justin!"

His fingers disappeared from view. "Are you mad with me?"

"Nay, love." She gritted her teeth, but her voice was calm again. "But I need a *real* key. Look on the wall."

"Meweeona?" he said in a singsong voice.

"Yea."

"You didn't say please."

"Oh, saints, Justin. *Please* look for the bloody key. I need to get out of here to stop the bad men."

"Mama says 'bloody' is a bad word."

Meiriona bit her tongue to keep from screaming. The last thing she needed was a manners lesson from a three-year-old. "And your mother is correct. I am sorry. Please help me."

She heard him scrambling around.

"I don't see one on the wall."

Tears of frustration stung her eyes.

"There's one in the lock, though."

"Oh, thank the holy virgin," she breathed.

"I can't reach it."

"Can you get a stool?"

"Meweeona, I gots to potty." Footsteps scrambled down the hall.

"Justin! Do not leave!"

"I can't wait! I can't wait!" His words were rushed, desperate. "I gots to go bad, bad, bad, bad, *bad*."

"Justin! Come back!"

Silence. She sank again to the floor in despair. Nothing to do but sit and pray the toddler would return.

The key was in the lock. Of all the vexing things. *Think, Meiriona, think. How does one remove a key from the other side?*

Meiriona nearly cried in relief when she heard the toddler scurry back to other side of the door.

"Meweeona! I broughted a stool."

Leaping to her feet, she pushed her ear against the

door, desperate to hear everything. "Oh, Justin! Thank the saints!"

She heard scraping against the stone, and her heart beat wildly.

"I gots it, Meweeona! Now you can pway with me."

With a gusty bang, the door sprang open and relief flooded her veins. Scooping up the toddler, Meiriona ran for her father's solar.

"I thought you were going to pway with me, Meweeona."

She rounded the corner, praying no one would see them. "Shh, love. We are going to play hide," she said, making up a tale as fast as she could. "We shall pretend I am still in my chamber and see how long it takes people to find us. I know a great place to hide."

She mounted the steps to her father's chamber, new hope blossoming inside her. If she could make it to her father's solar, she could take the secret passageway that led outside the castle walls. *Please, oh please, oh please.*

"Meweeona?"

"Shh, Justin. Whisper or they shall win."

"All right!" the toddler whispered very loudly. "I'll be vewy quiet."

Meiriona debated on whether or not to clamp her hand over his mouth. She'd send him off to his mother, but she knew the instant she sat him down, he would be screaming at the top of his lungs and alerting the entire castle of her disappearance.

Peering cautiously around a bend in the hallway, she was relieved when no one was in sight. Suddenly, hearing Uncle Pierre's voice, she jumped back.

Hope died.

"Oh, my Ioworth, my Ioworth, how could you leave me," he was saying, his words interwoven with sobs.

Tendrils of pity wound around Meiriona's heart. Footsteps sounded, and then a knight approached from the opposite end of the hallway. Meiriona shrank farther into the shadows, squeezing Justin in warning. The toddler's eyes rounded.

"My lord," the knight said, speaking to Pierre from the doorway. "You are needed at the gates."

"No!" Pierre cried. "No."

Meiriona motioned Justin to silence, praying the toddler would remain quiet.

"My lord?" the knight's voice sounded distinctly uneasy.

Pierre sniffed and spoke, but she could not make out his words.

Please, please, let them leave.

Shuffling ensued and more than two sets of footsteps pounded down the hall.

A miracle. An answer to a prayer. After counting to twenty, she lunged the final distance to her father's chamber, dashed inside, and closed the door quietly.

The room reeked of death.

"It stinks in here, Meweeona."

Gagging, she clamped her fingers over her nose, realizing that her father's body had not been removed from the room. How dare they leave him here! Why had Pierre not removed him?

Agony and fury took hold deep inside her. "I will set it all in order, Father. I promise."

The toddler stared at her father's lifeless form. "Is he . . . Is he dead, Meweeona?" he said, showing neither revulsion nor concern, but simple curiosity. Somehow the toddler's calm acceptance of death as a natural part of life made the horror of the situation more tolerable.

"Aye, love. He's dead." It hurt to say the words, but it was healing too. "And we must keep struggling because we are still alive."

Hurrying to a vanity chest, Meiriona tugged its edge until it pulled from the wall with a screech.

"Help me, Justin. I know where to hide. Here, squeeze behind here."

Pushing a heavy tapestry out of the way, she inched open a rusty hidden door. It groaned; likely the only person who had ever used it in recent years was Damien. Sweat broke out on her forehead. What if someone heard? She stopped and strained her ear toward the door.

"Meweeona, dead peoples can't hear. He won't tell anybody where we've gone."

A bubble of hysteria welled inside her. "Oh, Justin," she said, hugging him. "Thank the saints you are here with me."

The little boy beamed proudly at the praise, turning admiring cowlike eyes upon her.

"Swiftly, Justin," she admonished, pointing into the passageway. Grabbing a candle from the vanity, she thrust the boy into the dark hallway and followed after him, closing the rusty door with another squeal from the hinges.

The hall spanned, long and dank, before them. The lone candle illuminated only a thin circle of the path. A cobweb brushed her face. She tore it aside, but the sticky web clung to her fingers.

"I'm scawed of the dark, Meweeona."

"Be brave, love. Pretend you are a knight."

He didn't answer but wound his fist into her skirt.

For what seemed like an eternity, they walked. What would she tell Godric? Would she even be allowed to speak to him? What if she wasn't able to make her way to his camp?

Pushing her fear aside, she quickened her pace.

At last, they saw a sliver of light shining in the distance. Relief poured through her. She was almost there.

Blowing out a breath, she blinked in the sunlight when they reached the end of the stone passage.

Canvas tents propped around and the tops of several trebuchets poked through the nearby trees.

Picking up Justin, she raced toward the camp.

For a moment she wondered if she was befuddled for going to the Dragon like a slaughter lamb. Her stomach knotted with a mixture of anticipation and dread. What would she say to him?

Suddenly, from behind a rock, a giant form with wild red hair leaped at them. She started, clutching Justin tightly to keep from dropping him.

"Bear!"

"Milady." His voice was cold. He seized her wrist in his meaty hand. "Damien told us about the passageway. Godric said you might try to use it to run again."

She blinked several times, not understanding. "What do you mean?"

"I mean that you are to come with me. No more running." He tugged her forward harshly.

At once, her ire was riled. "Unhand me, you fool! I was running to Godric, not away from him!"

Justin squirmed in her arms. His face contorted, then he started to wail.

"Oh, Justin!" She clutched him tighter and gave Bear a scornful see-what-you-have-done glare.

"The bad men caughted us! Mama told me to stay in the keep!" he wailed in huge, loud cries.

"Hush, baby. Bear's not a bad man."

"But he only gots one arm!"

"Shh, love."

"Come along, lady." Bear released her wrist but pointed her forward toward the camp. "If ye were going there anyway, ye won't mind if I escort ye," he said in a tone that indicated he had not believed a word she had spoken.

* * *

The camp was located on the slope outside the front gates of Whitestone. Men milled about campfires, laughing, boasting, and slapping each other on the back. The steady snick, snick, snick of swords being sharpened bit into the chill air.

Justin clung to her neck, refusing to allow her to put him down even when her back and arms ached. A flock of butterflies bounced in her stomach. Would Godric believe, as Bear did, that she was trying to escape again?

She saw him across the grounds, his presence calling to her as it always had. He sat on a log near a campfire, intent on sharpening his sword, which lay across his knees.

He looked beautiful, calm and deadly. Her knees went weak and she fought the urge to turn and flee.

Saints, she would have paid a king's ransom to know his thoughts. Did he hate her? Did he miss her? Or, worst of all, did he not care at all?

"Ho, Master!" Bear shouted. "Look what I found in the castle's escape route."

Her stomach lurched when Godric's gaze snapped toward them. Anger flashed in his blue eyes before his features settled into a mask of indifference.

Slowly, with the stealth of a stalking leopard, he rose to his feet. "Countess."

"My lord." She set Justin on his feet. The little boy clung to her skirt.

Fury lurked beneath Godric's guarded composure. Like a striking cobra, he snatched her upper arm in a painful grip and hauled her close to him. "Do not call me that."

She swallowed. Justin let out a mournful cry as if it were him, and not her, that Godric was angry with.

"You silly fool," he said. "Did you think you could run? Do you think there is any place I cannot find you?" His voice was ice cold.

"I was not running from you."

"Cease, Meiriona! What sort of half-wit do you think I am?" Furiously, he thrust her toward Bear. "Take her to my tent. I cannot bear to look at her right now."

Tears stung her eyes. She blinked rapidly, refusing to let them spill down her cheeks. "Nay, Godric. Nay! You do not understand." She hurled herself at him, determined to make him see reason. "You cannot do this." Her dress caught on the heel of her shoe and she fell to her knees.

Bear sidled up behind her. Putting his huge paw beneath one of her arms, he dragged her to her feet. "Come on, lady. I'll show ye to yer quarters."

Godric turned aside, his back cold and unfeeling.

Pain, like a sharp knife, bit into her. How could he be so dispassionate after a night like they had shared?

"Wait! Nay! I brought you something."

Godric stared at Justin, who had wrapped himself in her skirt. "I do not need any more children." He bared his teeth and growled at the toddler.

Justin screamed. "Meweeona! Oh, Meweeona! Mama told me to stay in the castle!"

"Cease," she admonished Godric. "You are not helping." Turning to Justin, she picked him up. "He will not harm you. 'Tis me he's angry at."

The child clung tightly to Meiriona's neck.

"Please, Godric. 'Tis me you want. Let the child go back to his mother."

Godric's gaze flickered from Justin to her. "Nay." He turned to Bear. "Take the boy to Eleanor, the cook."

Justin squealed, nearly choking Meiriona. "Nay! Nay! They're goings to eated me!"

"Hush, love. He will not eat you." She sent a scathing look at Godric's back. "Just go with Bear. He will take care of you, and Eleanor is nice too. Mayhap she'll have a sweetmeat to give you."

At that moment, Amelina rushed from one of the tents. "Meiriona!"

Meiriona whirled and was pushed sideways as the little girl flung herself at her and wrapped her arms around her legs. "Wherefore are you here?" Meiriona asked, bewildered that Godric had brought his little girl to a battlefield.

"Papa ne'er leaves me behind," Amelina explained.

"Back to your tent," Godric roared, pointing at his daughter.

"Papa's been cranky," Amelina said in a loud whisper. She hugged Meiriona again. "Did you bring me a friend to play with?"

Watching Amelina, Justin shushed, but huge tears spilled down his cheeks. "Justin, this is Amelina. She will show you where to get a treat."

Justin blinked, but did not cry when Meiriona set him down.

Amelina snatched his hand. "Wanna play?"

"All right," Justin said, his eyes glowing now that he had a friend to play with. He allowed her to draw him away.

Bear herded the children toward what Meiriona supposed was the cooking tent. "Eleanor will return you to your mother shortly," Bear promised.

Thank the saints Justin was no longer wailing. "Think of it as a great big adventure," Meiriona called after them, wishing she could think of it that way as well.

Her heart lurched abruptly as Godric gripped her wrist, towing her toward a large canvas tent near the middle of the camp. She felt his men watching them, and she steeled herself against Godric's rage. She *would* make him understand.

Yanking her inside his tent, he thrust her upon his sleeping pallet. She landed with a soft grunt. Scrambling to a kneeling position, she faced the Dragon. "Please, Godric!"

He dug into a bag, retrieved a length of rope and stood before her. "Give me your wrists."

"'Tis unnecessary, sir."

He growled and grabbed her arm. "I am in no mood for argument." Winding the rope around her wrists, he knotted it tightly, then pulled her hands above her head and anchored the rope on a heavy trunk sitting near the pallet.

"Godric, hear me out," she pleaded.

"What did you bring me?" he snarled. His hair was wild, uncombed, its dark ends curled about his shoulders. He stood in front of her, hands on hips, looking like Satan himself about to welcome another sinner into hell. "I hope it is something more than your body. I have already sampled that and have no taste for poison."

Her heart caved in as if he had just kicked her. She searched his enigmatic features, trying to detect any softness. Finding none, she turned her gaze aside and stared at the heaps of pillows lying haphazardly around the tent.

"Spit it out, Countess. My patience is gone."

"Godric, you are frightening me."

"Good."

Her heart lurched. Where was the man who had told her he loved her?

"'Tis actually something you own already," she rushed out ere she lost her courage.

A flicker of curiosity crossed his features. "What?"

She gnawed her lower lip. "I wish you would cease staring at me as if you plan to eat me."

He grabbed her chin between his thumb and forefinger, and his lips lifted into a snarl. "'Tis exactly what I plan."

"Why are you doing this?"

He shrugged.

Glancing at the symbol of her castle encircling her finger, she prayed he would understand. The ropes bit into her flesh as she forced her wrists to face each other. Wiggling her father's ring back and forth, she slowly slid it down her finger. Grasping it carefully, she held it as high as her tied hands would allow. "This should belong to you."

"What is it?"

Taking a deep breath to steady herself, she spoke from her heart. "My father's ring. It denotes the owner of Whitestone."

He looked taken aback, as if she had just handed him a poisonous snake. Years ticked by.

"You are gifting me with your castle?"

"Aye." The ring slipped and tumbled to the pallet.

Godric sneered at it. "The castle is already mine."

If her hands had not been tied, she would have hit him. "Dammit, Godric, I know that." She twisted, trying to reach the ring. "I wanted you to have it."

He walked across the tent and sat on a makeshift stool made of wooden packing crates. "Are you telling me you came out the secret passage to give this to me?"

"Aye, you hardheaded man!"

He crossed a foot over the opposite leg's knee. "I do not believe you."

"Godric, listen to me!"

"If you wanted to give me a gift, why use the secret passageway? The lady of the castle is certainly able to use the front gate."

"Nay, Godric, you do not understand." She squirmed against the pallet, wishing she could touch him. "I was locked in my room."

He reached into a nearby crate and pulled out a flagon of wine and a wooden goblet in deliberate, controlled motions.

"Please, Godric. I thought you would understand."

"Understand what?"

"That I love you. I want to be yours."

"Nothing so deceitful as a woman," Godric snarled, flicking his gaze over her as if she were a disgusting worm.

A tear leaked from her eye, making its way down her temple and into her ear. "Did our night together mean naught?"

"The night you poisoned me?" he asked bitterly, pouring wine into the goblet.

"Oh, Godric."

'Twas not too late to salvage her pride. She could pretend her gift was just a bribe, another duty she performed for the good of her people. Blinking back more tears, she unlaced her heart. She had been a fool once, nay twice, to put duty first and run away from love. She would not do it again no matter how difficult he made it.

"I know you do not understand why I left, and I was a daft fool for doing so, but I love you. I want to be yours."

He growled. "You lie very prettily, Countess."

"Please, Godric." More tears stung her eyes. She leaned her head into her shoulder and wiped them as best she could. "You must believe me. I wanted to give you the ring so you would know that I trusted you to do right by my people."

He set the goblet aside and came forward. "My lady—" He bent over her, close enough she could smell the scent of the campfire lingering on his garments. "Do you truly trust me?"

She smiled. "Aye."

"Good." Slowly, he slid a dagger from his belt and held its cold blade to her throat.

CHAPTER 33

She started, and pressed against him. "What are you doing?"

Sliding his hand into her hair, he pulled her head back. "Silence, captive."

Deep within her, she felt a surrender. Whatever happened, Godric would not harm her or her people. Her lands were safe in his care, just as she was safe in his arms, even though he held a dagger to her neck and her wrists were tied above her head. Inhaling his warm, comforting scent, she closed her eyes and relaxed onto his pallet.

"You truly are not afraid, are you?"

"Nay."

He kissed her softly. "You should be."

Flicking the dagger downward, he slid the sharp point under the neckline of her kirtle. A ripping sound issued and he split her dress from neck to waist. She gasped, straining against the bonds holding her wrists. "Godric?"

He chuckled. "Shh. Trust me."

Desire coiled through her. "I do."

The dagger dipped lower, slicing her dress to her hipbone. Cool air caressed her stomach. The knife's point scratched the surface of her skin, sending a line of white-hot desire to her woman's core.

The world was dizzy. "My lord," she murmured.

He raked the pads of his callused hands softly down the newly exposed skin. A tremble of desire quivered through her. Abruptly, he grasped the edges of her gaping dress and ripped it to the hem. It pooled on either side of her.

"You are mine."

Her eyes flew open, watching him. His eyes were hard, focused, ruthless; desire boiled in them. This was no seductive Godric as he had been at their last coupling, but a man with a need to quench the fire burning just below the surface. Warm liquid seeped from her queynt, echoing his need.

"Godric—" Her voice was husky with desire. "I need you too."

He peeled down his breeks and tore the laces on his braies; his beautiful member, engorged and purple, sprang free. He fell atop her, his sex pushing inside her. "Meiriona, I cannot be gentle."

She wrapped her legs around his hips, pulling him farther inside her. "There is no need to be, my lord."

She gasped as he withdrew, then moaned contentedly as he slammed his member back inside her over and over, reveling in his need to possess her. His lovemaking was hard, fast, and rough. She knew he needed release for his pent-up anger.

She tightened her legs, trying to show him with her body how much she wanted to belong to him. Trying to show him how much she loved him and how sorry she was for running away.

He roared his climax, then his body stilled and he stared down at her. She whimpered when he rolled to the side, withdrawing from her.

"Godric, I need—" Her cheeks heated.

"I know."

She strained against the rope on her wrists. How frustrating it was to be unable to touch him.

"Meiriona—" His finger traced from her neck to

her swollen sex, the touch burning her overstimulated skin.

She wiggled, pulling against the ropes.

Hitching up his braies, he stood beside the pallet.

Coldness bit her skin at the loss of his body. "Godric? What are you doing?"

Icy darkness lurked in his gaze. "You may be a lying little vixen, but your body belongs to me."

"My lord?"

His lips were a cold, hard line. "I told you not to call me that."

Meiriona trembled. "Godric, please! What are you doing?"

"Merely taking what belongs to me, something I should have done years ago."

Hot, stinging tears welled in her eyes. How could he not understand? "With all my heart, Godric, I swear I do not lie." She glanced at the ring, still lying on the pallet. "Please take it."

Smoothing his breeks over his thighs as if wiping the feel of her off his hands, he stalked from the tent.

Less than two hours later, Godric sliced through her bonds and hurled a brown tunic and chemise at her. "Get dressed, Countess."

"Godric?" Coldness seeped through her.

"Silence, or I will gag you again."

Her heart ached at his anger. How could she show him her sincerity? Knowing that once his anger was quelled he would see reason, she dressed and determined to prove to him she trusted him and wanted him. Scooping up her father's ring, she tucked it into her bosom.

Moments later, one of Godric's brawny arms encircled her waist as she sat before him on his steed, worry stirring in her mind. His heat bore into her back.

The first pinks and oranges of the evening painted the sky, and Godric's mood had darkened even further. He was fierce and intent. His army followed behind him as they faced Whitestone, and her stomach churned with trepidation.

Her castle, tall and imposing, loomed before them. It grew taller by the moment as Godric marched his men up the sloped side of the mountain toward its massive wooden gates.

He called to his men, who were filed behind him in orderly rows, archers in front, horsemen and knights behind. With her father in command, Whitestone had been a strong fortress, but without his guidance, the castle would fall. Godric was too strong, too well armed. His men were too well trained, too battle ready for any other outcome. She prayed the skirmish would be short and surrender would come easily.

Slowly, as if reading the direction of her thoughts, Godric slipped his dagger from his boot. "Lean your head against my shoulder, Meiriona."

She complied, her heart racing. "Godric?"

The cold flat of his dagger chilled the skin of her throat. "Do not move," he demanded.

A nervous giggle erupted within her, drawing a scowl from Godric.

Then abruptly, trumpeters blared into the afternoon, announcing the army's arrival at Whitestone, and his attention turned toward the stone walls and the closed castle gates. Heads appeared over the tops of the parapets, looking like tiny black dots.

"Open the gates!" Godric's strong voice boomed into the morning. Bear's words came to her. *Milady, the master would give his own life rather than harm one of his own.* Please, please, she prayed, let her people surrender without a fight.

She leaned her head back, allowing him more access to her neck with his dagger.

"'E's got the mistress," she heard a high-pitched squeal say.

"Lady Meiriona?" another asked.

"Milady!" a third called.

"Open the gates. Now!" Godric ordered. He fisted his hand in her hair, and the flat of the cold blade pressed against her throat. Saints, she should have been scared out of her wits, but all she could think about was how the skin of her scalp tingled under his hand. Saints, she'd missed how he held her anchored to him at night with his hand twisted into the length of her hair.

The sound of footsteps scrambling across the ramparts echoed into the field. Helmet-covered heads popped up over the stone walls looking like black ants. Slowly, a white banner was raised atop the gatehouse.

Thank the heavens.

If only she could talk to her people.

Out of the corner of her eye, she saw Godric's dagger glinting in the sun. Long moments passed, and at last she heard the order to open the gate.

The portcullis creaked and clanked as the iron-covered lattice gate slowly rose. Godric spurred Vengeance forward. With her as a shield, there was no fear of any of the archers shooting him. She closed her eyes and heard the hundreds of feet of his men following them.

As they rode through the gate toward Whitestone's bailey, Meiriona glanced up at the four sets of eyes staring down at them through the murder holes. Tension stretched across the courtyard.

The soldiers' hands grasped their hilts with white knuckles and she could read the strain in the set of the men's shoulders. A white banner fluttered in the breeze.

Pierre limped into the courtyard, dragging his sword. Her heart went out to him. He was a crumpled old man who had loved her father too much.

Pierre glanced up at her. His eyes bore traces of hurt and betrayal. "I loved you," he said.

She licked her lips. With the dagger pressed to her throat, she could not lower her head. "'Twas not me you loved, Uncle."

"I taught you everything, bastard's whore."

Godric's arm tightened, whether to shield her or to possess her, she was unsure. "Pierre de Quéribus, the king requests your presence in London to answer the charges of high treason."

He sniffed. "Am I under arrest?"

There was a long pause. "Aye."

With a screech, Pierre hoisted his sword and lunged forward. Godric wheeled his horse away. Meiriona pitched sideways and felt herself falling toward the ground. Godric dropped the dagger and caught her. He hauled her upright with one hand while settling his horse with the other. "Easy." He squeezed her ribs. "Are you well?"

"Aye." Her heart leapt with hope that mayhap he was softening in his anger toward her. Glancing around, she saw men surrounding Uncle Pierre, swords outstretched.

"I loved you! I loved him!" Pierre screamed. "I will not divorce you!"

Godric motioned to one of his men. "Take him to the dungeon." Men scrambled to obey, and Meiriona watched her husband be led away.

"He is an old man," she whispered. "He will die in the dampness of the dungeon."

Godric dismounted and helped Meiriona down,

then tossed Vengeance's reins to one of his men. "Lady, mind yourself."

"He was my friend, my father's friend."

"You cannot have her for a wife," Pierre sneered over his shoulder. "You shall have to kill me. And if you do, everyone here will know what a coward you are for killing an old man."

Godric shrugged. "'Twould not be a problem for me, but it seems my betrothed has sentimental feelings toward you still. And I have no desire for a wife whom I am at odds with."

Hope burst in her heart at Godric's words. So he *did* still want more than an empty marriage. Determination to address her people filled her.

"My people," she said loudly, not giving herself time to think. "Attend my words."

Quietness came across the courtyard as men turned to look at her.

"You were loyal to my father; now hear *my* words. My people, many of you know that this man, Godric of Montgomery, and I were betrothed to marry. Perchance some of you know that the betrothal was illegally broken. The wrath of the king will assail us if we do not give him first claim on this land. This man is the rightful owner of Whitestone and you owe him your loyalty."

A murmur crossed the crowd. A few men set their swords on the ground. Others grasped their hilts, as if debating. Godric looked at her with an expression of astonishment.

"*However*," she continued loudly, "his claim is not the reason you should give him loyalty."

Bear shifted his weight and scratched his wooly red head.

"You should give him your loyalty because he is a kind, noble man, because he's a worthy ruler and our lands will prosper under his hand." She saw belief in the eyes of her people. Digging into her bosom, she retrieved her father's ring. "My father gave me this ring to give to a strong man worthy of Whitestone." She turned toward Godric, her heart pounding. Could she make him believe her?

His face was unreadable, but his eyes shone with interest and he thumbed his jaw.

Knowing he was softening, she sank to her knees in a position of fealty, holding the ring before her. "My people, as daughter of Ioworth, I swear fealty to Godric of Montgomery to obey my father's deathbed command . . . and because I love him and I cannot imagine life without him."

Godric watched the woman kneeling afore him, too astonished to move. Her passionate speech gnawed at the edges of his disbelief. She looked at him with hope and love shining in her eyes.

Please, she mouthed. *I love you.*

Stepping forward, he grasped the ring from her and slid it onto his finger. The crowd erupted into cheers. Taking her hand, he pulled her to her feet and kissed her soundly.

"Harlot!" Pierre snarled, his grey mustache drooping.

Meiriona pulled away from Godric, hurtled across the bailey, and slapped him across the face.

He tottered backward.

Godric chuckled. "Be thankful 'twas her and not me, old man."

Pierre opened his mouth as if to hurl another curse, but Meiriona touched his arm in warning. "My father is gone, Pierre. We must move on."

"You side with the enemy."

"Godric of Montgomery is neither my enemy nor yours. The crown gave this land to him. If you have any quarrel, 'tis with King Edward, not Godric."

Godric cleared his throat. "Verily, the lady speaks truth. The king wishes to try you for treason."

Limping backward, Pierre stumbled and had to be held upright by guards.

Reaching into his surcoat, Godric pulled out a parchment.

Pierre glanced at the papers. "What are those?"

"Annulment documents. I had them drawn up long ago. Sign them, and I will allow you passage to France."

Meiriona turned toward her uncle, hoping against hope that he would see reason. "Well? 'Tis more than fair."

Pierre, flanked by two guards, snarled at her. "You little traitor! Turning against your own father!"

"Uncle Pierre," she whispered. "Be practical."

"'Tis shameful!"

"Refuse this offer and it will not be my knife you face, but the king's torturers," Godric drawled.

Pierre paled, his crinkly skin turning a thin white.

"Sign the annulment papers, relinquish all claim on Whitestone and Meiriona, then leave England, ne'er to return."

Pierre turned desperate eyes on Meiriona. "How can you do this to me?"

"He offers you a chance that is more than fair. Take it, uncle. Live the rest of your life in peace, rather than in some cold dungeon."

Pierre stood still, and Meiriona feared he had not heard her. He stared into space as if seeing ghosts of the past.

"Well?" Godric prompted. "Your decision?"

Bear proffered a quill. Pierre glared at Godric, and Meiriona held her breath. Slowly, as if his fingers were made of iron, Pierre reached for the pen. In his familiar scrawling, beautiful script, he signed his name, releasing her as his wife.

Feeling dizzy, she let out the breath she was holding. She laid a gentle hand on Pierre's forearm. "Gramercy."

He jerked away and stood, leaning heavily on one of the men holding him. "I will prepare my things," he said stiffly.

As Pierre left to gather his belongings, Damien, purple cape flying, raced into the bailey atop a pale palfrey. Amelina and Justin sat before him on the horse.

"Meweeona!"

"Meiriona!"

"Damien!"

He swung down and helped the two toddlers off. All three of them hugged her. "I brought the extra horses from Montgomery."

Godric clapped the boy on the shoulder. "You will make a fine master horseman someday."

Damien beamed and dug into a pouch at his waist. Holding a small green object out to her, he raised a brow. "You forgot this, sister."

Meiriona stared down at her emerald hair comb and smiled, her heart leaping with joy. "Oh, thank the saints." She took the hair bauble and shoved it into her tresses.

"I found it in the rushes. Lord Montgomery found out about his mum throwing it at Master Godric."

"Throwing it at Godric!" Meiriona interrupted.

Godric hugged her. "She told me you hated me."

"I never said that."

"Lord Montgomery sent his apologies for his mum and also word that should she ever bother either of you again, he will deal with her," Damien said.

Turning, Meiriona wrapped her arms around Godric's waist and squeezed him. She ne'er wanted to release him again. "She is a nasty, bitter woman, just as you said."

Godric kissed her on the temple. "I have been so entrenched with women who do not know how to love, I could not believe in your love until just today."

"Please, my lord, never doubt my love."

"I do not, not now."

CHAPTER 34

Meiriona stared over the top of the parapets, watching Pierre and his small band of men make their way out the castle gates. Godric had granted Pierre leave to stay until her father's funeral, which had been mere hours after his men had taken command of the castle. Thank the holy heavens her father could now rest in peace.

Cold wind stung her cheeks. The air smelled of imminent rain. Godric stood behind her on the battlement, his arm wrapped possessively around her waist.

His hand tightened, pulling her body against his. "Are you sorry to see Pierre leave?"

"He was my friend. He was my father's friend." She sighed. "But, nay, I do not regret he is leaving." She turned in Godric's arms to face him. "What will you tell the king?"

Godric smiled, the merriment in his eyes softening his scars. "I will tell him that I am very happy with my new wife."

She splayed her hand across his cheek and smiled up at him. "I meant about Pierre. What will you tell the king about letting him go?"

"The truth."

"Will it bode ill for you?"

His fingers curved around her shoulder and he

pulled her close, brushing his lips against the soft skin of her eyelids. "Once the king understands your loyalty to me, surely he will forgive me for neglecting to bring an insignificant nobleman such as Pierre to London." He kissed the top of her nose, pushing her gently against the wall and holding her captive there with his large body. "I *can* assure him of your loyalty, can I not?"

Her eyelids fluttered open. "Verily, you know you can."

"Meiriona," he whispered, "you spoke of love. It was not just a woman's treachery to save her castle, was it?"

She studied his face, taking in his blue eyes and sickle scar. He looked vulnerable. "I think I have loved you since our first meeting. Godric . . ." Her fingers traced the scar below his eye. "Forgive me for my family. I am sorry for the part I played. You were right—I should have married you, long ago."

His hand closed over hers, and he held it to his heart. "Can you feel my heartbeat?"

"Aye."

"All the bad blood between us is in the past. What we have is now, in this living, breathing moment."

She twisted her fingers into his tunic and pulled his lips onto hers. The wind blew her hair about them, binding them together in a silky auburn net.

"I love you, my lord," she whispered.

"Meiriona, will you marry me?"

She stared at him for a long moment, too stunned to move. "You are . . . *asking* me?"

"Aye."

"Godric, the Dragon, is *asking* me?" She lifted one eyebrow. "And if I refuse?"

He wrapped his hand into her hair, drawing her close. "You will not."

Heat pooled in her core. "Arrogant blackheart."

His lips touched hers, gentle at first. She surrendered to his expert lead, and his kiss became urgent and demanding. His tongue swept into her mouth, teasing her until she was breathless beneath him.

"I will never get enough of you, Meiriona."

"Nor I you, Godric."

She found herself at once curious about the wooden chest and the instruments of pleasure which he had pulled from it before they had made love at Montgomery. Had he brought it with him? She had no doubt life with Godric would ne'er be dull or passionless.

"You belong to me," he said.

She laughed, being his possession no longer a frightful thing. "And you belong to me as well, my lord."

He swung her into his arms and carried her down the stairs toward their bedroom, newly decorated with trinkets from his great inventory of merchandise. She snuggled into his torso, loving his comforting, masculine scent. Kicking the door open, he strode across the rug and laid her across the bed. The mattress ropes moaned as he climbed beside her, his large body hovering above hers.

"I love you, my lady."

She grinned, her eyes twinkling in delight. Pulling the tunic from his muscled chest, she gazed up appreciatively at his tanned torso and yanked him down atop her. "Possess me, my lord. My heart already belongs to you. I long for my body to belong to you as well."

Godric chuckled, a deep appreciative laugh. Her heart felt as though it would burst with joy, and her quenyt felt hot and slick with need.

Rumpling her skirt over her thighs, he dragged her undergarments down her legs until she was naked and exposed afore him. Desire for him spiraled through her, and she wrapped her hands around the curves of his wide shoulders, pulling him close. "You are mine," she said.

"God's wounds, girl." In one motion, he unlaced his breeks and thrust himself inside her. "I am always and forever yours."

About the Author

Award-winning author Jessica Trapp believes a dynamic romance is one where two opposing characters are transformed into two people who share love and passion. Despite reading gobs of romance and science fiction instead of studying for biochemistry exams in college, she is a registered pharmacist. She lives in Houston, Texas, with her husband and son, who are as devoted to books as she is. When she's not reading or writing, she dances in an advanced Raks Sharki troupe (more commonly know as bellydance), putters in the garden, plays chess, and drinks copious amounts of hot tea. For excerpts of her novels, contests and more, please visit her on the web at www.jessicatrapp.com